THE MIRROR CHRONICLES

CIRCLE
OF STONE

Praise for The Mirror Chronicles series:

"I became totally immersed in an amazing world of painted words... breathtaking and an absolute joy to read. A book that you will reflect on for the rest of your life. Just like when you first read *The Hobbit* or took your first stroll along the story path of Terry Pratchett... An epic masterpiece."
Mr Ripley's Enchanted Books

"Johnstone effortlessly conjures up elaborate worlds rich in both magic and fantasy. *The Bell Between Worlds* has an enchanting quality that is capable of standing shoulder to shoulder with the likes of *The Chronicles of Narnia* and *His Dark Materials*... The narrative flows with ease and the story maintains excitement right to the end. This highly-charged adventure is a delightful page-turner for both children and adults alike."
We Love This Book

Books by Ian Johnstone

The Mirror Chronicles: The Bell Between Worlds
The Mirror Chronicles: Circles of Stone

Praise for *The Mirror Chronicles — The Bell Between Worlds*:

"Dramatic, with perils that are both real and colourfully described. Highly recommended." *The Bookbag*

"Not since *Harry Potter* have I devoured a fantasy world as much as this. I can tell Ian Johnstone will sit high up on the fantasy author list." *Readaraptor*

"Outstanding... Epic stuff. The best 'classic' fantasy I have come across so far from the last 14 years."
Magic Fiction Since Potter

"A beautifully written book, featuring a vividly imagined alternative world... Jaw-dropping." *Through the Gateway*

"Imaginative, intriguing and finely written. Great start to a new fantasy adventure trilogy. Very much looking forward to book two." *Goodreads*

IAN JOHNSTONE

THE MIRROR CHRONICLES

CIRCLES OF STONE

HarperCollins *Children's Books*

First published in Great Britain by HarperCollins *Children's Books* in 2015
HarperCollins *Children's Books* is a division of HarperCollins*Publishers* Ltd,
1 London Bridge Street, London SE1 9GF

The HarperCollins website address is: www.harpercollins.co.uk

1

ISBN 978-0-00-749117-9

Printed and bound in Great Britain by Clays Ltd, St Ives plc

MIX
Paper from
responsible sources
FSC C007454
www.fsc.org

FSC™ is a non-profit international organisation established to promote
the responsible management of the world's forests. Products carrying the
FSC label are independently certified to assure consumers that they come
from forests that are managed to meet the social, economic and
ecological needs of present and future generations,
and other controlled sources.

Find out more about HarperCollins and the environment at
www.harpercollins.co.uk/green

For Mum and Dad, who let me dream

PART ONE

The Valley

1

Safe Harbour

*"From the frothing talons of tempest a single craft emerged —
broken but afloat — drifting wearily to* safe harbour.*"*

THE TWO GIANT TREES towered above the others, their arms
outstretched as though claiming the ancient forest as their own.
But it was not only their size that made these mighty oaks so
magical, nor their drapery of white where the other trees wore
thin cloaks of orange and brown leaves. What made them
wondrous was their slow graceful motion. Like commanders
inspecting their troops they took a stately path between the lesser
trees, sweeping this way and that through the vast skeletal canopy.

And so it was that as the forest chattered and rustled and
chirped its welcome, the great masts of the *Windrush* brought it
to the end of its long journey.

The captain heaved at the wheel and the battered old ship
turned another bend in the river. He brushed back his ragged
mop of blond curls and peered through the pockets of evening
mist. He frowned and blinked.

"This is it..." he muttered, raising his head to look for his
companions. "This is it!"

3

Simia was sitting with her feet dangling over the side of the ship and did not look up.

"You said that three bends ago, Ash," she grumbled, throwing a pebble into the river. "And two bends before that."

"But it really is this time, I'm sure of it! Get Naeo... or Sylas... either — both of them!"

"Aye, aye, Cap'n..." grumbled Simia, giving him a wilting salute.

She made her way to the nearest hatch and disappeared below. Moments later her shock of red hair reappeared above deck and behind her another girl stepped into view. She looked about the same age as Simia but was taller and climbed the ladder lightly, with a longer, more graceful step. Her blonde hair was drawn back and held in place by a criss-cross of sticks, revealing a narrow neck and delicate features. As she stepped on to the deck, she fixed Ash with her piercing blue eyes.

He grinned and stepped down from the helm. "Naeo, look — look at the trees!" he exclaimed, striding past them both to the bow of the ship. "There's something about them — this *has* to be it!"

Simia and Naeo walked up and stood at his shoulders, staring out at the forest. Birds flitted from branch to branch as the aged trees hung over the swirling waters, dropping the occasional long-dead leaf. Above, the canopy ascended towards two hills, themselves blanketed in yet more forest. There was perhaps an odd quality to the light, a slight vividness to the mottled browns and oranges, but otherwise everything looked normal.

"Ash, they look just like the million other trees we've passed," said Simia, shaking her head. "Except these ones are getting really close — I mean *really* close — shouldn't you be at the wheel?"

The river curved away in a wide bend and the *Windrush* was

indeed drawing ever closer to the far bank. Ash sighed his disappointment, then pushed back from the handrail.

"Don't!" exclaimed Naeo suddenly. She looked up at him. "Wait."

She leaned forward and peered into the tangle of branches ahead.

Ash tensed. "If I don't go now, we're going to crash straight into—"

"Trust me," said Naeo, calmly. "We won't crash." She turned to them. "Just watch — we're expected."

Their eyes returned to the wall of branches, trunks, bushes and shadows that loomed ever nearer. They all took a firm hold of the handrail.

"I hope you're right about this...." said Ash, wincing.

As he spoke the long arm of the bowsprit passed over the far bank and disappeared into the forest, snapping branches and crashing through twigs as it went, sending down a shower of dried leaves. Ash and Simia exchanged a glance and braced themselves for the shuddering impact with the bank.

Simia pressed her eyes shut. "This is a bad idea!"

"Don't worry," came a voice from behind. "It'll be fine."

Sylas was standing back along the deck, near the hatch. He did not approach — throughout the journey he and Naeo had sought to be as far from one another as possible — but he smiled at Simia and took hold of the handrail by his side.

Everyone held on tight. A moment passed, then another. They heard the scrape of branches against the hull, felt the cool of the forest as they passed under the overhanging boughs, heard a joist creak beneath their feet. But there was no calamitous crash, no snapping of timbers, no sudden end to their long journey.

The *Windrush* sailed on.

They looked to their left and right and saw the floor of the forest passing them by: low bushes and huddling plants, saplings and tree trunks. They looked up and saw the canopy high above, brushing past the rigging, crowding the mast. It was as though the wilderness had opened its arms and drawn them in. The keel cleaved through the soft folds of earth and living things as though they were water, bearing its great weight onwards, towards the two hills.

Their eyes were wide with wonder and Simia shrieked with delight.

"How did you know?" she asked Naeo, breathlessly.

"Look..." said Naeo, pointing out into the forest.

They turned to where she was pointing and narrowed their eyes. At first they thought it was just a muddle of light, or perhaps an oddly shaped trunk, but then they realised that they were looking at a human figure. It was a woman leaning against a tree, her body draped in loose garments of the same drab colours of the forest: browns, oranges, greens, limes and yellows. The only part of her that did not blend with the thicket was her pale face, which almost seemed to float in mid-air, smiling at their wonderment.

"They're everywhere!" shouted Sylas, pointing out over the side of the ship.

Now they knew what to look for, they saw the pale glow of scores of faces, some peering from behind bushes, some high in the branches of trees, but most gathering alongside the great ship, as though guiding it in as it rolled and yawed ever deeper into the forest. They walked in two columns, left and right, stepping lightly between the trees, many peering back to the river as though to check that the *Windrush* had not been followed, others looking at its path ahead.

Simia ran from the bow and joined Sylas, grabbing his arm. "It's changing! The forest — look at it!"

Some distance ahead the trees seemed to be thinning, the shadows falling away, the colours brightening. They could see flecks of light between the foliage, scattering beams through the damp air. The ship dipped into the trough of a ditch and mounted the bank beyond like a wave, gaining new height. Every part of the brush was shimmering with the promise of a break in the forest, and as more and more people emerged to walk at the ship's flanks, they knew that they were nearing their destination.

The four shared excited glances as suddenly the final curtains of green and brown fell away. Evening sunlight poured down upon them, scattering the shadows and bathing the deck in a welcome warmth.

Before them lay all the majesty of Nature.

A huge lake stretched out as far as the eye could see. Its waters were bright and crystal clear and made the air smell sweet, and it was so still that the surface was mirror-like, reflecting the giant canopy of blue sky above. Only in the distance could they see any movement on the lake, for there, fogging the horizon, was a giant waterfall, sending up a smoke of ethereal mist. Rising steeply on either side were the two hills, carpeted with a thick forest that even now, in early winter, retained its green. Birds of all kinds soared above, turning in wide arcs on the gentle breeze, tipping their wings, playing on the thermals, darting between the treetops.

Sylas laughed with delight and grasped Simia's hand. At that moment the tired joints of the *Windrush* let out a brief complaint and Simia shrieked as the keel plunged into the cool waters of the lake, sending up a great sheet of spray on all sides. The vessel rocked backwards and lurched a little to one side, then righted itself. They heard a roar and patter, which at first they thought to be the falling water, but when they turned they saw that the bank was now crowded with a great assembly of Suhl, all of them clapping and cheering, smiling and shouting their welcome.

At their centre, one woman stood alone. She did not wear the forest hues of her fellows, but instead a flowing white gown – the gown of a Suhl elder. Her glistening grey hair fell about her shoulders, marked out by a braid of brighter colours. Her beautiful face was full of joy.

Filimaya raised her arms, gesturing to the Valley of Outs, and bid them welcome.

2
Sylva

" Sylva is a town as strange and beguiling as any in faery folklore, lost as it is in folds of earth, wrapped in a tangle of trees."

FILIMAYA EMBRACED SIMIA FIRST, holding her tight and bending down to kiss the top of her head. Then she went straight to Sylas and embraced him too, in a way that surprised him: not a formal greeting, but warm and heartfelt. For a moment he felt awkward, holding his arms at his sides. No one had held him like this since his mother had been taken away. But her warmth was infectious and slowly he drew his arms around her.

"Thank you for returning to us, Sylas," whispered Filimaya. There was a pause. "And who did you bring with you?"

Sylas turned. There, walking down the gangway from the ship, was Naeo. As was her way, she seemed at ease, her hands tucked into the pockets of her coat, eyeing the crowd of onlookers and paying little attention to the reunion.

"That's Naeo," he said, instinctively taking a step away from the gangway. "I thought... I thought you might know her. She's Bowe's daughter."

Filimaya raised a hand to her lips. "Of course..." she said. She took a step in the girl's direction. "Naeo, daughter of Bowe, my precious child! We thought you were—"

"Naeo is my Glimmer," said Sylas, abruptly.

Filimaya froze. The gathering of Suhl fell silent. Everyone turned to face him.

"*What* was that?" someone hissed behind him, and another: "Did he say his *Glimmer*?"

There was a gale of hushes, everyone straining to hear what was said next.

But Filimaya seemed lost for words. Her eyes narrowed a little, searching his face; she tilted her head as though struggling to understand. Then she glanced at Naeo, who returned her gaze without expression.

Finally Filimaya smiled. "Well you never cease to surprise us, Sylas!" she said. There were a few nervous laughs from the crowd. "You must forgive my awkwardness. I find myself entirely unsure how to address you both."

"The same as ever," said Simia with a careless shrug, as if it was perfectly clear. "Sylas is still Sylas and Naeo is Naeo. The only thing is—"

"We prefer not to be together," said Naeo. For the first time everyone turned to face her, taking in her slender features and calm, measured voice.

"There's no reason to treat us any differently," said Sylas. "It's just that Naeo and I... find each other... difficult."

"Madness, isn't it?" came a voice from beyond the crowd. It was Ash, strolling down the gangway from the *Windrush*. "All that blasted effort to get them together and now they can't *wait* to be apart!" He smiled and nodded at various faces that he knew, clearly enjoying his entrance.

Filimaya paused, clearly still preoccupied by Sylas and Naeo, her eyes shifting between them. Finally she turned to the young man and smiled. "Welcome, Ash. You still have your knack for timing, I see."

Ash's arrival was indeed a welcome distraction. Many of the Suhl were soon jockeying for position to shake Ash's hand, bidding him their personal welcome to the valley, and the same people then naturally turned their attention to the other travellers, swamping them with enthusiastic greetings. Simia in particular seemed to enjoy the deluge of well-wishers and beamed from ear to ear as she realised that she had achieved something approaching celebrity status. She walked around, offering her gracious hand to all who approached and many who did not.

Naeo, however, seemed far less comfortable. She shook hands and gave faint smiles, but she seemed distant and uncomfortable, looking at times tired and at others as though she wished to be anywhere else. Sylas too had slipped back a little into the crowd, distancing himself from Naeo.

Filimaya noticed this and raised her hands to call for silence. It took some while for the gathering to come to order.

"Friends! Friends!" shouted Filimaya. "Our guests have been travelling for days and who knows what perils they have faced. We must show them some hospitality and give them time to rest!"

A small hollow-cheeked man stepped forward. "But Filimaya, surely we can just ask a little of what they have seen?" he protested in a dry, wasted voice. "After all, the things we have been hearing on the winds have us all terribly worried! And just this morning the chatter among the birds has changed. I am no expert, but they would seem to suggest that Thoth is beginning to—"

Filimaya raised her hand in a calming gesture. "I understand your concerns, Dropka, and we all share them. But just look at our visitors! They are pale and they clearly haven't slept in days.

They have come here for sanctuary, not to be interrogated. What kind of hosts would you have us be?"

The man shrank a little. "I don't mean to be impolite," he said, dropping his eyes. "It's just—"

"I understand," said Filimaya, "of course I do, but there will be plenty of time for us to discuss these things tomorrow."

There was a general murmur of agreement from the gathering. The man gave a bow and quickly retreated into the crowd.

"Good, then!" said Filimaya brightly. She walked over to Ash, embraced him and gestured to a rather portly woman in the front row. "My dear Ash, please go with Kayla — she'll show you to some fitting quarters. I will come and see you later."

Ash nodded and hoisted his pack on to his shoulder. Filimaya turned to Naeo and smiled warmly. "Naeo, your father has become a good friend since the war and he has spoken of you often. I hope that in time we too can be friends." She held out her hand.

Naeo stared at the hand, then slowly and awkwardly she took it and gave it a quick shake. "All right," she said.

If Filimaya was surprised by this cool response, she did not show it. "Good!" she beamed. "Now, I take it that you and Sylas would prefer to sleep in different—"

"Yes," said Naeo and Sylas in unison.

Their abruptness clearly shocked Filimaya, but she quickly gathered herself and nodded politely. "Of course. Naeo, please go with Kayla and Ash. I'll come and check on you just as soon as I can." Finally she turned to Sylas and Simia. "You two," she added with a wink, "you can come with me."

Sylas and Simia smiled and fell in at her side. Sylas tried not to show his relief that they were not to be separated. After all they had been through together over the past few days, he knew he would feel a little lost without Simia. He saw in her glance that she felt the same.

"Thank you, everyone!" shouted Filimaya.

There were a few disappointed grumbles from the crowd, but soon enough everyone began to disperse, reluctantly and noisily, amid much chatter about the *Windrush* and its occupants, about the things Dropka had mentioned — the whispers in the leaves and the chatter among the birds — but most of all, about Sylas's strange declaration.

"Why did you have to mention *Glimmers*?" murmured Simia in his ear, jabbing him in the side. "Now everyone's completely freaked out!"

Sylas sucked a breath through his teeth and shrugged. "I don't know. It just came out!"

Filimaya led them up the grassy bank and into the cool of the forest. Many of the ancient trees were gigantic, with trunks as broad as castle towers and waist-high roots that rumpled the forest floor into a baffling, mossy maze. They crossed dazzling, sun-speckled glades and lively streams that bubbled between stones, singing watery melodies. They waded through seas of delicate ferns, between vast outcroppings of thickly scented bracken, over rich carpets of leaves and nodding flowers. Sylas was struck at once by how vital everything seemed, how full of life, even though the world outside the valley had fallen under the cloak of winter. Yet there was no sign of any of the people who had met them on the banks of the lake. It was as though they had simply disappeared.

Filimaya moved with all the grace and ease that Sylas remembered from his time with her in the Water Gardens; in fact she seemed even more vigorous, even more radiant, as though this magical place had returned to her some of her lost youth.

As they walked, they told Filimaya of their adventures; of their meeting with Espen and their long journey together across the Barrens, ending with Espen's revelations about the Glimmer Myth. Filimaya nodded as though entirely familiar with the Myth, just as Espen had predicted. They told of Espen's seeming betrayal at the Circle of Salsimaine and Bayleon's capture, of their escape to the city and their discovery of Paiscion and the *Windrush*.

At the first mention of Paiscion, Filimaya turned.

"Was he well?" she asked, anxiously.

Sylas nodded.

"And where is he now? Did he not travel with you?"

"You're jumping ahead!" scolded Simia. "You need to hear the rest first — you'll miss the best bit!"

Filimaya sighed. "I don't know why, Simsi, but I've missed you." She squeezed her arm. "Go on, then, tell me your own way."

Sylas and Simia took it in turns to finish the story, telling of Paiscion's astonishing discovery in the note from Mr Zhi, then Sylas's encounter with Naeo in the Glimmer Glass and Simia's decoding of the message "*So at last we may be one*" into Sylas and Naeo's names. Simia spent some time on this part of the story and rather exaggerated its importance, but even then Filimaya did not rush her.

As they began to tell of Naeo's rescue from the Dirgheon, Filimaya stopped in wonderment.

"You broke *into* the Dirgheon?" she blurted.

Sylas nodded. "It was the only way. I had to get to Naeo."

He described Paiscion's summoning of the storm, the encounter with Espen, the battle with Scarpia and their final escape, flying high over Thoth's city, borne aloft by Sylas's strange birds made from the ruined sails and rigging of the *Windrush*.

"We really flew, Filimaya!" said Simia. "As high as the clouds — higher even!"

"It sounds magical, Simsi," smiled Filimaya. She turned to Sylas. "Was it, Sylas? Was it magic? Or was it the science of your world? Of the Other?" She raised an eyebrow. "I ask because you seem to know quite a lot about both."

Sylas thought for a moment. It was still so strange to hear his own world referred to as "the Other" — if anything was *other* it was this place — this world — with its magic and its creatures and outlandish people.

"I think it was a bit of both," he said hesitantly. "Magic and science. The gliders seemed to work, but I don't think they would have flown like that if Ash hadn't summoned the winds."

"And so already the two worlds are becoming one," said Filimaya, almost to herself.

For a moment they walked in silence, each lost in their thoughts.

Finally Filimaya frowned. "So... you and Naeo *are* able to be together? You said you held hands. You shared a glider?"

"Then, yes," said Sylas. "I mean, it felt weird, and it hurt — here, around the Merisi band —" he held up his wrist to reveal the glistening bracelet — "but it was like, in that moment, we were *meant* to be together."

"And since that moment?"

"It's just been... difficult. To be around each other," said Sylas, shaking his head. "It's hard to describe why. It's like I start to feel... like the parts of me — my bones, my insides, even my thoughts... I don't know..." He trailed off.

Filimaya looked at him with concern.

"I keep telling him, I'm not sure they should still be together at all!" said Simia knowingly. She lowered her voice. "And Naeo's just a bit—"

"I'm sure Sylas and Naeo will be trying to work all this out

15

themselves in their own good time," interrupted Filimaya. She put a hand on Sylas's shoulder. "Come on, it's this way."

She led them through a veil of vines towards a denser part of the forest. As they passed through the long dangling strands, Sylas jabbed Simia in the side.

"I told you to keep out of it," he hissed.

Simia gaped innocently. "I was just being *honest*," she protested. "You seemed to think that was a good thing when we got here!"

Sylas said nothing and pushed on.

As the vines fell away they gasped. Here the tree trunks were as wide as houses and soared above them to new heights, like the columns of some grand and ancient citadel. Sylas and Simia craned their necks towards the canopy, trying in vain to see the topmost branches.

"So, tell me," said Filimaya in a casual tone over her shoulder, "where is Paiscion now?"

Sylas and Simia exchanged glances, as though neither wanted to reply.

"We don't really know," said Simia hesitantly. "He didn't come back to the *Windrush*."

"But he said he might not..." added Sylas, quickly. "And he said we shouldn't worry about him."

For a moment, Filimaya turned and gazed at them anxiously, as though hoping they would say more, but when nothing came she breathed in deeply and turned her eyes upwards. She watched the path of a fluttering bird until it was out of sight, but in truth, she seemed to be composing herself.

Eventually she looked down again. "Well, young Sylas Tate," she said, her voice sounding a little forced, "every chapter of your adventure is more extraordinary than the last. I marvel at all you have endured and discovered."

16

Sylas smiled, but that too was an effort. "The thing is," he said, "I still don't feel we know what we're doing. I mean, I've found out all about the Glimmer Myth, and I get that Naeo and I have... well, *everything* to do with it. And we've even managed to find each other, and to get away from Thoth and the city. But while we were on our way here, all I could think was, what next? Now that we're together, what do we do?" He frowned. "And the truth is, I still haven't managed to do the one thing I actually set out to do, which is to find my mum."

Filimaya regarded him closely for a moment and then raised her hand to his shoulder. "The truth, Sylas, is that you are at the centre of great things, and the greatest of things rarely happen when and how we choose."

Sylas gave her a pained look. "But it's all just so..."

"Frustrating? Yes, of course it is." She smiled and cast her eyes around her. "But you're here now, in the Valley of Outs, among friends and allies. We will help you to understand and to decide what comes next. I will call a Say-So especially. But right now, Sylas, Simia, you're exhausted. I'd love to stay with you and ask more, but now you need to go and rest. You can speak to us all, tomorrow, at the Say-So, once you have had a good meal and a decent sleep."

Sylas shifted his rucksack on his shoulder and allowed himself to feel the weariness in his limbs and the fogginess in his mind. Filimaya was right, of course. They had hardly slept all the way here — keeping watch, talking, going over all that had happened and what might come next. He looked up at her and nodded gratefully. "I'd like that," he said.

She gestured towards the forest. "So go on!"

Sylas and Simia looked where she had pointed. There was nothing there: just more ferns, bracken and tree trunks.

"Are we... camping?" asked Simia, failing to hide her disappointment.

Filimaya's laugh rang through the trees. "No, of course not —" she pointed — "*that's* where you'll be staying."

Sylas and Simia peered past her. She was pointing at a gigantic tree, which towered even higher than those around it and whose massive trunk was at least the width of a small house.

"Come on — take a closer look!" she said, setting out towards it.

They all walked slowly across the clearing, staring at the colossal redwood — its huge roots snaking over the surface like dragon tails; its vast, gnarled limbs reaching up into the canopy as far as they could see. But there was no sign of any shelter.

Then Sylas saw it.

In a fold of the trunk, between the joints of two great roots, there was an opening: a triangular slit where the flank of the tree had naturally grown apart. Sylas and Simia clambered over one of the roots and stood gazing up at the huge entrance, a grin of delight spreading across their faces. The lip around the dark cavern was smooth, almost as though it had been crafted that way, but there were no cuts or straight lines, no joints or nails. They could smell cool air issuing from the living cave, but it was not musty: it smelt fresh and a little sweet, like timber. And there, deep in the hollow, they saw a flickering light. Then another and another: little oil lamps, dotted around what looked like a substantial chamber.

Simia beamed at Filimaya. "We're staying in *there*?"

"Why not?" asked Filimaya, smiling. "This is how we live in the Valley of Outs."

Sylas frowned. "In trees?"

"In trees, caves, dells, on lily-rafts, behind waterfalls, beneath roots and hillocks, among the birds in the canopy. Wherever Nature opens herself to us. She is a very generous host, so there's never a shortage of places to stay!"

"She makes them for you?"

"Yes, but not at our bidding. We simply find them when we need them. The more we need the more we find, and I daresay that if we all left one day, they would disappear. Nature provides what is needed and nothing more." She smiled and looked about her. "And such has been our need since the Reckoning that this place has become something of a town. We call it Sylva."

Sylas looked around him but could see no sign of a town. There were no homes or walkways or streets, not even any people.

Simia could not restrain herself any longer. "I'm going inside," she said, tugging at his sleeve. "Are you coming?"

Filimaya was already turning to leave. "You'll find everything you need. Someone will come and get you in the morning," she said brightly, as she disappeared into the forest.

Sylas turned and eyed the dark opening, wondering at the mysterious forces that had made it. Then he followed Simia inside.

3

The Valley

"The spirit of the valley *never dies.*
It is the root of heaven and earth."

SYLAS STEPPED BEYOND THE threshold and gasped. It looked for all the world like the inside of a house, but instead of walls there were planes of living timber; in place of doors there was a honeycomb of oddly shaped openings, all seeming to be part of the tree, rather than cut by hand. Covering the floor there was a carpet of fine, spongy green moss, which felt luxuriously soft beneath the feet, and the hallway that he was now standing in — for that was what it seemed to be — was lit by lamps set into natural alcoves in the walls, so that it was well lit and cosy.

Sylas and Simia dipped through the nearest opening and saw to their delight a room set out with a table and chairs and alcoves containing cups, saucers, plates and all manner of things they might need to serve a meal. In a recess at their side there was bread and cheese; in another, all kinds of fruits; in another still, what looked like a cured ham wrapped in a waxy cloth. All this was lit by two more lamps and natural light that came in through a large slit high in the external wall. In the far corner, they could hear the tinkle of flowing water coming from a depression in the floor and when they looked they saw the glistening surface of an underground stream. Set neatly to one side was a pitcher and a set of glasses.

They rushed into the next room and found what seemed to be a lounge or parlour, but instead of a sofa the mossy floor was raised in one corner to form a comfortable platform covered with an even thicker layer of moss, to which someone had added a scattering of colourful cushions. They resisted the temptation to jump on it and ran into the next two rooms, where they found similar platforms that had been made into beds, with thick eiderdowns and feather pillows.

"How did they know to get this ready for us?" marvelled Sylas.

Simia lay back on a bed and closed her eyes blissfully. "Filimaya always kept at least one room ready for visitors in the Meander Mill. Not that I was ever allowed to *stay* in any of them." She yawned. "Yep, I'm definitely going up in the world."

Sylas grinned and laid his bag down, before heading to the dining room where he cut himself a piece of bread and ham. He took it with him to the lounge and sat back on the surprisingly soft and warm sofa, biting contentedly into his sandwich. He devoured it in seconds and then settled back to relax.

He smiled to himself as he thought how different this was from Gabblety Row – from the bricks and beams and winding corridors, from the growling roads at its corner and his uncle's grubby little apartment. He laughed at the thought of his uncle Tobias. What would *he* make of all this? He imagined that accountant's brain trying to make sense of it all, make it all add up, like a good tax return. Well, nothing about this world added up. It would defeat his uncle absolutely and completely, and something about that made Sylas happy.

He yawned and put his hands behind his head. What was his uncle doing now, now that he had no one to run his stupid little errands, no one to snipe at, no one to blame?

His eyes were just beginning to close when he heard a movement in the room.

He opened his eyes. Simia was leaning on what passed for the doorframe, chewing on an apple.

"What do you think you're doing?" she asked disapprovingly.

"What do you mean? I'm relaxing — I thought that was what you were doing!"

Simia was incredulous. "Isn't there a curious bone in your body? I mean, here we are in the great Valley of Outs, and all you want to do is have a kip?"

Sylas stared at her for a moment and then managed a weary grin. "Come on then," he said, hauling himself to his feet and brushing off the crumbs. "Let's go explore."

In the forest the sun was just setting, painting the trees with pink and orange, which only added to their magic and beauty. Walking alone they were free to wander and gaze all about them, to take in the sheer scale of the towering trees. But they also tried to look beyond roots and trunks and branches to find any sign of the town Filimaya had mentioned. And the more they explored, the more they discovered.

They saw the first of the townsfolk in the crevices and folds of tree trunks, in dark openings that now, in the failing light, showed themselves to be entrances to warm, glowing sanctuaries, where people sat around tables and laughed and chatted, where children played and argued and readied themselves for bed. And they saw homes in other, more unusual places. Sylas was the first to see one beneath the roots of a grand old tree, partly in the folds of the tree and partly underground. Then Simia saw one high in

22

the canopy, nestled in the crook of four intersecting boughs, wrapped all about with a lattice of branches like a giant nest. But these branches had not been cut or placed or woven. They were alive. They had grown that way.

They walked further into the forest and saw more and more of these strange dwellings high in the treetops, some beginning to glow with flickering lamplight. But what was even more magical was that they saw people walking from one to the other along the tops of the largest boughs, as though ambling through the roof of the forest was the most natural thing in the world. The more they looked, the more people they began to see, until they realised that the entire canopy was connected by a network of walkways. Some people walked quickly along the great branches, rushing to a late appointment or to get home for dinner; others walked beside a companion, chatting or taking in the evening air. One woman even walked along reading a book. But what Sylas found most surprising of all was the sight of children running between these great trees without a care in the world.

"Why aren't they scared?" he murmured, shaking his head in disbelief.

Simia followed his eyes and shrugged. "Nature wants to help us," she said matter-of-factly. "Remember what Merimaat told me that time? When I was trying to cross the river on stepping stones?"

Sylas remembered well Simia's story of Merimaat — the great, lost leader of the Suhl — her strange words sticking clearly in his mind: "*They aren't trying to trip you,*" she had said of the stepping stones, "*they're trying to help you.*"

"That's what the Suhl are brought up to believe," Simia continued, "that Nature is part of us and we are part of Nature. She's *on our side.*"

Sylas looked back up into the treetops in time to see an entire family walking almost directly overhead, laughing and joking, the children racing each other to the next trunk.

"Well *they* believe it, that's for sure," he said, under his breath.

They walked on, and as the sky grew darker they began to see a galaxy of orange lamplights dotted throughout the trees, casting a beautiful, magical light across the forest floor.

Soon they had reached the steep incline to one side of the Valley of Outs. They pressed on, hoping to climb high enough to look down on Sylva. At first they made good progress through the tangle of bushes and branches, but then, quite abruptly, the ground levelled off.

Sylas stopped. "This can't be the top," he said, glancing about. "We've only just started."

Simia pushed past and parted some branches. The ground ahead fell away. They shared a look.

"Odd," said Simia.

She pushed through the undergrowth and strode down the slope. "Come on, it must go up again in a bit."

They set out once more but had only walked a few steps when they came to a halt.

There, beyond a few branches of trees, was the valley they had just left behind. Lamplights blinked in the treetops, the occasional dark figure wandered through the canopy and just ahead was the stream they had crossed only minutes before.

Simia turned on her heel and marched past Sylas with a look of fierce determination.

"We must have circled back somehow. Come on!"

Sylas opened his mouth to say something, but then just turned to follow. They had only walked a dozen paces through the thicket before the ground again seemed to be levelling out. Again they

24

reached a clearing, and again they saw the ground falling away, and as soon as they started down the slope they stopped in astonishment — for there, through the bushes and wood smoke, were the same lamplights, the treetops and the familiar stream, babbling in the half-dark, seeming almost to mock them. They were back where they had started.

"I think I know what's happening here," said Simia, smiling suddenly. "You know why they call this the Valley of Outs?"

Sylas shook his head, perplexed.

"Because no one but the Suhl can find their way in. They always find themselves walking out again!"

"Right..." said Sylas, trying to get his head round it.

"Well, isn't this just the opposite? I mean, we're inside the valley, and perhaps the same magic that keeps other people out—"

"...is keeping us in!" exclaimed Sylas, a smile spreading across his tired features. "So however many times we try to climb this hill, and whatever point we try from, we'll always find ourselves walking back into the Valley of Outs!"

Simia put her hands on her hips and grinned. "Exactly."

Since they had gone as far as they could go, they sat down on a bed of dry leaves and gazed through the branches and bushes to the valley below, framed by the dark silhouettes of the two vast hills. The moon and stars lent everything a trace of silver: the distant hilltops, the curls of smoke rising from hundreds of fires, and somewhere below, only just visible through the fingers of the forest, the glistening surface of the lake.

For the first time they felt the true power of this place: the ancient and unfathomable magic that bound it together, from root, to trunk, to treetop — the magic that now held them close and would keep them safe.

"It's like a dream," murmured Simia under her breath.

Sylas nodded and almost without thinking he raised a hand towards the overhanging branches and opened his fingers wide. In the same instant, the twigs and leaves swept aside like the curtains of a stage, revealing the valley, the lake and the twinkling skies in all their majesty.

Simia's grin flashed in the half-dark. "Show off!"

Sylas laughed and started to close his fingers, but she reached out. "Don't," she said. "Leave it."

And so Sylas left the branches as they were, framing the most beautiful view either of them had ever seen.

They sat quietly, listening to the birds settling to roost and the animals of the night calling to the rising moon. To their surprise, these sounds suddenly faded, as though making way for something else. A moment later, they heard the sorrowful sound of a pipe. The music came from deep in the forest, and was quickly taken up by hundreds of instruments scattered throughout the treetops of Sylva: pipes, violins, guitars, horns, all playing as one.

Then the Suhl began to sing. Their words seemed to seep from the trees themselves, filling the valley with a mournful chorus:

> *In far lands of dark and high lands and low,*
> *I hear songs of a place where none ever go;*
> *Locked in the hills, 'midst green velvet folds,*
> *A treasure more precious than gem-furnished gold,*
> *For there dwell the Suhl, the last broken band,*
> *There dwell the lost and there dwell the damned...*

S

The thing throbbed and quivered, its glistening flanks oozing a sickening slime. It was a formless shape, a mess of organic sludge that barely cohered into a single thing. The tiny chamber in which it lived dripped the same oily filth and pulsed to the same quickening rhythm, as though it and the thing were one and the same: one sustaining the other. The air was thick and hot and wet. Trails of vapour rose and formed swirling, putrid clouds beneath the cave-like ceiling.

Suddenly there was silence.

The half-formed heart halted. The vapours ceased their constant movement.

The thing trembled. And then...

THUMP... THUMP...

THUMP-THUMP... THUMP-THUMP... THUMP-THUMP...

The thing swelled and receded. Something inside tensed and then a bulge moved beneath the glutinous surface. Then another: this time distinct and pointed.

The pulse accelerated, gaining volume, building and building, faster and faster until soon it was no longer a heartbeat but a rush of sound, a deafening percussion of panic.

Suddenly the thing erupted in frantic motion, twisting and stretching, turning and bulging. As the jelly was breached, more black mucous flowed down its sides and new vapours palled in the chamber.

And then, with a sudden surge, something forced itself upwards, striking the ceiling with a thud. It slewed to one side and then collapsed, slapping down into the ooze.

The heartbeat steadied and began to return to a measured pace. The walls ceased their throbbing altogether, for their work was done.

Something had been born.

It was partly submerged in the oily mire, so that it could almost not be seen. But in some strange contortion there was an arm and a hand — a human hand — and that hand rested against a human cheek. A woman's cheek. It twitched, the little finger tapping against the fine dark skin.

And then, slowly, the hand began to clench. The fingers curled, and as they did so there was movement at their tips, beneath the fingernails. Slow and slick, the points of rapier talons emerged into the gloom. They grew and grew, until they were almost half the length of the fingers. Until they scratched the woman's cheek.

The figure arched in a spasm of pain. She shrieked, her eyes wide and staring, the pupils drawn into narrow slits.

It was not a woman's shriek. It was the screeching wail of an animal.

4

Sorcery

"If sorcery *itself has form, it is the Black. The Black is all we cannot know; it is enchantment and it is despair."*

IT STARTED BEFORE THE first warming rays, in the darkness: a playful chirrup from a nearby branch, followed by an answering call. Then another, even nearer at hand, and another, building on the first, clamouring to be heard. Soon a mounting chorus filled the forest. Thousands of sparrows and swifts, finches and wrens, kites and kestrels, all raising their heads towards the crowning sun to welcome the new day.

And yet to Naeo, it was a strange, unwelcome sound — even now, even days after her escape. It was too clear and loud and shrill. In her slumber, she pushed at her heels and pressed herself even further back between the two rounded rocks, retreating into the shadows. And as the rays crept down the steps into her cave she coiled into a ball, wrapping her arms around her head, yearning for silence and darkness.

Silence and darkness were what she knew. They were her friends. They kept her safe.

She pulled her knees up a little further, murmuring as she turned her face into the cold stone.

"Naeo?"

It was a gentle, soothing voice.

"Naeo? I'm afraid I must wake you."

She groaned and twisted between the rocks, grazing her cheek. Her eyelids fluttered and she drew in a lungful of fragrant air.

Suddenly her eyes flew open. She sat up and pressed her narrow shoulders further back into the crevice. She glanced about the room, squinting into the shaft of sunlight, searching for the owner of the voice. But the light was everywhere, zigzagging between a dozen mirrors mounted on the walls, lighting the whole chamber. She covered her face with her hands.

"You're with friends, Naeo!" came the voice again, calm and warm. "Remember? You're in the Valley of Outs."

The beams shifted, turning away from the rear of the cave where Naeo lay, leaving her in shadows. She blinked as her eyes adjusted and then she saw Filimaya, kneeling only a few paces away, her aged face creased with concern.

"Have you slept here all night?" she asked, looking at the made-up bed in the corner of the cave.

Naeo shrugged. "I prefer the floor," she said. "I'm used to it." She pushed herself up, rubbing her eyes.

"Was it like that in the Dirgheon?"

"I suppose..." said Naeo, indifferently.

"Of course it was," said Filimaya. "I should have—"

"What's going on? Has the Say-So started?"

Filimaya frowned. She wanted to ask more, but thought better of it. "No, but it will be almost under way by the time we get there. We should go."

"Fine. I'll just change," said Naeo. She turned and walked to a driftwood shelf, pulling down the fresh clothes that had been laid there.

Filimaya was about to step outside, but as Naeo pulled off her top she froze.

She raised her hands to her mouth. The girl's back was terribly disfigured by a single scar, which ran all the way down her spine and across her shoulders. It was shapeless and mottled in the manner of burns, but marked out in greys and an inky black. In places the lifeless pigments seemed only to have stained her flesh, while in others they had pinched and raised the skin in a manner that could only have caused extreme pain.

"For the love of Isia!" breathed Filimaya. "What *happened* to you?"

"It's nothing," said Naeo, pulling down her tunic and turning abruptly. "Are we going?"

"Naeo, tell me what—"

"*It's nothing*," said Naeo, emphatically, walking to the steps. She reached down and picked up two short twigs, which she brushed off and then pushed into her hair in a cross, holding her long locks high above her shoulders. She looked back. "Really, I'm fine."

Filimaya watched her climb out of the cave before setting out after her. When she reached the top step she found Naeo waiting outside.

"Those are the marks of Thoth, aren't they?" she pressed.

Naeo sighed and nodded.

Filimaya shook her head. "He used the Black, didn't he?"

Naeo paused. "Yes," she said. "But it's fine. I'm fine. It's nowhere near as bad as what he did—"

She stopped, the words catching in her throat.

"As what, Naeo?"

31

"As the things he did to my dad."

Filimaya was aghast. "Oh, Naeo," she murmured. She reached out, but Naeo stepped away.

"Like I told you, I'm fine."

"Are your wounds painful? Is there anyth—"

"They're painful when I'm made to think about them!" For a moment Naeo glared at Filimaya, but then her features twisted with self-reproach. She turned away. "Look, shouldn't we be going?"

Filimaya looked at her calmly for a moment. "Yes, of course," she said.

She patted Naeo's arm and led her out into the dew-drenched forest. They walked over a stream, through a copse of saplings and between a gap in a thick tangle of bushes.

Soon they reached a clearing bisected by the mildewed remains of a fallen tree. Ash was sitting on it, kicking at the crumbling bark with his heels while chatting to Kayla, who had rested her considerable weight on a protruding branch.

"About time!" cried Ash. "It's freezing!" He breathed a cloud of vapour into the chilly air to emphasise his point.

Filimaya smiled. "The sun's up, so the valley will warm quickly. A perfect day for a Say-So." She squinted into the sun's rays. "Come, we must make haste!"

She led them across a field of drooping flowers, skirted a gully and then began to descend towards the lake. Pockets of mist gathered in the hollows and ditches, roots and dells, and the nearer they came to the water the more these wispy trails started to criss-cross their path, swirling about their ankles. When they finally reached the edge of the forest and gazed over the great lake, they saw nothing but a vast milky blanket, floating eerily over the surface as far as the eye could see. The morning sun had painted a pathway of luminous pink leading down the length of the valley to the gorge at its far end. There, the waterfall fizzed and smoked in front of the rising disc of gold.

"It's beautiful," murmured Ash, entranced.

"And more so every day," said Filimaya, setting off down the bank and into the mist.

Kayla grinned at Ash and Naeo. "OK, you two, time for a leap of faith," she said, then set out after Filimaya.

Ash and Naeo glanced at one another as the two women waded into the mist up to their waists, leaving twists of vapour in their wake.

"OK then," Ash shrugged. "I guess we'd better get our feet wet."

They wandered uncertainly down the slope into the impenetrable carpet of mist, all the while watching Filimaya and Kayla, expecting them at any moment to plunge into the lake. Naeo suddenly cocked her head on one side, then extended her hand out over the mists. The swirls ahead of them gathered, turned and rolled away, opening a path that revealed the mossy shore of the lake and led all the way to the women.

"Well, that's one way to do it," grinned Ash, clearly impressed.

Naeo gave a slight smile and a mock bow, then strode on.

They quickly made up ground and soon they saw what Filimaya had been heading for: a boat, moored to a stump at the water's edge. She drew to a halt and turned in time to see the remains of Naeo's strange pathway. She blinked and frowned, then raised her eyebrows at Ash.

"Ha! Don't look at me!" he said, nodding towards his companion. "I'm not the only trickster around here, you know."

Filimaya looked at Naeo and then broke into a smile. "Deftly done, Naeo." She waited a moment for Naeo to respond, but when there was only an awkward silence, she turned and pointed at the boat. "Well, come along. It's hardly the *Windrush*, but our journey is short."

They all clambered into the rowing boat and had soon seated themselves on the bench that ran around its hull: all but Ash, who volunteered to take the oars. The little boat glided over the glassy lake, mist rising at the bow and spiralling off into the air, catching the golden sunlight in a fiery trail. The passengers were just able to peep above the cloud, allowing them to watch the great valley drift past.

Naeo gazed up at the steep sides of the hills and the luxuriant forest that clung to their slopes. She watched a trio of swans drift over the canopy, then drop slowly into the mists of the lake, before landing softly on the water. She watched the sun climbing in the sky, flecking the treetops with a shimmering gold. She saw all of this beauty, but it felt far away, as though she was looking through a sheet of glass.

"You look sad," said Filimaya, who had been watching her across the boat.

Naeo gave no answer.

"Is it your father?"

Naeo turned and met her eyes. "He should be here. He should see this."

Filimaya smiled. "He did," she said. "Years ago, before the Reckoning."

"You were here with him?"

"I was. And he fell in love with this place. He found it as welcoming and healing as the rest of us." She was quiet for a moment. "But it made him curse his Scryer's eyes."

"Why?"

"Because Scryers see more clearly here than anywhere else.

34

Bowe used to say that when anyone was near, their feelings got in the way of the view!" she said, chuckling affectionately as she remembered. "He would leave Sylva and walk for hours just to get away from us all."

Naeo's face softened, but she said nothing.

"He'll come back one day," said Kayla, placing a hand on Naeo's arm.

Naeo stiffened. "Maybe."

"Well I for one can't *wait* to have a good look around," said Ash, in a timely effort at good cheer. He looked at Naeo. "Are you up for that? After the Say-So?"

Naeo shrugged.

And then she turned away, looking up at the steep sides of the valley. She pulled a long, well-worn bootlace from her pocket and without looking at it, wove it deftly through her fingers, quickly forming the complex weave of a cat's cradle between her hands. This simple twine was one of the things that had kept her sane in the long dark of the Dirgheon, taking her away from her thoughts, occupying her hands and her mind. And it showed, because without the slightest effort she threaded it into a web of stunning complexity, her fingers a blur as she gazed out at the valley, taking in its vastness and beauty. How different this place was to *that*, she thought; how light, compared with that despairing dark.

The valley was full of wonders, more stunning and majestic than she could possibly have imagined. And yet she had the strangest sense that she had already seen so much of it: that she had already walked through the giant redwoods; that she had seen dwellings in caves and dells, tree trunks and bowers; that she had seen all this lit by a thousand lamps in the dying rays of day. They were not memories, not even images in her mind, but fragments, like the elusive traces of a dream.

5

The Garden

"The garden defies expectations, not by breaking its promise, but by keeping it. It has a beauty that breaks the bounds of dreaming."

SYLAS WADED THROUGH THE mist at the water's edge, trying desperately to keep up with their guide while daydreaming about the wonders of the evening before. The enchanting sunset over the Valley of Outs and the lamp-lit forest seemed almost unreal, like a dream. Even now they warmed him on this chilly morning.

Their guide moved swiftly despite the thick mist, his long ranging steps more than a match for the quick-footedness of his followers. He never looked back, seeming to know exactly where they were: slowing when they fell behind and striding out when they drew near. He paused a few times to relight his pipe, which seemed prone to going out, but always he stayed well ahead.

Simia pulled at Sylas's sleeve. "Get him to slow down! I'm exhausted!!"

"Cat got your tongue?" whispered Sylas, adjusting the rucksack on his shoulder. "Why don't *you* ask?"

Simia eyed the young man leading them. She seemed unusually

reluctant to speak up. "I think he knows that we're tired —" she narrowed her eyes — "I'm just not sure he *cares*."

They both watched their guide as he mounted a boulder and dropped down on the other side amid a cloud of orange pipe smoke. He was not powerfully built, but had a sprightly, lithe figure and his long limbs swept with ease through the undergrowth. He had a perfectly bald head, which glistened a little from his exertions, lending new life to the ring of eyes tattooed into his scalp. They stared back unblinkingly, as though seeing their every move and thought. Sylas remembered the very same kind of tattoos on Bowe's head, but he was interested to see that there were fewer and that two of them, on one side of his head, were wrinkled and warped. It was as though someone had tried to burn them from his head.

"Stop fretting, we're nearly there," shouted the young Scryer, in a rich, accented voice. He did not slow or look around, but puffed out a cloud of orange smoke, which formed bright wisps in his wake.

"Told you!" hissed Simia.

They clambered up a small promontory that jutted into the lake, then skirted a towering cliff face. They became aware of a low rumble, which grew ever more noticeable, and when they looked out at the lake they saw that, although the morning fog was starting to clear, the surface was now clouded by great rolls and swirls of a new, finer mist.

"The waterfall!" exclaimed Simia, looking relieved. "We're at the end of the valley."

The young Scryer walked up to a great curtain of weeds and grasses hanging from the cliff face and turned to them. His gloomy features broke into a smile.

"Are you ready for this?" he asked, tapping out his pipe and tucking it behind his ear.

Sylas and Simia looked at each other.

"Ready for... what?" asked Sylas apprehensively.

Their guide pulled back the weeds and waved them into the darkness beyond. "For the Garden of Havens."

They peered warily into the cave and, to their surprise, saw a passageway sloping downwards to a bright opening, shrouded in more greenery. The walls of the tunnel had been worn smooth by the powerful currents of the river and, like so much in the Valley of Outs, seemed almost to have been crafted to suit its human residents, with a regular ceiling the height of a man and a gently inclined floor to allow an easy descent.

This time their guide let them go first. With growing excitement Sylas made his way down the slope, running his hands over the damp rock to keep his balance, treading carefully on the sloping floor. His hand drifted over empty space on one side and he felt a chilly breeze drifting from an opening. He turned towards it, assuming this was the path, only to find himself grasped by the shoulders and pulled back.

"Not that way!" growled the Scryer.

"Why?" asked Simia, peering into the tunnel. "What's down there?"

"Just the old mines," he said, pushing them both onwards towards the light. "They're forbidden now."

"Why?" asked Sylas, groping his way down the tunnel.

The Scryer sighed. "Because they're dangerous," he said. "Because of the Black."

Sylas was about to ask what "the Black" was, but as they reached the end of the tunnel the thunder of the waterfall surged, resonating in the rock and his chest. The air too had changed, becoming fresher and sweeter, carrying the fragrance of river silt. He drew up to the veil of weeds, which swung limply in a breeze from the bright world beyond. He paused for a moment, then pushed it aside.

The tunnel opened out into a cavernous bowl of rock, with the sky above and a sandy floor below. Its slick, curved sides rose ever more steeply until at the very top they slightly overhung, trailing grasses and vines into the vast space below. On one side could be seen the passing river as it flowed out into the lake, and beyond the ceaseless tumult of the waterfall.

Sylas's eyes took in the wonders of the bay before him. The walls were riddled with thousands of tiny rivulets and streams, waterfalls and springs which in places gushed playfully down to the river but in others splashed out over the rocky planes, forming a thin film over the stone. Between this endless motion was a garden of rich flowers and glorious ferns, livid lichens and lustrous bushes. This was a haven for Nature's most delicate and beautiful gifts.

But her finest creation of all was at the centre: a tree of gigantic proportions, whose ancient, crooked limbs had bowed almost to the ground under the weight of its giant leaves which even now, in winter, showed all the vitality of youth. There was only one sign of its age: dark veins running through its bark, which in places looked almost black, like the first tendrils of disease.

As the sun emerged from behind a cloud Sylas's eyes were drawn upwards to the myriad beams of sunlight which passed across the hollow a hundred times, rebounding from the smooth, wet surfaces. The light touched the upper reaches of the grand old tree so that it seemed to wear a halo of gold.

"I've heard about this tree," whispered Simia at his side, her eyes wide with wonder. "The Arbor Vital, they call it. The Living Tree. It just keeps going — no one knows how old it is."

"And yet it may not live much longer..." murmured the Scryer.

"Why?"

"The Black," he said, pointing to the trunk. "You can already see it."

"The stuff in the mines?"

He nodded.

"What *is* it?"

"Your guess is as good as ours," he said, scowling in distaste. "Think of it as corruption and disease, because whatever it is, it is evil."

Suddenly there was a sharp hiss above their heads. They looked up and to their surprise, saw a woman sitting on a narrow ledge of the cliff face. Her finger was pressed to her lips.

"Quiet!" mouthed the woman. "Please!"

The Scryer gave a brief bow of apology.

It was only then that Sylas and Simia became aware of the great gathering of people hidden in the folds of the gardens. Hundreds of silent figures were seated on mossy banks and ledges, perched on rocks and promontories in every part of the hollow, all of them looking down towards a figure standing near a boat at the water's edge. She held her hands aloft, commanding their attention, speaking in a soft but resonant voice that Sylas recognised straight away.

"So, my sisters and brothers, after all these years we have reached the fulfilment of Merisu's prophecy," said Filimaya, her voice echoing from the walls so that she could be heard easily. "It is a prophecy that most considered so far-fetched that it passed into the realm of myth. But this is the time that the Glimmer Myth foretold, the time when the separation of our worlds is finally seen for what it is — a rift in our very souls!"

The Garden of Havens rumbled with low mutters and loud

complaints. Sylas noticed the perplexity on people's faces; their worried frowns and troubled glances.

One elderly man sitting near the front rose to his feet. "But, Filimaya, do you really believe that the myth is true? That we each have an identical twin? One of these *Glimmers*? That one day we might even be made one?" He laughed scornfully. "Surely this is the wildest of fancies! That's why it's called a myth!"

There was a rumble of agreement from the crowd.

Filimaya nodded. "I understand your doubts, really I do. But let me say this clearly so that there can be no mistake." She lifted her eyes to the gathering. "Yes, I do believe the myth. Among others, I have believed it to be true for many years."

"Which 'others' do you mean, exactly?" demanded the old man.

"Well, you now know that Espasian believed, as did Paiscion, and Grayvel and..." She hesitated for a moment, seeming to consider whether or not to continue. "And Merimaat. Merimaat was quite certain that the myth was true."

Suddenly everyone cried out in astonishment. They turned to their neighbours in disbelief.

"*Merimaat* believed in all this?" asked the old man, looking more sceptical than ever. "Surely if she did, she would have shared it with us?"

"And so she did, Kaspertak," said Filimaya. "With some, at least. The Otherly Guild and the Salsimaine Retreat were set up to study the Glimmer Myth."

The aged man's mouth fell open. "But... they were going for decades — centuries!"

Filimaya nodded.

"We were told that they were studying the Other!"

"And in a way, they were."

He shook his head incredulously. "But they created the Bringer-Laws, the celestial maps, the —," a look of realisation formed across his face — "the Passing Bell!"

Filimaya smiled. "And so now you see how significant it was that Sylas was summoned using the bell! Which brings me back to my point. Regardless of who believed the Glimmer Myth before, Sylas and Naeo prove that somehow, for some reason, it is true. They are the living myth. They bring us hope."

"*What* hope?" shouted a fat man with red hair. "Forgive me, Filimaya, but what *use* is all this? How does it help us to know these things when we are here, hiding in the Valley of Outs, surrounded by our enemies? How does it stop the Undoing, or save our friends in the Dirgheon?"

"Haven't you been listening?" shouted a young woman from high on the cliff face. "Sylas and Naeo have powers beyond our dreams — they managed to escape the Dirgheon and defeat Scarpia. *There's* our hope!"

"So they're here to save us? They're a *weapon*?"

"Yes!" cried the woman to a murmur of excitement.

"No!" retorted Filimaya. "They're nothing of the kind! They're people, children, not weapons that we may use in our own defence. But they offer us the truth — the truth that we are more than we thought we were."

"But what does all that mean for *us*?" appealed the woman, throwing her arms out in exasperation. "We need help, not truths."

"We need both!" snapped Filimaya. She paused, controlling her rising temper.

Sylas shuffled nervously. This was not going well.

But then a familiar voice spoke up. "I agree with Filimaya. We're all missing the point." Ash strode out from beneath the branches of the tree. "We need to remember that before Sylas came, we were desperate. I mean, sure, we had the Meander Mill and some of us were managing to live openly by pretending we weren't what we are. But what kind of life is that? We had no future. How *could* we have a future when we had lost all that made us strong — everything that made us who we are?"

"We've still lost all those things!" shouted the fat red-headed man.

Just then Sylas noticed something strange. As the debate had become heated, so the light in the hollow had begun to dim. When he looked up, he saw that sure enough the beams of light were weak and faltering, barely reaching the upper branches of the great tree.

Filimaya blinked irritably. "Yes, Glubitch, but that was the old world. That was the world in which Glimmers were a myth. That was the world in which Merisu had broken his promise — in which the Three Ways had defeated the Fourth. Sylas and Naeo have shown us a *new* world — a world in which anything might happen, where we must question the very fabric of our worlds, and where Thoth's empire is built on sand."

"Yes, that's right!" shouted a stooped old man sitting near Sylas. There was a murmur of approval.

A very large man with a shock of black hair and gigantic sideburns rose from a rock near the river. "Ash and Filimaya are right, of course," said the man in a deep booming voice. "But we are still left with a question: what do we do with our new-found hope? And how can Sylas and Naeo help us?"

"Yes! Let's ask them! Where are they?" shouted someone.

"Let's see what they can do!" shouted another.

Again Sylas shifted anxiously. Naeo retreated beneath the tree.

"Listen! Everyone, listen!" said Filimaya, throwing her hands aloft. "It is up to us to decide—"

"How are we to decide anything without knowing what is possible?" objected the large man with black hair. He stepped forward and waved to the crowd. "We need to see them for ourselves — see all they are capable of — *then* we can decide a way forward."

Sylas noticed that the hollow had dimmed even further, so that now the beams of light were hardly visible at all.

"NO!" shouted Filimaya. "Ash has told you what they are capable of, and in any case, Sylas and Naeo have told us that they do not *wish* to be brought together. The challenge for us now—"

"Surely no harm will come to them?" cried someone from among the crowd. "They've done it before, so let us see it now!"

Suddenly the young Scryer pushed past Sylas and stepped out into the gardens. "You don't know what you're asking!" he shouted. "If you saw the connection between them with Scryer's eyes, you would not play with it like a party trick. It is a thing of colossal power — unknowable power!"

This gave everyone a moment of pause. The young man was clearly respected and his warning was taken seriously.

Kaspertak, the old man who had spoken earlier, rose slowly to his feet.

"Triste is of course right to be cautious, but I think on this occasion his Scryer's eyes cloud his judgement. By all accounts Sylas and Naeo are in control of their power — they have shown that in the Dirgheon. So what have we to fear? I say that we should see them together. Let us question them, at least." He looked directly at Filimaya. "I say it is so!"

"I say it is so!" shouted the large man with black hair.

"I say it is so!" cried Glubitch, followed by many others.

Suddenly the weight of opinion seemed to shift, and the voices of many uttered the all-important words: "I say it is so!"

For the first time Filimaya hesitated and Sylas's heart fell. He could see from her expression that she was powerless.

He turned and caught sight of Naeo. She too had paled.

Filimaya shook her head. "I truly believe this to be a mistake!"

"The Say-So has spoken, Filimaya," said Glubitch.

"Well, yes, I understand that!" muttered Filimaya, shooting him a fiery glance. She sighed. "So be it." She looked first at Sylas and then at Naeo, her face full of apology. "Sylas, Naeo, could you step forward, please."

Sylas drew a long breath and glanced at Simia.

"You'll be OK," she whispered. "You know what you're doing."

Sylas turned and raised his eyebrows. "Do I?"

He stepped out from the entrance to the tunnel and began walking across the floor of the hollow. People turned and moved out of his way, clearing a path to the boughs of the giant tree beneath which Filimaya was now standing. Naeo had already reached Filimaya's side and stood gazing up at the gathering with a look of defiance.

As Sylas stepped under the branches of the tree, he felt the first pang of nausea, and in the same instant he winced as the pain in his wrist suddenly shot up his arm. He reached down and rubbed the bone around the Merisi Band. Naeo did the same.

He kept walking. As he reached the trunk of the tree, there was a cry from somewhere behind him, and then another to his side.

"Look!" shouted somebody. "Look at the light!"

Sylas glanced up and saw several amazed onlookers pointing at the beams of sunlight that criss-crossed above his head. They were bending and warping, as if distorted by some massive magnetic force, twisted from their natural path.

And then there came another cry, this time above him. A

woman began to scramble down from her perch on the cliff face. "The water!" she screamed. "Look! The stream!"

Sure enough, the streams too were being mangled by some unseen force, curving and twisting, turning back on themselves, flowing against the pull of gravity, as if repelled by the two children. A clamour of frightened voices rose from around the hollow as people scrambled out of the path of crazed rivulets and wild waterfalls.

It was as though nature itself was being undone. Sylas felt his insides writhe and turn, his bones slide over each other, his thoughts begin to scramble. He looked down and saw that the Merisi Band was glowing like molten metal, shimmering as it burned into his wrist.

But then something changed. A new light fell on the Garden of Havens. The contorted beams of sunlight suddenly glowed and flared, burning with a new intensity. The shadows stretching across the gardens were dispelled, silencing the crowd. A fresh, white light illuminated the faces of the onlookers, the ancient tree was once again bathed in gold and green, as though it was flooding with new life.

"Stop this!" boomed a hard, male voice.

Standing at the cliff's edge was a dark figure, silhouetted against the bright blue, arms held high overhead.

Sylas and Naeo hesitated, neither knowing what to do.

"Sylas, Naeo! Move apart!" yelled the stranger.

They happily did as they were bidden, walking quickly to opposite sides of the tree. Instantly the rays of light shifted until they once again formed a web of straight lines, and the streams and waterfalls returned to their natural paths down the gullies and crevices of the cliff.

Filimaya was transfixed by the dark figure. Her hand rose to her mouth, and then she extended the other. Obediently, a beam of light drifted up the cliff face, illuminating the rock like a searchlight, passing over ledge and plant and stream until finally, it lit up the silhouette of the lone figure, bathing it in sunlight.

His robes and hair were a faded black, but his pale, sallow face shone in the ethereal light, revealing striking, high cheekbones, a heavy brow and eyes bright beneath round spectacles.

Filimaya's eyes brimmed with tears.

"Paiscion!" she whispered.

6

Born

"What weird homunculus is this, born *from the Dirgh's dark potion? It is like the ancient gods, forged of both man and beast, and yet it looks more a thing of hell itself."*

THE GHOR GUARDS STIFFENED and craned their long canine necks, reaching for scythe-like blades. There was a movement at the end of the passageway. The figure was hard to discern in the half-light of flickering torches. One moment it seemed to be human and the next animal; one moment walking and the next prowling, cat-like, with smooth predatory ease, spidering along the floor, riding up the walls. Alarmed by the pace of its approach, the commander swiped its blade over the flagstones, sending a shower of sparks down the passage.

"Who goes there?" it barked. The figure slowed for a moment and then reared up to its full height, its dark face flashing a white smile of long, cruel teeth.

It made a strange sound, a gentle rasp something like a purr.

"It's Scarpia, you fool!" came the reply.

And with that she was past his blade, gliding between their mighty shoulders and then rising up on her hind legs in front of the huge ornamented door. The guards turned in bewilderment, then stepped back into the shadows and bowed.

Scarpia raised a clawed fist and knocked at the door.

There was no answer, but she cocked her head and listened. She heard a beautiful but doleful music: a cello playing a bewitching lament. Its strains filled the air, the melody seeming strangely out of place in the deathly halls of the Dirgheon.

As she listened, the junior of the two guards quietly lifted its head to look at her — her powerful, feline limbs, part-clad in rich black fur; her crouching stance, halfway between standing and crawling; her long, sinewy neck, still showing the scars of many burns. But what most caught its attention was the distorted face — that disturbing blend of dark skin and black fur, revealing the angular jaw and heavy brow of a predatory cat, and beneath the brow: one human eye, the other pale and green, its pupil not round but drawn into a slit.

The green eye flicked to the young guard and a snarl gurgled in Scarpia's throat. With a sharp hiss she lashed out with bared claws, tearing savagely at its ear and making it yelp and whimper in submission.

"Do not look at me!" she hissed.

The guards turned obediently away.

In that moment, the cello finally fell silent and an answer came from behind the door. It was spoken with many voices: an unnatural chorus of men and women, young and old, boys and girls, all in perfect unison so that the words resonated down the passageway and sent a chill through those who heard it.

"Enter, Scarpia."

She did not hesitate but threw her head back and pushed at the door, stepping boldly into the half-light of the Apex Chamber.

The great hall was still, the only movement the flickering flames in four giant urns, one in each corner. Scarpia eyed the furthest one, the one now dented and marked, then recoiled slightly as though remembering her pain.

Her mongrel eyes scanned the room, searching for her master, past the dark pool at the centre of the room, tracing the rich tapestries, the long shelves of books, the great stone table topped with manacles and chains, before settling on an elaborate golden music stand and a lone figure sitting on a simple wooden chair, clasping an exquisitely made cello. Even through the many folds of scarlet robes, he looked cruelly twisted and bent and as he began to play again, his sharp joints protruded at ungainly angles. The hooded head was stooped low over the strings and while an emaciated hand danced the length of the fingerboard, the other guided the delicate bow with precision. The motion never slowed, even when he spoke.

"So, my child," came the voice of many, "you are reborn."

Scarpia's eyes flared. "If that's what you call this… this —" she gestured to her body with a clawed hand — "this abomination!" she snarled.

The bow halted and there was a brief moment of silence.

"Perhaps you would rather I had left you as you were?"

Scarpia hesitated, then her eyes narrowed and the standing fur on the back of her neck settled into a smooth, feline coat. A gentle purr rose in her throat. "No, my Lord Thoth."

"I would think not," was the quick reply. "There was very little left of you worth keeping."

For a moment Scarpia looked wounded: she sank a little on her haunches and her cat-like ears dropped back on her head.

"You will learn to appreciate your new form," murmured Thoth, coolly. "You are no less beautiful than you were."

Scarpia purred once again and lowered her head, as though

Thoth were stroking her glossy fur. Instead he resumed his playing, sweeping the bow over the strings. For some moments they were both lost in the strains of the cello.

"Do you know it?" asked her master.

Scarpia's ears rose and turned towards the cello. "The music? No, my Lord. Is it from the Other?"

Thoth nodded beneath his satin hood. "Their music has always been better than ours," he said, creating a complex medley of notes. "This is Elgar's great concerto. They say it is meant for an orchestra, but it is best played alone, don't you agree?"

He turned his head slightly in her direction, so that the shadow beneath the hood was partly visible.

"When *you* play, of course," purred Scarpia, edging towards him on all fours, unconsciously brushing up against a chair. She drew close to his skeletal form and sat on a cushion near him, drawing her tail around her. She eyed the bow as it darted through its final strokes, ending the recital as sombrely as it had begun.

There was a pause as the final strains of the concerto died away. Thoth remained hunched over his cello and for the first time his breathing could be heard: a deep, whistling wheeze.

He drew himself back in the chair and turned to Scarpia. For a moment, a flicker of lamplight penetrated his hood and part of his face could be seen. It was hardly a face at all, but rather a gathering of features, shimmering and shifting in the changing light. It was in constant flux: his narrow jaw suddenly seeming broad and then long and then narrow; the large sockets of his eyes momentarily waning to those of a child, then widening, then falling under an overhanging brow. All this took place in the blink of an eye, so that none of these features reached any definition at all. They were a blur, leaving a vague impression of shaded hollows for eyes, a protrusion for the nose and a wide gash for the mouth.

51

"And so to business," he said, his empty features stretching and moving as he spoke. "While you have been sleeping, I have been tireless. I have been reflecting and planning. I have decided that if we must be infected by this child from the Other, this young Sylas Tate, then we will take the good with the bad. We will reach into his mirrored world and take all that is rightfully ours! We will make these children rue the day they opened the way between the worlds."

A low growl rumbled in the back of Scarpia's throat and her tail flicked the air. "I want them to pay!" she snarled, baring her teeth and snapping at her own tail, which she then eyed with disgust.

"Oh, they will pay," murmured Thoth. "But they are strong. We must address our weaknesses, grow our muscle and sinew. And so we will bring forward our plans. We will find strength where they have found it. If they may cheat the division of the worlds, so may we."

Scarpia's eyes flared with delight and a purr rattled in her neck. "It is to begin now? All that we had planned?"

The Priest of Souls inclined his head. "It begins now."

Scarpia clawed the stone floor in excitement. "Tell me what to do!"

Thoth gave a low laugh. "You always were a happy predator, Scarpia." He gestured at her body with the bow. "Perhaps this is the form you were destined to take."

She seemed to consider this a compliment. Her scarred lips showed a wicked smile.

Thoth lifted the bow once more and placed it on the strings of the cello. "Do you know what draws me to this concerto?" he asked.

Scarpia looked at him inquisitively.

"War," he growled. "They say that Elgar wrote it in mourning, at the end of their great war." A cackle sounded in the void of his throat. "For us, it will be our call to arms!"

Scarpia's smile widened.

"Meet me in the birthing chambers," breathed Thoth, beginning to play. "You are not the only thing to have been born today."

7

The Merisi Band

"The Merisi Band is a clasp of intrigue, enclosing
mysteries that only its maker may ever understand."

WHEN PAISCION FINALLY EMERGED from the tunnel into the
Garden of Havens, the gathering was in a frenzy of excitement.
As people caught sight of him, there were spontaneous cheers
and cries of delight, then unrestrained, joyous applause from all
sides.

At last, the Magruman had returned.

But Paiscion himself hardly seemed to notice these attentions.
He smiled and nodded politely to all he passed, shaking any hands
that were offered and embracing those who lunged at him, unable
to contain themselves, but his eyes were fixed on the river's edge.
His eyes were on Filimaya.

For her part, she stood entirely still as she had since she had
first seen his face, her fingers at her lips, her eyes on his. When
finally he found his way through the last of the crowd, his pace
quickened and he half ran beneath the branches of the tree, then
pulled up and came to a halt shortly before he reached her. For
a moment he simply took in the sight of her, as if hardly believing

that she was there, and then he rushed forward and caught her up in a close embrace. They laughed and wept with joy.

Sylas smiled and glanced over at Simia. She was sitting on the side of the boat wearing a crooked smile, tears in her eyes.

"So it's true," he said, sitting down next to her. "What they said about Filimaya and Paiscion."

He waited for the inevitable rolling of eyes and sarcastic "obviously", but Simia just smiled, still watching the elderly couple.

After a moment she turned and looked Sylas up and down. "So… are you OK?" she asked.

Sylas said nothing, but looked pale and tired.

Simia leaned forward, peering at his wrist. "Did you see what happened to the Merisi Band?" she asked, reaching out towards it. "It was weird! For a moment, I thought it was going to…"

She trailed off and slowly her eyes crept up to his. "Have you seen?"

"Seen what?" He followed her gaze down to the Merisi Band. For the first time he saw that it was still glowing, not with a bright fire like before, but with a dim, rippling light, and running along the circumference of the bracelet was something that he had never seen before, stark and black against the light. It was a string of lettering that made no sense. But as he gazed at them the Ravel Runes began to show themselves, until soon they revealed true letters and words.

He blinked, frowned, then grew pale.

"So? What does it say?" asked Simia.

Sylas turned to look at her.

"It says, '*In blood it must end*'."

Suddenly the gardens fell silent. Sylas and Simia dragged their eyes from the Merisi Band to see Paiscion with his hands aloft, calling the assembly to order.

"Thank you! Thank you for your welcome," he shouted over the last excited heckles. "I apologise for my entrance. I had wanted to travel with my friends here, but I had a challenging time getting out of the city. I am sorry to say that there are dark things afoot in the city of Gheroth, and, I fear, throughout these lands. Thoth is gathering his forces and tightening his noose. I have seen new and foul creatures spilling from the Dirgheon, marching I know not where. I have seen messengers dispatched and received. And I have seen new patrols throughout the city, terrorising our poor sisters and brothers in the slums. All this in just the past few days. I need not tell you that such things have not been seen since the Reckoning."

A new and solemn quiet fell over the gathering. Faces paled and shoulders drooped, as though under some terrible weight.

"This is just what I have been saying!" shouted a tall woman wearing a long purple gown. "The winds, the birds, the waters, all have been telling us of new and terrible things beginning across the Four Lands! And the Black! It's everywhere — even here, in the Valley! The mines are full of it, and now the tree is infected…"

Paiscion turned sharply and looked towards the tree. His face darkened as he saw the fingers of black spiralling up the rumpled trunk.

"When did this begin?" he asked Filimaya.

"In the past days and weeks," she said, shaking her head sadly. "It seems to be rising from the mines. Nothing we've tried has stopped it — if anything, it gets worse."

"Indeed," said Paiscion grimly. "Whatever it is, the Black sinks its claws as deep as evil itself."

"But now, now we have reason to hope!" shouted someone from high above, to which everyone who heard nodded enthusiastically. "Our Magruman has returned!"

Paiscion frowned and pointed towards Sylas and Naeo. "My dear sisters and brothers, *here* is your hope! Surely you see that?"

There was only silence.

"But *you're* our Magruman!" came the same, anonymous voice from high on the cliff.

Paiscion turned his eyes to every part of the hollow. "I *am* your Magruman and I will serve you and the Suhl until my final breath. But Magrumen alone are powerless to stop the Undoing — these years of suffering leave us in no doubt of that. Even with the blessing of Essenfayle, we have failed to defend ourselves against our enemy and now, now that Merimaat is dead, the nation is weaker than ever — just as we enter what may be the final crisis."

A new hush fell over the proceedings, and those who moments before had glowed with excitement became quiet and reflective. Filimaya's eyes never left Paiscion's face.

"As you know," he continued, "since the Reckoning I have lived on the *Windrush*, in the shadow of our enemy, where he would never think to look. And there I watched and I listened. With the help of our sisters and brothers in the slums, I spied on Thoth and his agents, on the Ghor Command and the legions of the Dirgheon. I studied their plans and their works. I drew maps and kept records. But nothing I saw offered a way to free our people from their torments. That is why I never returned to you. But now, my friends, I am here." He extended an arm in the direction of Sylas. "I am here because of this boy."

All eyes turned to Sylas, who found himself shrinking a little between his shoulders.

Simia grinned. "He's talking about you!"

"You think?" he hissed.

"Let no one be in any doubt," continued the Magruman. "Sylas Tate changes everything. His arrival offers more hope than I ever dreamed possible in those dark days on the *Windrush*. He brings a hand of friendship from the Merisi — that sage order that knows many of the secrets of these two worlds and which has been our ally since the birth of our nation. He brings the wisdom of the Samarok and a mastery of Essenfayle that is quite miraculous. But he also offers something quite unexpected. He brings a promise of unity, of togetherness, of an end to the divisions that plague our world and upon which Thoth has built his empire. He shifts the lines of whatever battle may come."

A murmur of excitement rumbled around the gardens.

"You do all that?" whispered Simia sarcastically.

Sylas felt a little sick.

"But I'm telling only part of the story," said Paiscion, turning and walking towards Naeo. She looked at him warily, but he simply took her hand and drew her forward, presenting her to the gathering. "Because it was young Naeo here who called Sylas into this world. And for that we owe her an immense debt of gratitude. Not only because of what Sylas brings, but also because of who he is. You see, Naeo has shown almost unimaginable courage in doing what she has done. And that is because Sylas *is* Naeo." He turned on the spot, looking at the entire assembly. "Naeo *is* Sylas."

A surge of excited energy moved through the congregation and everyone leaned forward to try to improve their view. A thousand eyes shifted between the two children and a thousand minds struggled to comprehend what they were being told.

"But Paiscion, if I might say," said Glubitch, scratching in his red locks, "the reason we may have failed to appreciate the importance of these children is that it is hard to believe that they are what you say. They look perfectly *normal*! They don't even look the same, or behave alike — they're different. How can they be each other's Glimmer?"

Paiscion laughed. "I have absolutely no idea!" he cried. "But that makes it no less true. No one can doubt the truth after the events of the past few days."

Kaspertak stood. "And yet *we* have not witnessed these events!"

"I know, Kaspertak," replied the Magruman, "but we cannot ask them to show their gift. You saw what happened to the gardens when we failed to respect their power. If used wrongly, I believe it could cause great harm."

Sylas and Simia exchanged a look, then their eyes fell on the bracelet. The inscription was fading, but still visible.

IN BLOOD IT MUST END.

Simia looked up. "You have to show him!" she hissed. "It's important. It has to be!"

Sylas shook his head. "Not now," he whispered. "Everyone's already freaked out. This will only—"

"Well if you won't, I will!" She stood and took a step forward. "Paiscion!" she shouted. "You need to see this!"

8
The Choice

"Where is the choice when all must be brought into balance?
Which is the righteous path in two opposing worlds?"

PAISCION STOPPED MID-SENTENCE AND looked at her in surprise,
then followed her finger to the Merisi Band. He frowned and
started to walk over. "This had better be important, Simia
Roskoroy," he murmured.

The crowd began to chatter among themselves.

Paiscion drew up and looked from Simia to Sylas, then down
at the Merisi Band. He inclined his head a little.

"When did this inscription appear?"

"Just now," said Sylas, "when Naeo and I got close. The band
started to glow and—"

"The Samarok!" interjected Paiscion. "Do you have it with you?"

Sylas nodded. He reached for his bag, fished inside and drew
out the ancient tome.

Paiscion took it carefully in his hands. For some moments he
leafed through it, searching for something, apparently at random.

"Blood..." he murmured under his breath, "blood... blood..."

Finally he stopped and furrowed his brow in concentration,

apparently allowing the Ravel Runes to work their magic. Sylas saw the writing on the page writhe and shift again and again and again until finally, Paiscion nodded. His eyes snapped up to Sylas's.

"Here," he said, handing the Samarok back, open at the page. Then to Sylas's surprise, he turned on his heel and walked off beneath the boughs of the Living Tree, heading directly for Naeo.

"*Important*, you see!" grinned Simia, poking a finger in his side.

Sylas was too busy looking at the Samarok to reply. His eyes passed quickly over a page that seemed to be written almost entirely in verse, but before the Ravel Runes had time to reveal their meaning, he heard Paiscion speak.

The Magruman was now beneath the tree, talking to Naeo. There was a quick exchange and then, in some confusion, Naeo raised her wrist. She and Paiscion stared at the other half of the Merisi Band, still glowing faintly in the sunlight. For a moment they were motionless, then Paisicon's face filled with a knowing smile. Naeo was plainly bewildered. They exchanged a few more words and then the Magruman left her side and walked back out into the centre of the gardens.

By this point the Say-So had reached a high pitch of excitement, so that when Paiscion raised his hands he had to wait for silence.

"Sisters and brothers!" he shouted. "Sisters and brothers! Young Simia here has spotted something that may be very important to these proceedings." Attention shifted to Simia, who seemed fit to burst with pride. "As you may or may not have heard, when Sylas and Naeo first met, the Merisi Band split in two, forming a new bracelet for each of them. It seems that when Sylas and Naeo drew near one another just now, these two bracelets revealed a message, also in two parts." Paiscion opened his hands and grinned admiringly. "It is a message intended to reveal the way ahead. It speaks to us in this very moment!"

The Say-So erupted once again in excited murmurings and whisperings, followed by scores of hushes and calls for quiet. Everyone wanted to hear what Paiscion would say next.

"The inscription," he continued, "is simply this…"

He cleared his throat.

"*In blood it began. In blood it must end.*"

The gathering was silent long enough for Paiscion's words to echo from the cliffs and then the whispers began again – whispers filled with fear. Worried looks were exchanged, faces paled, heads were shaken in foreboding.

But the frightened murmurings fell away almost as soon as they had begun.

The Magruman was smiling.

He was standing with his arms crossed, waiting, with a broad grin on his face.

"Forgive me, Paiscion," protested Kaspertak, "but what is there to smile about? What can this be but a terrible prophecy?"

"It is a clue!" cried Paiscion. "A clue written by Merisu himself, for who but he forged the Merisi Band? And if it is a clue written by Merisu, where should it lead us but to the book he himself began all those centuries ago." He pointed across the gardens. "It leads us to the Samarok!"

Suddenly the entire Say-So was focused eagerly on Sylas and the book he held before him.

"I have just looked through the Samarok myself," continued Paiscion. "Using the Ravel Runes, I have searched for that same phrase. References to blood lead to many entries, but blood and beginnings lead to only one. An entry deep in the ancient histories – an entry I have never seen before. Sisters and brothers, it contains the exact message we have found on the Merisi Band!" He paused to allow more excited chatter to die away. "Now, Sylas, as the rightful bearer of the Samarok, perhaps you could read the whole entry to us?"

Sylas closed his eyes to overcome his nerves and to clear his mind. Finally he opened them and focused on the runes at the top of the page. Instantly they started to work their magic, changing from a nonsensical scrawl into intricate Ravel Runes, revealing their true meaning.

He read the first words: *"The Song of Isia."*

"Speak up, please!" shouted someone high on the cliff.

Sylas cleared his throat. "It's a song!" he shouted. *"The Song of Isia!"*

There was a new surge of excitement, with animated chatter, knowing nods and cries of, "Isia, of course!"

"Quiet, everyone!" shouted Filimaya, clapping her hands. "Let Sylas finish!"

Sylas turned his eyes back to the page, mastered his thoughts and read on:

> *"She sings from the skies,*
> *Through earth and the sea;*
> *She sings through the lies*
> *To both parts of me.*
>
> *She tells of old lore,*
> *Of dark and the light;*
> *She tells of a war*
> *Two children must fight."*

Suddenly the gardens were filled with more excited whispers. Sylas waited for them to calm before continuing.

> "She sings of two lands,
> Though one we can see:
> She tells of twin bands,
> To set us all free.
>
> She sings of the lines
> Of glove and the hand.
> She tells of a time
> For one final stand.
>
> But this time of sun
> Will end all too soon.
> Our hope quickly won,
> Will die in one moon.
>
> She sings from the skies,
> Through bare root and tree:
> She sings through the lies
> To both parts of me.
>
> In this her sad song
> A message she sends:
> In blood it began,
> In blood it must end."

He felt a slight shiver as he read the final lines, then looked up from the page to see hundreds of faces staring back. Paiscion was the only one who moved. He nodded quietly to himself, a smile growing on his lips.

"And so there it is," he said, almost to himself, his eyes bright behind his glasses, "our past, our present and our future!"

There were murmurings from the crowd, then someone cried out: "But I don't understand!"

Paiscion threw his arms wide. "The song tells us all we need to know!" he cried. "That all is coming to pass just as the great Merisu foretold! That Sylas and Naeo, these two children wearing twin bands, are destined to fight a great war for freedom! A battle to vanquish the lies that have divided our two worlds! Our two selves!"

"You see!" shouted someone by the river. "They *are* here to fight for us!"

Paiscion shook his head. "Not to fight for the Suhl," he corrected, "but for all humankind. For the freedom of all. For our right to be whole! The Suhl may be part of this war, but it will not be fought for us."

There were some whispers, but when no one spoke up, Paiscion turned back to the gathering.

"But the song tells us more than that. It tells us that there is no time to lose, that hope will die in one moon, which can only mean the moon that brought Sylas to us."

"But it's only just over two weeks before the new moon!" cried Glubitch, shaking his red locks. "It's full tomorrow. Surely there's no time for—"

"It seems that's all the time we have," said Paiscion firmly. "We will just have to use it well. Which brings us to the true purpose of the song: to tell us what must be done next."

"But I didn't hear any such thing," grumbled Kaspertak. "It's the usual Samarok gobbledygook!"

"And yet it was there, in the very title!" cried Paiscion. "Sisters and brothers, this is *Isia's* song! Can anyone doubt that she is at the centre of everything? That she was there at the beginning and that she knows the end? And is it really a surprise that she – the

Seer of Souls and the one power that Thoth does not control — that she holds the key to this prophecy?"

There were many nods of agreement and for the first time the congregation seemed to be one, muttering their assent.

Sylas listened to all this with growing astonishment and unease — fighting battles for all of humankind? Making the worlds whole? People whole? And in twenty days? It seemed ludicrous. But there was something else: a knot was forming in his stomach — a knot of frustration. The only people not being consulted on what should happen next were he and Naeo. What if they didn't want to do all this together? What if they just *couldn't*? They could hardly bear to be in the same gardens! And in truth, no matter how important all this sounded, he could not — must not — forget that his mother was still alive, languishing in some hospital somewhere in his own world.

"You are of course right," said an elderly woman near the Living Tree. "Sylas and Naeo should go back to the city and consult with Isia straight away."

Suddenly Naeo stepped forward. "But what if we don't want to travel together any more?" she asked abruptly. "What if we can't? You've seen what happens when we're too close! And it's getting worse all the time!"

The elderly woman wavered and sat down.

Ash stood and stepped forward. "In any case, I'd say it's not a great idea for them to move around together," he said. "Surely that's just what Thoth will be expecting? He'll have every Scryer he has looking out for them travelling together."

"But their power lies in being together!" said Kaspertak. "I thought that was the whole point!"

"Yes!" shouted someone else. "Wasn't that why Naeo summoned Sylas in the first place? So that they could be together? Change things *together*?"

"It's not as though anyone has done this before!" replied Naeo sharply. "How was I to know it'd feel like this? And anyway, who says we have to be together all the time? Why not just when it matters?"

The Say-So grew quiet. Paiscion took off his glasses and rubbed them on his handkerchief, deep in thought. Finally he placed them back on his nose.

"A conundrum," he said, wagging his finger as though finding his way through his thoughts. "But if Sylas and Naeo cannot do everything together — if they can only be together when it most matters — then perhaps only one of them can go to Isia after all. And if that is the case, I wonder if the other can use their time just as profitably…" He nodded and wagged his finger more vigorously. "I wonder if they can find a way to be together without harm… yes… or apart and together at the same time…"

"Paiscion, but you're making no sense!" grumbled Glubitch.

"I'm talking about the Merisi," said Paiscion, excited once again. "After all, the reason the Merisi created the Merisi Band was to keep the wearer from meeting their own Glimmer. *And* they created the Glimmer Glass — the mirrors that allow them to see their Glimmer!" He looked searchingly around the gardens. "Bringing Glimmers together and keeping them apart! If anyone understands the forces that draw us to and repel us from our Glimmer, it is the Merisi. And if anybody will know how Sylas and Naeo can make use of their gift without needing to be together, it is the Merisi!"

"Those Merisi inventions are mere trinkets," protested Kaspertak. "Cobbled-together mongrels of Essenfayle and science."

"How can you say that when you have seen what the Merisi Band can do?" retorted Filimaya. "And there's so much more!

67

We spoke earlier about the Otherly Guild — they spent years studying the Merisi's Things. They found them to have extraordinary power!"

Paiscion nodded. "As many of you know, I led the Otherly Guild and yes, among other things, we sought to understand the inventions of the Merisi — their miraculous and wonderful Things. They are more in number and greatness than we were ever able to understand."

Sylas had been listening to all this with growing realisation. "*Things?*" he repeated. "You mean the Things that Mr Zhi had when I met him? The ones in the Shop of Things?"

Paiscion grinned. "The very same."

Sylas's eyes grew wide. "So... you think if I went back to the Shop of Things, Mr Zhi might know... what? How we can be together while we're apart?"

"Quite possibly. Mr Zhi is the foremost authority on Things of all kinds, shapes and sizes," said Paiscion. Then he frowned. "Only I'm not sure that it is a good idea that you should go, Sylas. You are known in the Other and Thoth may expect you to return. In these perilous times, I think we need to do everything to defeat Thoth's expectations whenever we—"

"But when do we get to say what *we* want to do?" blurted Sylas, his frustration finally spilling over, his tone harsher than he had intended.

Paiscion blinked at him through his glasses, then he glanced at Filimaya. She simply nodded and crossed her arms.

"Young Sylas, I apologise," said the Magruman. He looked at Naeo. "Both of you, I'm sorry: this is of course *your* decision. We certainly don't mean to take away your freedom to choose your own course." He looked from one to the other. "So... what is it that *you* would like to do?"

Sylas hesitated for a moment, still a little surprised by his own outburst. And then something extraordinary happened. As Sylas opened his mouth to speak, so did Naeo.

"Find my mother," said Sylas.

"Find my father," said Naeo.

The congregation gasped and looked in wonder at the two children. Though the few words they had uttered were in unison, their two voices had not clashed: they had become one. And what they said was the same, but opposite. The effect was electric.

Perhaps the only people who did not seem surprised were Sylas and Naeo themselves. It was as though they had only heard their own voice.

Paiscion eyed them both with renewed fascination. "Of course!" he said. "Of course your parents are your priority and it is quite natural that you should want to find them." He frowned in concentration. "Perhaps there is a way that all of these objectives might be combined."

"I'm not saying that we can't do these other things as well," said Sylas quickly, starting to feel rather selfish. "I know it's important to talk to Mr Zhi – and to see Isia – but I can't just forget about my mother."

"And I can't leave my father in the Dirgheon!" said Naeo.

"Of *course* you must look for your parents," reassured Filimaya. "It adds to the challenge, but that is no reason not to try."

"*Really?*" said Ash. He walked to the centre of the hollow and looked at Naeo and Sylas. "I'm sorry, but I don't agree. If you do this – if you set out to find the very people you're closest to, you're far more likely to be seen by Thoth's spies. It was hard enough to get into the Dirgheon last time, and I'd wager my grandmother that he'll be more prepared now. Added to which, all the Dirgheon guards know what Naeo looks like."

Sylas and Naeo tensed and prepared for a fight. They knew that Ash was right but this wasn't rational, it was personal: how were they supposed to discard all the family they had left?

For a moment the meeting seemed to have reached another dead end. Many looked to Paiscion, hoping that their long-lost Magruman would know what to do. But it was not Paiscion who spoke next. Quietly and without anyone noticing, Simia stood up. She glanced anxiously at Sylas and then lifted her head to the great assembly.

"I have an idea," she said.

9

Friends

"In the Suhl, we have found allies and friends
with whom we might change the nature of the world."

THE THREE PRESSED ON, tracing the fringes of the great lake,
heading back towards Sylva. The young Scryer was soon striding
out in front, but this time he had not drawn far ahead: Sylas was
with him, his face set with determination and his arms pumping
furiously at his sides. It was Simia who was lagging behind. She
was scuttling on as best she could, but she was no match for the
Scryer, nor for Sylas in this mood.

"Oh, come on," she groaned, drawing to a halt, "slow down!"

Triste hesitated and eased his pace, but Sylas gritted his teeth
and stomped on. Then he stopped and turned back.

"I just can't believe *you* suggested it!" he bellowed. "I mean,
you, of all people! You know how much I want to find my mum.
And now instead I have to go back to the city to find Bowe! I
thought you were on my side?"

Simia flicked her fiery hair over her shoulders. "I *am* on your
side. And Naeo's, actually. But you've both got a death wish!"

"No, we haven't. We can look after ourselves!"

"Well, sure, when you're together! But isn't that the whole idea? We don't know what you'll be like when you're apart — in different worlds!" She stared at him steadily. "And anyway, the Say-So was never going to agree to you going after your mum — you could see that!"

"We'll do it anyway. I'm going after my mum and Naeo's going after Bowe, no matter what the Say-So decided."

"Then you're fools," said the Scryer.

Sylas rounded on him. "Oh really? You think so?" he yelled, his eyes burning.

Triste looked at him calmly, as though considering the question. He pulled the pipe from behind his ear.

He knocked it on the heel of his hand. "The Say-So is right — Thoth will be expecting you to look for your mother, and Naeo her father. He'll see you coming. And if he doesn't, his Scryers will."

"Thoth has his own Scryers?" said Simia incredulously.

Triste shook his head and pushed what looked like green moss into his pipe. "The ones he's captured and turned."

"Some of our Scryers are working for Thoth? How *could* they?"

Triste regarded her coolly with his weary, sunken eyes. "If you'd seen what we've seen," he said, "if you'd seen the Reckoning as we saw it, you might have despaired too." He puffed at his pipe. "For Scryers, more than any other, wars are a living hell. Too much pain. Too much loss." He took the pipe from his mouth and inspected the bowl, prodding at the strange tobacco inside. "Anyway, the point is, now that Thoth's Scryers know what to look for, they'll see everything I see."

"And what's that, exactly?" asked Sylas, still struggling to cool his temper.

Triste winced as his pipe sent up a new pall of orange smoke.

"If Naeo nears her father, or if you near your mother, you'll stand out like a bushfire on a dark night."

Sylas looked into the Scryer's large, shadowy eyes, then shot an angry look at Simia. He turned and walked to the water's edge, staring out across the lake. The mist had burned away now and the Valley of Outs was lit by the morning rays, but he hardly saw the beautiful waters or the majestic forests. He did not even see the small flotilla of boats on the lake, carrying the Suhl back to their homes. His thoughts were far away, with his mother, in another world. He knew that Simia was right — that the Say-So had been right — but that was irrelevant. For a few moments, when Paiscion had talked about going back to Mr Zhi, she had felt so *close*. Now she felt as far away as ever.

Simia walked up behind him. "I was just worried about you..." she said, quietly. "And I thought, in a way, if Naeo finds your mum — and you find Bowe — isn't that almost the same thing?"

"No, it's not," said Sylas, walking away. "It doesn't work like that."

"But you see, *that's* the problem," Simia called after him. "No one knows what it's like to be you. No one knows—"

She felt Triste's hand on her shoulder. The Scryer leaned down to her ear. "It's no good, not while he feels like this. Give him time."

"But I thought I was doing the right thing," she whispered, her eyes following Sylas. "I really did."

"Well, you were being a friend," said the Scryer. "And that isn't always easy."

She turned and looked at him. Her eyes explored his face and then, just for an instant, she looked surprised and confused, as though she had seen something unexpected. She opened her mouth to say something but seemed to think better of it and instead she wheeled about and set off alone.

The Scryer watched her go, tilting his head to one side as though trying to make sense of an impossible puzzle.

Then his brow knitted in a frown.

"How inconvenient," he muttered.

10
Hope and Despair

"...there, above her beloved valley, she surveyed
all the hope and despair *of the world."*

SYLAS WAS UNSURE HOW long he had been walking. For some time
he had trailed along the shoreline, following in the footsteps of Triste
and Simia. Occasionally he saw them climbing a headland or tracing
the edge of the woods, but he made no attempt to catch up.
Eventually he left their path altogether, walking into the shade of
the forest. He meandered between the trees in the general direction
of Sylva, but he was in no rush to get there. He needed to think.

Sure, Simia's idea made some sense: it would be the opposite
of what anyone would expect and the Scryers were much less
likely to see any connection — whatever that really meant. But
what did all that matter, compared to finding his mother? Being
with her, after all this time? Yes, Naeo might go in his place, but
that wasn't the same as finding her himself. In fact if it wasn't
him, would she really be *found* at all?

No, this wasn't even a good second best. They didn't understand.
He sighed. In truth, neither did he.

And these were the thoughts that dogged him as he ambled across the dried leaves on the forest floor and wound between the ancient trunks of the forest: *his* life… *his* mother… himself… what did those things even *mean* when he knew that Naeo was there, just through the forest. Another part of himself? How crazy did that sound!

He was still very far from understanding Naeo. His experience of her was sensation and emotion rather than anything real or tangible. He didn't even feel like he'd met her, not really. He remembered the feeling of warmth and joy when he had first seen her — of comfort and completeness when he had held her hand. Then the surge of energy — raw power, even — when she had stood at his side, when they had fought their way out of the Dirgheon. But since then, when she drew too near — as she had in the Garden of Havens — there was that awful pain, beginning in his wrist and becoming unbearable. Not like a wound, but more like an ache and the oddest sense that everything inside him was shifting out of place.

And although he had felt these things, these immense forces and feelings, for some reason he had thought very little of her. It was almost as if he didn't need to think of her, or perhaps his thoughts couldn't quite grasp her. She was still very much a separate person, and now it was that person, not him, who was going back to the Other.

He picked up a stick and swiped it against a tree trunk. It snapped in half and the crack echoed through the forest.

"What did that tree ever do to you?" asked a voice.

Sylas whirled about, his eyes searching the forest. But he already knew who it was.

The Magruman stepped out from behind a line of bushes. His eyebrows appeared above his spectacles.

"Sorry," said Sylas.

"Well, don't apologise to me! You didn't hit *me*!"

"Oh... no..." said Sylas. He turned back towards the tree, wondering if he was really supposed to say sorry to the trunk.

Paiscion let out a peel of laughter. "I'm only joking, Sylas!" he said, walking up and holding his hand out in greeting. "I'm sure that old giant can handle a tap on the backside!"

Sylas grinned. "Right," he said, taking the Magruman's hand.

Paiscion grasped his shoulder warmly with the other hand. He drew a breath and then looked about him. "Now, how did you find this place? Did someone tell you about it?"

Sylas shrugged. "No, I was just walking."

"Ha!" cried Paiscion. "Then we shall call it good luck, because you have stumbled on the very corner of the Valley of Outs that I wanted to show you!"

"I *have*?" asked Sylas, glancing around in surprise. This part looked just like any other.

A mysterious smile spread across Paiscion's face. "Step this way."

He led Sylas down a small bank towards the lake, then turned to one side. Ahead was a tree of even greater proportions than those around it, with a vast trunk that soared to an astonishing height above their heads. But it was not just its size that caught Sylas's eye.

He blinked and squinted. Its aged bark was deeply faulted and gnarled, such that the many ruts in its greyish brown surface coiled and twisted into countless patterns and shapes. But there, a little above head height, were some lines that appeared far from random. There were two gentle arcs, each side of a long, almost-straight furrow. The effect was simple, but unmistakable.

It was a giant feather.

"Do you like to climb trees?"

Sylas drew his eyes away from the symbol and looked up at

Paiscion. He frowned. "It's been a while," he said, "but I suppose so... why?"

Paiscion lifted his glasses off his nose and winked. "Well, imagine what fun it is when the tree is on your side."

"What do you mean?"

The Magruman shrugged. "Ask the tree to help you up. Someone with your gift should have no trouble at all." Then he raised his hands and gestured for Sylas to do the same.

"Now, just ask!" said the Magruman.

Sylas looked up into the great boughs of the tree, his eyes travelling up above the feather, up beyond the mighty trunk and into the heart of the canopy. And then he asked. It was only a thought — a fleeting flurry of words — but instantly the patchwork of orange and brown swayed a little and there was a hiss and swish as though the wind were racing through the leaves.

But there *was* no wind.

Suddenly, in a motion that was at once natural and utterly peculiar, the drooping branches of the tree swept down to the forest floor. Their powerful joints creaked under the strain, but the lowermost limbs fell with ease, then turned, brushing up their own fallen leaves, sweeping them towards Sylas and Paiscion. They flew up in a rush of yellows and browns, dancing about them in a great muddle of colour, and instinctively Sylas raised his hands to shield his eyes.

He felt something move beneath his arms.

He threw them down, but to his surprise, he felt the woody limbs sliding up into his armpits. Before he knew what was happening, they had taken the weight off his feet.

And then the grand old tree hoisted him into the air.

S

"Take whichever you want," echoed the voice of many.

Scarpia lowered her head and prowled across the passage to the nearest doorway. She snarled, dropping a little on her haunches and pressing her ears back against her head. Her sensitive nose had scented the Black and its stench was still strong in her memory. She peered into the chamber, her cat's eye adjusting quickly to the darkness.

There, in the centre of the stone floor, was a pulsating sack of slime. Protruding from its top was a massive head, half covered with dark fur, half with pale, human skin. Its ears turned at her approach and a low, gurgling growl rumbled in its throat, but its narrow eyes remained closed. It was a mongrel, but its angular, predatory features were clearly feline.

"Made in your own image, my dear," echoed the voices from somewhere further down the corridor. "For your own little army. You will need more than your mastery of Urgolvane in the Other. It will not be so powerful there."

Scarpia bowed, then turned and padded down the passageway after her master, zigzagging left and right as she glanced into chamber after chamber, each containing the same half-born forms.

"Thank you, my Lord," she said. "You are truly the master of Kimiyya."

"Of course I am!" was the abrupt reply. Then more softly: "Take whatever you need. Take the Scryers, if you wish. Take a Ray Reaper."

Scarpia's head snapped around. "A... *Ray Reaper*? Will it go with me?"

"It will go where I tell it!"

Scarpia recoiled a little, but still seemed unsure. "I would *like* to take one, my Lord," she said. "But I worry that... that it may not... obey me. After all, it was once a Priest of Souls, just like you."

Thoth whipped around, his cloak flying up about him. "The Reapers were NEVER like me! They are infidels and ingrates and fools!" he growled in barks and screams, his frail body seeming to swell. "They DARED to plot against me? To rise against me? The one who had led them to greatness, who had given them their power?" He spat dust from dry, empty lips. "They are lucky that I let them live at all! That I allow them their simpering dance with the sun and the moon!" He wheezed and panted, then lowered his head, seeming to shrink back down to his normal size. "Take Hathor. If nothing else, you will need him at the Circle of Salsimaine."

Scarpia bowed. "Of course, Great Lord," she said. "And he will do as I command?"

"He will do precisely as you command," was the quick reply, "or I will destroy what little of him is left!"

Scarpia purred and flashed a fanged smile. "Thank you, my Lord."

"Do not thank me!" barked Thoth. "Obey me!"

Scarpia bowed her head a little nearer to the flagstones. "I will not disappoint you again, my Lord," she said. "But do you not want me to leave some of this army with you?" She swept a clawed hand back down the corridor. "For your own... security?"

A dry chuckle sounded in the back of Thoth's wasted throat. He stepped up to the doors at the end of the corridor, seized the handles and threw them wide.

The whites of Scarpia's eyes flared. Beyond the doors was what looked like an infinite void — a passageway without end, flanked on both sides by hundreds, perhaps thousands of the same dark little doorways: the gaping mouths of birthing chambers.

Thoth drew the gash of his mouth into a crooked smile.

"I am prepared," he murmured.

§

"Just relax!" cried Paiscion. "It won't let you fall!"

Sylas winced as the crook of the branch swept out from beneath his armpits and dropped him on to a wide bough. He teetered forward, his arms circling in the air. He hardly had time to regain his balance before that bough too was sweeping him upwards, bearing him even higher into the crown of the tree.

He glanced across and saw Paiscion standing on a broad limb, being borne ever higher into the canopy, but that he was entirely relaxed, his arms resting at his sides, watching with amusement as his companion struggled and fretted.

Sylas tried to relax as another branch swept down from above and approached him head-on. Before he knew it, a fork was straddling his chest, lifting him beneath the arms and leaving him dangling in mid-air. Already he was in motion, sailing up between branches and somehow weaving a path between the twigs and leaves. He fought the urge to resist the tree — relaxing his shoulders, dropping his arms — and for the first time looked about him. The canopy was in constant motion, bearing them upwards with the deliberate but graceful path of its limbs, swaying this way and that in such a natural manner that if anyone had seen them from a distance they would have imagined the branches caught by the wind and thought no more of it. When he glanced up he saw to his amazement that he was already nearing the top: he could see a sparkle of daylight between the leaves.

"Nearly there!" cried Paiscion at his side.

And then, as quickly as it had begun, it was over. Sylas was dropped on to one final limb, which swayed to allow him to gain his balance and then drifted up towards a large bough above his head. As it came level, it slowed and then halted, allowing him to step off.

Panting and sweating, he found himself at Paiscion's shoulder.

The Magruman smiled at him and nodded over the edge of the wide bough.

"Have you ever climbed such a tree?"

Sylas peered over the edge. His head swam as he saw most of the canopy far below him. He could not see the ground at all.

He squatted down and had to resist the temptation to wrap his arms around the bough. "No," he said, with a dry throat. "I really haven't."

Paiscion laughed and slid a hand under his arm, drawing him back to his feet. "The longer the drop," he whispered in Sylas's ear, "the greater the reward. Look at that view!"

Ignoring his wobbly knees, Sylas followed the Magruman's gaze. The rolling roof of the forest was far below, the billowing clouds of orange, green and brown flecked with the golden sun. And there, framed by the leaves of trees and stretching almost as far as the eyes could see, was the vast span of the Valley of Outs.

"I've never tired of this view and never will," said Paiscion wistfully. He drew a long breath. "It reminds me of her."

Sylas pulled his eyes away. "Her?"

"Merimaat," said Paiscion, as if it should be obvious, "the mother of our people. This was her retreat, her hideaway." He nodded along the branch of the tree. "Well, to be more precise, *that* was her hideaway."

Sylas turned and his eyes grew wide.

"Wow," he whispered.

There, crowning the very pinnacle of the tree was what looked like a gigantic nest. But this nest had not been made by the peck and weave of birds, nor by the labour of men, but rather by the tree itself. Each of its uppermost branches had become part of the structure, bending and looping into the floor, walls and roof of a glorious chamber. Its outline matched the curves of the tree, such that from a distance it would look like nothing unusual. But from here, it was a thing of wonder. The branches formed regular, looping beams and curling struts, the leaves blanketing the roof to form a perfect shelter, and some of the branches seemed to have grown in generous, empty arcs, to create two huge windows and a doorway.

"Come along," said Paiscion, stepping along the bough. "It is best seen from the inside!"

Sylas spread his arms wide and teetered along the branch behind the Magruman, trying not to let his eyes drop into the void below. Finally he stepped with relief into the strange hideaway.

He found himself standing on a soft, springy surface, a tightly woven web of twigs and leaves so dense that there was only the odd gap, through which he spied the long drop below. Around him was a beautiful, domed structure, in which there appeared to be no straight lines, no clasps or fixings. It looked to have just grown that way, weaving around the space as though it contained something precious and untouchable. And yet that space was entirely empty, except for four chairs — two facing out of each huge window — and a table at its centre, which was also bare except for a small wooden box.

"She would often sit there in the morning and watch the sun rise over the valley," said Paiscion, pointing to one of the chairs at the nearest window. "And in the evening, she would sit and watch the sunset." He turned to the other window. "Take a look — it's quite special."

Sylas walked over the pleasing carpet of leaves to the giant opening. This view was almost as striking as the other, but it was quite different. Below, the beautiful canopy of trees stretched away over to a range of lower hills, where it thinned and darkened.

His eyes followed the glistening trail of the river as it snaked through this forest, following the course that he and the *Windrush* had taken only the day before. The further his gaze travelled, the more he felt a creeping dread and then, sure enough, he saw the dying fringes of the forest bleeding into a vast grey expanse. Parched and hungry, the Barrens sucked the light from the sky so that the entire horizon was a giant, senseless strip of drabness, showing no breaks, no features, no promise of anything beyond.

But then Sylas squinted and leaned forward, peering into the nothingness. There *was* something. Its sharp peak was just visible through the sickly atmosphere of dust and ash. A perfect triangle of shadow: the apex of a pyramid.

He felt a chill run down his spine. The Dirgheon.

Paiscion sat down in the chair at his side. "'The hope of the world through one window', she would say, 'and its despair through the other'." He looked grimly towards the horizon. "I hate that view. A wasteland of lives and souls... the place where Merimaat herself would finally lose her life in the Reckoning... and beyond, just there through the endless grey, Gheroth, Thoth's city." He glanced at Sylas. "He never used to show it such interest, you know — this city he calls his own and has turned to darkness. Until recent years, he was far more interested in other parts of his Empire. He's only blighted Gheroth with his presence since the Reckoning, gloating on all he has won, all he has destroyed. Making sure that he finishes the job. I sometimes think he'll be there in that hideous Dirgheon of his until the last of the Suhl draws their final breath."

As he listened Sylas found himself back in the stinking dungeons and dank passageways of the Dirgheon, the filth and stench of the thousands of cells, the warren of corridors and staircases leading only into darkness. And he thought of the moment when he and

Naeo had reached the pinnacle of the pyramid, when they had seen Bowe reaching up to wave them away while above him, that diabolical figure in crimson robes gazed out at them, peered into them with a blank and empty face...

He swallowed and drew himself back to the present. He walked around the chair and sat down.

"So, why did you bring me here?"

Paiscion glanced across at him. "It's what she would have done," he said, taking off his glasses and cleaning them on his robe. "Merimaat said this place helped her to see more clearly."

"See what?"

The Magruman placed the spectacles back on his nose. "To see what was important, and to remind herself that those important things —" he nodded towards the Valley of Outs — "those things we most treasure — that they come at a price. They always come at a price." He looked back at the Barrens.

Sylas gazed out over the blanket of grey. He could sense where this conversation was going. "You're not just talking about the valley and the Barrens, are you?" he said. "You're talking about what was decided in the Say-So. You're saying that my mum comes at a price too."

The Magruman inclined his head. "Perhaps my point is rather obvious, Sylas, but it is important." He turned back to the wastes. "On a clearer day, you know, even this view improves. When the light is just right, when the Dirgheon casts no shadow, you can see the Temple of Isia, glowing in all the grimness."

"You mean, the place I'm supposed to go," said Sylas irritably. "The place I have to go instead of finding my mother."

"Quite a price to pay, you are thinking, aren't you?" asked Paiscion.

Sylas nodded.

"Well it is a sacrifice — that is for certain — but it may not be quite as heavy a price as you may think. Did you see it on your way through the city? The temple?"

"Yes," said Sylas trying to lose the edge in his voice. "A white tower — it was strange — sloping sides and two platforms at the top."

"Strange, and beautiful," said the Magruman. "It's modelled on the Djed Pillar, an ancient symbol of stability. Only right, because Isia is perhaps the only stable thing in this world of ours. Many have dreamed of going inside, of meeting Isia. But she rarely shows herself and even then, only on the platform at the top of the temple."

"So... who is she?" asked Sylas, leaning forward, his elbows on his knees.

"Well, now we're getting to it!" said Paiscion with a smile. "No one really knows where she hails from, but she's been around at least as long as Thoth himself. They say she's young and beautiful in appearance — and kind, unwaveringly kind — Thoth's nemesis, if you like. Although she never takes sides — she doesn't involve herself in the ugliness of the world."

Sylas frowned. "If she doesn't get involved, how can she be so good? Why's she so important?"

"She may not interfere, but that's not to say that she isn't at the centre of our lives. There's something that has always drawn people to Isia — something deeper and more important than our daily lives, than our skirmishes and battles, even the Undoing."

"So she's a leader or... what, some kind of... god?"

Paiscion shrugged. "Some people believe that, yes. She certainly has unique insights into the human soul. Much has been made of her teachings, her predictions, her pronouncements. I daresay you will find many of them in the Samarok. She has extraordinary vision."

"So she sees... like a Scryer sees?"

Paiscion shook his head. "Like a thousand Scryers who never sleep. They say she sees further than the four horizons and deeper than thought or feeling."

"And you think she knows about the Glimmer Myth?"

"Well, you read the song in that book of yours," said Paiscion, nodding to Sylas's bag. "She knows about the Glimmer Myth, certainly. And about your place in it? Quite probably."

"And you think she'll speak to me?"

Paiscion laughed. "Sylas, you're a boy from another world, one half of a reunited soul and the fulfilment of the Glimmer Myth. She won't be able to resist you."

11
Duty

*"Twelve priests bound by duty to their king,
and to each of them, three indentured Magrumen.
This is all it took to bring the world to ruin."*

FILIMAYA'S EYES SPARKLED LIKE jewels of the forest.

"Beautiful, isn't it?" she said.

Naeo climbed the bank and stepped up to Filimaya's side. Below, scores of little streams and rivulets wove their way across the forest floor, twisting and turning, rolling and leaping. At the base of the slope they joined the still waters of the lake amidst a great muddle of bubbles and spray, which sent a pleasant mist back up the bank and laced everything in a glistening dew.

"This is what we tried to recreate at the Meander Mill," said Filimaya. "Did you hear of our Water Gardens?"

Naeo shook her head. They sounded familiar, but she had no idea why.

"Ah well," said Filimaya, "they're gone now, like so much else. And so this is it: our last retreat, our patch of things."

"There are still plenty of us in the slums," said Naeo, picking up a stick and poking at the bank. "And in the Dirgheon."

"Yes, there are, but that's no way to live," said Filimaya with a sigh. "It sometimes feels as though we are clinging on to this world, doesn't it? As if we might lose our place in it altogether."

"Well, that's just what he wants, isn't it?" muttered Naeo, swiping the tip of the stick into the nearest stream.

"Yes. Indeed," said Filimaya wistfully.

She stepped over the torrent and began making her way across the labyrinth of rivulets. After a few steps she stopped and looked back at Naeo. "But that's part of what makes Sylas so exciting, so hopeful, isn't it? Like the Bringers before him, he brings us a promise of a world without Thoth, without the Undoing, without all the suffering our people have endured."

Naeo stepped out to follow. She sensed where this conversation was heading. "I suppose, but that still doesn't make me want to go to his world."

"Really? You're not the least bit curious? A world without Thoth, where you're entirely free? Like everyone else?"

Naeo shrugged.

"A place without Essenfayle or the Three Ways, where summer is winter and night is day? Where people drive carriages without horses and light torches without flames; where they fly—"

"No! I'm not interested!" snapped Naeo, drawing up sharply. "I don't care about any of that! My father is still *here*! And — and worse than that — he's in the Dirgheon, probably half dead or... or worse." She paused, her heart thumping and her eyes burning. "And it's my fault!"

It was a huge relief to say it. She had thought about little else since her escape.

It was her fault. *Her fault.*

The memories came in flashes: stark and clear. There he was, chained to a stone table, covered in sweat and blood, arching with

89

pain whenever his tormentor drew near, screaming until his voice trailed away. She remembered the few quiet moments, those precious moments of reprieve when Thoth would write, or take up his cello, or even leave the room, when her father would turn to her with those large green eyes.

How she loved those eyes.

And in that generous gaze she had felt him saying it would all be all right, felt his strength, his warmth. But she had seen the tears trickling on to the stone. And she had known their meaning. She had seen the despair in those tears.

And what had she done? She had left him behind, she had taken flight, rising on the magical winds above the pyramid. She had seen him there, on the pinnacle. Her beautiful, strong father, raising his bloodied hand to wave them away. And above him, that murderous figure in crimson robes, that empty, merciless face.

Then she had turned in the night sky, and fled.

She pressed her eyes closed and tried to hold that final moment in her mind. When it became too much, a sob escaped her lips.

An arm curled around her shoulders and drew her close. She pushed away at first: she didn't want to give in to it — she had to be strong. And she didn't deserve comfort — where was her father's comfort? But there was something about Filimaya's presence that caught her off guard, that made her feel safe. It was almost as though, in some small way, Filimaya brought her father closer.

So she didn't fight any more.

They stood for some time surrounded by the streams, neither of them speaking: Filimaya holding her, Naeo with her arms at her sides.

"It's not your fault, you know," said Filimaya, finally.

Naeo shook her head. "Thoth wouldn't even care about my father if it wasn't for me. I should be trying to find him." She pulled away and looked up at Filimaya. "I know it doesn't make any sense, not to anyone else. I mean, Espasian and I brought Sylas here so that we could change things, so that he and I might do something *important*. But the thing is —" her voice broke but she forced herself to finish — "the thing is, whenever I pictured a better world, a world after the Undoing — a world without Thoth — I always pictured seeing it with my dad. I think I did some of this — all of it, maybe — for him. To be with him — safe and free."

Filimaya drew some strands of blonde hair from Naeo's face. "I do understand," she said. "We often say that we would move mountains for those we love. In your case, you have the chance to do exactly that: you have the chance to change the world." She held out her hand to lead Naeo across the next stream. "Tell me, what do you know about Sylas and his mother?"

Naeo shrugged. "I know she's in hospital — a place run by the Merisi. And I know that she has something to do with this world."

"That's all true," said Filimaya, stepping on a stone in the middle of a stream. "But you are talking about Sylas's mother. My question is, what do you know of her and *Sylas*?"

"What do you mean?"

"Well, do you know that Sylas thought her dead for many years, just as your father thought he had lost you?"

Naeo shook her head. "No, I didn't."

"Did you know that she suffered the most appalling dreams and nightmares, so that people thought she was mad? That Sylas had to watch her suffering, and that finally he saw her drugged and taken away?"

Naeo winced and slowed her step. "Why are you telling me this?"

"Did you know that the last time I saw your anguish, the last time I saw that kind of devotion, was when Sylas told me about

91

his mother? When he told me that the only thing that mattered to him was finding her?"

Naeo shifted uncomfortably. "No, I didn't," she said. "What are you trying to say?"

Filimaya turned and looked earnestly into her eyes. "I'm trying to say that his love for his mother *is* your love for your father, that his search *is* your search, that your lives are the same life." She took both of Naeo's hands in hers. "I'm saying, Naeo, that if you find Sylas's mother, *he* will find her; and if Sylas—"

"...if Sylas finds my father, I'll find him too," said Naeo, shaking her head. "But how? I'll be in the Other and my father will be here!"

Filimaya placed a hand on Naeo's cheek and smiled sympathetically. "I don't quite know, Naeo. These are the things the Glimmer Myth doesn't tell us." She paused, considering her words. "What I do know is that you are both one wonderful whole. Your lives are entwined, and if it is not safe for you to go to your father — as it is not — then Sylas may go in your place."

Naeo looked deep into her eyes. She wanted to argue, to say that she owed it to her father whatever the risks, and that no one, not even Sylas, could take her place in this. But as she opened her mouth to speak the words failed her. Any way she tried to say it, it just sounded hollow and selfish.

Just then she saw a movement ahead. She peered beyond Filimaya and saw Ash's lithe figure sprawled on the grassy bank on the far side of the waterways. He grinned at her and waved.

"Do you know," he shouted, getting to his feet, "it's taken you two longer to cross this dribble than it took Moses to part the seas!"

Filimaya laughed. "Well, we had the saving of worlds to talk about." She set out over the last of the streams, drawing Naeo alongside her.

"Funny you should say that," said Ash, rummaging uneasily in his crop of curls, "because I have something I want to talk to you about. Both of you."

Filimaya narrowed her eyes. "Really?"

Ash beamed. "Really. I just wondered if you had decided who's going to go with Naeo? Into the Other, I mean?"

"I don't need anyone to come with me," said Naeo sharply. "I'll be fine alone."

"Well, I'm afraid I'm going to have to disappoint you both," said Filimaya, "because—"

"Uh-uh! I'm going. And that's final!" cried Ash, wagging his finger in protest. "Naeo, where you're going, you'll need someone with... resources, someone who knows their way aroun—"

"But you don't know your way around, Ash," said Naeo. "You've never even been to the Other, have you?"

"Well, no," said Ash, grinning and crossing his arms, "but where my kind of cunning is concerned, one world is quite the same as another. And anyway, Filimaya, haven't I shown myself a worthy travelling companion? Didn't I get Sylas safely across the Barrens? And I know him — and Naeo — better than anyone else here. Yes," he said, with a finality that suggested the decision was his own, "if anyone's going to go to the Other, it has to be me!"

Filimaya sighed and looked down at Naeo, who shook her head imploringly.

Ash leaned between them. "If you coop me up here, Filimaya, I'll make an unbearable nuisance of myself. I'm already planning to set up a pub on the *Windrush*. 'Two Sheets to the Wind' I'll call it. And that's just—"

Filimaya raised her hands in surrender. "OK, OK, Ash," she said. "I'll talk to Paiscion. Not because of your bluster or because I owe it to you, but because," she turned and looked at Naeo

93

earnestly, "you really do need some help, and Ash has proven himself a very useful companion to Sylas."

Naeo groaned, then glared at Ash. "Well, he'd better not get in my way! I'm used to being on my own!"

"Yes, we can all tell that," said Ash out of the side of his mouth.

"Really?" she said, defiantly.

"Yes, really."

Filimaya gazed out over the tranquil waterways and sighed. "What have I done?"

"So you see," said Paiscion, leaning forward and gesturing out of the window, "your journeys are not separate. As you seek Bowe, you must know that Naeo will be in search of your mother — your efforts are her efforts — your travels are entwined."

The Magruman stood, leaving Sylas staring over the forest to the dark horizon, trying to make sense of his emotions.

"But there is one thing that will set your journeys apart," said Paiscion, returning to his seat.

"You mean, other than that we'll be in different worlds?"

"Well, yes, there's that," said the Magruman with a shrug. "But there's also this." He held out the wooden box that Sylas had seen on the table. "Take it. It's a gift."

Sylas glanced up at the Magruman, then reached out and took it. "Thank you," he said. "What is it?"

"Open it and see."

Sylas turned the box between his fingers. It was made of driftwood so worn by its watery travels that all of its surfaces were perfectly smooth and its corners rounded, making it pleasant to the touch. The lid had been beautifully crafted so that at first Sylas could not see the join, but after a few attempts, he managed to position his thumb in the right place and prise it up. It came away with a slight hiss of air and revealed a cushion covered with rumpled green satin.

There, in the centre of the fabric, was a single white feather.

"Do you recognise it?" asked Paiscion, peering keenly through his thick glasses.

Sylas laughed in surprise and delight. "Is it... is it the feather from the *Windrush*? The one we made dance when you were teaching me Essenfayle?"

The Magruman smiled warmly. "It is," he said. "But it's not quite the same as it was. Go on, pick it up!"

Sylas reached into the box and took the feather between two fingers. As he lifted it, he saw a small glass pot of thick black fluid, sealed with a cork stopper. He took a closer look at the shaft of the feather and saw that it had been shortened and cut, so that it looked like the nib of a pen.

He raised his eyes to Paiscion. "You've made it into a quill!"

"You have a story to tell and you need the right tools to tell it!" said Paiscion. "I assume you still have the Samarok?"

Sylas nodded and then his eyes widened. "I should *write* in it?"

Paiscion looked astonished. "Of course you should write in it, Sylas, you are the last of the Bringers! It is you who must write the final chapter of their chronicles."

"But what would I write?"

"What is to come. You have read the beginning, now you must write the end." The Magruman frowned. "Oh my, that sounds rather like the inscription on your bracelet, doesn't it? How strange... it must be on my mind."

The smile faded from Sylas's face and his eyes dropped to his wrist. In the short time since the Say-So he had almost forgotten about the inscription. In fact, the gathering had never even discussed it in their excitement about the song in the Samarok.

In blood it began, in blood it must end.

"What do you think it means?" asked Sylas. "'In blood it must end?'"

Paiscion shook his head solemnly. "I can't be sure, Sylas, but the song speaks of a war still to come. Wars are never waged without the loss of blood."

Sylas frowned at the band, trying to see the inscription, only to find that it had vanished. "But why pick those lines in particular?" he asked. "I mean why are they so—"

He was interrupted by the sharp snap of a twig somewhere below the window.

Paiscion launched himself out of his seat and pulled Sylas back into the hideaway, then he whirled about and stood in front of the window. They heard another sharp crack, then a hiss like someone cursing under their breath, and finally a hand appeared on the bottom edge of the window. To the sound of another loud curse a mop of red hair rose into view, followed by a small, weather-worn face.

"Simsi!" cried Sylas, rushing past Paiscion to offer her his hand. "What are you *doing*?"

Simia glared up at him with narrowed eyes. "I'm here..." she paused to brush twigs and leaves from her hair, "I'm here to say don't you *dare* hatch any plans to go without me!"

Sylas gaped at her for a moment and then he laughed out loud. He walked to the window and reached down to haul her up. "Simsi, you got me into this! Do you really think I'm going anywhere without dragging you with me?"

Simia's pouting lips grew into a wide grin.

12

Exodus

*"...like the exodus of ancient times, she led them thence,
to those fateful plains of Salsimaine."*

THE ANCIENT DOORS OF the Dirgheon thundered as the vast bolts
were drawn back, growling their complaint at the city. As they
inched open, putrid air gushed through the crack, pooling down
the wide steps. The creaks and groans sounded out like a fanfare
as the opening grew wide.

And then they came.

First the sounds, not close but somewhere in the depths, out
of sight: the quiet *chink, chink, chink* of chains; the padding of soft
feet; the scraping of claws against stone. And then the panting of
giant lungs, the hiss of air between teeth, the deep guttural rasps
of canine tongues.

Suddenly there was movement in the shadows and they
prowled out into the half-light, their gargantuan heads lolling from
side to side as they drooled from muzzled jaws, their keen yellow
eyes searching the streets below. Chains trailed from wrought-iron
collars fastened around their massive, muscular necks. Thirty,
forty, perhaps fifty Ghorhund passed in three rows, all straining

against their bonds as they paced silently between the gigantic doors. And behind came their handlers: brooding, deadly, marching across the stone in perfect unison, making no sound. At times the Ghor appeared human, but they were too large, too powerful, and they moved with a chilling, predatory ease that betrayed their canine blood.

They were not alone, for they shared their formation with their slighter, sleeker cousins: half-breeds of a new and curious kind — sometimes upright, sometimes thrown forward, loping on lithe limbs, their watchful eyes drinking in the darkness, seeing all. Some purred with satisfaction as they saw the city spread out below, while others hissed and prickled at their hound-like companions, baring their claws when they drew too close. And each of these creatures grasped the chains of a single Ghorhund, occasionally giving them a vicious yank to keep their charges in check.

This was no ordinary outing, no swift assault upon the slums. It was a quiet, well-planned exodus.

Then there were new sounds: the grating of metal wheels against stone, the clatter of harnesses, the snap of reins and soon a dazzling medley of red and gold passed between the giant doors: a beautiful chariot constructed of ornamental armour, riding on massive, heavy wheels of solid oak. And there, standing resplendent at the reins, was Scarpia, her hood thrown back to reveal her strange, disfigured beauty and her teeth flashing white as she snarled at her newborn horde.

But although she was clearly in command, she was not alone. She seemed to be leaning away from something strange and unearthly at her side, something transparent and ghost-like. The structure of the chariot behind it was still clearly visible and yet it seemed to draw the light, creating an amorphous blur, like a trick of the eye. But what made its presence certain, its being beyond doubt, was its shape. It had all the proportions of a man, standing tall and still at Scarpia's side.

Then, just for a moment, the light of the moon played across it, tracing its edges in silver. And in that moment the dancing light picked out a face wrapped in rotten rags. The face was flat, revealing no sign of a nose, and its eyes were but empty voids, staring blackly over the city. The wide gash of a mouth lolled open, swinging loose between threadbare bandages.

A Ray Reaper.

Scarpia turned and eyed it with something between fear and distaste, and when it turned towards her she quickly averted her gaze.

Behind came a humbler crowd: men carrying boxes and bags, sleeping rolls and tents, and with them, the lesser beasts — pack-horses and mules, livestock to eat.

As Scarpia's chariot reached the brink of the steps, she paused. She gazed out over the city — across the huddling pyramids of rooftops, over the cowering slums, through the gathering palls of smoke. She peered beyond, out into the wasteland, into the expanses of the Barrens, to where she knew it lay.

The Circle of Salsimaine: gateway to another world.

She threw her head back and let out a half-human cry that became a wail. As her legion surged ahead, she flicked her tail and the chariot leapt forward, clattering down the steps and careering into the streets below.

S

It was not so much a chorus as a symphony. Birds of every kind sang to the top of their lungs, each adding a joyous strain to the cacophony of chirps, tweets, squawks and trills. The sound moved in waves across the lake, ebbing and flowing, as though the two sides were vying with one another to raise the more glorious song.

Paiscion closed his eyes and listened, letting it wash over him. To his ears, it was the most beautiful music of all: Nature's music – the song of life and light. How long it had been since he had heard it, and how it now restored his spirits. He took deep draughts of it, letting it fill him to the core.

So lost was he in the dawn chorus that he did not notice Filimaya coming to sit down on the fallen tree, at his side. She was there for some moments, just enjoying being there with him, until finally she placed a hand on his. He knew her touch at once. He simply turned his hand over and slid his fingers between hers. They sat like that for a while longer, knowing that they may not have many more moments like this. That things were changing. That the Glimmer Myth was finally coming to pass.

That here, in this place, they would make their final stand.

Filimaya gazed at the *Windrush*, moored against the bank just a few paces away. She looked at its shattered decks, broken hull and shredded rigging and suddenly felt an overwhelming affection. This poor, benighted hulk wore all the scars of her people – all their pain and indignity, their wounds and losses. The *Windrush* had seen the worst of their horrors, been there on the darkest of days. And despite all her strength and craft and valour, the ship showed it. The woes of the Suhl were etched into her timbers and written on her sails.

"What will you do with her now?" asked Filimaya, breaking their silence.

Paiscion drew a long breath. "I shall make her all she can be."

She smiled. "Prepare her well, my love. She will be our Ark."

Suddenly she drew her hair from over her shoulder and ran it through her fingers until she came to the purple braid woven tightly into the silver strands. She began picking at it, unravelling the coloured threads.

Paiscion looked across and frowned. "What are you doing?"

"I'm giving you something."

He shook his head. "No, they're yours to—"

"They mustn't be hidden away any longer, they should be flown high for all to see." She pulled them carefully out of her hair. "They will be the first threads of a brave new flag — a flag for our people, for what is to come."

Paiscion gave her a tender smile. "What do you have in mind?"

Filimaya pointed to the broken ship. "The standard of the *Windrush*!"

Even as Sylas and Simia stepped out from their tree house, the forest felt different. There was a hush, an expectation, a sense that they were being watched. And of course, they were. Hundreds of eyes peered between branches and through leaves, trying to catch their first glimpse of the travellers. Children sat fearlessly on the boughs, their feet dangling as they pointed and whispered. Many of them looked on enviously, wishing perhaps that they too were allowed to join the adventure, to travel to the great city of Gheroth — perhaps even to meet Isia herself. Most of the adults were quieter and more thoughtful, gazing down with worried expressions at these two tiny children upon whom rested so much.

Triste was leaning up against a tree puffing on his pipe, just as he was the day before, but today he was wearing a heavy coat and as they approached he hoisted a large pack on to his shoulder. He nodded impassively as they approached.

"Are you... coming with us?" asked Simia, completely failing to hide her disappointment.

Triste regarded her through tired, sunken eyes. "I am. Didn't Paiscion tell you?"

"No," she said, bluntly. "He just said *someone* would be coming along."

Triste shrugged. "Well, it's me. They thought you might need a Scryer."

"Sure," she said, walking past him and on, into the forest.

Sylas watched her go, shaking his head, then turned and grinned. "She'll warm up. She was like that with me at first."

"It's OK," said Triste, setting off after her. "I see more than you think."

Sylas frowned. He wasn't quite sure what that meant. He sighed, adjusted his own pack on his shoulder and walked after them.

The further they walked, the more faces they saw peering down at them from the canopy, and they began to realise that the entire community had turned out to see them go. Simia threw back her shoulders, drew her huge coat about her and walked as tall as she could, enjoying her place in the lead. Sylas nodded politely to the many children who waved and adults who bowed as they passed. He was struck again by the warmth of these people: the kindness and generosity in their faces, the open innocence of their features. And yet he also saw in them something darker: the sadness and resignation of a people who knew that, for better or worse, their time was drawing near.

He was so busy looking about him that he almost stumbled into Filimaya and Paiscion as they stepped from the trees.

"Morning!" cried Paiscion. "And what an exciting morning it is!"

Filimaya slid an arm around Sylas and Simia. "How are you feeling?"

"Ready," said Simia boldly.

"And you need to be," said Paiscion. "Have you said goodbye to Ash and Naeo?"

"Haven't seen them yet," said Sylas. Then he paused, lowering his eyes. "But they're coming."

He had begun to feel the familiar pang of pain in his wrist, the sickness in his belly, the sense that something was amiss. And sure enough they all soon saw Ash's full head of blond locks winding between the trees and beside him Naeo's tall, slim figure, walking with all her usual grace. Both of them were wearing heavy coats and carrying bags over their shoulders.

As they drew closer Naeo slowed and stayed back. Sylas too stepped away and walked to the far side of the group.

"I guess this is goodbye!" cried Ash, striding up to the gathering.

"You remember everything I told you," said Filimaya, embracing him, "about the Other, and about those tricks of yours. The Three Ways are strictly off limits there. They could get you into—"

"I've already forgotten," said Ash, breaking into a playful grin. He squeezed her hand, then turned to Sylas and Simia. "OK, you two, see you afterwards. I trust you're going to make as much mischief here as we're going to make there!" He winked playfully and leaned closer. "But just look after yourselves," he whispered, glancing at Triste. "I won't be there, and these Scryers are no match for a Muddlemorph and sorcerer like myself."

Simia grinned. "You be careful too. And don't eat their food." She screwed up her nose. "Like I said to Sylas, it can't be... natural."

Ash laughed and patted his stomach. "My diet starts here!"

As everyone said their final goodbyes, Filimaya walked over to Naeo, who was still standing at a safe distance. Before she even drew close, Naeo raised her hand.

"I'm fine," she said. "I just want to go, if that's what I have to do."

Filimaya opened her arms and drew her close. "Well, I know you don't need this, but I do."

Naeo looked puzzled and awkward, but she returned the embrace.

"Take care of yourself," said Filimaya, stepping back. "And remember what I told you. Try not to worry about your father. I know that Sylas will do all you would do."

Naeo looked unconvinced. "I hope so," she said.

Paiscion wandered over and took both her hands in his.

"Now remember what I said about the Circle of Salsimaine. Get there as quickly as you can — don't give Thoth any more time than you have to. And when you're through, remember to look for—"

"You think I'll just... know what to do?" said Naeo.

"At the Circle?"

She nodded dubiously.

"You'll know," he said dismissively. "You summoned the Passing Bell! The Circle of Salsimaine will be no challenge at all. When you're through, remember to look for our friends — if you don't find them, they'll find you. And whatever happens on the other side, remember this: we are in a race against a dying moon. Keep to our plan and do not delay. Is that understood?"

He lifted his glasses and eyed her closely until she nodded.

"Then you're ready. Filimaya, perhaps you could guide Naeo and Ash out of the valley?"

Filimaya nodded and turned to leave, but Naeo stood rooted to the spot. She was looking across the clearing, searching for Sylas. The impulse confused her. It did not come from a thought, nor a feeling: it was a need — a powerful, consuming need.

Sylas was already looking at her.

It was a peculiar moment, a moment when as individuals they were unsure what to do, but something beyond them, something between them, left no doubt at all.

They each turned and walked towards the other.

Everyone fell silent, transfixed by what they saw. Paiscion opened his mouth to call them away, but stopped himself. The people in the trees craned their necks and leaned over branches to get a better view. Children ceased their chatter and adults held their breath. They, like Paiscion, could see that this was not like the Say-So. There was something different in their manner, in the way they held each other's gaze. They were single-minded, confident, fearless.

As they drew close they slowed, extending their hand to the other.

Their fingers touched, their palms met and they held on.

The instant they came together the bands of silver and gold around their wrists morphed, losing lustre and form. The edges became blurred as though they were no longer solid but shifting vapour. Then, sure enough, the band around Naeo's wrist issued a wisp of silver, curling up into the air like a trail of smoke, and in that moment Sylas's did the same, sending forth a twisting tendril of gold. It was as if the two parts of the Merisi Band were reaching out, trying to become one.

The forest fell absolutely silent. Not a normal quiet — the kind of quiet that consumed the forest at night, this silence was complete: birds ceased their singing; animals stopped their foraging; the breeze fell away. Nothing shifted or called or breathed.

And while the world fell still, in Sylas and Naeo, there was a storm. A violent, ravaging storm like before, when they had met in the Dirgheon. They felt sick to their stomachs and winced from the pain in their wrists, but at the same time something else grew within them, something greater than their physical selves, something that caught them up and consumed them.

It was the knowledge that each was the other. It was a pact — a certainty that one would do for the other whatever they wished for themselves.

But it was also something else.

It was the joy of being whole.

13

The Way

*"The great Leo Tsu warned us that the way
is shadowy and indistinct, that it is dim and dark.
But within, he said, is the essence."*

THIS WAS A NEW kind of forest. It was lower, thicker and darker than the majestic woods in the Valley of Outs and it pressed in on all sides, smothering sound and clawing at clothes. Naeo and Ash pushed on through the dense undergrowth, panting from the exertion. To make matters worse, their route took them across a range of hills: it was only midday and already, this was the fifth they had climbed.

"I'm not saying that Essenfayle isn't the best of the bunch," said Ash, pausing for breath and pulling a stray leaf out of his hair, "I'm just saying that the Three Ways have their place too. And together, you have to admit that the Three Ways are more than a match for Essenfayle. The Reckoning proved that."

Naeo turned to him. "And I'm just saying that you're very sure of yourself."

"What's wrong with that?"

"Nothing. I'm sure of myself too. And you're wrong."

"Ouch," said Ash with a grin. "Feisty one, aren't you?"

Naeo shrugged and carried on climbing.

"I've been wondering," persisted Ash, setting out after her, "how come you're so pushy? I mean, Sylas is confident in his own way, but—"

Naeo wheeled about. "Did you ask to come because you were short of someone to talk to?"

Ash looked at her blankly and shook his head.

"So *stop talking*," snapped Naeo. With that she turned and continued her climb.

Ash pulled a face. "This is going to be such fun," he murmured.

They climbed for what seemed an age: clambering over tree roots and boulders; squeezing through bush and thicket, scrambling up banks thick with leaves. The forest hummed and squabbled and squawked around them, the air humid and close. This was the highest hill so far, but with ravines and steep slopes on either side, they had no choice but to carry on, no matter how hard the going. At one point they stopped and ate some lunch, but Ash again found his attempts at conversation futile. Naeo ate quickly, then gazed off into the forest, weaving the bootlace between her fingers, crafting her cat's cradle until he was ready.

As they resumed their climb, Naeo felt a familiar ache inching upwards from her lower back, following the contours of the black scar. The pain was never far away, but it had become more persistent in the past days, and had only worsened with the effort of the climb and the constant rubbing of her pack. She adjusted it so that it hung from her front, but even then, the pat, pat, pat of her loose hair grew unbearable and she soon had to ask Ash to stop. She foraged around in the undergrowth and found two suitable twigs, then coiled her hair behind her head and slid them through it to hold it fast.

"Lovely," said Ash, sarcastically. "Are we expecting company? Making a public appearance perhaps?" He made a show of looking around.

Naeo gave him a steady look. "Just a sore back," she said, setting out again.

"Well, of course," he said, shaking his head in bewilderment. "The wrong hairdo can be a devil for your back."

It was well into the afternoon before the ground finally started to level off and they allowed themselves to believe that they were nearing the top. They noticed the forest begin to lighten and then, to their relief, they saw a break in the branches and twigs and the grey glow of the open sky. Within moments they were dragging their weary limbs into a clearing and hauling their packs gratefully from their shoulders.

They looked out on a dismal view. Gone was the winter sun and the bronzes and reds of a forest clinging to autumn. In their place they saw a brooding, melancholy scene: a blank wall of grey sky descending to a granite horizon; the rolling, featureless terrain of minor foothills sprawling out on to an empty dust-swept plain as far as the eye could see.

"Ah, the Barrens," said Ash with a dramatic sigh. "A tonic for the soul!"

Naeo did not smile. The deathly landscape brought back distant memories that were all too real. She remembered the last, terrifying days of war; she saw the surge of armies and the heavens burning with fire; she felt the thunderclap of explosions and the raking sting of howling winds. But most of all she remembered the voices: the screams, the sobs, the last murmurings of despair.

Her eyes filled with tears and she turned away.

If Ash noticed, he did not show it. He was looking up, trying to make out the position of the sun through the cloud. Finally he shook his head. "We're going slower than we expected," he said. "We'll have to get a move on if we're to get to the Circle of Salsimaine on time."

"So what do you suggest?"

"Well, we'll have to pick our feet up, I suppose."

Naeo crossed her arms and gazed out over the lowland hills, tracing the folds and undulations, valleys and dells. Ash was right, it was their first morning and already they were falling behind.

She rocked thoughtfully for some moments and then she frowned, her eyes exploring the terrain.

"I think we can do better than that," she said.

Ash raised his eyebrows. "How? Don't tell me you want to fly. I'm not flying again in a hurry."

"No need," said Naeo, walking off down the slope. "We have Essenfayle."

"Well, yes, we do, but how does that—"

"Stop talking," said Naeo. "You'll put me off."

She drew up short of the fringe of trees where a small stream was bubbling off between the trunks, laid her pack on the floor and rolled up her sleeves.

Ash approached from behind. "What are you doing? Not a *Groundrush*?" he exclaimed. "It's not worth it! It'll only get us to the bottom of the hill."

"Not just to the bottom of *this* hill," said Naeo, confidently. "It'll get us on to the Barrens."

Ash chuckled and crossed his arms. "And how exactly will it do that?"

"Remember what you said about Essenfayle?"

Ash shrugged.

"And remember I said you were wrong?"

He nodded slowly.

She raised her arms. "Well this is why."

In a way, it was beautiful: a sinuous snake of silver winding along the valley floor, bordered on both sides by frosted branches and leaves, which drooped into the water as if to taste the muddy gruel. Its wide arcs cut through the very heart of the forest, carrying the three travellers through its wildest and most secret parts, where animals shrieked, insects scuttled and birds twittered, filling the canopy with a pleasant echo.

But Sylas was thoroughly ill at ease.

It wasn't just that his back and shoulders were aching or that the canoe felt flimsy and unstable. It was also that he had absolutely no idea what he was doing. After a morning of frustrating meanders from bank to bank, he had finally mastered the steering, but even after lunch he was still much slower than the others. He only occasionally saw a flash of Simia's red hair as she disappeared around another bend and he was certain that he was irritating Triste, who had insisted on guarding the rear and so was always just over his shoulder.

"Use slow, steady strokes," Triste had suggested. "Hold the paddle lower, around the neck. Dip the blade deeper into the water."

That had helped, but Simia continued to forge ahead. And then he had an idea. He thought back to the attack on the Meander Mill and their flight in a flotilla of boats, when Filimaya called upon the river to form a mighty wave to carry them all to safety. Why couldn't he do that? He closed his eyes and extended one hand behind the boat as she had, sending his thoughts down into the waters. He felt their chill creeping into his chest, their dark enclosing his mind, their swell flooding through his stomach. And then he called them up from the deep, up through the swirling currents until they surged behind his boat, rising in a small, perfectly formed wave. He felt a rush of excitement as the canoe lurched forward, borne on by the river itself. And then, even as he grinned in celebration it all went wrong. The sharp bow plunged deep into the waters. The boat came to a sudden halt while the wave continued, lifting the stern and throwing it around in a graceless pirouette. It left Sylas drenched, clinging to the sides and facing completely the wrong way. Facing a very unimpressed Scryer.

"Just use... the... paddle!" said Triste impatiently. "That's what it's for."

"I just thought that Essenfayle might—"

"Your gift isn't a replacement for a perfectly good paddle." The Scryer fixed Sylas with an intent stare. "What you have, Sylas — your feel for Essenfayle — is a sacred thing: a thing not to be trifled with."

"I didn't think it would do any harm," Sylas grunted in embarrassment.

"It would if a Scryer's out looking for you. Don't forget, we see *connections*, and those as strong as you are able to create can be seen miles away. Keep your tricks to yourself until you really need them, understand?"

Sylas nodded. "Sorry," he mumbled.

"Good then," said the Scryer, squinting downriver. "In the meantime, you'll just have to put your back into it. At this rate your friend will be knocking at Isia's door before dinner."

Sylas dug his paddle in and turned himself around. Simia was so far ahead he could barely make her out and even as he watched, she disappeared around a bend.

He cupped his hands and shouted: "Simsi! Slow down!"

When Simia showed no sign of stopping they both plunged

their paddles deep into the river and set off after her at a feverish pace.

"She's mad to leave us so far behind," grumbled Triste. "Mad!"

In truth, relations between Simia and Triste had only become more strained since they had left the valley. At lunch she had continued to talk to him as though he was more hindrance than help and now, even though he had implored her to stay close for her own safety, she seemed wilfully to be extending her lead.

"She's like this," said Sylas, panting as he struggled to pick up speed. "Feisty. Always doing things her own way. She has... you know —" he grinned — "sharp edges. But it's never boring."

"Well, I'm not against feisty, but I am against stupid," said Triste archly. "She has no idea what's around that bend. I can't Scry so far ahead and even if I could, I wouldn't be able to warn her. She could paddle straight into a shoal of Slithen — or worse."

Sylas thought back to the hideous reptilian creatures that had chased them from the Meander Mill. "*Worse* than Slithen?"

Triste looked surprised. "*Much* worse."

Sylas glanced into the murk of the river and wished he hadn't asked.

"I guess she's just tired of waiting for me," he said, pulling his eyes away.

"No," said the Scryer. "It's not you, it's me."

"*You?* Why?"

"Because she doesn't want to be near me."

Sylas laughed. "I think that's a bit—"

"I remind her of her father," said Triste, stopping his paddling.

"Her *father*? What makes you say that?" asked Sylas.

"I *see* it," said Triste, tapping his tattooed skull. "Whether I want to or not."

Sylas searched his face. "Is that what you meant this morning... 'I see more than you think'?"

Triste nodded. "Just bad luck, I suppose. Especially since she was so close to him."

"She was. *Very* close," said Sylas. He gazed ahead. "That's his coat that she wears all the time."

Suddenly he felt unforgivably selfish: he had almost forgotten about her father. Over the past few days he had spoken endlessly about finding his mum and Simia had just been doing her best to help — it couldn't have been easy for her. Was that why she had said nothing to him about Triste? Because he was too wrapped up in his own problems? His own mother? At least his mum was still alive.

Poor Simsi.

As though sensing Sylas's darkening mood, the bright winter sun faded above their heads, not because it was late but because a blanket of grey cloud had rolled in, obscuring it from view. The forest too seemed drained of its colour, losing it to the thirsty grey skies. Its bare canopy no longer rang with the sounds of its residents, but had fallen silent and still — a stillness that they knew.

The Barrens were drawing near.

14

The Tempest

"High upon the headland stood a tiny girl,
turning Neptune's own tempest *to her will."*

AS SYLAS'S PADDLING FINALLY grew more confident, Triste no longer insisted on following him and drew alongside. When he thought he might not be noticed, Sylas could not resist the occasional glance over at the Scryer — and most of all at the strange tattoos around his scalp. He was drawn to the two mutilated eyes — the ones where the skin seemed to have been burned or twisted until they had lost their shape, almost as though they had been closed behind mangled lids.

"If you're so interested, you should ask," grunted Triste without turning.

Sylas dropped his gaze, horrified that he had been seen. But then, of *course* he had been seen.

"I was just wondering what happened to your tattoos," he said. "The eyes... the ones that look... burned?"

Triste let out a long sigh. "I tried to close my Scrying eyes. It was the first time I ever used Kimiyya. It'll be the last, I can assure you."

"Why would you do that?"

"Why wouldn't I?" said the Scryer with a bitter laugh. "I became tired of seeing as a Scryer sees. Like I told Simia, wars are no place for Scryers. Normal people see all the violence and the death and the suffering, which is awful enough. We see great tides of anguish and oceans of hate. We see despair and loss surging like great waves over the battlefield." He looked at Sylas with his dark, tired eyes. "You see the broken bodies; we see the breaking of hearts again and again and again until the entire world seems full of sadness and pain and grief, until there is nowhere to hide, no hope of sleep. Until all we can dream about is being able to close our eyes."

Sylas had stopped paddling several strokes back, and now just gazed at Triste as he rowed on. He hadn't really thought about what had been said by the lake — he had been too consumed by his own emotions — but now he understood. What a torture it must have been to be a Scryer during the Reckoning. He thought back to Bowe at the Meander Mill, struggling with the gathered emotion even of a Say-So... what must it have been like when people were gathered to kill and be killed. He shuddered. How insensitive his question seemed now.

He dug in with his paddle and set out after Triste, but he could not quite bring himself to draw alongside. He felt too ashamed.

They travelled on in silence, passing deeper into the dreary landscape, and only spoke again when they finally caught up with Simia. As they rounded a bend, they saw that she had pulled into the outside bank, her red hair sharp against the drabness of the forest. Sylas noticed how quickly he was gliding between the trees and saw that the entire river was surging forward, swirling and churning as it veered around the bend.

And then they heard the unmistakable roar and thunder of rapids. The air became cool and moist and carried traces of spray, as though to warn them of what lay ahead. When they drew near to Simia, they found themselves having to back-paddle to control their speed.

The river divided, turning slowly away to the right while the left bank fell away down a slope, spilling the winter flood in a deluge of frothing, bubbling water over the rough ground beyond. They could not see all the way down, but even in the topmost stretch there were giant standing waves, deep, churning whirlpools and great eruptions of angry foam.

"This should be a bit more interesting!" grinned Simia over the roar.

"We won't be taking the rapids," said Triste firmly. "We'll follow the meander – the two stretches join up again later."

Simia's face fell. "We took the meander on the *Windrush* – it took ages!"

"The canoes are fast enough. And anyhow, we're going downstream now."

"But the rapids will be so much quicker!"

"And much more dangerous," said Triste, his tone final. "The stakes are too high to take that kind of risk."

"Well, I'm going down the rapids," announced Simia, launching herself out from under the trees. She plunged her paddle into the water and wheeled the canoe around. "Sylas, are you coming?"

Sylas dropped his head between his shoulders. "Simia," he sighed. "Triste's right, and anyway I'm not as good in a canoe as you are."

"You'll be *fine*. It can't be very long." She looked from one to the other. "Look, if you won't come I'll go on my own and meet you later."

"Simsi, it just doesn't make—"

"Oh, come on, Sylas," cajoled Simia, pushing back into the

main current. "Think of everything we've done together! This is nothing!"

Later, Sylas would struggle to understand why he gave in. Perhaps it was because he was still feeling a little guilty about her father, or because he didn't want her to think him a coward, or because he was genuinely worried that she would attempt the rapids alone. Whatever the case, it went against all his better judgement.

He shrugged and said: "OK."

Triste whirled about in disbelief. He grabbed Sylas's boat. "Don't, Sylas! It's insane!"

"It'll be OK," said Sylas with more confidence than he felt. "We'll take it one stage at a time. Anyway, you heard her, if we don't go she'll try it alone."

"Let her!" shouted the Scryer. "You're too important to risk this kind of nonsense!"

"Yeah, because I don't matter! I'm just here for the ride!" said Simia, with fire in her eyes. "That's what you think, isn't it?"

Triste let out a long, exasperated sigh.

"Come on, Sylas, let's get going," said Simia, heading off in the direction of the rapids.

Sylas looked from Simia to the Scryer, then dipped his paddle.

Then he said: "Let's just get this over with," he said.

It was a tumult of rocks and stones and trees. Naeo was thrown this way and that, hurled from bank to boulder, slammed against tree and trench, as she snaked across the forest floor.

The pain in her back was almost unbearable as the scars were snagged and pummelled, but she closed her eyes and pushed it from her mind. There was no time for pain — no time to think — this was all instinct: instinct for earth and forest.

She felt the ground beneath her and the trees above, the folds of soil and root, the barest beginnings of bank and slope and drop. They were part of her now.

Her father's words echoed in her mind: "I see the hearts of men, but you see so much more! You see Nature herself!"

And so she did. It had always been this way, since she could remember. When her thoughts and feelings reached into the world around her, they found their true home. They became lost in the currents of streams, the pulse of animals and the fibre of living things. And yet she did not *feel* lost. In fact, it was like opening her eyes wide — like seeing the world true and clear, with its thriving mesh of connections: mighty trunk to tiny leaf; raindrop to raging sea.

And she did not just see these connections, she *felt* them.

The forest wrapped itself around her thoughts and bowed before her feelings. She flew across moss and leaves as though they lay down before her, shaping themselves to her will. The stream carried her at impossible speeds, banking left, then right, then heaving her into the air before catching her on a mossy bank and sending her on, down the hill. Ahead, a constant flux of trees, bracken and bush warped as though seen through a lens: shifting and arching, turning and stretching, drawing her on and on and on.

It was like no Groundrush that Ash had ever seen. Not that he saw much of it, because he spent most of his time on his face, or peering between his knees, or with his eyes pressed closed, pleading for it to end. It was slicker, faster, more savage than anything he and his friends had conjured in their youth. This was no childish toy. This was the unbridled force of nature.

And that was not all. Somehow, by some new trick, Naeo was forging the Groundrush even as they careered down the hillside, feeling out the route in an instant and clearing the path ahead in what seemed the blink of an eye. But there was something else that Ash had never seen before: the Groundrush did not take the quickest path down the slope but traversed it, following not the simplest route but the one that travelled the greatest distance, threading between obstacles, keeping them high, allowing them to whisk along the shoulder of one hill until they joined up with another, avoiding the valleys, hollows and dells.

He was lost in an endless tumult of water, leaves and undergrowth, his limbs flapped about him and his mass of curls were plastered across his face, but Ash knew that everything was as Naeo wished it to be. Somehow, by some miracle of Essenfayle, she was taking them all the way to the Barrens.

Icy waves scythed like teeth, thrashing the side of Sylas's canoe, sending the bow leaping into the air. Then it turned and twisted, plummeting downwards into a deep grey hole, almost pitching him overboard. As the hull ploughed into the depths, he dropped the paddle and clung to the sides. The river spat him back out, but only sent him lurching backwards into a whirlpool, spinning him round once, twice, and then slamming the boat against a wall of water. He heard Triste somewhere behind him.

"The paddle!" he screamed. "Use the paddle!"

Sylas reached down and grabbed it from the bottom of the boat, but when he jabbed it over the side, it flailed in nothingness — he had been launched high into the air and the paddle simply wafted through the spray. When he looked down the length of the hull, he saw to his horror a gigantic wall of foam. It was the surface of the river, far below him. He felt a sickening sensation of weightlessness, his stomach rising into his chest.

Then a crack on the side of the head.

The last thing he saw was his rucksack flying over his shoulder.

She could see them now — just there, ahead — unfolding in endless waves of grey. The Barrens beckoned like an open grave, calling them on past the last few skeletons of trees. And yet to Naeo, they seemed far away, as though they were behind a sheet of glass, because something was happening to her — something deep inside her. It sucked the air from her lungs and whipped her thoughts into a frenzy. It was a gathering, terrifying, all-consuming panic.

The moment it gripped her, she lost control. The path ahead fogged as quickly as her thoughts, the little stream spilled haphazardly down the hillside, the curtain of shrubs twisted back into shape, the ground once again became rutted and treacherous. And although she saw this, she could do nothing. She was still behind the sheet of glass, her mind and body fighting some unseen horror. She opened her mouth to scream but in that instant her feet caught a rock and she was thrown high into the air, somersaulting over a line of blackened bushes and sent sprawling into the grey mud beyond.

All was silence, blackness and cold. Bone-shattering, skin-pinching cold.

Sylas tumbled in the dark, a massive force pushing him ever downwards. Currents clawed at his clothes and forced water into his mouth and nose. He felt his body flip over and over until something hard and solid smashed against his shoulder. He cried out in a gush of bubbles and then, to his horror, he realised that he had no air in his lungs. He thrashed the water, but it was futile — he had no idea which way was up.

Then, suddenly, a shimmering glow. Not so much light as the promise of it — a lessening of the blackness. And in the midst of the shade and shadow, something sharp and distinct: a hard, black edge.

A shape. A hand.

It grabbed him by the chest — or was it his throat? — he could not tell. All that mattered was that in the midst of the tumult and the horror, something — somebody — had hold of him. He could feel their strength heaving him up, fighting all that would drag him down.

As his lungs were about to burst and his eyes bulged, his world erupted with a blinding light, a rage of noise. But these things he hardly noticed, because at the same moment he heaved air into his lungs — wonderful, beautiful, life-giving air that flooded his floundering body with energy and purpose. He threw his hands up, dug his fingers into something soft, and clung on. As the intensity of the light faded he saw a new shape, a face, peering down at him, shouting something.

"I've got you!" said the voice. "I've got you!"

Naeo hit the ground hard, slamming her shoulder into the hard-packed earth. She tumbled over and over in mud and twigs and dirt, twisting awkwardly and catching her knee on a stone as she went. She yelped with pain and threw out her hands, clawing at all that flew past, trying desperately to stop.

Finally she slid to a halt, spluttering into the mud, gasping for breath. She lifted her head and heaved air into her lungs.

And then she heard heavy steps pounding the earth behind her. Strong hands turned her over and a face peered down. It was plastered in mud and pale with fright.

"I've got you!" Ash panted. "I've got you!"

15
Undone

"The Suhl are a people of two parts:
of dark and light, of loss and hope. They suffer
the Undoing, but they are the last to be undone.*"*

THEY SAT SHIVERING AT the water's edge, neither of them saying a word. Simia was hunched forward, her elbows resting on her knees and her wet hair a curtain around her face, hiding her features from view. Sylas simply stared out at the endless bubbling churn that had so nearly taken his life. He felt at once impossibly weary and intensely alive, as though these were the first few moments of a new life: precious and fragile. Even the throbbing pain in his temple was somehow welcome — it meant he was still here. He felt a trickle of blood rolling down his cheek and did not wipe it away. He savoured its warmth, its tickling touch.

He looked upstream and saw the splintered remains of his canoe laid over a boulder, and a little nearer, the wreckage of Simia's, which barely looked like a boat at all. The only recognisable part was the tip of the bow, hanging from a low-lying branch like lifeless fruit.

He looked over at Simia and saw how she had folded into herself, alone and shivering and full of shame. He knew he should be angry with her but he wasn't. He was just glad she was there; broken and bruised, but there.

"You have to get warm!" said Triste, emerging suddenly from the bushes. He dumped a load of firewood by their feet and immediately set about making a fire. "Get your heavy clothes off – quickly! Lay them over the rocks by the fire."

By some miracle, the Scryer's flint and tinder were dry and within moments he had started the fire. When Sylas and Simia had laid their clothes out on the rocks, they joined him, warming themselves by the flames. Still no one spoke.

When their fingers had warmed a little, they busied themselves checking through their belongings. Sylas found his bag drenched but intact and with a sinking heart he opened the drawstring and reached for the Samarok. The cover felt strangely dry and as he leafed through its pages, he found them surprisingly untouched by the waters.

Finally they all sat back in silence, basking in the radiance of the flames as they grew into a blaze. Simia stared blankly into the flickering light.

"I'm so sorry," she said, finally. Her voice was just a whisper. She lifted her face and looked at Sylas with tears in her eyes. "So... so sorry."

Sylas reached across and took her hand. It was as cold as stone. He knew that she had tried to come back for him, that she had only fallen in because she was trying to reach him – Triste had mumbled that much – but he had no idea how long she had been in the water. By the feel of her, it had been far, far too long.

"It's OK, Simsi," he said. "We got out of it, didn't we?"

"Barely," grunted Triste.

Simia turned to the Scryer. "I'm really sorry," she repeated. "I don't know what we'd have done without you."

"You'd have drowned!" growled Triste, fixing her with his piercing blue eyes. "And the hopes of the Suhl would have drowned with you!"

Simia dropped her head. She made no sound but tears rolled down her cheeks.

Sylas shifted uncomfortably. "She didn't know how dangerous it was," he said. "It was as much my fault for agreeing to go."

"Yes, it was," said Triste. He lifted an ember from the fire and pushed it into the bowl of his pipe, then puffed away, trying to light the damp tobacco.

Sylas stared at him reproachfully for a moment and then looked down. He knew the Scryer was right, but why couldn't he give them a break? What was done was done.

He looked up to see Triste eyeing him closely, as though he knew exactly what he was thinking. He was a Scryer: of course he knew.

"You need to dress that wound before it gets infected," said the Scryer, pointing to Sylas's temple. "A little Salve should help."

Sylas had almost forgotten the gash on his head. Instinctively he reached up and touched it, wincing as he felt a long seam of broken skin.

Triste reached into his pack, drew out a small bottle and threw it across. Sylas pulled out the cork and poured a little of the contents on to his fingers. He recognised the bright green fluid — it was the ointment Filimaya had used to heal his knee back at the Meander Mill; how long ago that seemed now. As he dabbed it on his forehead he felt the same miraculous cool, soothing sensation reaching deep into the wound. The rutted skin seemed to dissolve beneath his fingertips, and in moments the pain began to ebb away.

Triste cleared his throat. "I'm interested," he said through a cloud of purple smoke, which smelt a little of raspberries, "how is it that you are so different from Naeo?"

Sylas looked up. "What do you mean?"

"I mean that from the little I know of her, I can't imagine Naeo being persuaded to risk *her* life canoeing down rapids."

"She wouldn't *need* persuading," mumbled Simia beneath her hair.

Triste thought about this for a moment. "Perhaps," he said, "but whether she would refuse to go, or go of her own accord, she's still different."

Sylas didn't like where this was going. He still found it difficult to talk about Naeo. She occupied a blind spot in his mind: a dark, confusing place he hadn't allowed himself to go.

"I suppose you're right. But I don't really think about it." He picked up a loose stick and tossed it on the fire.

Triste looked surprised. "*Really?* You're not intrigued?"

Sylas shrugged. "Nope. And I doubt she thinks about it either. It's strange... I mean, to me, it's like she's not quite... there." He shook his head. "No, it's not that. It's more like she's not... real."

Triste clamped the pipe between his teeth and leaned into the fire to warm his hands. "And yet the connection between you is so *strong*. Even now."

"You think so?"

"I know it. I see it. To a Scryer, it's blindingly obvious."

Sylas felt even more uncomfortable. "*What* do you see?"

Triste smiled. "Ah, well to understand that, you need to understand a bit about Scrying." He stoked the fire, sending up a shower of sparks. "When I look at people, I see two things: first, their image, just as you see; and second, what we call their *aura*. Now the aura isn't a visual thing at all — it's something that we Scryers see in our mind's eye. The best way to describe it is a gathering of colours, all clustered around the person we're looking at. The colours have different shapes or forms, and it's the combination of colour and form that tells us what someone is feeling — the connection they have to people around them." He paused and looked at Sylas intently. "So, ask me what I see when I look at you."

"What do you see?"

"Everything."

"*Everything?*"

Triste nodded, his features unusually animated. "It's like a cloud... no — more than that — an *explosion*. An explosion of colour! In you, I see every colour and every shape I have ever encountered."

Sylas shifted again. He was getting that familiar feeling that someone else knew far more about him than he did. "Really?"

"Yes! Why do you think I asked to come along with you?"

"You *asked* to come?"

"Of course I did! Whether you know it or not, you and Naeo change the rules — Thoth's rules — the ones that say all we can look forward to is suffering, that the best we can hope for is survival." He blew out a long trail of smoke, a bright contrast to the grey riverbank. He looked at Sylas earnestly. "For the first time since the war, you've made me wonder if there might be something worth seeing in this dying world of ours: something new and hopeful. Something that makes me glad of my Scrying eyes, rather than wanting to scratch them out."

Sylas stared at him. "So..." he blurted, "these colours and shapes — the ones you think are so important — do you know what they mean?"

Triste leaned forward on his elbows. "I don't *think* they're important, they *are* important. They mean that you aren't just

127

connected to Naeo by your feelings towards her, like you would be with most people. After all, you say you don't feel *anything* towards her." He took a deep draw on his pipe. "No, with you it's different. I think you're connected to her in every way, all of the time."

Sylas shrugged. "Well if I am, I don't know about it."

"I suppose there's no reason you should," said Triste, lowering his pipe and heaving himself to his feet. "But you certainly should be something else."

"What?"

Triste arched an eyebrow. "Intrigued. *Very* intrigued."

"I don't know for sure," murmured Naeo as she dripped a few more drops of Salve on to her knee. Then she looked up. "I think it was Sylas. It was like... like I could feel what he was feeling. And it felt terrible... cold... frightening. Like I was trapped and couldn't breathe."

Ash squatted down next to her, searching her face. "Do you think he's all right?"

Naeo thought for a moment. "Yes, I do," she murmured. "He... must be."

"Why?"

"Because *I* feel all right."

"Oh," said Ash, looking surprised. "You look terrible."

"Thank you."

"No, seriously," he said, looking her up and down. "Terrible."

"Thanks, Ash, but I'll be fine. My knee's already stopped bleeding."

"I wasn't talking about your knee," said Ash. "I was talking about your back. When you fell you looked like the pain was killing you."

128

"I just winded myself," she said, making a show of rolling her shoulders. A searing pain rattled up her spine and across her shoulder blades making her wince.

"See!" cried Ash.

"It's just... an old pain," said Naeo, lying. The pain was familiar, but there was something new about this: it was sharper and more intense, as though the Black had seeped that little bit deeper into her flesh.

Ash narrowed his eyes. "Just let me take a look. A little Salve might help that too."

"Never helped before."

"Well, you weren't bruised and battered before. That was a heck of a fall. Come on, let me try."

Naeo eyed him cautiously. "OK," she said. And then for the briefest moment she looked a little vulnerable, even girlish. "It's not pretty."

"Take a look about you," he said, picking up the bottle of Salve. "This isn't the place for pretty."

He sat down behind her and waited. Hesitantly, she undid the bottom buttons of her shirt, then lifted it above her waist.

Ash's breath caught in his throat. He wasn't sure what he had expected to see, but this was not it. There were no cuts, nor scabs, nor bruises, rather a thick, swollen scar picked out in deep, ebony black. It traced her spine, and just beneath her shoulder blades fanned out like the branches of a tree. Perhaps it was the depth of its colour, or its shape, or the fact that it was raised proud of her smooth white skin, but it looked almost... alive.

"Is this..." The word failed him, until he remembered to breathe. "Is this... the Black?"

She nodded without turning.

"Who did this to you?"

"He did. Thoth."

"Why?"

She laughed mirthlessly. "Like he needs a reason." She was quiet for a moment. "To make my dad tell him what he wanted to know."

Ash gazed at the back of her head and shook his head incredulously. He poured a generous dose of Salve on to his fingers. "And what was that?"

"Who my mother was."

He paused with his fingers next to her back.

"And who *was* your mother?"

Naeo shrugged. "She's dead," she said. "And that's all he needed to know. Are you finished yet?"

Ash laid his hand against the scar, held it for a moment and then pulled it away. He leaned down for a better look and then his eyes widened. The bright green Salve was not lying over the scar but rather draining into it, trailing away as though caught up in some unseen current. Even as it joined the flow, its brightness faded and then went out, until there was no trace of green at all. It had been consumed, becoming one with the Black. The scar was unchanged.

He sat up and looked anxiously at the back of her head.

"Yes, I'm done," he said.

"Did it work?"

He paused. "I think so, yes," he said.

"Liar," she said, standing up. "But it's OK. It's the Black — I'm not sure there's anything to be done."

"Well, we'll see about that," he said, getting to his feet. "But it's not going to be easy. I don't think anyone knows for sure where the Black comes from. Or what it's for."

"Well, I don't know what it's for exactly, but I do know who's behind it," said Naeo, smiling weakly, "even if I wish I didn't." She sighed and began working on her buttons. "So, come on, what are we going to do?"

"About what?"

She nodded out across the Barrens. "About Grail. What do you think? Through it or around it?"

Ash turned and followed her eyes towards the ruins below them.

In truth Grail was not a town. It was not even the ruin of a town. It was like a ghostly apparition, a haunting memory of what once had been. It had the look of something ancient, something that had almost given up its place on this earth, sliding slowly into the dust. Entire streets now appeared little more than gatherings of rubble, marked out by occasional ramshackle walls or the buckled remnants of a cobbled road.

"I say straight through it," Ash said firmly, glad of the change of subject. "Sure, it has a reputation, but that was years ago, when it was still thick with the Kraven. I'm sure there's nothing to worry about now."

Naeo hesitated. She didn't like it, not one little bit.

The few buildings that still stood were missing their roofs and at least one wall, giving them a ghoulish aspect. But what made this awful place even more depressing was the grey. The Barrens had swept through the remains of roads and plazas, homes and temples, parks and markets, coating them all in a deathly blanket. This was a tragic place. A place best left alone.

"It just doesn't feel right," said Naeo. "It feels like... like *death*."

Ash nodded and rummaged in his hair. "That's just because it's deserted. Look, whatever the risks, it'll be safer to camp in Grail than on the open Barrens."

"Grail," muttered Naeo, shaking her head. "I can't believe they called it that."

"A happier time," said Ash thoughtfully. "I remember how excited my father was when we—"

"Come on then," said Naeo, striding off down the hill. "If we're going to do it, let's do it."

Ash watched her go. "Sometimes I very much prefer your other half," he said, under his breath.

16

Remember

"To see is to remember, *so they have learned to close their eyes."*

THEY WALKED DOWN THE open hillside, leaving behind them the last traces of forest. Gnarled roots gave way to broken stones and pounded ash, and they felt the sorrowful gloom pressing in on them. But it was as they entered the town that Naeo's heart failed. Perhaps it was the skeletal carcasses of buildings with their gaping doors and windows, or the blasted walls, scarred by a ferocious fire that she did not dare remember. Or perhaps it was Thoth's glowering, empty face etched deeply into the crumbling stone. Whatever it was, they found themselves drawing closer to one another, walking as far as possible from the buildings and shadows, trying not to see too much or look too close. There were too many memories here: too much they had tried so hard to forget.

They passed a row of broken buildings, glancing warily into the recesses, trying not to notice the belongings of those who had lived there: furniture carved from the woods of the forest, now splintered and charred; broken pottery; faded murals on the walls. One mural showed an image of the Valley of Outs between the two forested hills, and in the foreground, the lamplights of Sylva twinkling in the trees. But there was something scrawled across the centre of the mural in black ink or soot. It was a long-beaked bird, hunched like a vulture over the valley as though preparing to feed. The Ibis: the symbol of Thoth's private legion. They turned away and fixed their eyes ahead, walking swiftly past.

They reached the end of the street, passing the shattered timber columns of a once-grand building. As they rounded its corner they suddenly halted and stared.

Ahead of them was a wide plaza strewn with dried weeds. At its centre was a giant statue, towering towards the bleak grey sky. They knew at once what it was. They remembered it from their childhood, from their schoolbooks and their parents' tales: the Monument of Maat. But it was different from how they remembered it, not only because it was broken and defaced, but also because like everything else, it was in shadow. Its smooth, lovingly carved surface was shrouded in the same miserable gloom as the buildings and rubble. In the past this effigy of Merimaat had glowed, seeming to draw to its surface the barest traces of light. It had been as much a beacon as a statue — a reminder of her presence, her teachings, her love. Now its white stone was covered with freakish, illiterate scrawl and every part of it was chipped or mutilated. An entire arm had been hewn off — the arm that had held the Maat feather; the feather of truth. Both now lay discarded at the corner of the square, the feather in pieces beside the broken remains of delicate fingers. Merimaat was left with only her other, withered hand, turned upwards with an empty palm in that way that Naeo had always found so strange, so mysterious.

But worst of all, those who had attacked the statue had taken her face. Her beautiful face. It had been set upon by a thousand chisels until nothing remained of that gentle smile, those generous eyes, that radiance.

"Why would they *do* that?" murmured Naeo.

"So we don't remember," said Ash, his voice empty. "So we don't hope."

They gazed at the broken statue, trying to understand the hatred that had done this. It was as unfathomable as any atrocity of the Undoing, but there was something worse about this. As Naeo looked at the monument, this beautiful image that had once stood for joy and togetherness and hope, a thought wrapped itself around her like a blanket of ice.

It had been made into a new kind of symbol.

It was a monument to despair.

Sylas laughed and shook his head. "What is it with you and water, Simsi?"

Simia smiled guardedly. "What do you mean?"

"Well, the whole reason you got caught up in this was that you threw yourself off the side of a wave *into* my boat, and now you throw yourself out of—"

"It's not funny!" snapped Simia, dropping her eyes.

He gave her a sidelong look. "Not even a bit?"

"No," she said firmly. "If I hadn't been so pig-headed, we wouldn't have to walk the rest of the way." She kicked at a weed. "It was stupid!"

"Don't be so hard on yourself. You couldn't have known it would turn out like this and anyway, as Triste said, we needed to leave the boats behind soon enough anyway. The river isn't safe near the city."

"Sure, but we wouldn't have had to walk through this!" said Simia, pointing ahead.

They were on marshland, surrounded by clumps of sparse undergrowth and undersized trees, and between them countless

135

pools of filthy, stinking, greyish-brown water. There were still occasional signs of life — a bird flitting between rotting stumps; a broken branch bearing a few green leaves; the splash of something moving in the marshy mud. But there was no doubt that the Barrens were drawing near. These scant sightings of life had become fewer and further between and the dying light was now taking on a greyish hue, killing all the remaining colour. Worst of all was the stench: the chilling, musty scent of rotting vegetation and putrefying sludge.

They picked their way as carefully as they could between the deepest pools, following Triste's sure-footed, loping step, but even then they occasionally stumbled into pools of slime that sucked thirstily at their boots.

It was slow going and already the night was drawing in. As the sky passed through deepening shades of grey, they gave up hope of finding their way on to dry ground before dark. Triste slowed his pace, searching for a place to camp and what scarce dry firewood could be found. Sylas and Simia soon joined the hunt, each scavenging for the smallest piece of wood or brush.

Simia spotted a large branch and bent down to pick it up, but as she pulled at it she felt it yanked out of her hand. She lifted her head in surprise only to see Triste looming above the reeds, hoisting the branch over his shoulder.

He smiled down at her. "We'll share it," he said.

She grinned and walked on beside him as they continued through the swamp.

"Triste, I just wanted to say again how sorry I am. It really was—"

"It's done," said Triste dismissively. "No need to go over it again."

He went to move on, but Simia held on to his arm.

136

"I need to explain why I was so pig-headed — why I've been so rude to—"

"I understand."

"No, you don't. You see... the thing is—"

"I remind you of your father," said Triste softly. For the first time he gave her an unguarded smile — a smile that banished his gloominess and the dark rings beneath his eyes — a smile that was warm and compassionate. "I understand."

Simia's mouth fell open. "You... You saw..."

"I'm rather good at what I do."

Simia grew pale. "You *Scried* it? When?"

"A while back, before we set off."

Simia turned away.

He put his hand warmly on her shoulder and turned her back round.

"Don't be nice to me," she snapped, glaring at him. "It makes it worse."

"Sorry," he said, taking his hand away.

Simia looked him full in the face, now so close, so very close. Her eyes travelled over his features, taking in the angular jaw, the shape of his mouth, the darkness around his eyes, and then the eyes themselves: deep eyes — the eyes that opened her wide.

Her hand rose haltingly towards his cheek. But then she seemed to think better of it, snapping it away again.

"It's all right," she murmured, walking off into the marsh. "It's not your fault."

Triste started out after her, but Sylas, who had overheard the exchange, came up behind him and pulled him back. "I'll go," he said.

Triste nodded. "Not too far. I'll set up camp here."

Sylas followed her, but did not try to catch up, staying several paces behind. How strange, he thought, that here they were again, on the Barrens, and this time it was Simia who was in tears and he who was trailing behind. At least he could follow her example, because she had known exactly how to be. He walked with her for a while, winding through scrub and mud, wandering on towards the feeble, lifeless smudge of a setting sun.

When finally she sat down, he sat down too. They were silent, listening to the occasional croaking of a frog or the chirrup of a grasshopper – perhaps the last living things in this ghostly place.

"I miss him, Sylas," she said eventually, her voice thick. "I miss him so much." She took hold of the lapels of her father's coat, pulling it tight to her chest. She fought her tears, and when they came, they came in deep, swelling sobs that wracked her body but made no sound. These were tears she had shed many times before, quietly, so that no one would know, tears she had first shed not far from here, somewhere on the Barrens. But then she had been alone.

Sylas shifted to her side, putting an arm around her shoulder and pulling her closer. His gaze followed hers out across the desolate terrain, past the twisted silhouettes of famished trees, out towards the dying sun.

But he saw none of that. All he saw was his mother's face, soft and warm but far away, like she was behind glass. Like in the picture still hanging in his room.

"I know, Simsi," he said. "I know."

The last light had almost died and the marshes were still. The grasshoppers had ceased their song and the rodents and slithering creatures stirred no more.

They were glad of the fire, while it lasted. Exhausted by the trials and traumas of the day, Simia had already curled up next to it and fallen asleep. She had barely even kept herself awake to eat their dinner of stew and bread. Triste was somewhere out in the darkness, searching for more firewood. The flames were already burning low and it was important to keep it lively while they slept, to deter any animals. And so Sylas found his eyes drifting from the fire to the shadows, wondering what kind of creatures would live in such a place. Eventually he decided that he didn't really want to know.

He reached over to his bag and brought out the box that Paiscion had given him, and the Samarok, drawing both closer to the fire. He laid the Samarok carefully in his lap and then pulled open the lid of the box. Placing the box gently down again, he unscrewed the bottle of ink and picked up the quill. It was as light as air but it felt substantial, because what it lacked in weight it gained in other ways: the elegant shaft; the fine detail of the nib; the fact that it just felt important, as if it was destined to write great things.

Tentatively, he dipped the nib in the ink. He glanced down at the Samarok, seeing its beautiful stones glinting in the firelight, then flicked through the rough-edged pages to the very back. There, after the last entry, were two blank sheets that he had never noticed before. They were unmarked on either side, but that would still only give him four pages to tell his whole story – even the parts that were yet to come. He blew out his cheeks – that would be a challenge.

He lowered the nib opposite the scrawl of the last writer then closed his eyes and tried to concentrate. Not only did he have to think about what to say, but he assumed he would also have to write in Ravel Runes, which he was not even sure he could do. He cleared his mind as best he could, thought of his first line and then tried to picture the runes that would make up the first two words. In his mind they were even more fluid and shifting than they were on paper, but when he thought he had grasped them well enough, he opened his eyes and lowered the nib. Wincing as it scratched the precious page, he began.

To his surprise the quill moved swiftly and fluently, completing the first rune in three confident strokes. He did not pause to examine his work because he was already on to the second, and then the next word. Only when he had finished these two words did he stop and cast his eye back. Even as he looked the runes altered, taking a new, more coherent form:

"My name"

He smiled. This wasn't as difficult as he had thought. He closed his eyes again, concentrated for a moment and then resumed his writing. The quill moved more gracefully than before, and soon it was looping and dancing across the page. This time he looked back as he wrote, his eyes tracing the runes he had written even before the ink was dry, seeing them shifting and morphing. The effect was startling at first but beautiful, and Sylas felt his heart quicken.

Moments later he had completed his first two sentences and he turned the book towards the firelight, admiring his handiwork. He read the words out loud:

"My name is Sylas Tate and I am not a Bringer. I am my mother's son, and that seems to be enough."

He lowered the book and grinned; that was a good start.

Suddenly a low, barely audible hiss seeped out of the night.

"I am my mother's s-s-s-son!"

Sylas started. Then he heard it again, this time from the other side of the camp.

"I am my mother's s-s-s-son... that should be enough."

He sprang to his feet. "Simia!" he shouted. "Simia, wake up!"

She looked up with bleary eyes, pushing back her blanket.

"Did you hear it?" he whispered.

Simia said nothing, her eyes searched the darkness beyond the halo of fire. Then it came again — a low hiss — louder this time, closer.

"*Do you h-h-h-hear it?*"

"The fire!" cried Simia, looking frightened. "Get closer! Quickly!"

"Why? What is it?"

"Just come! Now!" She kicked at the embers, sending up a shower of sparks.

"*DO YOU H-H-H-HEAR IT?*" echoed the voice in the dark.

17

Death

*"And so it seems certain: the Undoing is not just about empire or culture
or politics or greed. For the Suhl, it is about life and* death.*"*

THE NOISES CAME FROM all sides. It was not one sound but several
— a chorus of eerie whispers drifting around them, taunting them,
moving close and then sliding away.

"Little ones-s-s..." hissed one voice.

"So s-s-s-small," whispered another.

As Sylas peered out into the darkness, he saw a mist forming
before his eyes. It passed away as quickly as it had formed, and
then reappeared. His breath was clouding in front of his face.

"Why's it so cold?" he murmured.

Suddenly he felt an overpowering chill clawing through his
clothes and biting his face. It was a vicious, painful cold that
passed quickly into his bones and seized his muscles.

He turned to Simia and shouted through clenched teeth:
"What's happ—"

Then something hit him. It came at him from the front, colliding
head-on. It was not solid nor could he feel its touch. Instead it
seemed to enter him, passing through skin, flesh and bone, bringing

with it a new, paralysing, hideous cold that lodged itself in the very centre of his chest. There it lingered, spreading outwards through his torso and limbs, infusing them with an awful, aching emptiness, smothering all feeling and warmth. As his limbs faltered and he began to stagger, his mind was filled with a horrifying nothingness: a black, meaningless void that felt like madness.

He flailed about, trying to tear himself free, but there was nothing to cling to. He tried to scream, but he had no voice.

Then, as quickly as it had entered him, he felt it sliding away, pulling at his organs as it released him: slowly, reluctantly. He felt his teeth being drawn towards the back of his head, his tongue straining towards his throat, his eyes pressing into his skull. He had the strangest sense that his very thoughts were being raked from his mind, as though whatever was in him was trying to gather them up.

He staggered forward and as he did so he saw Simia fall on to her hands and then crumple into the dust, her limbs limp.

"Simsi!" he cried.

He turned towards her, taking her under the arms, but as he did so he was struck again, this time in his side. The cold moved more quickly than before, surging into his body, knocking the wind from his lungs. He let go of her shoulders just as he felt the emptiness claw into his mind. This time it swamped every part of him, seeping into thoughts and feelings.

And then a light burst out of nowhere, making him heave his heavy arms to protect his face. It bathed the swamp in a wide orange halo, burning into the night, driving back the darkness. Through his fingers he saw a ball of fire hovering above the ground, flames licking around its edges and sparks leaping from its surface. He could feel its warmth on his face, banishing the cold from his cheeks. At the same time the thing inside him seemed to recoil and shift, as though trying to find a place to hide. His heart shuddered and his lungs turned in his chest and then, in a dragging motion that drew him upwards, the thing rose through his shoulders and his skull, tearing at his thoughts as it passed.

Finally, miraculously, it let go. He slumped forward on to his hands, taking great gasps of the freezing air, trying not to be sick. He turned to see Simia next to him, her face ashen and expressionless as she did her best to stand up, then fell again. He looked back towards the fading light and saw Triste standing beneath the fire, legs braced wide and arms aloft, his face contorted with pain. Between his hands he held a bundle of wood and brush that writhed with flame, spitting angrily at the night and crackling as it burned. Sparks fell on to his shoulders and glistening head, burning cruelly as they touched his skin.

"Run!" bellowed the Scryer. "Follow the fire!"

He rotated his shoulders and extended his arms and suddenly a tongue of flame burst from the side of the blazing orb, snaking out into the blackness. It struck the top of a nearby stump, setting it alight, and then careered onwards, carving through the night.

They hesitated.

"GO!" cried Triste, "before they take us all!"

For a moment Sylas and Simia looked at one another. Then they ran. They ran with leaden limbs, still frozen to the core, with unruly legs that hardly seemed part of them any more. They ran blindly, wildly, with eyes only for the trail of fire, trying not to think of what crawled through the dark around them. The tentacle of flame fizzed and crackled, spat and snarled as if it were lashing the dark, but to Sylas and Simia it was a friend at their shoulder, leading them on, lighting their way. They ran so close to it that its heat seared their skin and its light blinded them, but they never drew away. What lay beyond was far, far worse. When Simia fell, Sylas pulled her to her feet and when Sylas stumbled, she hauled him on.

As they ran the tongue of fire became a tendril and the tendril became a trace. It flickered ever more dimly as it curled through the darkness, casting less and less light. And then they saw its end, flicking like a serpent's tail.

Sylas felt a surge of panic — surely they hadn't run far enough? And as though in answer, he heard another whisper somewhere behind: harsh and ghoulish. His heart began to fail, when suddenly he remembered Triste's words on the river: "*Keep your tricks to yourself until you really need them.*"

He cast his hand out towards the finger of light, closing his eyes, searching for the flames. At first he flailed in the darkness and cold, but then he felt them, burning through his veins, flickering in his mind's eye: weak and failing, but there. He caught them up, nurturing their light and heat, gathering them in his chest before sending them out, along his arm, his hand, his fingertips, out into the night. He opened his eyes and saw the trail of fire flare and spark, twist and stretch. For an instant it pulled itself thin and bright, surging on and on.

And then, suddenly, it went out.

They both drew up panting then whirled about, peering into the night.

"You've put it out!" cried Simia.

Sylas whirled about, looking for the flames. "I thought... I thought I could—"

"You can't make fire where there isn't any!" she snapped. "That isn't how Essenfayle works!"

The darkness drew in upon them, threatening them from

every side, leaving them open and defenceless. They expected the whispers at any moment: the chill against their skin, at their throats, around their hearts.

But as they paced about they realised that something else had changed. The ground underfoot was firmer and dryer, and they could no longer smell the damp and rot of the swamp, just the faintest smell of burning and dust.

"We're on the Barrens," panted Simia. "Triste found the way!"

"Will they follow us?"

"Not if we can make a new fire!"

He heard her scrabbling around in the dust and then the clatter of wood against wood. He bent down, laying his hands quickly on a piece of driftwood.

"What about Triste?" he hissed.

"The Kraven will have him by now!" said Simia, her voice full of fear. "We're his only hope!"

They scrambled through the blackness, pulling at dead roots, chafing their hands on rocks, listening without wanting to hear, knowing that the whispers were not far away. And then Sylas saw a flash in the night — a flintlock spark illuminating Simia's terrified face. He staggered over to her and dumped his sticks just as the tinder took. There was a momentary flare and then the tiniest, most delicate flame sprang up. It was no larger than a fingernail, but their lives depended on it.

They gathered around, shielding it from any breath of wind. Slowly — too slowly — it took, snaking through the dead grass and twigs, blooming into life. They nursed it, laying twigs gently, tenderly over the growing flames.

Sylas glanced up. "I feel..." he stopped, trying to control his chattering teeth. "I feel... dead, inside."

"That's the Kraven," said Simia, shivering and turning to look out into the darkness. "That's what they do. They steal your life away."

"What *are* they?"

He saw her face crumple as she fought back her tears. He reached out, but she pushed his hand away.

"I'm all right," she said firmly. "But *Triste*! He's out there on his own! With *them*!"

Sylas laid more wood on the fire, feeling the first warmth from its flames.

"What is it he's up against, Simsi?" he asked, as calmly as he could. "What *are* they?"

There was a brief silence. "Dead people."

18

The Kraven

*"The Kraven do not see and they do not hear.
They do not feel, or think, or do. All that they are is stolen."*

IT WAS A COLD that pained the limbs and froze the air in her lungs. It surged upwards, curling icicle fingers around her throat, and then it started to squeeze. When her eyes flicked open she knew it was no dream, for there were the fingers, giant and marble-white. Her mouth gaped wide, somewhere between a gasp and a scream, and then it came: an avalanche of air cascading into her aching chest, filling her with a sudden explosion of life.

Then she saw a shadow above her.

"Are you OK?" It was Ash's voice and it was full of concern. "You're white as a witch's frock!"

He took her by her collar and pulled her out from under the broken hand of Merimaat's statue, where they had decided to make their bed for the night.

Naeo's chest heaved and she panted violently, trying to force air into her lungs. She felt the pain clawing through her back, rippling through the black scar.

"So c-c-cold!" she gasped.

Ash felt her hand and looked shocked. He glanced over at the fire, but it had almost died and they had no more wood. He grabbed his rucksack.

"Last time I did this I got into a whole heap of trouble," he mumbled, grabbing a large stone and planting it in front of Naeo. He parted her curtain of hair and winked at her. "But what's a bit of Kimiyya between friends?"

He spooned something from a jar on to the stone, sprinkled it with a little ash from the fire and then cupped his hands on either side. The substance on the rock hissed and then spat out a puff of acrid smoke before bursting into a piercing white flame.

"Easy as that," he said, proudly. "Mustard... tastes good, saves lives."

The small flame grew and gave off a burst of radiant heat. Naeo shuffled closer.

"So are you sick?" he asked, putting his blanket over her shoulders. "Is it your back?"

Naeo shook her head, her teeth chattering. She swallowed to regain her voice. "No... not really. This is different. I feel so cold. So... dark." She looked up at Ash. "I'm frightened this time... for Sylas."

"You think something's happened to him?"

"I know it has."

Ash searched her face, hoping she would say more, but she just looked blank and dazed.

They sat quietly, staring into the white flame. Naeo slowly began to feel the heat penetrating her icy skin, restoring the barest traces of pink to her cheeks. The pain in her back started to ease, returning to the usual, bearable ache.

Finally Ash drew a breath and turned to Naeo.

"Well, we just have to carry on. Triste knows what he's doing," he said, sounding rather like he was trying to reassure himself as much as Naeo. "I'm sure they'll be OK. My job is to worry about you, and you need to get moving — a bit of hiking should warm you up."

Naeo looked unsure.

Ash thought for a moment and then narrowed his eyes. "OK, you're right, let's stay here for a while," he said, slipping his arm around her shoulders and drawing her close. "We should get you warmed up first."

Naeo pushed his arm away and heaved herself to her feet. "No... thanks. I'm OK. Let's just go."

Ash smiled to himself and began packing away their belongings.

The chill climbed Sylas's spine. "*Dead* people?"

Simia was still facing away from him, looking out into the night, searching for any sign of Triste.

"People who died in the Reckoning," she said. "On the Barrens."

"They're still here?"

"Some of them. Less and less these days. We were unlucky to run into them."

"The Kraven," murmured Sylas, still finding it hard to believe what Simia had told him.

"There are lots of names for them, but Kraven is the one that's stuck."

"What... other names?"

Simia turned back to him, her face still a ghastly shade of white. "Wraiths, spectres, ghosts..."

"*Ghosts?*" murmured Sylas. "You're saying that ghosts are *real*?"

"Very real."

Suddenly there was a noise out in the darkness. A quiet, almost inaudible wheeze followed by a deep groan.

Without breathing they inched closer to the fire, waiting for the voices and the cold.

Then again, a deep groan.

They exchanged a glance.

Sylas grabbed Simia's arm. "Get ready to—"

But he was cut short, because suddenly there was movement — a shifting of shadows. Then footsteps — heavy and faltering — coming towards them.

When the wraith appeared, its large body was stooped forward, bent almost double; its limbs flailed wide, its clammy white skin glistened in the firelight. But it did not whisper. It was silent. And it looked at them with wide, tear-filled eyes. Then they saw more eyes, tattooed across its naked scalp.

"Triste!" they cried in unison.

The Scryer stepped into the halo of light, his arms hanging limply at his sides. He opened his mouth to say something, but then he simply exhaled, pitched forward and fell at their feet.

§

The Ghor commander stood quietly, dutifully, its giant head held high, its mighty shoulders snapped back to attention. It stood so still that it barely seemed to breathe, its muscular, fur-clad limbs held tightly to its sides. It was able to stay in this stance for hours, days if necessary. But it was ready to rouse itself to arms in an instant. It was all in the training. And the breeding.

But while its body was still, its blue, almost-human eyes were lively and sharp, passing along the long rows of books, reading their spines: the titles and authors, written in hieroglyphs, cartouches, runes and letters; in Egyptian, Greek, Persian, English and other languages it did not know. And here, in Thoth's library, it need never look at the same book twice. The shelves disappeared into the darkness above and into the gloom on both sides. The bookcase was vast, limitless: a repository for all books written by all hands of all ages. The commander marvelled at the omniscience of its master, at the magnificence of his intellect: so many of these volumes scribed by his very own hand. The scribe to the gods themselves.

How proud it was to serve.

"You are loyal, Anubikan," rasped the voice of many, echoing down the corridor of books. "I shall reward your devotion one day. I shall show you a book from the Beginning. A book that tells of the very first of your kind. The god in whose image you were created."

The commander allowed itself a twitch of the neck, a glance towards its master.

"My Lord," it growled, with a slight bow.

Its master had promised this many times, a fact both knew all too well, and yet each time it was a new gift, a new joy. Its reverent eyes traced its master's seated form. That bony, frail figure, which would be nothing without the folds of its cloak. It watched the skeletal fingers guide the quill with expert ease, the curling fingernails and discoloured fingertips stained by the flow of lifetimes of ink, ages of wisdom. It peered into the darkness of the hood, trying to glimpse the beauty of its master's face: that face of all men, but so much greater than them all.

"I shall be with you in a moment," boomed Thoth, as though aware of the admiring gaze.

Of course he was aware. Anubikan fixed its eyes ahead, reproaching itself for disturbing its master. It bit its tongue angrily until it tasted blood.

Several minutes passed before Thoth finally spoke.

"You have something to tell me."

The commander snapped its snout up in the air, stiffening its limbs until they burned. "Yes, my Lord."

"Well, go on."

"Your carriage is ready and the Hund have been despatched ahead. The other Dirghea will be readied for you well before your arrival."

There was a brief silence. "Yes, that is as I instructed," said Thoth with a note of impatience. "What else?"

Anubikan cleared its throat with a hacking growl. "It seems the Scryer was telling the truth about the child's mother. She must be dead. She is not in the cells, we are sure of it, and none of our spies have seen her among the Suhl scum."

"The slums?"

"Nothing, my Lord. We have searched them thoroughly."

"No one knows anything? You're certain of it?"

"Yes, my Lord. We made an example of some of them to be sure. Nothing. The only slave who had heard of her said she was dead."

"Let me speak to the slave."

Anubikan shifted uncomfortably. "My Lord, she died. Under interrogation."

There was an extended quiet, a quiet that set the commander on edge.

"She was convincing, my Lord. The mother is dead."

"You had better hope so," snapped the Priest of Souls.

The commander swallowed and clicked its heels.

"And there is no more word about this book? The book they call the Samarok?"

Anubikan shook its head. "Sorry, my Lord, no. We interrogated several of the Scribes as you instructed, but they claim to know nothing of its contents."

"Indeed..." muttered Thoth, sounding unconvinced.

"One suggested that it was not of this world. That it is from the Other."

"No doubt," growled Thoth, "but I would still have it. Such a book should be here, in my library."

"Yes, my Lord. We will find it, my Lord."

"Leave me now, Anubikan," breathed Thoth. "I have one more thing to do before we leave."

Anubikan bowed deeply and heaved its powerful limbs into motion, striding towards the great brass doors.

"Do you know the name of the book I will show you? The book of your ancestor?"

Anubikan turned on its heel and shook its head. "No, my Lord." In truth, it did. Its master had told him the name many times, at moments such as this. Moments of displeasure.

Thoth raised his hooded head and turned, showing the barest trace of a pallid cheek.

"The Book of the Dead."

19

Never Look Back

"The law of the Passing is simple: never look back.
Your way is onwards now; on, into another world."

> *With a hey-ho and an open yawn,*
> *We'll wander out this morning!*
> *Singing hey-ho to the scarlet dawn,*
> *Among the birds a-calling!*
> *And a hey—*

"ASH."

"Yes?"

"Do you have to?"

"I thought it would cheer you up."

"It doesn't. It makes me feel worse."

There was a brief silence.

"No accounting for taste," muttered Ash.

They had been walking for what seemed like hours, though they had no way to tell how long for sure. The sun was still not up and they knew that, even when it was, it would be shrouded in grey. Naeo's limbs were still leaden, but they had been warmed a little by the trudge. Ash had been right about that — it had been best to get moving.

The journey had been arduous. It was not just the jarring of the hard-packed dust, or the blind stumbles into dried-up creeks or fissures. These things were tolerable. It was the completeness of the dark that most drained the spirit. It was an unnatural darkness; oil-thick, without pigment or shade. There was no moon, no distant star, no glow of a far-flung town or camp. There was no buzz of insects, no song of cicadas, no tinkle of water, no rush of wind. The Barrens was not a place at all. It was an absence. It had been a place once — Naeo remembered all too well when she had lived on the plains of Salsimaine — but that time was gone, and with it the place. There was only one thing for them on the Barrens now, one thing too large, too strong, too powerful to be swept aside. The Circle of Salsimaine. And they could not reach it soon enough.

It felt strange to yearn to reach the place that would take her so far from everything she had ever known, and from her father. How unthinkable to be leaving him behind — leaving him *there*, in the Dirgheon. And yet she didn't feel the awful, searing guilt that she had before. Perhaps the conversation with Filimaya had helped, but it was something else too. At some point in the hours of walking she had realised that this was what he would want. He would want it because this was safer for her. More importantly, he would want it because of something he had said to her once. And here, in the endless dark and silence, it came back to her as though she had heard it yesterday.

They had been walking through the wood near their home. She tried not to think how near to that place she might be right now — now it was just another expanse of dust. They had been talking about the tree house they would build together. They had talked about such innocent, unthinking things in those days. And they had a pretend argument about who would be lookout, in their fortress in the trees — pretend, because who would make a finer lookout than a Scryer? And then they had talked about Scrying, and her sadness that the gift had not passed to her (because then surely she would be a better lookout than he). But her father had suddenly become serious, and had taken her by the shoulders and looked at her earnestly.

"I would give it all — all I have seen — to see with your eyes." She had laughed. "Why?"

"Because you are the better part of me, and you will see a better world." His grip had begun to hurt. "You must never look back, Nay-no! Never look back!"

He had said it so fiercely — so much had he meant it — that it made her shiver even now. *A better world*, Naeo mused. Is this what he could have meant? This strange journey? Or had he just meant that she sees the world differently?

Whatever the truth, she knew he would prefer she was opening her eyes to the wonders of the Other, than trailing back to the horrors of Thoth's city.

"'Never look back, Nay-no'," she murmured.

"If you're finished talking to yourself," said Ash suddenly, "you may want to take a look!"

Naeo lifted her eyes and instantly felt a flood of relief. There, high above the plain, was the silver disc of the full moon, muddled with wisps of cloud. When she looked about her, she could see the rolling, featureless surface of the Barrens, marked out in dim shades of silver and grey. Finally they would be able to see their way.

But there was something else. Something on the muddy horizon: bold and distinct. It resembled a collection of broken, decaying teeth, assembled in regimental rows. Some pointed towards the moon, others were capped across their tops, forming an arch.

Naeo drew up sharply. "The Circle of Salsimaine!" she whispered.

She felt a surge of energy, and for the first time in hours warmth flowed through her veins. They picked up their pace, striding out towards their goal. Ash struck up a song once again, and this time she joined him:

> *"With a hey-ho and an open yawn,*
> *We'll wander out this morning!*
> *Singing hey-ho to the scarlet dawn,*
> *Among the birds—"*

And then they halted and fell silent.

There was a movement out on the Barrens, beyond the stone circle.

It seemed at first like a heat haze, or a trick of the light, but neither were possible: not here on the Barrens. And then, in the heart of the rippling, shimmering motion — lights. Just two at first, blinking feebly. Then another, and then three more. Suddenly there were fifteen, twenty lights strung out across the horizon. Between them, the first shapes appeared: low and hunched and dark. Naeo felt a shiver as she saw them rolling from side to side, heaving and loping. She knew that prowling gait all too well: Ghorhund, running at full sprint, running directly towards the Circle of Salsimaine.

Then, between them, others began to materialise through the night mists: taller and leaner, moving with a longer, more measured stride, their formation precise and purposeful.

And finally, at the very centre, a shape that dwarfed the others. A solid form with wheels, led by a great entourage of bounding creatures: a feverish churn of life. Riding high in the rear, a tall elegant figure held an arm aloft, wielding an unseen whip, driving the charge.

"Run!" cried Naeo, stepping out in the direction of the stone circle.

Ash hesitated. "*Towards* them?"

Naeo wheeled about. "What choice do we have? We have to get there first! Run!"

20
What You Are Not

"What you are not, the rest of you may be."

TRISTE'S EYES STARED UP at them wildly, searching, imploring.

"Run!" he cried. His teeth were chattering. "I s-see them!"

He strained to sit up as though wanting to flee, but there was nowhere to go but the dark. He settled back as he had many times before, closing his eyes for another few moments of exhausting visions.

Simia could hardly look at him. His head and hands were covered in burns from where he had held the fire, and where he was not burned, his flesh was white and icy, glistening with a cold sweat. The Salve they had applied to his injuries seemed to be doing little to help — it was never very effective on burns, and these burns were so deep, so severe. Gone was Triste's sombre calm and instead he looked restless, like a frightened child. Even the warmth of the fire seemed of little comfort — if anything, he seemed to be getting worse.

"I did this," mumbled Simia. Her face was pale and streaked with tears, her expression blank and desperate. Sylas reached out to take her hand, but she pulled it away.

He wanted to console her, but he had to attend to Triste. He leaned over, bringing his face close to the Scryer's, forcing him to look away from the darkness.

"What can we do, Triste?" he asked softly.

The Scryer seemed to see him for a moment, frowning slightly, but then his eyes drifted back to the darkness. His face crumpled. "I *saw* them," he sighed, tears welling in his eyes. "I saw them!"

Sylas shifted again, trying to catch the Scryer's eye. "Triste! Look at me!" he pleaded. "Tell me what to do!"

The Scryer blinked and looked confused, as though fighting some internal battle. Slowly he seemed to focus.

"Water…" he whispered. "Cold…"

Suddenly they were both in motion. Simia riffled through their bags for their blankets, flinging the contents on the floor in her haste. Sylas fetched his water bottle, threw the stopper to one side and brought it to Triste's lips. The Scryer drank weakly but thirstily, then nodded his thanks.

As Simia arranged the blankets, Sylas lowered Triste's head on to a rolled-up tunic and then leaned over him again, stopping him from looking out into the night. Slowly, the Scryer seemed to settle a little, his eyes losing their wild stare, his body relaxing beneath the blankets. And then, with each passing minute, he came back to himself. As the darkness and confusion receded, he seemed to become aware of Sylas for the first time.

"You made it," he said in a feeble voice.

"Thanks to you."

Triste coughed and wheezed then glanced around him. "Simia?"

She knelt down next to Sylas, her face strained. "I'm so sorry! This is all my fault!" The tears started to flow again. "If I hadn't—"

161

Triste pulled a hand from beneath the blanket and held it up to her lips. Sylas flinched when he saw how badly burnt it was, livid in the firelight.

"They could have found us anywhere," said the Scryer. He touched her cheek. "You're not to blame."

"But I made us—"

"You kept Sylas safe. That's all that matters. It was just bad luck."

Simia tried to take hold of his hand but he winced and drew it away, laying it back on his chest. She looked stricken and helpless, her hand wavering in the air.

Triste fixed her with his doleful eyes. "Will you do something for me?"

"What?"

"Sit with me while I sleep," he said with a weak smile. "Lie next to me, if you like. Keep me warm."

Sylas glanced at Simia warily — he knew how she could be when people got too close — but she did not hesitate. With a steady look as though daring him to say anything, she made a pillow of a bundle of clothing and laid down next to Triste. In truth she was not close enough to give him any warmth, but the young Scryer seemed contented, or pretended to be so, for her sake. He shifted his stiff limbs until he was as comfortable as he could be and closed his eyes.

Sylas stood up and moved a little closer to the fire. He had almost forgotten how cold and numb he felt, and it was good to be nearer to the glowing embers. He sat down as close as he dared, letting the fire do its work on his aching limbs, then he stared out into the darkness.

He tried not to listen for voices, but they seemed to have gone. Perhaps they had somehow managed to elude the Kraven in the marshes, amid all the confusion and Triste's strange, magical fire.

Or perhaps – his eyes drifted across to his companions – perhaps they had taken all they needed from Triste.

The Scryer looked peaceful now, lying on his back, breathing slowly and deeply, but Sylas remembered their first sight of him entering the camp. He had looked half dead: gaunt and pale, whispering wild words in a tongue Sylas did not understand. He shuddered as he remembered his own encounter: the raking sensation as they had drawn themselves out of him, leaving less than they had found. And perhaps because of that sense that they had taken part of him away, he found himself even keener to understand. What were they? Where did they come from? Why were they here?

He glanced at Simia, wondering if he might disturb her, but she was asleep now, lying on her side, facing away from Triste but nestled close, so that her back was tight up against him. And then, even as he watched, she turned over and unconsciously threw an arm across the Scryer's chest.

Sylas smiled and looked away. And then something glinted in the corner of his eye, something among the things that Simia had scattered in her hunt for the blankets. It was the Samarok, the gems on its cover winking by the light of the flames. He fetched it, dusted it down and took his place by the embers.

He opened it at a random page and started to turn through the entries, his eyes tracing the handwritten runes, now accustomed to their shape and form, reading them with ease. But after he had scoured four pages, he bit his lip and frowned. This wasn't going to be easy. He knew that the Ravel Runes should be able to take him quickly to any mention of the Kraven, but he first had to find a reference to them. He rubbed his cheek, deep in thought. Or did he? Paiscion had only taken moments to find those lines from 'The Song of Isia' – had he really just chanced across them?

And then he remembered. He remembered those final moments in the Den of Scribes, when Fathray had shown him the true power of Ravel Runes: their power to connect meanings, not just words.

He turned the next page and the next, until something caught his eye and then he began to read:

> *"...how many generations now dead and gone have passed their lives in ignorance of this singular and simple truth..."*

Part of him wanted to read on, but instead his gaze rested on a single word, the word 'dead'. Then he turned his thoughts back to the marshes, when the Kraven had attacked, when he had first felt their deathly touch. Even as he called all this to mind, the runes began to move: the delicate tendrils turning and stretching, the coils unravelling. Within moments the entire page was writhing, its neat lines of Ravel Runes unfurling into a new entry. As it became still, his eyes travelled back along the new line and he began to read:

> *"...and who knows what such things might tell us about the dead – about spirits and ghosts and superstitions that have long tested the boundaries of our imagination..."*

With a tingle of excitement he rested his eyes on '*spirits and ghosts*' and once again, he cast his mind back to his encounter with the Kraven. The runes responded more quickly this time, their loops and coils unravelling in an instant. The entire page blurred and then settled to a new entry.

He smiled to himself: he was getting better at this.

"...though my rational mind tells me it cannot be so, it seems clear to me now that the mythical things we have come to know as ghosts and wraiths and spirits, are the very same deathly creatures that the Suhl and the Gherothians call the Kraven."

He raised his eyes and for a moment stared out into the darkness. It felt like a world of secrets was opening itself to him. He steeled himself and dropped his eyes to the page.

"Here in this world, like all supernatural things, these ghosts have found their full and true form. They are as much a part of this world as the Suhl, or Essenfayle, or Thoth's creatures, or the Three Ways; and just as things of magic and folklore flourish in the endless possibilities of this world, so do the Kraven."

Sylas felt the chill returning to his limbs and he threw another bundle of wood on to the fire. He shuffled a little closer and carried on reading.

"But because here the Kraven walk the earth like men, because they are as much a feature of the night as the stars or the moon, they can be known. They can be studied and understood And this brings me to my most astonishing discovery: the discovery that they have their roots in the division of our worlds, and perhaps in the Glimmer Myth itself."

Sylas's fingers were quivering now, partly from cold and partly excitement.

"The Kraven speak with varied voices, they behave in different ways, but one thing is common to them all: they gather in places of violence, places where lives have been torn away. Indeed, the truth of the Kraven is reminiscent of our own ghost stories: tales of murder victims haunting those who killed them, of dead soldiers roaming the battlefields upon which they fell. And so we must ask ourselves, what if all our superstitions about ghosts are founded on a truth? What if the Kraven are part of our world as well as this? What if our own ghosts – however rare, however diminished and misunderstood – are real? After all, it makes a certain kind of sense that the two worlds should be twinned in death as well as in life. And so, as the guardians of the Glimmer Myth, we must ask, does the Myth help us to understand not only how we are in life, but also in death? Surely it must. If we all, each of us, have our twin, our Glimmer in the other world, living as we live, what happens when one part dies an unnatural death – suddenly, violently – and yet the other remains alive?"

Sylas had stopped breathing.

"The answer, I believe, is the Kraven."

21

Doubt

"Why do we so **doubt** *ourselves? Why do we seek comfort as we do from priests and soothsayers and clerics? I have begun to wonder if the answer lies somewhere between the worlds..."*

THEY RAN AND STUMBLED and fell and cursed and ran again. They ran until their chests heaved and their muscles burned, until their vision narrowed to a tunnel and all they could see in that tunnel was the Circle of Salsimaine.

They still had not been seen, shrouded as they were in the darkness of the Barrens, and now they were drawing near. But so was the approaching host. The creatures were beyond the stones, picked out by pinprick torchlight: the glint of harnesses, the glow of fangs, the bounding lope of their charge. Around fifty Ghorhund devoured the last stretch to the stones followed by at least the same number of Ghor. But in this dim moonlight Naeo doubted her eyes, because many moved with a lithe and supple sprint that barely disturbed the dust. Their motion was ranging and cat-like, light and nimble: they hardly seemed to be Ghor at all.

"It's going to be close," panted Ash, wiping dust from his eyes.

"I'll have to distract them while you... you do whatever it is you're going to do."

"Whatever that might be," grunted Naeo.

Ash slowed his run.

"What do you mean?"

"Just that I'm not sure what I'm going to do," gasped Naeo. "I don't know... how the stones work, exactly."

Ash threw his arms wide. "*What?*"

"Well it's not as though anyone *told* me!" snapped Naeo. "Filimaya said I'd know and I believed her!"

"And now you think you can't do it?"

"What do you want from me? I'll do my best, just buy me a bit of time!"

Ash looked at her darkly and then out at the approaching creatures.

"Good thing the future of our world doesn't rest on a half-baked scheme and a kid who doesn't know what she's doing!"

Naeo threw her eyes in the air and ran on.

Ash watched Naeo's slender form disappear into the darkness, then his eyes shifted to the imposing stones of Salsimaine, now just a short sprint away. He pressed his hands together in a mock prayer. "This place will be the death of me," he sighed.

He peeled off to his right and spurred his tired limbs to another dash. He skirted a deep fissure wide of the stones and near to the greatest number of the enemy. When he thought he had run far enough, he chose a wide part of the crevice and jumped down into its shadow, dropping as far as his waist. Then he went to work.

He pulled his pack from his back and thrashed through its contents until he found his water bottle, then he laid it at his feet and shaped the loose dust around it so that it stood upright. He

168

pulled the stopper out and took several paces backwards and squatted down. Already he could hear the low thunder of the approaching Ghorhund and the dry walls around him were shuddering and bleeding wisps of dust into the air. He only had a few more moments.

"I know you wouldn't approve, Paiscion," he muttered, "but in this godforsaken place, who really cares?"

With that he closed his eyes and began.

Naeo skidded to a halt by the Scrying Rock. She felt the earth shake under the charge of creatures somewhere out in the darkness. She yearned to turn and see how close they were, but she could not look, not now — she knew she had to trust Ash. She had to focus.

Her eyes ran over the vast structure of jagged stones, edged in the silver of moonlight. It was beautiful and majestic, but at that moment it just filled her with dread and helplessness. Somehow she had to make it open itself to her, bow to her will. She had to ask it to do something that she could hardly even conceive of. It had to take her to another world.

When she thought back to the Passing Bell, she realised how different that had been. Espen had been with her, guiding her, helping her to feel her way to the bell. And then the whole thing had been much easier to understand. It couldn't have been more personal. It had been intimate and familiar, like reaching into herself.

There was nothing familiar about this. She thought she would have so much more time to think this through, to work out what the stones needed from her.

She felt the thunder in the earth as the Ghor drew ever closer. Her heart pounded, her mouth was dry, and she felt panic rising in her chest. She pressed herself back into the cold, hard stone of the Scrying Rock and closed her eyes.

"Calm down, Nay-no," she said quietly — the way her father had said it. "*Calm down!*"

There was something about that silly name that took her back to him, that helped her to steady her breathing and gather her thoughts. She cast her mind back to the Passing Bell, to the web of fire that she and Sylas had mastered in the Dirgheon, to the power between them in the Garden of Havens: if she could do *those* things, surely she could do this. She just had to do something new, something different. Something... bigger.

Much bigger.

Her gaze travelled from the stones up to the silver disc of the moon, still half shrouded by a wisp of grey. She knew that the stone circle had been built to harness the power of the sun and the moon... the moon *must* have something to do with it. In fact, perhaps it was as simple as that!

With a surge of new confidence, she took a step forward and raised her eyes to the moon.

"Right then," she murmured, feeling a tremor of excitement. "Let's see about this other world."

She lifted her arms above her head, her hands gathering around the moon, and then she did the things that came so naturally to her. She closed her eyes, slowed her breathing and freed her imagination. She let it take her up on a silvery ray of moonlight, gliding into the night sky above the Scrying Rock and the wasted Barrens. She saw the perfect stone circle laid out below her, the Ghorhund bounding towards it and a single chariot bearing a slight lone figure, wielding a whip to drive the charge. All this disappeared below her into a dim grey mist before she turned her eyes upward, to the beautiful face of the moon.

It glowed ever more brightly now, blazing in her wide eyes, bathing her in silver light. And as she felt its delicate power flowing over her body, she drew her hands aside, peeling away the trails of cloud, the murk and mist, the fingers of dust and grime that reached up from the Barrens. She cast them away as lightly as the air and opened the way to the moon.

And then she opened her eyes.

The last traces of cloud curled away from the moon, leaving it bold in a pitch-black sky. It sent down a cascade of pale light upon the Circle of Salsimaine, gilding the rough-hewn stones with a new grandeur, giving them an unworldly quality. And in that moment, with the great stone circle dancing in an outlandish silvery moonlight, another world seemed close and possible.

Naeo held her breath, waiting for the stones to shift or the earth to open or some unutterable magic to bring her world crashing down.

But there was nothing. The giant rocks stood tall and still and immovable, as though mocking her childish tricks.

She felt another surge of panic.

As her hands fell slowly to her sides, she heard a sound that made her blood run cold. It was a low, feral howl that started with a single voice and was soon joined by many, each adding volume and pitch until the Barrens echoed with the haunting lament. It was the cry of the Ghor, and with it something new: a screeching wail falling away to a carnivorous growl.

Her skin prickled. Despite herself, she had to turn and look.

She recoiled in astonishment. Out in the darkness of the Barrens, taller than the standing stones, was the beautiful figure of Merimaat. The new light of the moon played across her serene features, her shimmering gown, her long flowing hair. She gazed

171

out towards the circle, implacable, wise and invincible, surveying her creation with a gentle but protective eye.

Hope surged into Naeo like electricity. A bewildered smile formed on her lips.

But as quickly as it came, it fell away. She saw how Merimaat held her head, a little to one side; she saw how her arms were outstretched with open palms, one withered and one fine but strong, holding a feather; she saw the too-perfect shape, the too-true form. And then she knew what it was. It was the statue — the one they had seen broken and defaced in the ruins of Grail — now restored to all its splendour. But this was not made of stone. Its features rippled and shifted in the breeze.

As she realised what it was, the howl of the Ghor and the Ghorhund swelled to a feverish battle cry. They charged at Merimaat and leapt into the air, gnashing at her flanks, tearing at her limbs. And at the moment of impact, as their jaws snapped closed, her giant form lost its shape, broke into swirls and trails of vapour and disappeared into the darkness.

Suddenly Naeo heard heavy footsteps to her side and she threw herself back against the Scrying Rock.

Ash came tearing towards her, his expression somewhere between fear and jubilation.

"I don't think she'd mind, do you?" he panted. "Ready to go?"

Naeo opened her mouth but nothing came.

The triumph drained from Ash's face. "*Not*... ready?"

She shook her head.

Together they turned and gazed hopelessly at the Circle of Salsimaine, and realised it would be the last thing they ever saw.

22
Faith

"The difficulty with Glimmers is one of faith*.
Once you accept that they are real, everything about
them starts to make a ghoulish kind of sense."*

SYLAS HAD TO READ it again to grasp the meaning of it.

*"...what happens when one part dies an unnatural death
– suddenly, violently – and yet the other remains alive? The
answer, I believe, is the Kraven."*

He shook his head, but he knew it had to be true. His skin crawled
at the certainty of it.

*"We are intended to live and die in union with our Glimmer,
but that bond can be broken. I believe that under some
circumstances one half of us may be destroyed – killed in
battle or some other violent act – leaving the other alive. In
such cases, the two parts of our soul are not free to act
together, and so they are torn apart: the one, to live on; the*

other, to become one of the Kraven, until such time as their Glimmer is ready to follow."

Sylas gazed into the fire. Those poor souls, cast adrift on the Barrens, waiting to be set free. No wonder they sought out the living; no wonder they yearned to take the life of another.

He shuddered and closed his eyes. It was too cruel, too awful.

Lying back, he propped his head on the box containing the quill. He needed to sleep, and that meant thinking about something else. He picked up the Samarok again, looking for lighter topics he might explore. He rested his eyes on the word 'Glimmer' and cleared his mind of all thoughts of ghosts and Kraven and death. Instead he thought of Naeo: her familiarity, her otherness. He thought of her face, so similar but so different; her character, so obvious but so surprising.

The Ravel Runes sprang into life once again, turning and shifting, opening themselves to new words, new meanings. A moment later a fresh entry had formed. He began to read:

"What we must also come to understand is how these Glimmers are connected to us and how they are separate. We must understand how their fortunes affect ours. When our Glimmer is blithe, are we sad? When we are hopeful, are they despairing? And what of knowledge? Do we find that we know the same things as our Glimmer? Or is their experience entirely their own?"

Sylas glanced over at Triste's sleeping form, remembering his questions by the river. "Aren't you intrigued?" he had asked. Why had that question been such a surprise? Why had he not known how to answer?

174

He yawned and rubbed his eyes, but he had to read a little more.

"There are many questions, but there are certainties too. The knowledge of our Glimmer brings us hope. It makes us whole. It tells us that we are as full and true as all the great pairings of Nature: as life and death, man and woman, sun and moon. It unlocks within us something clear and bold and true. It lays the worlds before us and tells us 'what you are not, the rest of you may be.'"

Sylas was still breathing in the final words, when the ancient book fell and shut and he slipped off to sleep.

"If you're going to do something," yelled Ash, "this would be a very good time!"

They ran wildly, without hope, blindly following the narrow path of moonlight that led to the Circle of Salsimaine.

The darkness on all sides was alive with movement, with black shapes running, prowling, jockeying for position. The Ghor and Ghorhund closed in behind and on both sides, their bodies thrown forward, their hungry mouths dripping drool into the dust. The other, slighter creatures prowled between them, filling the few remaining gaps. There were hundreds of them and they were everywhere.

The only way was ahead now, into the stone circle.

Still Thoth's creatures did not attack. They were waiting for something, poised for a command. Perhaps for that reason, their snarls and growls had fallen away, leaving only the horrifying sound of claws swiping the dust, collars pulling at reins, teeth snapping.

And then Naeo understood. The chariot came careering across the plain, driven by a hooded figure, pulled by a baying team of Ghorhund. Even in the silver moonlight she could see its ornamented gold and its vivid red trim, and it filled her with a new dread. It was Scarpia's chariot, and it could only be her, risen from the dead in some new and abominable form. And then the chariot bounced and leapt and the hood fell away to reveal the Magruman's dark and beautiful features — the same but somehow different — her unmatched eyes wide and her teeth bared.

It would soon be over.

Ash had seen her too and he reached out for Naeo's arm.

"It was an impossible dream, Naeo," he said, more earnest than she had ever seen him. "It's not your fault."

But Naeo did not turn or slow, she kept running.

She looked at the Circle of Salsimaine, at the rays of the moon and the parting in the skies, and she knew that this was the moment. The moment upon which everything rested. The course of the two worlds, the passage of history, her life, Sylas's life.

And in that moment, as she thought of Sylas, it was clear to her that she had been wrong all along. She had thought that this was different from the Passing Bell, from the things she had done with Sylas; that this had nothing to do with her connection to him. But she realised then that it had everything to do with him. That in ways she could not understand, all the strength she had found to do the things she had done had flowed from Sylas. From her knowledge that he was there; from a sense she had that together *nothing* was beyond them. Somehow she had forgotten him just when he was most important, when she was trying to leave her own world and enter his.

And then some new words entered her mind — unfamiliar

words — but they came to her as her own: "*What you are not, the rest of you may be.*"

She closed her eyes and forgot about the running and the Barrens and the horror of the attack. She did not see Scarpia tearing through her own troops, knocking them aside, her eyes wild with fury, or the strange, transparent being leaping from the chariot. Instead she returned to the moon, feeling its radiance, its stillness, its calm. She gathered its rays, turning them to her cause, sweeping them across the Barrens to the Circle of Salsimaine. If she had looked she would have seen those ancient rocks as they had been created to be seen: bright, beautiful and terrifying. But she did not look. She had turned her mind to something else.

To the key to another world.

To Sylas.

As Scarpia screamed her command, as the massed horde closed in and Ash reached the first of the standing stones, Naeo filled her mind with her second self.

In the same moment, something happened to the great stones of Salsimaine. The last remaining arches no longer bridged a void of darkness and dust. Instead they spanned a pool of moonlight. A shimmering, rippling surface of moonlight.

Naeo reached out for Ash and took his hand.

They ran towards the light.

And then they were gone.

Epilogue

THOTH STOOD ON THE white marble steps before the pure, rich elixir. Before the Black. Its glassy surface was clean and true, a perfect mirror, reflecting the only image that was worthy of it: the motif of his face, painted in oils on the ceiling, its gaping eyes glaring into the mystical pool below.

His thin, grey fingers grasped the silver vessel and held it out over the depths, pouring out a silvery trail of water. Then he grabbed the golden urn, tipping its contents in too: no more than a sprinkling of dust, falling lightly through the air. Both substances disappeared as soon as they touched the silky black surface, causing no splash, no disturbance. Finally he lifted the candle from the tray, stooped his aged shoulders over the pool and lowered the flame to the liquid, allowing the two to meet for the briefest moment.

Instantly the flame spanned outwards in an arc of fire, igniting the surface. A sheet of blue-white flame bubbled above the Black, sending up bright fingers of clean white light. Then, slowly, he crouched down next to the pool, easing his hooded face down so that the dancing flames lit the recesses of his hood.

"O darkness deep, O black despair, I give water, earth, fire and air!" he growled. Then he breathed out in a wheeze.

Suddenly the fire roared and the flames leapt high into the air, illuminating the painting of his face. As the fire crackled and raged, the Black began to change. Its surface churned and as it did so, bubbles rose to its surface, sending up black vapour, which mixed with the flames like black tongues of fire.

Thoth began to laugh: a dry laugh that filled the Apex Chamber and echoed out of the openings, out into the night. It was a laugh of triumph at all he had achieved and all he was about to achieve.

In response the pool began to heave and dance, slapping against the white marble sides. The Black rose in peaks that first muddled with the flames and then surpassed them, reaching up and up towards the painting of their conjurer.

"Rise, my friends!" bellowed Thoth. "Join me!"

The peaks of oily fluid ceased their rise and fall and began to broaden, lifting and bulging until they took distinct shapes. Some grew a protrusion near their top, a jutting growth that came to look a little like a snout, and from that smaller bulges rose, climbing into points, like ears. A clutch of canine heads found their form, and below them giant shoulders, chests and torsos, arms and legs, glistened among the flames. Elsewhere other figures began to take shape, those with slighter builds and human features. Then came the details: cloaks and crowns, beards and necklaces, long flowing locks and the hard edges of armour. All were made of the thick, fluid darkness, drawn up from the fiery pool of Black.

Then these monstrous figures came to life. Black lids blinked over black eyes, black tongues ran over black lips, black fingers smoothed the curls of black hair. These were no statues or effigies: this was a congregation of Ghor and human, man and woman, priest and warrior.

With one motion, the figures bowed deeply, leaving trails of dripping blackness.

Thoth raised his arms in greeting. "Welcome, faithful friends, Guardians of the Four Lands," he boomed. "You will return to your duties before long, but you will find this time well spent. I bring you here through the Black to talk — to talk of high things, to talk the talk of gods!"

The freakish gathering shifted at these words, some leaning forward, some making another slight bow. All were transfixed.

"Our forefathers gave to us a broken world of Upper and Lower Kingdoms, of rival tribes and warring nations. They gave us lands bathed in blood. But this empire, my empire, has brought great change. Now, all these blessed lands are united under a single crown. My crown. The Sekhemti."

He gestured to the top of the marble steps where a beautiful crown rested on a jewelled table. Its tall white centrepiece was surrounded by a dramatic, deep red outer ring, which swept high at the rear, making it both grand and imposing. He waited for their black eyes to return to him.

"But we all know that there is a division that runs deeper than the rest," he continued, "a division that defies the dominion of the Sekhemti. It is a cleft in our world, a rift between lands of immeasurable size and power, lands that span from the rising to the setting sun. We know them simply as this, and the Other."

The gathering became agitated, their expressions betraying their excitement. One of the Ghor licked its black fangs with a long, black tongue as if scenting prey.

"For centuries we have allowed this second land, this 'Other', to abide. We have allowed it to pen its own languages, indulge in its own cultures, devise its own rule and allegiance, its own kings and gods." He turned with a flourish of his cloak. "This we have done in the name of peace."

The listeners nodded and growled their agreement.

"But I have been watching. I have surveyed with a caring but careful eye, because I know my fellow humankind. I know that trust is rarely rewarded." He opened his palms in resignation. "And so it has come to pass. The day has come when our enemy the Merisi and their petty followers have risen against us! When they and the last rabble of the Suhl seek to steal our peace and rob us of our blessings! When they seek to gain dominion over a united world!"

The mightiest and blackest of the Ghor rose up with a snarl and very nearly surged out of the pool that sustained it. The rest screamed their outrage, shaking their fists with a spray of black slime.

"Yes, my friends! Heresy!" bellowed Thoth with the terrifying voice of many. "Treason! For are they not created in *our* image? Do they not live by OUR borrowed light? Are they not our lesser half, our *discarded* half?" His hands were trembling now as he punched the air and cast his eyes upwards, to his own image. "They must bow to *us*! Ours shall be the Upper Kingdom, and theirs, the Lower!"

The black figures threw their arms in the air in unison, shouting out a hacking chant, revering their master, feeding on his rage.

"Friends, we have prepared well! You know what you must do. Return to your lands! This is our moment to take from the Other what they would take from us!"

Then he lowered his hooded head and swept his arms wide.

"Begin the harvest!" he growled.

PART TWO

The Yin and
the Yang

23
What Magic?

"What magic is this that forges wonders from the humble earth and raises cathedrals in the sky?"

SCARPIA EASED HERSELF DOWN from the broken chariot, and as she did so scores of canine and feline heads bowed into the dust. She snarled and fell on to all fours, spitting at the shattered axle. One of the wheels lay on its side next to the giant stone arch. The other was still attached, spinning at an angle. She whipped around and caught it between her teeth, growling as the timber shattered in her mouth. She prowled on, brushing against the stone as she entered the arch, sniffing the dust where they had disappeared, scratching the surface with her claws. Finally she raised her head, ears back and rapier teeth bared, and screamed her fury.

She leapt into the air, claws slashing the sides of the stone until she gained purchase, then bounded up. She mounted the top of the arch, rearing high and gazing down at the Circle of Salsimaine, searching for any sign of her quarry. There was nothing but dust and stone. The hairs bristled at the back of her neck and she began to lope along the horizontal stones, padding from one to the next, peering down at every shadow and edifice. When she was satisfied that there was nothing to be done, she accelerated to a sprint, bounding over the final stones to bring her full circle, back to her waiting commanders.

She rose on to her hind legs and gazed down at them imperiously.

"Where is the Ray Reaper?"

There was a moment's pause while eyes searched and feet shuffled, then the ranks of Ghorhund parted, bowing their heads once again as something passed between them. It was not so much a figure as a presence, an apparition. It could not be called a man, but it moved as one, its indistinct outline appearing to walk with legs that were not there, swinging arms that could barely be seen. Then the moonlight shifted slightly, catching the edges of rotten rags hanging loose from twisted limbs and a narrow, misshapen jaw. The only part of the creature that did not appear covered by these decaying bandages were gaping black holes for eyes and a mouth.

It did not rush but took its time, clearly unaccustomed to command. As it reached the circle, it paused to look at the chariot and then up at Scarpia's graceful figure, silhouetted by the moon.

Scarpia seemed to shrink a little in its presence. "Hathor, reaper of rays," she said respectfully, "now is our moment of need."

The shapeless form was still for a moment, then it inclined its head.

"Speak your will," it said in a voice of dust and flames.

She gestured to the stone circle. "Are you able to open the way between the worlds?"

The creature threw back its half-seen head and cackled. "Am I *able*? Able to do the work of a child?"

Scarpia opened her mouth to reply, but the creature had already turned to the stones. It lowered its rag-ridden head.

186

The assembled beasts were still and expectant. Scarpia turned a little to look between the stones.

Then the Ray Reaper made a sound: a gravelly murmur that became a rasping hum. It could hardly be called a voice — it was made of the sounds of sand against rock, wind over dry grass, the crackle of flames — but somehow these sounds formed a note, and the note became a chant. It was without words or melody, but there were vowels and there was rhythm, and as the moments passed it gained pace and volume and became an incantation: a spell as old as the great circle itself.

Something began to change. The shadows cast by the stones were moving, creeping over the dust, sliding out across the plain. They did not drift in the same direction, but separately, each shadow seeming to follow its own path as though the moon had split into many moving sources of light. And yet there the moon was, above, still shining bold and bright. Some of the Ghorhund whimpered and took a step back, but their handlers snapped their reins and barked or snarled for silence. All eyes were on the shadows, watching in wonder as they made the ground swim in shifting shades.

Scarpia purred with delight and lifted her eyes to the heavens. She knew that it was not the shadows that were changing, nor the great circle of stones: it was the light of the moon. Its rays no longer obeyed the laws of Nature. They were a writhing mass, moving around and between one another, turning and bending until they began to gather into a single pillar of light: a deluge of moonbeams.

There, in the centre of the Circle of Salsimaine, they merged into a pool of light: a pool that soon bubbled and spilled, splaying outwards towards the stones and as it reached them, splashed up like waves against some unseen barrier, filling the arches with a dazzling silver.

The watching horde at first shrank away, wincing in the fierce light. But soon, as they saw the Circle of Salsimaine bathed in a magical glow even bolder and brighter than was conjured by the human child, they turned and edged forward, sniffing and growling, their pale eyes alive in the fire. Then they raised their hideous heads and howled a triumphant howl.

§

Naeo and Ash stood on trembling legs, blinking into the searing light. They still held hands — clinging so tight that it hurt. That was the only way they knew the other was still there in the sudden, dazzling radiance of day. With their other hands, they steadied themselves on the cold stone of the arch.

As their eyes adjusted they looked around them. They were still beneath the arch of stone, but it was lit by warming rays. The sky above was crystal clear and blue, with only a few scattered white clouds, some of which looked oddly long and straight, like the sweep of a celestial pen across the heavens. All about them were the great stones of Salsimaine, but they looked different. They were still in disarray but they were not shattered or broken, rather they seemed worn, tumbledown, neglected. Their edges and corners were smoothed off or coated in lichen and some had sunk into luscious green grass, as though easing themselves to sleep. Others had disappeared altogether, consumed by the elements or swallowed up by the pasture.

They blinked and looked down at their feet. *Pasture?*

Ash turned to Naeo and took her by the shoulders, his eyes wide with excitement. "I think you did it!"

Naeo's face was slack and pale. "I think so too," she murmured.

And then she smiled. It was the first time he had seen her smile: her face softened and for a moment she looked as young as she actually was.

188

Suddenly there was a movement to one side and instinctively they took a step backwards, retreating between the stones. Then they saw a figure — a human figure — walking directly towards them.

"Hey! You two!" said the man in a nasal accent. "You're not supposed to be in here! Get back outside the cordon!"

Before them was a tubby, stooped man who stared at them with an expression of astonishment and annoyance. He was wearing a peculiarly neat black outfit, with a matching jacket and trousers, a pristine white shirt with a stiff collar and, strangest of all, a brightly coloured strip of fabric hanging round his neck and knotted at his throat.

Something crackled and barked, and the man coolly reached behind him, unclipped a black box from his belt and brought it up to his mouth, pressing a button on its side.

"Yes, I'd grasped that, Tasker, I'm with them now," he said into the box. "They look... well... *lost*. I'll bring them out." He replaced the box on his belt and beckoned to them, his eyes lingering on their rough, crudely woven clothes. "Come on, I'll show you the way."

With that he marched past them and led them back through the arch. As they turned and followed, they saw to their relief no expanse of dust, no baying multitude, no Scarpia. Instead there was another stretch of grass and then a crowd of people gathered on what looked to be a walkway skirting the outside of the stones.

The people were quite the oddest that Ash and Naeo had ever seen. They wore a startling array of colours, of all kinds of fabrics, shapes and styles. Some wore what looked like blue trousers, which looked far too tight to be comfortable, while others sported dazzling white footwear marked with garish designs. Many held up more little black boxes, but not to their ear as the young man had done, and instead to their eye or to their face. It was all quite unsettling. Naeo and Ash stayed close to one another as they followed the official.

"You'll have to keep to the path, like everyone else," said the official, raising his voice so that the onlookers could hear. They parted to make room.

As Naeo stepped between the people, many regarded her with apparent distaste. She had a cursory look at herself and saw why: next to the sharp colours and bright whites of the strangers' garb, their own drab, ill-fitting clothes looked very strange indeed. To make matters worse, they were also splattered with mud and caked in the dust of the Barrens.

As soon as the official moved away, Ash pulled Naeo to one side. "We should get away from here before they ask questions," he murmured in her ear. He nodded out past the stones. "North. They said we should go North, along the river."

They had to push through a large gathering of children who seemed oblivious to them, largely because each seemed to be listening to some kind of contraption clamped over their head, covering both ears. As they passed they could just make out tiny little voices muttering and squeaking into the children's heads: it was all too bizarre and they pushed through as quickly as they could. As they emerged, they had to step past a middle-aged woman who seemed to be their teacher. She wore the oddest hat, which seemed to have flowers growing from its brim, but she looked at Ash and Naeo as though *they* were the freakish ones and drew one of the children away, as though shielding him from barbarians. Ash instinctively smiled and nodded, but the flower-topped woman regarded him through narrow, distrustful eyes and hurried the child away.

They rushed on, drawing clear of the last of the crowd and setting out along the pathway that curved off around the great stone circle. But just a few paces later, having checked that no one was watching, they stepped off it, heading out across the grassland. Soon they were jogging down the hill towards open fields.

"Oi, you!" It was a male voice, somewhere behind them. "Stop!"

Ash grabbed Naeo by the arm. "Run!"

They sprinted off as fast as they could, bounding over the soft pasture towards a row of chest-high posts that ran across their path.

"Hey!" came the voice again, more urgent now. "You can't go that way!"

In the same moment, they both pulled up, slapping their feet down in the turf. They had almost run headlong into what looked like a giant spider's web. There were long, silvery strands between the wooden posts and whatever creature had made it had left nothing to chance: the lines were woven together with incredible precision, regular and equally spaced, with no gap large enough for a person to pass. Ash reached out and touched it tentatively, snapping his fingers away as soon as they came into contact.

"It feels... cold," he said, bewildered. Then he reached out again and ran his fingers along one of the pale filaments. "Like metal."

They both cast a dismayed glance along the web. It stretched all the way around the stone circle. At its top, two horizontal strands threw out jagged barbs to catch anyone who tried to scale the boundary.

"What did I tell you?" came the voice again.

Ash took a couple of paces back from the fence and threw his arms out towards it, his brow furrowed with concentration. His hands began to shake, but nothing happened.

Naeo turned at him. "What are you doing?" she hissed. "We've only just got here and you're already breaking your promise!"

Ash showed no sign of giving up. "Just a little Urgolvane! But it's strange. It seems... *harder* here."

In front of him the mesh bowed a little and started to glow a feint red, as though heated to an extreme temperature.

"You *can't*, Ash!" said Naeo, moving in front of the fence and pulling his arms down. "It's not safe! Remember what Filimaya said — even Essenfayle isn't—"

They heard someone striding up behind them and the distinctive sound of jangling keys. "Oi! Cloth-ears! What do you think you're up to?"

They turned and saw their pursuer standing with his hands on his hips. He was wearing the same uniform as the other official, but his was immaculate and it was finished with shiny black shoes. He was a young man of small build, standing little taller than Naeo, but he carried himself with confidence, shoulders back, feet planted well apart. His features were equally bold, with a strong jaw, a handsome, animated face and bizarrely styled dark hair that rose in carefully arranged, architectural tufts.

He seemed to size them up in a moment and his attention had already moved on to the fence, which was still bulging a little in the middle and retained the barest traces of a glow.

His brow furrowed, his gaze returning to the intruders and passing quickly over their clothes, their dirty faces, their bags. "Let me see your tickets."

Naeo adjusted the crossed sticks in her hair. "Tickets?" she said, as if it were a strange question.

The young official cocked his head on one side. "You don't have tickets, do you?"

"We got a bit lost," said Ash, with a carefree laugh. "We didn't mean to come here at all. We just stumbled into it, really."

The official raised an eyebrow. "You were just wandering around Salisbury Plain and you stumbled into Stonehenge?"

Ash shifted his gaze past the stone circle and saw an endless rolling horizon of open grassland, as vast and open as the Barrens. He should have given that a little more thought.

"Yes, that's right," he said, turning back to the young man's forensic stare.

For a moment the two just held each other's gaze, weighing each other up, each refusing to look away first.

Then, without dropping his eyes, the official reached to his belt and unclipped the little black box.

"Wait a minute," said Ash, panicking, "we really haven't broken any..."

He stopped. The young man did not raise the black oblong to his mouth, instead he swapped it between hands and clipped it on to the other side of his belt. He rummaged in a hidden pouch and brought out something small and green, which he unfolded and slipped over his fingers, pulling it up over his wrist.

Ash and Naeo knew it in an instant.

The young man's face broke into a smile, revealing for the first time a bright golden tooth. He stretched out his hand in greeting — a hand clothed in a beautifully embroidered green glove.

"You're... *Merisi*?" breathed Naeo.

The stranger grinned and nodded. "The name's Jem Tasker," he said, shaking her hand, "but everyone just calls me Tasker."

§

After all the silence, the long dark quiet, it was almost more than the man could bear. It was a deafening cacophony: a rage of noise. There was the scraping of claws against rock, the rasp of snarls and barks, the *chink, chink, chink* of chainmail. It seemed an endless procession, marauding down the broad passageway, some of them at an urgent march, some running and jostling, pounding the flagstones, making them shake and thunder. The echoes only made it worse, capturing the sound and throwing it back again and again and again.

He curled into a ball and waited for it to be over.

And eventually, it was. The rampage of an army became the lope of a trailing few, and finally there were just the echoes whispering down the empty passageway. He lay there for some time, he could not tell how long — time had long since lost its meaning. He knew only the unending dark and the silence. And what he had to do.

He pressed his delirious mind to action, working to remember his limbs, numb and remote, as though no longer part of his body. He pushed back the tide of weariness, and he moved. He pushed an arm that was not his out of his hiding place and paused. He breathed in shallow gasps, face into the stone, collecting himself for the next push. He closed his eyes and prayed to Merimaat for hope, to Isia for courage, and then he struck out with the barest remembrance of shoulders, the dream of legs and toes.

He felt the flagstones slide beneath him, the cold grit biting into his face, and he was glad of the pain. It meant he was on the move. It meant he was alive.

24
Wonders Scientific

"In the end, there is little difference between the wonders of magic and wonders scientific.*"*

SUDDENLY, AFTER EVERYTHING, NAEO's heart failed. She gazed into the tunnel entrance and it was like peering over a precipice. Her head swam and she struggled for her breath.

"I can't," she said, flatly.

Tasker regarded her coolly. "This is the way out."

"I won't!" she said, closing her hands into fists.

Ash raised his hand to stop Tasker from saying more. "Just give her a moment," he said quietly.

Tasker looked her up and down irritably. "What's wrong with her? I thought you guys had just…" He nodded back at the stone circle. "I mean, what's a tunnel after *that*?"

Ash gave him a steady look. "She just needs *a moment*."

Their guide shrugged, fingering the strip of fabric hanging from his neck. "OK, sure, we wait," he said, glancing about him. "But we can't be long."

Naeo hardly heard this exchange. Her eyes were fixed on the long slope ahead, dropping away into the tunnel and then disappearing below the earth. She sensed the weight of soil and turf and rock above, felt the lowness of the ceiling, the walls pressing in. She saw the throng of people emerging from the gloom, weaving and jostling, leaving no space, no escape.

It had caught her by surprise — a sudden and crippling terror of a simple tunnel. She could not even think why it was happening.

Ash stepped in front of her and lowered his face. "It's not the Dirgheon," he said, gently, seeing her more clearly than she saw herself. "Look, there are lights. *Scientific* lights — there'll be no dark corners, no darkness at all."

He stepped out of the way and Naeo looked doubtfully towards the opening. Sure enough there were lights, not only on the walls but — somehow — built into the ceiling, and these were not like any torches or lamps she had seen before. These did not flicker or dance or burn with an orange flame: they were just *there*. They were perfect strips of luminescence — white light, like the light of day. And the more she peered into the tunnel, she saw that although it was dimmer than the bright sunlight, it was filled with this miraculous light.

Ash was right about the Dirgheon. Since her escape, she had not been anywhere that reminded her of the soulless, deathly cells and passages that had been her home for those long years. Nowhere with its cold, hard edges; its brooding walls and ceilings that left no room for life.

Before she had time to think about it, she took hold of Ash's sleeve and started walking, pulling him along beside her.

"Let's go," she said.

Tasker gazed after them, shaking his head. "Right you are, Princess."

After a moment he pulled the green glove off his hand, pushed it into his pocket and then slipped past them to lead the way down the slope.

Naeo's eyes never left the magical strips of light. She stared at them until her eyes hurt, until all she saw was their radiance. This was *so* different from the Dirgheon. This was magical. This was science.

More than once she collided with someone passing by and more than once someone snapped at her, telling her to watch where she was going, but still she kept her eyes on the lights. Ash stayed close, leading her through, weaving deftly towards the well-lit exit at the other end.

It seemed an age before they emerged from the tunnel and climbed another ramp, feeling the fresh outdoor air once again. Naeo's shoulders started to relax and her breathing returned to normal. She let go of Ash's sleeve, leaving it creased and mangled, and turned to thank him, but he was already looking ahead at Tasker, who was still on the move, darting to the left, through some double doors.

They followed him into a small building, which seemed to be some kind of entrance hall. The brightly lit space hummed with activity but they had little time to take it in as Tasker strutted on, walking confidently past the ticket office, shoulders swinging and arms ranging from his sides as though he owned the place. His eyes were everywhere, choosing the path ahead, trying to keep them as far from visitors and staff as possible.

"I don't know where you find the cheek," he grumbled loudly enough to be heard. "The rest of these visitors have to pay. Don't they tell you that on those fruit-loop websites?"

They didn't reply — they knew it was all for show.

When they reached the entrance Tasker slowed a little and an ugly official frowned as they approached.

"Entrance only!" she whined in the tone of one who used those words many thousands of times a day. "That way for the exit!"

"They're with me, Trace," said Tasker. He leaned towards her and whispered conspiratorially in her ear. "Wannabe druids." He threw his eyes in the air.

The pug-faced woman turned her pinprick eyes to Ash and Naeo. "I swear they get younger every year," she said in a monotone, already losing interest.

Naeo heard all this, but her attention was elsewhere. She was gazing at the queues of people waiting patiently to buy tickets, taking in their odd appearance and their chatter in the languages of another world. But it was what they were doing that most caught her eye. Some held those little black oblongs in front of them — smaller than Tasker's — and they stared at a rectangular glow at its centre: a muddle of colours, shapes and scripts. To her amazement, they occasionally touched or swiped the radiance with a finger and it would shift and change: a new set of shapes and texts taking its place. What was even more peculiar was that some would then raise the oblong to their ear then suddenly burst into conversation, as though talking to the strange black box. It was baffling.

Ash shared a bemused grin with her, but then straightened his face. "Don't *stare*," he hissed.

Tasker reached out for a silver handle, which seemed to be suspended in mid-air, but as he pulled on it they saw that it was fixed to a door made of a thick sheet of perfectly clear glass. It swung lightly on its hinges, letting in a gentle breeze.

"After you, Princess," he said, sweeping an arm in front of him.

Naeo glanced at him irritably — she wasn't keen on her new nickname and was a little unsure how she had earned it.

She stepped outside but then drew up sharply and gasped.

There, arranged in neat rows across an enormous slab of dark rock was an army of bizarre creatures, each standing about her height, each sporting a glistening colourful livery. Her first thought was to run back inside, but Tasker slipped past her, calm and unfazed.

"Come on," he said.

She blinked and looked more closely. This was no ambush. The creatures were still: not the stillness of a predator lying in wait but complete stillness — the stillness of something that was not alive at all. And something started to come back to her — the memory of another strange magic from the Other that she had once read about in a schoolbook.

"Cars!" she murmured, her breath quickening with excitement.

They were far stranger than she had imagined, not least because they were things of contradictions: massive and still, like a boulder worn smooth over countless years, and yet, somehow swift-seeming, with purposeful lines suggestive of speed. They looked designed, with all the marks of man-made symmetry and precision, but they also seemed to have been born — seeing with two silvery eyes, huddling over four circular feet, poised for a sprint.

"You won't get far here without a car," said Tasker, strolling towards the nearest row of vehicles. He pulled something out of his pocket and a large blue car honked and flashed its orange lights.

Ash jumped out of his skin and eyed the car as though it had just spoken to him. He turned to Naeo. "And you think *my* magic is weird…"

Suddenly a black car hurtled towards them from the near distance, roaring down a long smooth surface beyond the stationary cars. It moved at implausible speeds but with poise and grace — there was no judder nor bump, no trail of fire or smoke, no sign of effort at all. It seemed almost to be gliding above the earth and yet its four wheels were firm and solid on the surface. It was upon them in a moment and then it was gone, whistling off across the plain.

Tasker did not flinch. He turned and looked at them both for a moment, witnessing their shocked faces and wide eyes.

"Guys, it's just a road," he said, glancing over his shoulder. "Listen, you already *look* weird — you're going to have to stop *acting* it. Things are going to be strange — just go with it. If you carry on like this, someone's going to have you locked up."

Ash bristled. "Have you *been* where we come from?"

"What's that got to do with anything?"

"Just that if you had, you wouldn't think—"

He was cut off by a new sound, a sound so jarring and out of place that it instantly set their nerves on edge. It came from somewhere behind them — in the distance — from the stone circle.

Even as they turned Naeo and Ash knew what it was. The growl became a wail and the wail became a howl. It was at once canine, like the lament of a mountain wolf, and yet somehow controlled and conscious, like the cry of a human being. It echoed between the rocks and spread over the green plain, announcing something animal and wild.

Something inconceivable.

Something from another world.

25

Unthinkable

"The Merisi are the keepers of a gate that must remain closed.
The thought of free passage between the worlds is horrifying.
Invasion is simply unthinkable*."*

A SHARP CRY GAVE way to a chorus of terrified screams and suddenly they saw a crowd surging from the stone circle towards the tunnel, obscuring their view of the scene. Some voices rose above them all, shouting commands, appealing for calm, but they had no effect: the crowd pressed on, driven by fear and panic. The screams and shouts came nearer and all at once the glass doors flew open and people began pouring out, scrambling towards the cars. Some ushered children in front of them; some fumbled with bunches of keys or with the strange black devices, raising them to their ear, shouting. The woman with the flowery hat burst through the doors amid a shower of petals. She was carrying a red-faced child, who was the only person among the crowd who did not look terrified. He looked delighted.

Tasker took them both by the arm and shoved them in front of him.

"We're going! Right now!"

In a couple of strides they were by the blue car, and Tasker reached out and pulled a handle in its rear flank. A door flew open to reveal a long cushioned seat and before they knew it they had been bundled inside and the door slammed shut with a muffled clunk. Immediately the screams and shrieks and shouts were silenced. They could still see the terrified faces running past the windows, mouths chattering, parents calling out for their children, but somehow the car rebuffed these sounds, sealing Ash and Naeo in an eerie quiet.

The door in front of them flew open, letting in a brief burst of noise, and Tasker leapt into the front seat, heaving the door closed behind him. He pushed a key into a small slot and then turned it.

The car roared.

Ash and Naeo braced themselves against anything they could lay their hands on. Suddenly they wanted to escape the growling cage of metal, but before they could do anything Tasker grasped a lever and rammed it forward. All at once the vehicle lurched ahead, mounting a bank between the rows of cars and the road. They were all thrown back in their seats as it dropped down on to the long, smooth road of rock. With nothing in its path, the beast snarled and took off at the pace of a trot, and then a canter, and then it tore away at a racing gallop. Naeo grimaced as the seat pressed against the wounds in her back, but she was too scared to give it much thought.

She turned to the window and saw the unthinkable.

The sun's rays plunged from the sky in a muddle and weave, spiralling erratically between the rocks. But more worrying still: the stone circle had been transformed. The void of the standing arches now rippled with golden sunlight, shimmering and shifting like the surface of water. The blaze brought forth things of darkness and shadow, crouching and crawling from the ether. Their half-blood shape was unmistakable: powerful, sloping necks, high canine ears, the muzzles of wolves and the lithe, powerful stance of a predator.

Naeo shook her head. "This can't be happening!"

The creatures looked smaller than she knew them, less than the height of a man, but they had lost none of their menace, none of their terrifying, chilling intent.

And now they were here, in the Other.

How could this be? How could they be showing themselves like this? In broad daylight? This went against all the rules, all the teachings. Even for Scarpia — even for Thoth himself — this was unimaginable. And yet there they were, breaching the way between the worlds.

Around the Ghor, the muscular forms of the Ghorhund clawed and fought for position. Among them slunk the smaller, slighter beasts, prowling like cats between the growing forest of black limbs and drooling jaws. Already they were spilling outside the circle, some straying on to the open plain, others lunging towards the fleeing visitors before being called sharply back to heel. They were wild but disciplined, as though waiting for something.

"Stay low," said Tasker. "We have to drive past the stones to get away."

But as they drew near the circle one of the Ghor seemed to catch a scent, falling on to all fours and prowling forward, ears alert, muzzle in the air, before finally looking straight up at the blue car as it roared past.

"GET DOWN!" yelled Ash, throwing himself down on the seat.

But it was too late. The beast lifted its half-human head and let out a bloodthirsty howl that turned the heads of all the assembled creatures. Already it was in motion, hurling itself forward and snapping at the air as a pack of Ghorhund fell in behind it. They gathered speed, ripping at the pasture and sending clods of earth high into the air, baying like hunting hounds.

"Faster!" shouted Naeo, her eyes wide and desperate. "They're going to catch us!"

Tasker slammed his foot down and rammed the large lever forward. "I'm trying!" he cried, desperately eyeing the mirrors.

For a moment the car lost pace but then it growled, the wheels screeched and it lurched forward at an even greater pace. But still the creatures were gaining on them, pounding the earth and yelping with excitement. Some tourists ran in panic across their path and for a second it looked as though they would be trampled, but the Ghor bounded into the air, clearing the tallest of them by a hair's breadth. The pack of Ghorhund followed, throwing themselves skywards and arching over the terrified clutch of tourists, knocking two of them over as they passed.

Now they were nearer than ever. Naeo could see their yellow eyes, their glistening fangs, their snarling snouts wet with drool. The Ghor leader hurled itself over the grassy bank and landed on the road just a few strides behind the car. It lost its footing, its claws skating over the smooth surface, but then it dug in, scouring the grey rock.

The car was still accelerating – the moan of its engine building to a whine – and for a moment Naeo thought they would make it. But then the beast seemed to summon new energy and it launched itself, claws and jaws outstretched, towards the car. It hung in the air, its hideous, half-human features straining, its tongue lolling from its mouth.

And then it struck.

As the rear window shattered, the entire car shook with the force of the blow and then it fishtailed, swinging left and right, wheels screeching.

Tasker had to fight to keep control, and Ash and Naeo were thrown from their seats, smashing up against the side windows. Naeo cried out as the wounds across her back screamed. Through shards of flying glass, they saw the creature's wide yellow eyes and its black hands clawing at the metal frame, twisting it out of shape as it struggled to keep hold. As the car veered wildly from left to right, one of the beast's limbs was wrenched free and it swung wide, only to slam its claws into the side of the car. It gave a vicious snarl and its furred face grimaced with pain, but somehow it held on. With herculean strength it began crawling up the car's flank, tearing at the metal as though it were paper-thin. Naeo watched in horror as it trailed blood and drool up the side window, drawing back its black lips and baring its fangs as it prepared to smash its way in. Ash was dragging Naeo away from the window, trying to put himself between her and the beast, when she heard Tasker cry out.

"Hold on to something!" he screamed. "Anything!"

Instinctively her eyes shot to the road ahead. There, on the other side of the road, hurtling in their direction at an incredible speed, was a giant vehicle, wheels thundering, engine screaming. It would be passing them any second. Naeo knew instinctively what Tasker was going to do and she tightened her grip on the headrest in front of her, indicating to Ash to do the same.

In the instant that the colossal vehicle whisked past, Tasker jerked the steering wheel. The car swerved dangerously, throwing driver, passengers and beast to one side.

There was an almighty crash as they sheered down the side of the larger vehicle, jostling with its gigantic wheels, ripping at its bodywork. For a moment all was noise and destruction — squeal and boom and judder — and Naeo thought it was over, that this was the last she would know. She pressed her eyes closed, hugged the headrest and waited for the inevitable.

And then there was quiet.

Suddenly the only noise was the buffeting of wind and the hum of the car.

She opened one eye. Then two.

She blinked at the daylight, took in the blur of passing cars, and the breeze coming in through the gaping hole in the side of the car. Then she turned to look where Ash was staring, open-mouthed, at the mayhem out of the back window: the giant vehicle veering down the road, the black body of the Ghor tumbling over and over down its centre, crashing into the other chasing Ghorhund, sending them flailing and tumbling, letting out yelps of pain. Soon all were littered across the road like the fallen on a battlefield.

Naeo turned to Ash, a grin slowly forming on her lips.

He wiped a trail of blood from his brow. "I love these car things," he said, grinning and patting the seat.

"WHAT THE HELL JUST HAPPENED?" bellowed Tasker, swivelling round in his seat and steering the mauled vehicle with one hand. His eyes were wild, his face beaded with sweat and his sculpted hair skewed to one side.

"I have no idea," said Ash in all honesty. "We knew they were chasing us, but we didn't think they'd come through the circle. I don't think they've ever done that before."

"You're not kidding they haven't!" cried Tasker, turning back to the road to take a corner and inadvertently knocking a lever that sent two arms sweeping across the front window. He cursed and wrestled with his controls, setting off a loud honk and various lights. He turned to glare at them. "JUST TELL ME WHAT'S GOING ON!"

Naeo blinked at him calmly. "That's what we were saying," she said. "We're not sure. I mean, we know why *we're* here, but

206

we have no idea what they're doing here. They weren't just chasing us. They were with Scarpia and she seemed to be—"

Tasker raised a hand for silence. "Did you say *Scarpia*?"

"That's right. Thoth's Magruman. You know what a Magruman is?"

Tasker laughed mirthlessly. He rummaged in his pocket and brought out his small black oblong, then swept a finger over it so that it flared into life. He tapped his thumb over the glow a few times, then raised it to his ear.

Ash and Naeo watched in fascination.

"Hi, it's me," blurted Tasker suddenly, apparently to someone in the oblong. "No, listen!" He took the oblong away from his ear and stared at it as a tiny voice twittered from one end, then brought it back to his mouth and shouted: "PLAGUE!"

The twittering fell silent, then spat out one word.

"Yes, PLAGUE!" repeated Tasker.

More twittering.

Tasker gritted his teeth. "Just tell everyone. I'll explain when I get there."

26
The Time Machine

"Science is a measured magic, but a magic nonetheless.
It unravels the secrets of space and time *and natural law,*
and weaves them into endless possibility. It is the stuff
of magic forged by invention and machine.*"*

TASKER SHOVED THE OBLONG back in his pocket and gripped the wheel. Then he began riffling anxiously through his hair. "This is bad. Very, very bad," he muttered.

"Where are you taking us?" asked Naeo, leaning forward. "We need to follow the river — to town."

Tasker took a deep breath. "To start with, I'm putting as much distance between us and them as possible. Once I know it's safe, I'll circle back and take you to town. I daren't go direct — if those things set off at a pace, they could cut us off."

He looked up at a little mirror attached to the ceiling of the car and gazed at his passengers. There was a moment of silence. "So who *are* you people? I mean, apart from bad luck?"

Ash raised his eyebrows. "I'm actually known for having quite excellent luck," he said petulantly. "This is a very bad day for me."

"Who ARE you?"

Ash grinned. "I'm Ash. This is Naeo."

"And you're Suhl, right?"

"That's right."

"Well, that's something." Tasker went quiet for a moment, glancing in the mirror. "Do you know anything about a boy who made the passing about a week ago? A boy called Tate — Sylas Tate?"

Naeo grasped Ash's arm.

"What do *you* know about Sylas Tate?" she asked suspiciously.

Tasker's eyes narrowed. "Just that a lot of people are worried about him."

"What people?" asked Naeo.

"Plenty of people. But I think the name you're fishing for is Mr Zhi."

Naeo rocked back in her seat and smiled at Ash.

"Sorry to be so cautious," she said, "it's just—"

"We live in dangerous times," finished Tasker. "Yes, so it seems. So... Sylas?"

"He's fine," said Naeo. "But he... well, we *all* still have questions about who he is. And why he came. We thought Mr Zhi might be able to help us."

Tasker arched an eyebrow. "Well, from what I hear, he hoped Sylas would find the answers for himself." He looked for a reaction in the mirror, but Naeo was giving nothing away. "But you'll find out soon enough. You're in luck — Mr Zhi is still in town."

"In Gabblety Row?" asked Ash, keenly.

"That's the place."

Ash sat back and patted his knees. "You see?" he exclaimed. "Good luck! I just can't help myself!"

Tasker and Naeo both mumbled something under their breath as the car drove on towards their destination.

§

Scarpia squinted towards the horizon, raising a panther's claw to shield her eyes from the dying sun. Her mongrel gaze missed nothing of the scene: where her feline eye failed, her human eye saw all. She saw ten small groups of black figures, each at a sprint, spanning out across the wilderness, following the contours and ditches, streams and hedgerows, so that they seemed no more than evening shadows. In the distance she saw the great stone circle lit by a gathering swarm of scientific lights, their frantic blinks and darting beams betraying controlled panic. And all around the stones were her very own Ghorhund, unleashed from the chariot to bring forth their mayhem: howling at the lights, tearing the vehicles like tin cans, ripping at fences. One stood high on the stones, silhouetted against the setting sun, baying at the strange machine that thrummed and stuttered as it circled in the sky.

She purred deep down in her throat. Everything was going precisely to plan. Some of the Ghorhund would be taken or killed — it was to be expected — but by then it would be too late.

She glanced up at the cobalt-blue sky, now adorned with pink-trimmed trails of cloud. Soon it would be night. And what a night it would be.

Her night.

She dropped her eyes to the peaceful river at her side. "Come, Lord Hathor," she purred. "Let's see if our friends are at home."

She bounded off down the bank, leaping over bushes, ducking beneath branches, weaving between trees until, a moment later, she disappeared completely.

There was a brief, uneasy stillness, and then something shifted in the undergrowth, whispering like a breeze over dead leaves.

Suddenly a bush rustled, a branch darted to one side, and then, with all the force of a desert wind, the Ray Reaper moved off, cleaving down the bank, snapping trees in half like twigs and shattering all that lay in its path.

§

As Naeo stared out of her crystal window at another world, she felt a new electricity coursing through her veins.

None of it seemed real: not the rich verdant countryside; nor the neat hedgerows dividing fields that heaved with crops, planted in straight-edged rows by some impossibly careful hand; nor the regimental lines of giant metal frames, rising high into the sky and spanned by thick black ropes – defence perhaps against some unimaginable scientific foe.

Cars whisked past them at just an arm's reach away, travelling so fast that if she had not seen them approach and disappear, she would have doubted they had been there at all. It was their speed that made all this truly magical, truly of another world. It was more than just a thrill: it challenged everything they knew. The distance they had already travelled broke every law of Nature. This car was not just a way of getting where they were going: it was a machine that gobbled time.

As Naeo watched it all fly by, she realised that she had never felt so alive.

"Not far now," said Tasker, breaking her daydream. "The good news is we're coming from a direction they'd never expect. The bad news is we don't know what to expect either."

They dipped briefly into a tunnel and then climbed a long ramp that led back towards the light. At the top they joined an enormous road of terrifying speeds with two vehicles travelling in each direction. Despite their death-defying pace, the cars passed so close that Naeo could see the occupants as they whizzed on their way. It was some kind of orderly madness. Naeo and Ash sank in their seats.

"This may be pushing my luck too far," muttered Ash.

Tasker laughed. "No need for luck," he said. "*I'm* driving."

The car surged on and, as Tasker had promised, they soon started to see the strange structures of a town: familiar ones at first, with sloping roofs and chimneys — although they were higher than normal and oblong. Naeo wondered what it was with this world and oblongs... they were *everywhere*. Soon these blockish buildings gave way to larger, more imposing structures, which jutted skywards with silky smooth, angular flanks of grey, or shimmering, gleaming planes of glass. Some rose to such heights that they would have rivalled even Isia's temple, though these were not so proud — so different from all around them. Instead they jostled in a great muddle of brick, stone and glass, shouldering aside the smaller dwellings. Like the road, this place spoke of business and impatience, of people short of space and time.

The town made Naeo nervous but excited too. It was gloriously chaotic, filled with shapes and colours and sounds — sounds that penetrated even the strange cocoon of the car. People milled about on the streets, clothed in the myriad colours of another world. Although they seemed rushed and anxious, they appeared to have no work to do. None of them had any real burden to carry, none seemed to be plying a trade. There were not even markets or stalls to speak of. It was all quite bewildering. But then, Naeo was getting used to that.

The road became even busier and, with less and less space to manoeuvre, the cars began to slow. Soon they were arranged end to end in growling rows, grumbling and honking and blinking their frustration.

"Where are they all *going*?" asked Naeo, shaking her head.

Tasker laughed. "I sometimes ask myself the same thing," he said, running his hand through his thick locks. "Right now, I just wish they'd get the heck out of our way."

The cars inched forward, rolling past huge, brightly lit frontages of glass displaying all manner of wares that Naeo would never have dreamed of: bizarre clothes, strange machines, more little black oblongs. As they turned a bend they passed a huge display of larger oblongs, each alive with blinking, disjointed snippets of the world, dazzlingly clear and true, but somehow flat and unreal, cutting between faces and landscapes, things of nature and wild, psychedelic explosions of colour. Naeo and Ash grinned at one another excitedly. To them the Other seemed so steeped in magic — a place of such endless possibility — that they wondered how Sylas could have been so amazed by Essenfayle or the Three Ways.

Naeo's eyes suddenly narrowed. Some of the oblongs in the window were showing an image of what looked like the stone circle, from the point of view of somewhere high in the sky. Just as she was about to point this out, the images disappeared and cut to a woman speaking and pointing frantically.

Naeo turned to her companions. "Did anyone just see—"

"What in the name of Isia is *that*?"

Ash was looking in a different direction, jabbing a finger into the window pane next to Tasker's ear. He was pointing at a man gliding past at the same speed as the car, wearing the strangest and most questionable outfit he had ever seen. He was clothed all over in a garment so tight that, were it not covered in splashes of luminous colours, they might have thought him naked. The strange clothing was stretched wafer-thin across his torso, down his arms, over his hips and thighs, leaving only his lower legs and hands free. But it was the man's transport that had caught Ash's attention. He was sailing along on a flimsy-looking contraption of only two comically large wheels, one directly in front of the other, leaving no support on either side. By all the laws of Nature, he should have fallen into the path of the passing cars.

"That," said Tasker, looking surprised, "is a bloke on a bike."

"A *bike*..." repeated Ash reverently. "And how does he hold it like that? I thought you people didn't use Urgolvane?"

Tasker turned suddenly in his seat. "Whoa, now!" he cried. "We don't speak of those things here!"

Ash threw his hands in the air. "Calm down, no one can hear us!"

"That doesn't matter!" snapped Tasker. "We just never, EVER talk of those things. They're forbidden — understand?"

"So you don't even *mention* them? The Three... you know?"

"No, never."

"Well that'll be tough for Ash," murmured Naeo, still staring out of the window. "He's a bit of a fan."

Ash glared at her. "So what if I am?"

She grunted and shrugged. "You know what I think."

Ash looked away, pursing his lips as though struggling to hold his tongue. "Well, in any case, all this secrecy is irrelevant if you ask me. Now that Scarpia's here, the cat is well and truly out of the bag... so to speak."

Tasker sighed and rubbed the back of his neck. "You might be right," he said.

The traffic slowed to a crawl and for some time they just edged forward in silence, each lost in their thoughts. Naeo found herself playing with the Merisi Band around her wrist. It was only after a while that she realised it felt strange — lighter somehow — and it took her some moments to work out why: the pain had gone. From the beginning it had hurt, and never more so than when she was with Sylas. And now — now that she was as far from him as could be — there was nothing. It was a relief not to feel the pain any more, but in the same moment she felt oddly uncomfortable.

The traffic noise swelled around them as they approached a large junction controlled by curious towers of red, orange and green lights. As peculiar as these were, her eyes were drawn to a tumbledown building made of stone, which seemed a little reminiscent of some of the grander buildings in their own world, with columns and high stone arches. It was just as decayed and decrepit as many of them too, with no panes in the windows and weeds and ivy growing up the cracked walls. Naeo spotted an old, faded sign in its overgrown gardens. It read: 'Church of the Holy Trinity'.

"Well, here we are," said Tasker, nodding to the building on the other side of the road. "Gabblety Row."

Naeo and Ash scrambled to the other window and peered out.

There it was.

It was a tumbledown improbability of a building, which had no real right to be standing. Nothing about it made sense: not the crumbling red bricks, which wandered and wavered in confused rows; not the misshapen windows, some of which actually lunged out from the side of the building, held precariously on a forest of brackets; not the crazy framework of dark brown beams, which were arranged at such weird angles that they looked like a giant game of pick-up sticks. But despite its frailties, Gabblety Row also looked timeless and substantial. It was a place that had been as it was for many years gone and would be so for many years to come, shrugging off the noise and rush of the roads, the precisions of modern life, the breathless pace of things.

"It's a grand old place, in its own way," said Tasker respectfully. "One of our own, you know."

Ash frowned. "What do you mean?"

"I mean, the Merisi built it."

Ash looked surprised. "I didn't know the Merisi were into *building* things."

"We're into more than you can imagine," said Tasker. "But Gabblety Row was less about the building than the ground it sits on."

Ash peered at its foundations. "How so?"

"It's built over a Slip," said Tasker as the lights changed and the traffic began to move.

"A what?"

"A Slip — a missed stitch," he said as though it should be clear. "A gap. A hole."

"What *kind* of hole?" interjected Naeo.

"A hole between the worlds, of course."

Naeo and Ash stared at him in silence, then leaned over to get a better look.

"That's why it's such a tumbledown," continued Tasker. "Poor thing barely knows which world it's in. They built it to plug the Slip." He turned and gave them a knowing look. "Dangerous things, Slips."

They cornered at the junction and swept past the building, seeing the frontage of shops: a bustling bakery; a dismal undertaker marked 'Veeglum & Retch'; a locksmith and carpentry shop, and finally: a dark, unlit premises whose faded sign could no longer be read.

Naeo knew what it was without being told.

"The Shop of Things," she murmured.

Tasker glanced back and smiled. "That's right," he said. "And Mr Zhi is waiting for you."

27

War

"But know this: in the last, it will come to War. *War is inevitable."*

SYLAS OPENED HIS EYES, blinked and thought he must be dreaming.

It was light. Wonderful, life-giving light. It was more of a feeble glow than a dawn — the usual grey smudge of the Barrens — but it was day, and it meant that their trials were over. He pushed himself up on his elbows. There was something else different too: a tingling lightness in his wrist, a warmth that made him look down at his arm. It was only then, when he saw the Merisi Band, that he realised that it was not so much a sensation as something missing — the pain that had become second nature, that had told him Naeo was near. He had not been without it since he was last on the Barrens, walking into Thoth's city. But now it was gone.

She was gone.

He was certain. He could feel it — not just in his wrist but somewhere deep inside. It was a lack of something, an absence that left him feeling strangely exposed. Naeo was far away. She was not even part of this world. She had passed into the Other.

He heard a noise and glanced across the ashes of the campfire.

Simia was lying on her side, propped up on one elbow, curling a lock of red hair around a finger. She had been watching him.

"Something wrong with your arm?" she asked huskily.

Sylas sat up. "No, it's better than it's been for ages," he said, yawning and stretching. "The band doesn't hurt any more."

Simia raised her eyebrows. "So what does *that* mean? Is she OK?"

"Yes, but she's gone. I don't know how, but I just know — they made it."

"Well at least part of this adventure is going to plan," came a whisper from the other side of the fire. It was Triste, speaking in a dry, broken voice.

He pushed back his blankets with closed fists and strained to sit up. Simia rushed to help him, but he waved her away, preferring to do it himself. His burns looked a little less livid in the cool light of morning, but he was still a shade of himself.

He was silent for a while, gathering his strength. Sylas made a support for his back and Simia brought him some water. They exchanged an anxious look.

"Did you get any rest?" asked Simia as she sat next to him.

Triste gave a wheezing laugh. "I'm not sure I'd call it rest, exactly," he said, fixing her with his bloodshot eyes. "Dreams... *strange* dreams." He frowned as he remembered. "Or perhaps... perhaps they weren't dreams at all."

"What do you mean?" asked Sylas.

The Scryer sipped at his water and shook his head. "All that darkness — all those shapes in the blackness, flowing from it..." His eyes snapped up. "It was the Black, I'm sure of it. It was as though... as though, with that chill in my veins, with that darkness in my heart, I could see it for what it was." He looked down and shook his head again. "No, no that's not it. I could see *through* it. I'm sure of it... I could—"

Simia leaned forward and said softly: "Perhaps you should get some more rest before you—"

"No!" snapped Triste. "You need to know what I saw!" He turned his eyes to them both, agitated now. "He was *using* it... using the Black to span the void, to speak across seas and mountains and deserts... *impossible* distances..."

"Who?" asked Sylas.

"Thoth!" cried Triste, his eyes wide. "I couldn't see him, but I could hear him. And he wasn't alone. The Black brought him his generals, his priests — the leaders of the four lands! They were all gathered together, feeding on the Black... sustained by it..." His face slackened and he seemed to lose focus, drifting back into his nightmare.

Sylas leaned forward. "What were they doing, Triste?"

"Preparing for war."

Sylas and Simia stiffened.

"What... what kind of war?" breathed Sylas.

The Scryer turned to him, his features dark and sorrowful. "A war to end all wars. A war of worlds."

Icy fingers crept up Sylas's back. "No..."

Triste nodded grimly.

"A war between this world and... and *mine*?" asked Sylas, the breath leaving his lungs.

"I fear so."

"But *why*? What's my world ever done to him?"

"Does Thoth need a reason for anything?" muttered Simia defiantly, but she too had grown terribly pale.

Triste took another sip of his water. "And yet, if you think about it," he said, "Thoth has every reason to attack your world. Here his power is unrivalled, his empire stretching to the very borders of the four lands. But beyond those borders, beyond the

219

great divide between our worlds, he has no control. No dominion. And there —" a little of the sparkle returned to Triste's eyes — "there he faces a foe greater than any he might have met before, a foe whose science reaches up into the skies and down into the seas: a foe with power beyond imagining."

"So why start a war?" asked Simia. "It makes no sense."

Triste coughed as he tried to drink some more water and hunched over to regain his breath. "Think about it," he said finally. "For many years we've suspected that Thoth's war on the Suhl was only ever about the Other, that the Suhl's only crime was that we control that final border — the border between the worlds. That was enough to make him wage war on everything that we are. That's how much he fears your world. We were never the threat. The Other — *that's* what he's afraid of!"

"But why attack the Other if he fears it?" pressed Simia.

Sylas had been listening with growing horror. "Because of me," he said.

Triste lifted his eyes and looked at him. Sylas could see the pity in his eyes. "I'm afraid so," he said. "You have made the threat very real. And not just by coming here. Thoth knows Merisu's prophecy, and that if it is true, you will one day—"

"—bring the two worlds together," finished Sylas, staring into the embers.

Simia looked from one to the other. "And so... so Thoth thinks he has nothing to lose!"

"And everything, *everything* to gain," said Triste. "A whole new world of treasures and possibilities and powers and..." he trailed off, seeming reluctant to continue.

"And... what?" asked Sylas.

Triste's features darkened. "In my dream, Thoth spoke of the worlds as an upper and a lower kingdom, as in ancient times. A kingdom of the strong, and one of the weak. One for the rulers and one for the ruled."

Sylas's stomach turned. "Slaves..." he said.

Images whirled through his mind: images of his own world, of the things that he had always thought would go on forever. Suddenly they seemed so distant, so frail. Because of him. He saw busy streets bustling with cars and people, children playing in parks, the lively comings and goings of Gabblety Row. He thought of his friends in the terrace — Sam Clump the locksmith, Mr Buntague the Baker — and for a moment he even thought of his mean-spirited Uncle Tobias, hunched over his desk, lost in his world of ledgers and balances and numbers with no idea that it could all come crashing down. He thought of the kindly Mr Zhi in his wonderful Shop of Things. But finally, painfully, he saw that precious, sepia-tinted memory of his mother, the memory he had kept so close and that, over the past few days, had started to feel so alive and real once more... so *possible*...

What would happen to her now? Would Naeo ever be able to find her? And if she did, would she be in time?

Triste watched him closely and seemed to see his thoughts. "You have to go," he said resolutely. "You have to go right now! Find Isia, find out what she knows, and then do what you have to before it's too late! Time is up against us, more than we thought."

Suddenly Sylas remembered the song in the Samarok, Isia's Song: "*Our hope quickly won will die in one moon,*" he murmured.

"Yes!" said Triste. "And that's why you have to go!"

"You mean *we*," interjected Simia, looking from Sylas to Triste. "*We* have to go."

The Scryer smiled and shook his head. "No, I won't be coming. Look at me, I'm a mess. I'll stay here until I have the—"

"No, you won't!" cried Simia, horrified. "You can't! The… the Kraven! They'll be back as soon as it gets dark!"

"Not if I have enough firewood to keep me going."

Simia gawped in disbelief. "But you're too weak to be alone!"

"I'm not, Simsi, but I *am* too weak to walk across the Barrens. At best I'll slow you down and at worst I won't make it at all. You have to go on alone."

28
Home

*"It is a warming thought, that each of us has
another home in another world."*

SIMIA LOOKED AT SYLAS, then back at the Scryer. "What if I stay
with you and Sylas goes on alone?"

Sylas shot her an anxious glance but nodded. "Yes, I'm sure I
could—"

"NO!" insisted Triste. "You need all the help you can get. You
both have to remember why we're here, and now more than ever.
You *must* reach the Temple of Isia, for all our sakes."

Sylas and Simia looked at each other helplessly. This seemed
so wrong, so cruel, but as hard as they tried, neither could think
of any other way.

"We're wasting time," said Triste. "If Naeo has made the
passing as planned, things are already unfolding. You need to get
on."

There was another pause.

"Sylas, tell me you'll go!" snapped Triste, wincing with the exertion.

Sylas lifted his eyes and let out a sigh. "I suppose we don't
have a choice."

Simia glared at him, but he knew she wasn't angry — she was blaming herself. He held her gaze for a moment and soon she looked away.

They ate a sombre, meagre breakfast, talking through what they were going to do. Afterwards Simia gathered up the belongings that had been strewn about the previous evening and moved some provisions between the packs, then began digging a proper fire pit. Sylas went off foraging for firewood. It was so much easier by the light of day, and he was soon carrying a decent haul of dry and almost-dry wood.

He gathered three loads, and each time he returned to camp Simia had made more and more progress with the fire pit. She was engrossed in her task, her hair matted with sweat. This pit would be deeper and better than any she had dug before. Triste tried to tell her to slow down, that that bank did not need to be that high, that the pit need not be so broad or so deep, but she was not listening. It was as important to her as it was to him.

Before long she was putting the final touches to the earthen ring and Sylas was packing the wood around the outside, so that Triste would be able to reach it easily but it would be well away from the flames. Then he checked on Triste.

If anything the Scryer looked worse. He was propped up against the bank, his eyes half closed and a faint wheeze passing his lips. Sylas rekindled the fire, placed a small pan of water over it to brew some tea, and adjusted the blankets.

As he handed Triste the cup their eyes met.

"Tell me," said the Scryer. "Do you still feel her? Naeo — do you know she's still... there? Now she's gone?"

"Yes, I think so," he said. "I know that she made it."

The Scryer nodded. "I can't see a connection," he said, taking a sip of tea, "but I'm sure it's still there. It must be good to know that she's with everything that matters: your own world, your town, your home..."

Sylas realised that the Scryer was right. Even now, the thought of Naeo — the sense of her — was strangely consoling. It gave him hope. He allowed himself to think of her drawing near to the town — perhaps even there already, walking up to the tumbledown terrace of Gabblety Row, peering in the window of The Shop of Things. And for an instant he felt that in some curious way he might be there himself, opening that door of possibilities once again. And then he had another thought that was more hopeful still. He felt a flicker of warmth in his stomach, a stirring of excitement.

Perhaps, just perhaps, she was near her now. Near his mother.

All this Triste saw in Sylas with his tired, failing sight. He saw the exquisite wisp of belief and the faint flicker of a half-formed hope. He witnessed the searing red glow of a son's love for his mother.

He reached out and took Sylas by the wrist, his fingers closing around the Merisi Band. "Not far now, Sylas," he said. "Not far now."

Sylas drew a long deep breath. "Perhaps," he said.

The Scryer's eyes were still at work. They saw the slightest trace of something else, something he had not seen before: a trail of silver that left Sylas and headed off into the nothingness, disappearing into a place he could only guess at.

Triste frowned. He closed his eyes and tried to open his mind to it, but the more he tried the more indistinct it became.

Even as he reached for it, it was gone.

The 'Closed' sign slapped against the glass of the door as it shut behind them. They stood in the gloom of the dusty interior, listening to the off-key chime of the shop's bell. Their eyes wandered over the high piles of crates and parcels arranged in haphazard rows trailing off into the dark recesses of The Shop of Things. The crooked glass behind them sprayed the room with the contorted rays of sunset, flooding it with sepia tones, like an old photograph.

"It's a weird old place, Gabblety Row," said Tasker in a low voice. "Stuck in a time of its own. It's almost like time leaks out of it…"

Ash scoffed. "Leaks where?"

Tasker turned to him and arched an eyebrow. "I don't know. Somewhere between the worlds, perhaps." He took a sharp breath then added breezily: "Anyway, come on! No time for the tour! Mr Zhi's rooms are upstairs," he said, strolling off between the nearest stacks.

He led them through the extraordinary Things towards the back of the shop. While the majority were still sealed inside their parcels, some lay half unpacked in their crates, offering a tantalising sample of the shop's wares: Things of wood and glass and iron, Things of colour and of grey, oblong Things and spherical Things, large Things and Things as small as a fingernail. At the end of one row, Naeo saw what looked like a plant erupting from the straw of a crate, unfurling leaves of parchment upon which were written thousands of rows of tiny runes and scripts. She desperately wanted to stop and try to read it, but Tasker and Ash had already disappeared. She tore her eyes away and ran to catch up.

The Shop of Things was just as magical as Sylas had said and suddenly she was struck by a thought of Sylas, here, in this peculiar shop, among these very wonders. How strange it was to think that he had been here just a few days ago, before she had summoned the bell. And what a thought, that this dilapidated

226

building had been his home for all those years, the years that she had been in the Dirgheon. It wasn't that the building itself seemed out of place — in fact it seemed almost familiar. It was more the peculiar sense that by being here, she was looking back in time, back across the years of Sylas's life. And in a way, *her* life.

When she reached the back of the shop they were waiting for her next to a door.

Tasker looked impatient. "Are you with us, Princess?"

"Why do you keep calling me that?" she asked, irritated.

"No reason!" he muttered before darting through the door and climbing the staircase beyond.

"Take it as a compliment," said Ash with a shrug. "He barely speaks to me at all."

As they climbed the crooked stairs, the sound of string music met their ears. It was a beautiful ebb and flow of notes played by a single instrument, rising up the scale only to tumble back down again, settling like leaves before being caught up once more and sent skywards. It soon filled their ears, though it was resonant rather than loud, reverberating in the old timbers of the building.

Just as they were nearing the door at the top of the stairs, Naeo's blood ran cold.

She *knew* that sound: the dulcet notes, the sustained sound of horsehair against gut, the occasional squeak as a finger slid down a fingerboard.

It was the sound of Thoth at play.

29
Mr Zhi

*"*Mr Zhi *wears the power of kings as lightly as a gossamer crown.
For him, wisdom is just to think or speak; miracles are just to do."*

NAEO EDGED UP THE stairs, hardly breathing.

Tasker's demeanour, meanwhile, had changed. His usual
boldness seemed to ebb away so that he returned to his rightful
size. His arms fell to his sides, his shoulders slumped a little, his
movements became smaller and more careful. He lifted his hand
to the door, hesitated for a briefest of moments, then knocked.
He paused and then went in.

The music flooded into the staircase, echoing down the tight
passageway far more loudly than Naeo had thought possible for
a single cello. She shrank away until Ash reached back and drew
her into the amber glow.

She stepped into a large room lit by several windows at either
end. At the very centre, an elaborately embroidered rug had been
laid on the floor, upon which sat a small old man, his legs crossed
with surprising suppleness, his head bowed in concentration. He
was dressed in a rather crumpled, dowdy old grey suit, which
combined with his littleness to make him easy to overlook. The

only distinctive features of his dress were his slump of a green hat and the length of fabric hanging from his neck, both of which were a bright green. Neither went with the suit.

Naeo could not see his face — his head remained bowed as he listened to the music — but she knew at once who it was, and the thought sent a shiver down her spine.

Mr Zhi.

There he was, sitting right there, on the floor. She cocked her head on one side. For such a great man, he seemed beguilingly slight and humble. In fact on the face of it, there was nothing particularly remarkable about him at all.

When he showed no sign of acknowledging their arrival, her eyes started to drift around the room. At one end, between two windows, was the smallest tree (or at least, the smallest fully grown tree) that Naeo had ever seen. Despite its size, it looked as twisted and gnarled as an ancient oak, leaning a little to one side as though it had begun to stoop with old age. Nevertheless, its miniature leaves seemed very much alive, quivering and vibrating with the music, dancing to its melodies.

Then she saw why — on either side of it, two narrow black oblongs were inexplicably alive with notes and chords. It was only then that she realised that they were in fact the source of the music, as though two tiny cellos, along with tiny bows and tiny cellists, were somehow crammed inside.

Ash too was staring at the oblongs, his eyes full of wonder. "Science!" he said, in a reverent tone. "The *Fifth* Way!"

Still the music played, building now to a crescendo. This was like no music she had heard Thoth play: it was beautiful and heartrending, simple but evocative — and she realised that she could no more think of Thoth when she listened to this than she could imagine Mr Zhi in the Dirgheon. The instrument may have been the same, but here, in Mr Zhi's rooms, it expressed something utterly different, something that filled her with hope.

Her eyes passed along the many bookshelves, crammed with volumes of all shapes and sizes. These were unlike the usual drab cloth and leather bindings she knew from the great collections of the Scribes: these were bright and various. The shelves were a celebration, alive with possibility and knowledge, brimming with the fascinating words of this astonishing world. How she wanted to take a look. She was considering walking over when suddenly the music came to an end. The strains of the cello fell to a single low note that hung in the air, then lifted to a final chord.

All at once and apparently without any effort, Mr Zhi rose to his feet. He did not put down a hand or even uncross his legs. He simply rose, smoothed down his rumpled suit and smiled.

"Please forgive my meditations," he said, cheerfully. "When I heard your news I felt the need for a little Bach. He settles my spirits. Welcome! Welcome!"

He went first to Naeo, holding out his hand, upon which she now noticed a beautifully embroidered velvet glove in the same shade of green as his hat and necktie. As she reached to take his hand, he slipped his fingers forward a little and she felt them brush the Merisi Band. His eyes twinkled.

"I am Mr Zhi," he said with a smile, his eyes full of warmth and welcome.

"I'm Naeo," she said, finding herself unusually nervous. "Naeo Bowe."

Mr Zhi raised his eyebrows. "Welcome, daughter of Bowe. Your father is a fine man, I hear. Perhaps it is he who taught you your love of books?" His eyes shifted to his bookshelves.

Naeo glanced at the books. "I... Yes, I..."

"You must take a look at them, once we have dispensed with

the formalities," he said, turning to Ash. "Hello," he said, extending his hand.

"Hi, I'm Ash. Ash Dagglegar."

Mr Zhi shook his hand warmly and peered into his face. "Pleased to meet you, Ash," he said. "So, you are rather a fan of our science?" He frowned. "And of the Three Ways?"

Ash rummaged in his hair. "Well, I wouldn't say—"

"There is much to admire," said Mr Zhi graciously, "in *all* of the Four Ways."

"Right! There's plenty to admire in Essenfayle," Ash said, defensively. Then he added: "I just happen to think the others have a little more... punch."

Mr Zhi arched an eyebrow. "Punch?"

Ash nodded. "Punch," he said, a little less confidently. He glanced at Naeo for support and immediately wished he hadn't. She just crossed her arms and threw her eyes in the air.

Mr Zhi turned and beamed at Tasker, holding out both his hands, which the younger man took up. "Jeremy! Good to see you."

Tasker smiled and bowed. "And you, Mr Zhi. I hope I—"

"You've done very well," said the old man. Then he frowned. "Only... what on *earth* have you done to your hair?"

Tasker glanced at the visitors and flushed, raising his hand to his sculpted locks. "It's the fashion," he said. "Just to fit in."

Mr Zhi was unimpressed. "How extraordinary!" he exclaimed and quickly turned away. "Now, my good friends, please come and take a seat over here."

He led the thoroughly unnerved gathering to the other end of the room. There they found a cluster of worn but homely old armchairs and a large sofa, surrounding a low table brimming with sandwiches, cakes, fruit and a perfectly arranged tray of tea for four.

"I prepared a few morsels in case you were hungry," he said, motioning them into the seats. "But I am afraid we must talk as we eat. If our visitors come in this direction, which I fear is inevitable, they will be here before long."

"You know about them?" asked Ash.

Mr Zhi shrugged. "Just what Jeremy told us over the phone and what I have already seen on news reports."

Ash and Naeo exchanged a baffled look.

Mr Zhi smiled. "Forgive me, you will not be familiar with such things! Suffice it to say that one of the gifts of science is that she allows us to whisper further and faster than the wind!"

He took his seat and began pouring the tea. "Now, to business. I think it would make sense if I first tell you what I do know, so that you can then tell me the rest." He finished pouring the tea, set the teapot down on the table with a clink of china, and looked at Naeo. "I know that Naeo is the most important person, bar one, that I will ever meet." He reached over and took her hand. "And I know that she is Sylas's Glimmer."

Tasker set his cup down on its saucer with a clatter.

Naeo's eyes never left Mr Zhi.

"That's... right," she said.

Tasker threw himself back in his chair. "I asked you if you knew anything about Sylas! You didn't tell me that you were... well..."

"A princess?" murmured Ash, arching his eyebrow. Tasker blinked at him irritably and turned away.

"Is Sylas well?" asked Mr Zhi, ignoring them.

Naeo thought for a moment. "Yes, I think he is," she said. "We've been apart for a while, but yes, I think he's OK." She reached for the Merisi Band, rolling it gently around her wrist. "He feels... more distant than he has since..."

Mr Zhi smiled. "Since you raised the Passing Bell," he said.

Naeo nodded and smiled. She was surprised again, but less so.

Somehow it seemed right that Mr Zhi should know so much of her. She found it rather comforting.

"Only to be expected," continued Mr Zhi. He settled back in his chair with his cup of tea. "Now, if you don't mind, I would like to hear everything that has happened since Sylas made his passing. I don't need to hear the detail, but please don't miss anything of importance."

Naeo blew out her cheeks. How was she supposed to tell him everything that had happened to Sylas? She barely knew the details herself. She glanced at Ash.

"Mr Zhi," said Ash, leaning forward, "perhaps it would be easier if you let *me* tell you what has happened. You see, Sylas only found Naeo a few days ago."

"As you wish," said Mr Zhi.

Ash swallowed down the remains of a piece of shortbread, gathered his thoughts and began.

As Sylas's story unfolded, Mr Zhi crossed his legs, drawing his feet up on to the chair and closing his eyes as if to improve his concentration. He did not move a muscle except to give a slight smile at certain points in the story, such as Ash's first encounter with Sylas at the Mutable Inn — when he had conjured the plume like a master of Essenfayle — or Sylas's brave speech to the Say-So, when he had told them not to fear what they do not understand.

"Do not fear what you do not understand," murmured Mr Zhi. "There's much to be said for that!" He smiled and waved for Ash to continue.

When Ash told of Sylas's stand on the river the old man gave a knowing nod, and again when he described the chasm he created on the Barrens, as though these displays of power only confirmed what the old man had known all along.

Tasker, meanwhile, had stopped eating, laid down his cup and sat hunched forward, engrossed in the tale.

So involved were they in Ash's account that they did not notice Naeo rise from her seat and walk back across the room to the towering shelves of books. She knew Mr Zhi did not need her — after all, holding court was Ash's special talent — and her instinct to leave had been overpowering. Ash was drawing near to the part of the story where she made her appearance and that made her feel strangely uncomfortable, as though what he would reveal was too close, too intimate. Of course, she knew that it was more about Sylas than about her, but it was all so intensely... personal. Her connection with Sylas was fogged and fraught — full of questions that still needed answers.

So instead, she lost herself in Mr Zhi's books.

She tilted her head to one side and ran her eyes along the first shelf, trying to read the titles, but they were written in a language she could not decipher: an angular and yet intricate alphabet, made up of many strokes of the pen. She soon gave up on that shelf, turning to those above and below, but with some disappointment she saw that they too comprised more books written in that curious script. She moved on to the next bookcase and found the titles instantly discernible, if impossible to understand. She mouthed them as she read them:

Tao Te Ching
The Tao

She blew out her cheeks. The lettering was familiar, but the words they formed were *weird*. She read some more from the shelf below:

Origins of Taoism
Finding the Way
Yin, Yang and the Two Worlds.

"The Two Worlds," she repeated under her breath. Intrigued, she took the book off the shelf and looked at the cover, which bore a strange symbol:

It was simple and yet complex, stark and yet beautiful. She stared at it for some moments, marvelling at its apparent symmetry, its capturing of absolute opposites. Finally she opened the book and began leafing through it, flicking through many densely worded pages in peculiarly orderly writing, which looked as though it had been written by a machine rather than a person. She tried to read a few passages, but was soon befuddled and bored by the dry, academic style, and she turned back to the cover. That symbol reminded her of something, but she could not think what.

Only then did she realise that Ash had stopped talking.

"Beautiful, isn't it?" came a kindly voice at her ear. Mr Zhi was peering over her shoulder. He sighed. "They call it the Yin Yang symbol."

Naeo glanced over to see that the others were watching.

"Er... yes, it is," she said, a little embarrassed to have been caught snooping. "What does it... what does it mean?"

"Well you might ask," said Mr Zhi with a grin, "because it has much to do with everything!" He gestured at the shelves she had been looking at. "Much of the philosophies of the East follow the beliefs of the Merisi, and none more so than Taoism, which created this symbol. It is Taoism that has the Merisi heart."

"Taoism..." murmured Naeo. It meant nothing to her. "Why?"

"Because Merisu, our great father, made his home in the East. He had much to do with the nurturing of their beliefs, and particularly those of Taoism: two opposing forces, all in harmony and balance, just like our two worlds!" He tapped the cover, pointing to the segments of black and white. "Just like you and Sylas." His finger moved to the two dots, one black and one white.

"So —" Naeo frowned — "this Yin Yang thing is about the two worlds? About me and Sylas?"

Mr Zhi smiled. "Almost certainly," he said. "Our divided worlds and souls are the source of so many beliefs."

"So... people here *know* about the two worlds? I thought the Merisi kept it a secret?"

He laughed. "Thankfully, knowing and believing are different things! We have done a fairly good job of preventing the *knowing*, but less well at preventing the *believing*. When you are keeping the greatest of secrets, there will always be stumbles along the way, stumbles that leave room for fables and legends and myths and folktales. They are part of the struggle to understand."

Ash peered with interest at the book. "So let me get this straight... some of your myths and legends are about our world, and people don't even know it?"

Mr Zhi smiled. "Many of yours are too, but I am no expert on those. I am, however, rather an expert on our own superstitions." He cast his hand across to the next bookcase, which was heaving with a collection of new and old volumes, all stuffed irregularly on the shelves as though they were read often. "This is my own little library on the topic!"

Naeo walked across and read some of the titles.

Another Look at Déjà Vu
The Truth About Ghosts, Wraiths and Spectres
Where there are Werewolves
Tales of the Bermuda Triangle

Secrets of Stone Circles
Doppelgangers: Our Mirrored Self
Alchemy: the Science of Magic.

Most meant nothing to Naeo, but she nodded politely. "So these superstitions... you think they're better than knowing the truth?"

"A very good question, Naeo," said Mr Zhi. "No, I don't think so at all. Superstitions divide people: only truth unites them. People can hold all sorts of strange ideas about the very same thing, but only one of them is the truth — that's why, in the end, the search for truth is the only way. But the truth of our divided worlds... well, that is a strange and unpalatable truth indeed, one for which our world has not been ready."

Ash took down one of the books. "I've never understood what you're so afraid of," he murmured, leafing through the volume. "*We* know about the two worlds and it never did us any harm."

Mr Zhi seemed surprised. "That's because you are the Suhl, the people of Essenfayle!" he exclaimed. "You understand the power that exists between all natural things! Essenfayle allowed you to discover the links between our worlds, but it also gave you the wisdom not to meddle with them. Until now, at least." He looked at Naeo. "Now it seems that everything will change."

"But if that's true," said Ash, "if everything is about to change... what about your world? Is it ready?"

Mr Zhi's face darkened. "I think it has to be."

Naeo did not notice: she was still working through the bookcase of superstitions, engrossed in the volumes, mouthing their many strange titles under her breath. It was something her father had taught her: "Say them to yourself," he had once said. "If you listen closely enough, you may hear the meaning. It's trying to get out." Like so much of what he had told her, she had never forgotten.

"What are those ones?" she asked, pointing to a high shelf which strained under the weight of a few mighty volumes. "More fables?"

Mr Zhi looked up at them and thought for a moment. "Those are different from the others. They are books of religion. They have still been written to explain what we don't understand, but they are not simple superstitions. Those ones have a greater power."

"What kind of power?" asked Ash with sudden interest, trying to read the titles.

"The power of true belief," said the old man. "Of absolute faith."

Naeo frowned. "What makes them so special?"

"Ah well, quite," said Mr Zhi. "And there are many answers to that question — one man will tell you one thing and his brother will tell you another. But the Merisi think that it is because we need to believe."

"*Need* to believe?"

Mr Zhi nodded. "Because we doubt ourselves."

"Why do you say that?" asked Ash, surprised.

The old man did not answer. His eyes were fixed on Naeo.

Naeo felt a shiver trace her spine. *She knew why*. "Because we're not whole," she said.

Mr Zhi smiled. "And so we come to the truth. The truth of our doubting and our broken souls."

Naeo frowned. "But... but I still doubt myself... like anyone else. And now I know Sylas — I know he's there."

"But *do* you?" probed Mr Zhi, his smile broadening. "Do you really know he's there? Perhaps there is more to knowing Sylas than you have yet dis—"

He stopped and tensed. In the next instant they heard the bell in the shop below, followed by rapid footsteps between the stacks of Things, and a thundering rush up the staircase.

They all turned to face the door.

A tall, thin figure strode through the door. Despite his height, the man's movements were silent and smooth and, combined with his apparel of black jacket over a black shirt with black trousers and black shoes below, he gave a very convincing impression of a shadow. A long, evening shadow. Two large, piercing eyes blinked at them from a pale, open face.

Mr Zhi gave a slight bow. "Naeo, Ash, this is Franz Veeglum."

The stranger gave a small bow and Naeo and Ash nodded in response.

"Zer is little time, Mr Zhi," said Veeglum in a thin, dry voice. "Ze noos reports are coming in sick and fast. Zey are everywhere, and at least some of zem are coming zis way."

"It was to be expected," said Mr Zhi calmly. "Did you speak to our friends?"

Veeglum inclined his head. "Zey are expecting us."

"Good," said Mr Zhi, turning to Tasker. "Jeremy, we will take your car. Please go and bring it around to the back of the terrace so we will not be seen." He turned back to Veeglum. "Franz, you come after us, in the other car. In the meantime, please wait with our guests — I have a few Things to collect from the shop before we go."

He started to walk off towards the staircase.

"But... where are we going?" asked Ash, bewildered.

Mr Zhi turned and laughed drily. "Young man, I'm sorry! There is so much going on that I've quite forgotten my manners! We need to go where we should be safe for a while — a place where we can lay some plans. It's one of the Merisi sanctuaries. I think Sylas may have mentioned it to you: Winterfern Hospital."

Ash shook his head.

"The hospital has one particularly special resident," said Mr Zhi as he reached for the door handle. "Sylas's mother."

30
The Lost Legions

"Such a battle is not won by heroic deeds nor the cunning of command. It is lost *in the blood of men, measured out in* legions.*"*

IT WAS THE RHYTHM that kept the man moving: the regular draw of a shoulder and push of a foot, the slide of a hip and the scrape of fingernails. He measured the distance in grunts and pants and moans of pain. As long as he kept the rhythm, he felt safe from all that sought to pull him back: the Black in his veins, the chill in his limbs and, worse than either of these, the constant threat of despair. And despair was what he feared the most. He knew that if it nested in his heart, all would be done.

Draw, push, slide, scrape.
Draw, push, slide, scrape.

Every ten pushes of a foot, every twenty painful draws of his shoulder brought a break in the endless dark of the passageway. To his left was an opening, lit dimly by a shaft of light descending from the ceiling. He knew what that shaft of light would show him if he looked. He would see the interior of a birthing chamber: the thick flood of black ooze sliding down its walls; the bubble and gloop of a viscous floor; the drip, drip, drip from above. And at the centre, rising from the floor or hanging from the ceiling, there would be the pulsating form, still wrapped in its mucous shell: the thing being born. He would see one of many shapes, some familiar and some unknown. He knew the stoop and snout of the Ghor and he recognised the broad, muscular mass of the Ghorhund. But the majority of the chambers housed new and sinister forms: the lithe figure of something slender and cat-like; the strange, angular wings of something that hung from the ceiling and chattered in its fitful sleep; the spiked spine of something scaled and reptilian; and in many, the vast bulk of something that barely fitted into its chamber, something that bulged and strained with sinew and muscle.

He had seen so many of these shapes that he had lost count, and soon he had simply stopped looking. To look was to despair.

He had seen the birthing chambers before, he had even watched them at work, but he had never seen anything like this, *numbers* like this. These were no usual spawn — a new regiment of guards or skirmishing force of common Ghorhund — these would not replace anything that came before. This was a new army — an army of unthinkable scale and power. It would dwarf anything the Priest of Souls had produced before, even for the Reckoning. It was an army born for war.

And yet where was the foe? Thoth had defeated and destroyed all in his path. The Suhl were as good as extinct. What war was left to fight?

He pushed on, heaving his shoulder forward. He could not think of it. He must not think of it. He must think only of the rhythm.

Draw, push, slide, scrape.
Draw, push, slide, scrape.

He blinked. There was a change somewhere ahead: a low

murmur of many sounds, a shift in the damp, stale air. He could make it out now: a pale opening — an end to the passageway.

On he pushed, his rhythm quickening now, spurred on by the promise of a change, of an end to the endless darkness.

Draw, push, slide, scrape.

Draw, push, slide, scrape.

And then, suddenly, he sensed something.

For a moment he froze, listening. Then he threw himself flat.

The stone beneath him shuddered, the rock moaned; and then came an unimaginable sound.

It began with the deep, resonant report of a horn, starting low and rising to a deafening pitch. It echoed from the walls, shattering the silence, blasting down the empty passageway. It slammed into him like a blow to the face and body, rattling through him and humming in his lungs. Then, as it started to fade, came a devilish chorus: a forest of cries and yelps, growls and snarls. They built to a triumphal roar that drowned the horn in a thunder of voices.

The opening flared with light: light like the light of day.

He pushed on, quicker now.

Draw, push, slide, scrape.

Draw, push, slide, scrape.

On and on.

And then he was there, out into the light, on to a balcony with staircases leading down to the left and right. Ahead, through the balustrade, he could see a vast hall lit by a growing slit of light — a precious aperture of daylight which grew and grew before his eyes as two giant doors swung open.

There was a tremendous roar of voices from below and he looked down, into the bowels of the great hall. It writhed before his eyes: a swaying mass of bodies, Ghor, Ghorhund, Slithen, Tythish and myriad other creatures he had never seen before. And somehow, in this heaving mass of creation, there was order. The beasts formed two immense columns, scores of bodies thick and hundreds long, led by twenty or thirty baying Ghorhund, which even now strained at their leashes, heaving their handlers towards the light. And as they reached the threshold, the twin columns stepped forward as one, surging in a steady, rhythmic lope in time to a deep, discordant chant. They threw up row upon row of fluttering flags: flags of red and black, emblazoned with a hollow face and empty eyes — the staring face of Thoth.

Espen slumped against the stone, giving in to his despair.

"Isia help us!" he whispered, raising his hands to his face.

S

It had been terrible leaving Triste behind. They had walked for a while in a painful, heavy silence and then they had stopped and looked back, peering through the grey haze. They had seen little: just the rise of Simia's earthen ring and the dome of Triste's head resting against it, the tattoos just visible, staring after them.

He had not moved since they left him and that only made them feel worse. Would he even have the energy to build the fire when he needed to? They had left a bundle of kindling and firewood just next to his foot so that he would only have to push it with his heel until it rolled on to the embers, but would he even be able to do that? They had fed the fire with lumps of wood so that it would smoulder for hours, they had done everything they could think of, but would he even be conscious when he needed to be? When it mattered most? When the darkness came?

Then, after that last look back, they had turned away with heavy hearts wracked with guilt, and they had broken into a run. It had felt as though they were running away. But what else could they do?

And so there they were again, alone together on the open Barrens, running towards the city, their thoughts with the friend they had left behind. Their minds inevitably turned to Bayleon, to that fateful night at Salsimaine when he had given himself up to let Simia run free. It was little wonder then that when they saw the great stone circle far off to their left, glowering broodily through the grey, Simia fell a little behind. Little wonder that tears stung her eyes, that she cursed herself under her breath.

Sylas too had been struck by the sight of the Circle of Salsimaine. For him, it was like a glimpse of home, beckoning him back to familiar things, to Naeo's journey rather than his own. But he tried not to give in to those thoughts. He knew that now more than ever he had to keep his focus.

They had to continue, to Gheroth, and Isia's temple.

Sylas led them into one of the deep fissures in the earth, running ahead, darting left and right as the steep sides leaned and lunged, striking out one way and then the other. It was so much easier than before, in the dark, when they had had nothing but their instincts to guide them. Now, by the light of day, they ran even faster, tearing through ditches and the dried beds of streams, through cracks and crevices, feeling their hearts pound, their lungs burn. It was a release from their dark thoughts, a chance to forget what they had done.

Simia shrieked as she barged past, taking the lead, and he knew to let her. This had been her domain in those long months after the Reckoning, and it showed. As she gained speed, she used the walls, riding up on them as she cornered at speed, leaning over at incredible angles as she leapt from bank to bank, her red hair billowing and dancing ahead.

At first Sylas struggled to keep up, but then he took himself back to that night, to what she had told him — "*you're linked to everything: the air, the Barrens, the earth in these riverbanks. You need to feel them — know where they are just as they know where you are.*"

And that is what he did. He felt dust and earth, rock and riverbank, and as he did they opened up to him, folded around him, rose up beneath his feet, corrected his path, prevented his fall. He charged up on to a near-vertical wall, running over it as though it were on the flat, using it to make the next corner. His blood coursed and his heart thundered. After all they had been through, he suddenly felt so alive.

Then he skidded to a halt.

The path ahead was almost straight, leading between two high banks that glinted and glistened with metal. Swords lay bent and broken on the surface, daggers littered the dust, shields and armoured plate tumbled down the banks. To one side, the torso of a suit of armour lay upside down on the ground, its occupant missing: lost to the fires that had made the Barrens.

This was not just a riverbed, it was a grave.

He felt sick as he started to jog through it, trying to keep his eyes to the front, trying not to imagine what had happened here. How had Simia just kept running? Why hadn't she even slowed down, turned her head?

He realised he already knew the answer. She was used to it. This was where she had been forced to live in the aftermath of the Reckoning, among the shattered remains of armies, the skeletons of military might. For her, these had become the things of daily life.

"Poor Simsi," he murmured.

He broke into a run, picking up his earlier pace, glad to be on the move again. He was relieved when he finally saw the flash of Simia's red hair up ahead. She was sitting on another shield projecting from the wall, kicking at the dust with her heel.

"Where've you *been*?" she asked as he ran up.

"Sorry, I got a bit distracted," he panted, gesturing to the fragments of armour that lay about her like so much litter.

Simia looked around. "Why? You've been here before."

Sylas looked at her blankly. "Well I couldn't *see* it before, could I?"

"I suppose not," she said with a shrug. "Anyway, never mind. We're through it all now."

Sylas turned sharply. "We're at the city? Already?" He reached up to the top of the bank and started to pull himself up to take a look.

"Don't!" hissed Simia, dragging him down.

Sylas pulled himself free. "Why? What's wrong?"

"We've got a problem."

She put a finger to her lips and then walked on, crouching to keep well below the rim. Sylas watched her go, realising that whatever it was, it was very close. He bent down and followed.

They rounded a corner and crawled along a straight ditch, pushing up against the wall so as to avoid a steady flow of sewage. The further they went, the more Sylas became aware of the sounds of a city: the low rumble of carts rolling over stone, the murmur of voices, the endless jostle of people and things occasionally punctuated by a child's cry or the singsong of a distant trader calling for custom.

Finally Simia stopped and pointed to the top of the bank. Sylas rose as carefully as he could, his nose trailing over the dust until his eyes peeked over.

There, across a narrow expanse of litter-strewn earth, was Gheroth, Thoth's city. It was just as dark and imposing as he remembered it, sweeping off to the left and right as far as he could see, and to the front rising in layer upon layer of jumbled horizons:

first, the ramshackle hovels of the slums; then above, the smoking disarray of timber housing; and above that, the mighty towering, stone structures at the heart of the metropolis. Finally, looming above it all, was the vast dark pyramid of shadow – the Dirgheon, its stark edges jutting high into the sky.

But Sylas's eyes were drawn to a scene much closer at hand. Standing shoulder to shoulder at one of the entrances to the city were three inexplicably tall figures, towering over a long line of city folk who were waiting to pass. Each of the three had exactly the same features: broad but rounded shoulders thrown menacingly forward over those that queued before them; extraordinarily long arms that moved at a speed so fast they were little more than a blur as they gathered papers from those they met; and huge, plate-like hands that seemed to boast far more than five digits a piece – though Sylas could hardly be sure, such was the speed with which they moved.

But the most striking feature of these creatures was their face, which seemed entirely out of proportion. Their long, hooked noses occupied a good half of it and their fierce, bloodshot eyes took up much of what was left. Their mouths were mean and thin-lipped, and by contrast, their wrinkled ears were utterly prodigious. If there were anything to be overheard, spied upon or sniffed out, these were the creatures to do it.

"The Tythish!" whispered Simia at his ear.

"What are they doing?"

"Checking papers," she hissed. "They do this kind of thing a lot, particularly around the slums, but not like this, not *three* of them in one place. And there are more – look!"

He followed her eyes to other dark openings of the many lanes leading onwards into the heart of the city. Each and every one of them was spanned by the enormous, spider-like forms of the

Tythish, looming over waiting crowds, searching with their prying eyes, pawing with their many-fingered hands. It seemed that no one and nothing would escape them.

"I've never seen so many," murmured Simia, shaking her head.

Sylas sank between his shoulders. "They're looking for us, aren't they?"

She nodded. "Uh-huh."

"So what do you think we should do?"

She rested her forehead against the dust. "We have to get past them."

"Great idea!" said Sylas, raising his eyebrows. "*How?*"

Simia said nothing, but glanced behind her. Sylas looked, but all he could see was the thick ooze of sewage flowing along the bottom of the ditch.

His eyes travelled slowly back to hers. "No!"

She sighed. "Oh yes."

31
Things

*"Like those before him, he seems to know which
of his magical* things *will work for which people."*

THE ROADS WERE QUIETER NOW. As they drove out of the town, Tasker was able to drive at greater and greater speeds, swinging confidently around the corners so that the wheels screeched. There were fewer people on the streets too. The only ones they had seen had been gathered around the shop with the glowing oblongs in the window – 'televisions', Mr Zhi had called them. A gaggle of young people were pressed up against the glass, watching a succession of quick-fire images, some of which had looked fleetingly like the stone circle, while others showed men – soldiers, perhaps – in uniforms of green camouflage. Others still showed the head and shoulders of a wide-eyed man or woman chattering frantically, gesticulating behind them.

But while the televisions had seemed full of life and drama, the town had been quiet. At one point a whole convoy of white cars with luminescent orange stripes had suddenly rushed upon them with blue lights flashing and strange, shrill wails shattering the calm, but they had been gone in an instant. Shortly afterwards,

Naeo thought she had heard a buzzing, humming stutter in the sky, and two or three long shadows had passed across the car, but she had not seen what caused them. She would have asked Mr Zhi what they were, but there had been too many other things to talk about. In fact, ever since they had left the Shop of Things they had been plying one another with questions, about the strange things they had seen, about Gabblety Row and Sylas, about the Merisi and the plight of the Suhl.

Naeo had been telling Mr Zhi about the Reckoning – about the great fires that had in large part decided its outcome. She told him about the clouds of hot ash that had ravaged the land, coating everything living, dead and dying in a deep, smothering blanket that left nothing but grey wastes. Mr Zhi had raised his hands in resignation, unwilling to hear more. He apologised for his sensibilities, then turned away and stared at the road ahead, quiet and thoughtful. Naeo thought that he looked even smaller, if that were possible.

A chattering, rhythmic music broke the silence as it had a number of times on their journey, and Tasker fumbled in his pocket for his little black oblong. Now, as on the other occasions, he raised it to his ear and listened to a quiet but frantic voice. He nodded and murmured in response, "Still on the move? How far?" And then: "More? How many?" He glanced at Mr Zhi, but the old man simply raised his hand, indicating that he understood but would not speak. "It'll have to wait until Winterfern," he said. And so it was each time the oblong burst into life: Tasker would speak calmly to the person in the oblong, imploring them to wait until later or to meet them at Winterfern, while Mr Zhi would remain quiet and thoughtful.

They drove out into the open countryside, and as the sun painted its final cheery tints on the horizon the conversation took a new turn.

"So this Winterfern... is it a hospital?" asked Ash, looking out at the rolling hills ahead. "A real one?"

Mr Zhi turned a little in the front seat to face him. "In the sense that it makes people well, yes, it is real. But it is hardly ordinary."

Naeo pulled her eyes away from the scenery. "Why?"

"Everyone at Winterfern is a little like Sylas's mother. They all suffer from a little too much *truth*."

Naeo frowned. "How can you have too much truth? You mean, about the two worlds?"

"Yes, though it is normally far more specific than that. Far more... individual." Mr Zhi smiled, seeming to realise that he was not making a lot of sense. He turned a little more in his seat. "You see, an unexpected run-in with the Other can be a very traumatic thing. If someone is unfortunate enough to chance upon some part of the truth without preparation, without explanation, well, that can be quite terrifying. Devastating, even."

Ash leaned forward. "What parts of the truth do people see?"

Mr Zhi sighed. "That's what makes these problems so difficult to prevent and to treat. Each case is individual... personal. Some might just have vivid dreams, glimpsing things that they shouldn't really see – things perhaps that their Glimmer has seen. Others are unfortunate enough to see those things when they are not even sleeping – those poor souls hardly know whether they are coming or going. But those that tend to suffer most of all are the ones who go one step further – those who actually witness something they shouldn't. Something not of their world."

"Some people actually cross over?" asked Naeo.

"Not necessarily, no. One doesn't need to leave this world to have a dalliance with one of the Four Ways. Imagine living an ordinary, magic-free life, and then one day somebody pinches you or irritates you and somehow, without raising a finger, you throw a chair at them."

"Urgolvane," said Naeo, glancing at Ash. "That happens? *Here?*"

Mr Zhi nodded. "Rarely, but it does. Or perhaps one day you are sitting a test at school and suddenly you find you know all the answers, but not because you did the work: because your neighbour did."

"Druindil…" said Ash, looking confused. "But I thought you said you didn't have the Four Ways here?"

"Generally, we don't; we don't witness any of the wonders of your world. But it happens. Like anything so unnatural, the division of our worlds is imperfect. It breaks, not because of how it was made, but because it was made at all. We call the breaks 'Slips'. They take all sorts of forms: places, things — Slips even happen in people's minds. And that's where the Merisi come in."

"To stop it from happening?" asked Naeo.

"If only we could!" the old man exclaimed with a sad chuckle. "No, but we can help in other ways. We care for those affected by the break in the worlds — and that is just what Winterfern is doing. We also keep others from being affected, which means keeping the division as orderly — and as secret — as we can. That's why we built Gabblety Row over a Slip, for instance. To hide it."

"Like I told you," said Tasker.

"Yes, thank you, Jeremy," said Mr Zhi. "Which brings me to the Merisi's third and most important task. I said we don't have the power to stop it from happening, but we can help those who have. Those who may actually be able to end this abomination once and for all."

Naeo narrowed her eyes. "You're talking about me and Sylas, aren't you?"

"Not to put too fine a point on it," he said, with a smile.

Ash cleared his throat. "All this is great but *how* can you help Naeo, exactly?"

Mr Zhi's eyes flicked to his. "Well, quite! You have an excellent way of getting to the point, young Ash. If you weren't on the wrong side of things, I'd make a Bringer of you!"

Tasker scoffed.

Mr Zhi's smile faded. "Please forgive Jeremy. He only recently completed training for the Merisi himself and perhaps the pains of that journey are yet to fade. Is that right, Jeremy?"

"You could say that," he muttered.

Mr Zhi's voice suddenly changed. "And yet the memory is not so strong that you remember your manners!"

Tasker glanced at Mr Zhi and flushed. "I'm sorry, Mr Zhi," he said, shrinking a little in his seat.

"Pride is your weakness, Jeremy!"

Ash allowed himself a quiet smile at Tasker's expense.

"And if you don't mind me saying, Ash, I sense that it is yours too," continued Mr Zhi.

Ash's face fell and he too shrank a little.

"But Mr Zhi, *can* you help?" pressed Naeo. "Paiscion thought you'd know what to do. The truth is, I thought when Sylas and I found each other things would just... happen ... get better. But they only seem to have got worse."

Mr Zhi sighed deeply. "I know it's hard to hear, Naeo, but no one has all the answers. We know that you and Sylas are special — we even know what you might one day achieve — but as for *how*... well, that *is* more difficult. Some things must come from the doing and not the asking. That was why I couldn't tell Sylas more before he left me. If I had, he may never have begun at all. Or worse, he could have ended up a patient at Winterfern... like his mother."

Naeo stared at Mr Zhi. Was that all he was going to tell them? After everything they'd been through to get here? She looked at Ash and saw that he was thinking the same thing.

The old man smiled. "But Paiscion was right — we *can* help a little. The Merisi have many of the answers that you seek and Isia will have others. But there will be plenty of time to talk about those things at Winterfern."

Naeo breathed a sigh of relief. "Thank you," she said, watching as Mr Zhi rummaged for something in a compartment of the car. She exchanged a glance with Ash, before continuing. "And there was something else. Paiscion thought that you might *have* something. A Thing. One that might help us to—"

"It's strange that you should mention that," interjected Mr Zhi, turning back to her. He raised two packages above the back of his seat. "Because I brought two Things from my shop. One for each of you, as it happens."

"You... you *knew*?" said Naeo, reaching for the package — yet another oblong, wrapped in brown paper.

"Young lady, *everyone* needs one of my Things," said Mr Zhi, his eyes twinkling. "But these are not just *any* Things. As I told Sylas when I met him, I consider it my particular talent to know which Things are for which people."

Naeo turned the package over in her fingers, feeling a sudden thrill of excitement.

"Thank you..." she said quietly, without lifting her eyes from her gift.

The Thing was small and very light and it made no sound when she shook it. She tore the paper away and allowed the rather plain little object to fall into her hand. At first she thought it was just a simple wooden box — a container for something else — but when she turned it over, she saw two plates running down its length, one white and one black, each inscribed with a series of glistening runes, and between the two plates was a delicate needle, made of a bright metal, perhaps gold. While everything else about the box was unremarkable, the needle was exquisitely intricate, ingeniously hinged at one end and rising in metal swirls and hair-thin strands to the tiniest, most precise point, which was held in a minute clasp.

"That, my dear, is a very special Thing," said Mr Zhi, marvelling at it over the back of his seat. "It is called a Glimmertrome."

Naeo slid her finger along the length of the needle. "What does it do?" she asked, reaching for the clasp.

"Don't touch that!" exclaimed Mr Zhi, lurching towards it. "My dear, I'm terribly sorry, I should have explained before you opened it! The Glimmertrome is a rather powerful Thing and mustn't be used lightly. You see, that needle, when it is released, will rock from side to side, a little like a metronome — do you know what one of those is?"

Naeo shook her head.

"It's of little consequence," said Mr Zhi, lifting the Glimmertrome and pointing to the white plate. "When the needle is released, it swings very slowly, passing first over one plate and then back across the middle point to the other. Then it will repeat to a precise rhythm." He rocked his arm back and forth to demonstrate. "But what is remarkable, what is truly *magical*, is what the bearer experiences as that happens. They will see with their own eyes when the needle rocks to the white, like so —" Mr Zhi tilted his hand to demonstrate — "and when it swings to the black they will see—"

"What their *Glimmer* sees..." whispered Naeo, her face filled with wonder.

"Precisely!" cried Mr Zhi.

Ash's eyes grew wide. "Do you know what this means?"

"I can be with Sylas while we're apart!" exclaimed Naeo. "Just like Paiscion said!"

Mr Zhi laughed and clapped with delight. "So it is what you needed?"

"It's *exactly* what I needed!" said Naeo. "But why do I have to be so careful with it? Can't I just see what Sylas is doing right now?"

Mr Zhi opened his palms. "No, because the Glimmertrome works both ways," he explained. "When the needle swings back, Sylas will see what you see."

Naeo furrowed her brow. "No matter what he's doing?"

"Precisely. You can imagine how dangerous that can be."

Naeo nodded slowly. "So I should only use it when I really have to?"

"Only when you have no other choice," said Mr Zhi.

For a moment he watched Naeo, seeming to enjoy her wonderment. Then he turned his attention to Ash.

"Ash, you haven't opened your Thing."

Ash pulled his eyes away from the Glimmertrome and grinned excitedly at Mr Zhi, like a child with a new toy. He turned the package over between his fingers, then he shook it next to his ear. It made a barely audible *gloop*. He tore the paper away and his eyes widened when he saw the gleam and shimmer of the brightest gold. The Thing fell heavily into the palm of his hand. It was not a ball, but a large egg, made entirely of a polished metal that seemed a little like gold, yet was more luminous and reflective. Ash stared at his distorted reflection in its surface, turning it carefully between his fingers.

"Thank you, it's… shiny," he said. "What is it?"

Mr Zhi laughed. "As I have been saying, that is for you to

discover. All I will tell you is that this is a Thing for a true master of magic: someone like yourself. Someone for whom Essenfayle is simply not enough."

Ash beamed, delighted by the sound of Mr Zhi's gift. He shook it again. "Sounds like there's something inside."

"Ah, well, that is where the true gold lies!" said Mr Zhi, patting Ash on the knee. "You'll see!"

For some time Naeo and Ash sat quietly looking at their gifts — first their own and then each other's — wondering at their craftsmanship, trying to think how and when they might be used. Meanwhile Mr Zhi turned to the road ahead and started a quiet conversation with Tasker. Outside, the terrain had changed. The open plains had given way to gentle hills, which in turn had surrendered to deep ravines and high, forested hilltops. The road was no longer a great sweep of rock disappearing to a point in the distance, but instead it rolled through endless loops and turns, winding along hillsides, twisting along valley floors, climbing through high passes. And as the landscape changed, day gave way to night. The last pinks and ambers died from the horizon and the deep blue of the cavernous sky dissolved into a star-filled black.

Soon the sway and drone of the car and the comfort of its seats had lulled Naeo and Ash into a doze, and from a doze into a deep, exhausted slumber. The precious Things slipped from their fingers, only to be caught up by Mr Zhi and wrapped carefully in their brown paper for safekeeping. Before he turned away, he allowed his gaze to rest for a moment on Naeo's sleeping face, on her narrow features and long eyelashes, her slight care-worn frown that was too old for her age.

"Remarkable," he said to himself, with a shake of the head.

Tasker seemed unaware of this. "They're frantic back at

Stonehenge, you know," he said, biting his lip. "It's everything we feared — worse than we feared."

Mr Zhi nodded. "I know," he said.

"So shouldn't we be—"

"No. In the dark we must look for the light."

Tasker glanced at him. "What do you mean?"

"I mean, Jeremy, you must learn to see what is under your nose," said the old man, with strained patience. "Tell me, why do you call Naeo 'Princess'?"

Tasker looked sheepish. "I don't mean anything by—"

"Tell me anyway," demanded Mr Zhi.

Tasker scratched his chin. "She's just a bit *difficult* — you know, sure of herself... for someone her age."

Mr Zhi sighed and shook his head. "Well, if you could get past your pride and stop worrying about how you expect to be spoken to, you would see that she has every reason to be that way."

"Because of what she's been through?"

"Because in a very real way, she *is* a princess. She and Sylas can do anything they choose. They are the miracle we've been waiting for."

Tasker's eyes travelled to the rear-view mirror: to Naeo's slender face glowing by the light of a full moon. His eyes lingered for a while before returning to the road.

Naeo heard none of this; her dreams were as deep and vivid as ever. She dreamed of her father's face as she had last seen it, streaked with blood and tears; of the misty lake in the Valley of Outs and the broad expanse of the Barrens; of Scarpia, bounding across a green plain, followed by machines that buzzed in the air; and then again of her father, gazing up at her on the day of the Reckoning in pride and wonder as she turned mighty waves against the Priest of Souls.

Her mind reached ahead, to the Winterfern hospital, to a woman with a face she knew but did not know. For a moment this image, this unknown face ebbed and flowed, merging with the face she knew so well. With the face of her father.

Then both faded to nothing.

In their place came the darkness: waves of it, thick and deep. And as she was touched by it, she felt the Black ripple beneath her skin. It sent out spears of pain that scoured her back and made her scream a silent scream. And then it pulled her down.

Down and down into the dark.

32

The Black

"If it is true that all things have their equal answer — their opposing form — then that of knowledge and light must surely be this evil and confounding slick of Black."

SYLAS STARED INTO THE darkness. The opening was no higher than his waist, fringed with yellowing vegetation and a foamy scum, and from it crept a brownish sludge streaked with black. It brought with it a stench so foul that it made him gag. He took Simia's lead and covered his nose with his sleeve.

"*Really* though, Simsi?" he said.

She shrugged. "It's not far — we just need to get past the checkpoints — a street or two — then we can come up."

His eyes travelled back to the tunnel. It was a disgusting, foul little sewer, but he was a little surprised at just how much it made his skin crawl and his throat tighten. It was not so much the stench — though that was bad enough — it was something about the inky blackness that set him on edge.

"What... what about if we just made a run for it? We could duck past those Tythish things and... lose ourselves in the slums. You know the slums so well we could—"

"You're kidding, right?" said Simia, incredulously. "I know the slums and I know the Tythish! They don't miss a thing — not ever. And don't let their size fool you, they're as quick as lightning — with those arms and legs they can crawl straight over the slums like spiders if they want to." She shuddered. "We wouldn't stand a chance."

Sylas was still eyeing the opening. "Maybe I could use Essenfayle to get us through," he murmured.

"How? Break the earth in two like you did on the Barrens? Between those buildings and streets? With all those people around?"

Sylas glanced over. "All right... I see your point."

"Anyway, we're trying to get in quietly, aren't we?"

He sighed and nodded.

"It'll be *fine*," she said. "I used the sewers loads when I was living in the slums."

"You did?"

"Well, three or four times."

"In my world, that's not loads."

"Well, it's loads here," muttered Simia. "Come on, we can't waste any more time."

Sylas sighed. "OK, I'm right behind you."

They both glanced up at the sky as though wishing it a fond farewell, took a deep breath and ducked inside the opening.

The world was suddenly cool and black. He found to his relief that the ceiling was a little higher inside so he was not quite bent double, and there was a brick ledge to one side of the stream of sewage that they could use as a path. However both ceiling and ledge were coated in a noxious slime that squelched underfoot and dripped on their heads and shoulders. The stench was abominable — so bad that he could taste it on his tongue — and it clung to the back of his throat. But still it was the darkness that unnerved him, which was strange — the dark had never bothered him much before.

"So apart from the god awful smell," he whispered, his voice echoing from the walls, "is there anything... *else* down here?"

He saw Simia's shadow pause up ahead. "The Slithen sometimes."

"The *Slithen*? You didn't tell me there were—"

"Relax! They don't bother patrolling this far out — the sewers are a labyrinth. All false tunnels and pitfalls — they don't think anyone knows a way through."

"But... you do?"

"Yeah," said Simia, walking away. "Pretty sure I do."

Sylas shook his head. "Great," he murmured.

They clambered on, quickly leaving the dim grey light far behind. Now the real challenge of walking in the dark and staying out of the sewage began. At first Sylas tried to use his elbow to guide himself along the wall, keen to avoid touching the slimy bricks, but after a couple of slips he let his fingers trail over the wet, slippery surface and chose not to think too much about it. A little further on his hand passed over a cool, dark opening, but he heard Simia pushing on ahead so he carried on too, wincing as he stepped across the junction, half expecting to plunge deep into the mire. After that came another junction, and another, and soon enough he developed a feel for it, becoming more confident of the surface underfoot and the distances across the passageways. He picked up his pace, trying to keep up with Simia, who was scurrying like a sewer rat, turning left and right and left again, bounding over junctions, hurrying along narrower and narrower tunnels.

And then she stopped.

Sylas drew up behind her, almost slipping into the channel of sewage.

"What's up?" he whispered.

"It's... a dead end."

"It's a *what*?"

"A dead end," said Simia, her voice wavering a little. "But I don't understand... I was sure that this was the way!"

They both turned and peered back the way they had come.

"Simsi, tell me you know your way back..."

Silence.

"*Simsi!*" he hissed.

"What do you want from me?" she replied. "Yes, I think I do, but then I thought I—" She stopped. "Did you hear that?" she muttered.

"What?"

Suddenly Sylas felt her hand on his arm. She was gripping it tighter and tighter until it hurt.

"*That*..." she whispered.

He strained his ears. For a moment all he heard was Simia's 'that' echoing down the tunnel. But then he heard it.

A squelch, then a drip, then a ripple.

It was far away — back in the adjoining tunnel — but it seemed to be getting closer.

"What do you think it is?" he breathed, as quietly as he could.

"I don't know," whispered Simia.

For a moment they were frozen, listening to the sounds getting ever closer.

"Well, we can't stay here," murmured Sylas. "Let's go."

"*Towards* it?"

"What choice do we have? We're cornered if we stay here!"

Simia hesitated. "OK."

They started creeping back up the passageway, hardly daring to breathe. Sylas's mind was racing: would Essenfayle work down here? Surely not. What would he use? The walls and ceiling were brick and what else was there? It seemed madness to be heading towards the sound, but surely it would be worse to be caught in a dead end?

They moved ever more slowly, listening to the sounds just ahead, somewhere beyond the blanket of darkness.

And then the sounds fell silent.

Sylas froze. He felt Simia's hand around his arm again, holding him back.

Then there was another sound. Not like before but a hiss, followed by another.

Simia's hand relaxed a little.

Another hiss.

Suddenly and to Sylas's astonishment, Simia squeezed past him.

She paused for a moment, then in a husky voice she called out. "Suhl!"

Her voice rang down the tunnel. After the quiet of the past minutes it seemed far, far too loud. Recklessly, stupidly loud.

For what seemed an age they listened to it disappear into the labyrinth.

And then it came back.

"Suhl!"

They both started. It was not Simia's voice but a male one, deep and strong.

Simia edged forward and Sylas followed, a step or two behind.

They were there now, at the junction with the other tunnel. Sylas could feel the change in the squalid, heavy air — in the way the sound of their footsteps echoed off the walls.

264

Simia put a hand on Sylas's chest, then she turned back towards the unknown voice.

"Who knows the way to the light?" she asked.

Sylas was still wondering what this meant when the answer came.

"Merimaat," said the voice. Then it added: "How does she lead us?"

"With a withered hand," said Simia quickly. "What is her name?"

"Truth," said the voice. There was a brief silence. "What myth is no myth at all?"

Simia seemed surprised by this. For a moment she was quiet, then she said, "The Glimmer Myth?"

The male voice grunted: apparently this was the right answer but he seemed unimpressed. "And who is come to us?" he asked.

Again Simia hesitated.

"Who is come to us?" asked the voice, louder this time. "From the Other?"

This seemed to have taken Simia off guard. She began to murmur something, then seemed to change her mind. Finally she said: "The boy."

"His *name*!" insisted the voice.

Simia cleared her throat. "Sylas. Sylas Tate."

There was a laugh from the darkness and the sound of shifting fabric, feet squelching on the bricks. "You had me worried for a moment!" said the voice, now more friendly. A hand patted Simia's shoulder, and then Sylas's.

"The name's Takk and this is my daughter, Faysa."

"Hello," said a young female voice.

"Hi, I'm Simia." She paused and squeezed Sylas's arm. "And this is Ash."

Takk grunted. "I'd say it's a pleasure to meet you, but nothing's a pleasure down here. Where are you headed?"

"Just trying to get into the city — past the checkpoints," said Simia.

"Aren't we all!" said Takk, seeming amused. "We have three bags of dried meat and a whole bunch of letters the Tythish would love to get their hands on. What are you bringing in?"

"More letters," said Simia. "From the valley."

"From the *valley*?" The voice had a new tone of respect. "They'll go down a treat in the slums!"

"I hope so. It's taken us a week to get here."

"Not surprised. Strange times... evil times. More vermin around than I've ever seen before. Ghor, Ghorhund, Slithen, Tythish... others too. They say the birthing chambers have never been busier. And it's not just here in Gheroth — we were in Setgur before and it was just the same. Whatever's going on, it's happening right across the empire."

"Dad," whispered the girl, "we shouldn't be talking so much! Can't we just go? I hate it down here."

"Yes, Faysa, yes, you're right," said Takk. "We shouldn't tarry any longer than we need to. Slithen everywhere." He paused and then asked: "Do you want to walk with us? I know a way out not too far from here."

"Thanks," said Simia, needing no encouragement. "I think I may have got us a little lost."

Takk had already started off up the passage. "You don't want to get lost, not in these tunnels. And watch your footing. It's not just sewage you have to watch out for these days."

"Really?" asked Sylas, compelled to break his silence. "What... else is there?"

Takk grunted in distaste. "The Black. It's coming up everywhere.

We don't know where it's coming from, but it's there, all mixed in with the sewage. And once you get that stuff on you... well, it's horrible stuff. Horrible."

With that, he and his daughter marched on, leaving Sylas and Simia staring into the blackness at their feet, shuddering as they thought of the number of times they had nearly let a foot slip into the sewage. They hoisted their bags on their shoulders and set off in pursuit.

33

Before The Storm

"With canvas set and banners high,
Ten thousand souls prepared to die;
And with their sighs and songs forlorn
Held close the calm before the storm*."*

THOTH HUNCHED LOW OVER the cello, his hood hanging just inches above the fingerboard, his bony body almost in a crouch. He held the bow loosely at his side, its tip resting on the floor, an emaciated finger tapping a slow rhythm on the handle.

But that was the only movement, the only sound. All else in the Apex Chamber was silent and still. The two imperial guards at Thoth's sides did not speak, nor shift, nor breathe. The pool of Black glistened mirror-smooth before them. Two vast tapestries on the adjacent walls hung flat and limp in the stagnant air. Even the clock was quiet, its catches and cogs moving in curious silence.

All was a hush. There was only that finger, tapping out the final seconds, measuring out the calm before that greatest of storms.

And then the finger stopped its tapping. Thoth lifted the bow and placed it on the strings. The very air seemed to leave the chamber.

Then the clock chimed.

Instantly Thoth swept his arm back and the cello groaned into life, breathing out the first haunting notes of Elgar. He rocked in his seat, his wasted body rolling with the building melody, his spindly fingers dancing over the fingerboard. And as the music reverberated around the chamber, the pool rippled in response. With the swell of the tune, the Black erupted upwards, growing into a hideous form with snout and stoop, claw and tooth. Even as the dripping oily mass turned into a giant canine beast, it lifted its muzzle and opened its mouth as if to speak. Black tongue rasped and black throat hacked, but they produced no sound to disturb Thoth's tragic melody. The creature made a silent speech, then bowed.

Thoth inclined his hooded head in response, then murmured something to the Ghor guards. At once they snapped to attention, then each strode to one of the two tapestries. They caught up a bronze pin from a table at their side, then spent some moments searching for a specific place on the complex design before them. Each was a colossal map of a world, complete with continents and oceans, rivers and seas. The two were identical but for the thin twines of silver, dividing the great sweeps of land into kingdoms and nations. In these, they were utterly different.

The guards traced their claws across embroidered coastlines and close-stitched rivers, over the threads of mountain ranges and the gilded braids of seas. And then they found their mark. The first lifted its bronze pin and fixed it to a coastal town labelled 'Tastintrice'. The second, to a town in exactly the same place on the same coast in another world. It was marked 'Hamburg'.

Thoth continued to play, stridently now, swaying with the music. Before him the Black was in motion too, creating a new form, a human form. It quickly took the shape of a woman decked

269

in a black headdress, liquid black robes and dripping black jewels. She too made a silent speech and then a deep, ceremonial bow.

Without pausing, Thoth inclined his head in reply. Then he lifted his shaded eyes.

"Fisslak legions to Carnac, Brittany," he said in a thousand voices.

Instantly the two guards reached for another pin and began their search. The first made its way quickly to a large peninsula near to the centre of the map and sank its pin into a town called Fisslak. The second found the same peninsula on the other map and set its pin in a region called Brittany, next to the larger label 'France'.

By the time they turned, another form had risen from the Black: a bullish beast with the crest of an imperial general. Hardly had it reached its full height before it began to speak with a silent, forked tongue, which dripped oily Black as it spoke. Even as it gave its report, another, human form was growing at its side and, as it finished its speech and sank back into the Black, a further Ghor head rose from the smooth surface. Soon figures were rising and slipping away two and three at a time, each taking its bow and then delivering its message.

All the while Thoth stooped over his cello, sweeping the bow back and forth, conjuring a mounting swell of sound: a mournful, poignant melody, composed by a master from another world. Every few bars, with the ebb of the music, he inclined his head and spoke.

"Finistander raiders to Warsaw…" he said in a swell of voices.

"…Krak company to Hong Kong…"

"…Fuska guard to Moscow…"

"…Reserve Imperial Troops to New York…"

The two Ghor guards were in constant motion now, searching

the maps, finding the labels that marked the points of passing in each of two worlds, taking a moment to check that they had each found exactly the same point on the map.

Only then would they set their pin.

And so they plotted the charts of war. Pin after pin after pin.

S

Takk seemed to know exactly where he was going. He took many turns, branching off at junctions and making his way with ease down the twisting tunnels. He hesitated occasionally, often to wait for his companions, but also to listen. Each time he resumed his march without saying a word.

At one point they came to a particularly spacious tunnel that was standing height, which came as a relief to backs and necks. Simia took the opportunity to break the silence. "So you know about him?" she said in a loud whisper. "About Sylas Tate?"

Takk laughed. "Everyone's heard of Sylas Tate!"

"Yeah, of course," said Simia quickly. "But no one knows much, do they? No one seems to have actually *seen* him."

"No, they haven't. But I tell you what, the Swillers and Luggers up at the Dirgheon saw what he did," said Takk, pausing in the passage. "Not that night, but they had to clear up the mess the next day and they'd never seen anything like it. There was a huge fire right in one of the halls, slam bang in the middle of the Dirgheon. They said those imperial guards — and the Magrumen — AND the Dirgh himself — none of them knew what hit 'em! They're trying to say now that it was a lightning strike. Hogwash — it was Sylas Tate! They reckon he and his friends killed Scarpia and maybe one of the others. I reckon they'd have finished the Dirgh if he hadn't thrown all he had at 'em!"

"Really?" said Simia, sounding appropriately excited.

"Yeah, and that isn't all! They say this boy proves that the Glimmer Myth is true. They say he's the one—"

"*Dad!*" hissed Faysa somewhere in the blackness. "You're *talking* again!"

There was a brief silence. "You're right, Fay," he said. "Let's keep moving." He cleared his throat. "We can talk later."

He turned and headed off up the passageway.

Sylas followed in a daze. It was weird to hear himself described as some sort of hero, and yet in the same moment he felt a little pride. He had hardly had a chance to think of everything that had happened in the Dirgheon, but now as he walked through the dark, he found himself remembering the great lattice of fire that he and Naeo had conjured, the excitement he had felt, the togetherness, the power.

The tunnel became narrower and lower, the ceiling trailing long sinews of slime that soon drenched their clothes. They were forced to stoop even lower until the reek of the sewage filled their mouths and nostrils and made their eyes stream. Then, just as it started to be unbearable, Sylas thought he saw a faint glow ahead. Then he was sure: there in the distance was a pale stream of light from somewhere above. For the first time he could see the silhouettes of his companions — the tall, wiry Takk leading the way with bags over each shoulder; the tiny form of Faysa at his heels, labouring under a single, oversized sack; and Simia, picking her way nimbly behind them. As they drew nearer, Sylas noticed a welcome change in the air, which became fresher and more breathable with every step.

Then Takk stopped dead in his tracks. "Shhh!"

His sharp hiss echoed off into the blackness.

They crouched and held their breath.

For a moment Sylas thought it was another false alarm, but

then he heard the unmistakable *gloop* of something moving through the sewage behind them. Something large. Then he heard a loud *slop*. Then somewhere nearer, a splash.

Takk dropped his bags, letting them roll into the sewage.

"Run!" he shouted. He lunged for Faysa and hurled her sack to one side then pulled her roughly down the passageway. He glanced back. "I said, RUN!"

Sylas and Simia threw themselves forward, scrambling down the tunnel as fast as they dared. But their thoughts were behind them, in the dark. With the sloshes and splashes and slaps. The sounds of not one but many bodies swimming through the ooze — the sounds of Slithen on the hunt.

He could see the way out now — a timber ladder at a junction in the sewer, with a tunnel on either side. Takk was already there, hoisting Faysa over to the ladder and then launching her into the air. For a moment she flailed hopelessly, but then she grasped the rungs and scrambled quickly out of sight. Her father turned then, revealing for the first time his drawn, pale face, his patch over one eye, his shock of red hair. He beckoned furiously to Sylas and Simia, and then his gaze travelled past them into the shadows. His one eye widened and for an instant he hesitated, then he turned and hurried up the ladder.

"Run faster!" he screamed over his shoulder.

Sylas felt prickles down his back. He watched Simia scrambling down the last part of the tunnel and leaping across the channel to the ladder. She started her climb but only a few rungs up, she turned back.

Her eyes went first to Sylas, then beyond him, into the tunnel. She went rigid, her features taut with fear.

"No! Sylas!" she cried.

"Go!"

She shook her head.

"GO!" he screamed.

For a moment she seemed paralysed, but then she pressed her eyes closed and heaved herself up towards the light.

In the same instant Sylas was there, leaping across the channel of sewage to the ladder. But instead of scurrying up it, he paused, turning just for a second to look back down the tunnel.

The Slithen were just yards away, filling the narrow passage, slithering one upon the other as a single mass of pale grey limbs and reptilian scales. Glassy eyes and tooth-riddled mouths gaped, snapping at their prize; slippery limbs flapped and writhed, scrambling through the ooze, straining to be the first to grasp a human neck.

There was no time.

It was too late to run.

34

Time

"When it begins, our greatest enemy will be time *itself."*

No TIME.

No time for Simia to finish her climb, no time for Sylas to begin his.

He felt the stones vibrating beneath his feet as the Slithen hurled one another against the walls in their thirst for blood. He saw pink, slavering mouths and tongues slapping and trilling with excitement. He heard squeals of triumph.

There was no time. No hope of escape.

Was this really it? Was this how it was all to end, here, in the sewers of Gheroth? How could that be, after everything he had been through?

He pressed himself back against the ladder and forced himself to concentrate, to remove himself from the moment and turn inwards.

There, he found the things that Takk had said: the memories he had brought back. He found that feeling of being at Naeo's shoulder, standing their ground with a carpet of fire above and the winds at their backs. He remembered what was possible.

And as he watched the Slithen close those final yards, he knew exactly what he had to do.

He squared his shoulders, raised his arms and pressed his eyes shut.

His mind reached out into the dark, into the tunnels left and right, wide and far, into the deep, dark silence of the sewers. He saw a swamp of fetid filth and evil sludge, filled with everything the world would like to forget, filled with slime and scum and froth. But in his belly and his bones he felt the waters that bound these things: the cool and quiet flood that ran beneath the city in a thousand creeks and rivulets.

He knew these waters. He knew them from the Aquium in the Meander Mill and from the river that had borne him away. He knew what they had done for him then, that they were open to him. That they were waiting for him.

And so he drew them in, heaving them into his chest like his very own breath.

And then he exhaled.

They came with a thunder and howl that made the passageways bellow like giant horns of war. They came as a screaming fury of water and waste, spiralling and swirling, twisting and foaming until they crashed into just two tunnels: the tunnels at Sylas's sides.

It was the winds that hit the Slithen first – the foul, stale air of the sewers that rushed ahead of the waters in a mounting hurricane. These alone stopped the creatures in their tracks and sent many somersaulting backwards into the darkness. The rest stared with wide, black eyes, their faces contorted with fear. The twin torrents flew past Sylas and clashed with an almighty thump, tearing off towards the Slithen, devouring all that lay in their path.

Sylas opened his eyes and threw his hands forward, guiding

the deluge, keeping it from his own tiny refuge. All he could see was a passing blur, but he still knew it, controlled it. If the Black was there, it was held by the mighty tide, turning in the same twisting current. And then, slowly, Sylas turned one shoulder, let one arm drift back to grasp a rung. He slid his toe on to the lowest step and pushed himself up, leaving his free arm outstretched a moment longer. Then suddenly he was climbing, rung after rung, scrambling up towards the light. The great flood closed in beneath him, swamping the little recess, surging up into the shaft. But Sylas was well ahead, clattering up the ladder. He was almost there. The air smelled sweet and pure, the light poured down on his shoulders, the roar of the waters began to fall away.

But then he saw Simia.

She was trying to pull herself through a broken grille at the top of the shaft but her coat was caught: skewered on one of the iron rods. She pulled and twisted but her trusty coat would not give way. She looked down, screaming something at him but he could not hear.

The waters below him were wild now, untamed, forming giant plumes of froth and foam. With his hands on the ladder, he was powerless to stop them, and so he scrambled on up the ladder until he was at Simia's feet. He heard her sobbing as she fought to free her coat, kicking at the bar.

"Sylas, I can't..." she gasped. "I can't... get it... loose!"

And then she stopped. He looked up and saw a wiry figure silhouetted against the light, two strong arms reaching down, taking Simia's hands, heaving her up. And as she squirmed to safety, Sylas watched the buttons of her coat shear away, falling past him and down into the torrent. And then came the coat itself, torn and limp, fluttering down the shaft before he had a chance to reach out. For a moment it rode the maelstrom — her beloved coat, her father's coat — dancing on the crowns of foam. And then it was consumed.

Sylas watched this until he heard Simia's scream from above. Only then did he see how close the waters were: three rungs below. Then two. He turned and threw himself up the final steps, heaving himself through the grille and then finally, over the rim into the world of light. He lay there on his back, panting, staring up at the darkening sky, which in that moment seemed like a glimpse of heaven.

He pushed himself up on his elbows and saw that he was in a deserted back alley, fringed by ramshackle timber dwellings. His companions were sitting with their backs up against a disused wall: Simia with her arms around her knees, staring at the dirt; Takk and Faysa huddled close to one another, holding thin hands. They were staring at him, clearly bewildered, mouths a little open, faces slack and white.

Faysa swallowed and murmured: "You're... him!"

"You are, aren't you?" said Takk. He blew a low whistle. "You're Sylas Tate!"

Sylas glanced nervously up and down the lane, then he nodded.

Takk brushed down his coat and rose slowly to his feet, his one eye never leaving Sylas. He walked over and held out his hand.

"I'm... honoured," he said.

Sylas laughed. "The honour's all mine," he said, shaking Takk's hand. "You saved us down there."

"And you saved us all!" said Takk, shaking his hand ever more vigorously. "How did you... how did you *do* that?"

"I don't really know," said Sylas with a smile. "I don't understand it myself..." He trailed off as his eyes drifted over to Simia and found her staring up at him. She looked exhausted, her expression empty and sad, her shoulders trembling a little in the cold.

He started unbuttoning his coat. "Here," he said, "you need to keep—"

"I don't want it," said Simia sharply. Then she softened her voice. "I mean, thanks, I'm fine." She climbed wearily to her feet. "Come on, we should be going."

"But won't you come with us to the slums?" asked Takk, obviously disappointed. "People there would love to see you. And we can give you a good square meal! We may be a bit short of dried meat, eh, Faysa, but we can still put on a decent—"

"No, thank you," said Sylas, still looking at Simia. "Simsi's right, we need to keep moving."

"Well, at least let us help you. Where are you going?"

Simia shook her head. "We shouldn't say."

Sylas looked at Simia for a moment, as if deciding something, then turned to Takk. "We're going to see Isia," he said quietly.

Takk's mouth fell open and then his narrow face broke into a smile. "Of course you are!" he said, with a chuckle. "Of course you are!" He tapped the side of his nose. "Don't worry, your secret is safe with us!"

"I know," said Sylas, smiling as he reached down for his bag. He felt around in the dirt for a moment before hoisting it on to his shoulder. As his fingers brushed his neck, he noticed that they were cool and oily. He glanced at them and saw a trace of black slime across his fingertips. He scowled and wiped them on his coat.

"Was that stuff black? On your fingers?" asked Takk, looking alarmed.

"Yeah, but it's gone, look," said Sylas, showing him.

Takk peered at them closely with his good eye and grunted.

He reached for his belt, unhooking his water bottle. "They should be all right," he said, washing Sylas's fingers, then returning the bottle to his belt, "but wash them again when you get the chance. Can't be too careful with the Black."

"Come on, we need to go," said Simia, who had already started up the lane, calling over her shoulder, "thanks."

And then she was gone, walking swiftly away.

Sylas turned to Takk. "Sorry. It's the coat — it was her dad's."

"No need to explain," said Takk, watching her go. "We all know what it's like to lose what's important." He clapped him on the shoulder. "It looks like you'd better be going. Good luck!"

Sylas nodded his farewell to them both, then he ran after Simia.

When he reached her, she was standing at the end of the lane, gazing past him, watching Takk and Faysa gathering their things. They took one last look into the grille of the sewer, talking excitedly, then wandered off between two timber houses. Before they were out of sight, Faysa took her father's hand. He lifted it up and pressed it to his lips.

"It's not fair," said Simia in a small, flat voice. "None of this is fair." She was trembling in the cold.

"I know, Simsi," he said. Then, putting an arm round her shoulder, he said: "Come on. Let's do this."

35
The Place of Tongues

"What enchantment attends this Place of Tongues, where thoughts and dreams are borne up like leaves upon the wind?"

NAEO STIRRED IN HER sleep. For a moment it felt like she might escape that darkness of lonely cells and dank corridors and half-seen monsters: that darkness of the Dirgheon. She felt like she was rising to the surface, drifting up through layers of murk to a distant light. She could see grey somewhere above — a wide, cloud-covered sky — and for a moment she was filled with hope: hope that she might wake, that the nightmare might be over.

And then came the Black.

Like before it shifted under her skin, making her want to scream. But this was worse. It fogged her mind like it had in those first days, rising in plumes of nothingness until her thoughts had no space, until she felt she was losing herself. And in the same moment, the pain surged up her spine, scything up and up, spanning her shoulders. This time it did not stop. It climbed until it reached the nape of her neck, then turned like a twisting dagger and planted itself deep in her flesh.

She jolted in her sleep, pressing herself back into the car seat, trying to ease the pain. And then, even in the shades of her dream, even through the fog of the Black, she prayed to Isia for help.

Sylas winced. He cocked his head to one side and rubbed his neck. That seemed to help the pain a little, but it still felt strange, as though something was shifting under his skin, plucking at his nerves. He rubbed it again, and then forced himself to leave it alone. Right now there were more important things to worry about.

They were at the centre of a broad street beset by rattles and clatters, shouts and rumbles — all the life and chaos of the city. Ox-drawn carts, pack horses and carriages whisked by, churning up the muddy street while an endless throng of people rushed to and fro, making their way between shops and taverns and market stalls.

"Not far now," Simia said, pressing on.

Sylas wandered after her through the crowd. He felt completely unprepared to reach the temple... his mind was still in the darkness of the sewer. He could still smell the stench on his clothes, see the Slithen writhing through the tunnel, feel the foul waters coursing through his body.

And then he felt it again, something rippling just beneath his skin — a sharp, shooting pain through his neck. But there was something else too: a numbness and fogginess that crept up the side of his face, through his skull, into his thoughts until his mind began to drift, as though it was no longer his own.

Suddenly something slammed into him from behind.

"Out of the way, numbskull!" growled a bearded trader on horseback, sliding his boot back into its stirrup. "You'll get yourself killed!"

Sylas lowered his eyes and hurried away. What had he been

thinking? Standing stock-still in the middle of a street? How stupid could he be? When he caught up with Simia, she was standing with her arms crossed looking distinctly unimpressed.

"Gawping again!" she whispered. "I thought you were over that?"

"I thought so too," snapped Sylas, still angry at himself. "It's just my neck —" he started rubbing below his chin — "it feels really.... weird."

Suddenly he stopped. Simia's eyes were fixed on his neck and her mouth had fallen open. "What... is it, Simsi?"

"Your neck," she said. "Did you touch it? When you had the Black on your fingers?"

Sylas shook his head and was about to say no when he remembered that brief, slight sensation of wetness as he had lifted his bag. He felt his gut tighten.

"I... might have done. What *is* it, Simsi?"

Simia seemed to struggle to find the words, then she said: "You have it on your neck... like a spider." She looked back up to his eyes. "It wasn't there back in the lane. It must have grown since then."

Sylas touched it again and for the first time he felt a slight rise, like a vein beneath his skin. "How bad is it?"

"Well it's not good," said Simia. There was a softness in her voice.

Sylas did not like that softness. He saw it in her eyes too and that frightened him. "Well... I guess I can't do anything about it now. Not until we get to the temple." He hesitated, trying not to panic. "Can I?"

Simia drew her eyes away from his neck. "I don't know. I suppose not." She turned and took a quick look down a lane at her side. "Come on, it's this way."

She led him down the shadowy lane crammed with traders behind carts and stalls, all of them selling what looked like necklaces threaded with symbols of wood and bone. They navigated all the bother and bustle with ease and quickly reached the far end, where Simia finally slowed to a halt, looked around her and stepped into the shade of a porch.

"What are you doing?" Sylas asked, pushing in next to her.

"I'm letting you gawp without being conspicuous." She nodded back over his shoulder. "You'd better take a look."

Sylas felt a tingle down his spine and turned slowly, following her gaze.

Ahead of him, through a grand opening at the end of the lane was a huge expanse of pristine white marble flooring, so pure and bright that he had to squint. The stone was smooth and polished so that it showed the reflection of all who walked on it: a faint, shimmering double beneath their feet. But most were not on their feet at all. In the centre of the vast square of white stone, hundreds if not thousands of people knelt, all of them facing in the same direction, bowed over so that their foreheads rested on the cool marble. None of them stirred — they were entirely still except for their hands, which moved feverishly over strings of symbols, turning them through their fingers. These were the necklaces the traders had been selling in the lane — not necklaces at all, but some kind of beads, aiding the worshippers in their prayer.

The square was utterly silent except for the ebb and flow of thousands of hushed voices, whispering a jumble of millions of words, which merged to create an incessant murmur and hiss. The effect was entrancing.

"Is all this for Isia?" he asked.

Simia nodded. "This is the Place of Tongues. They come here to worship her."

His gaze drifted over the thousands of hunched backs and he wondered at the devotion of the congregation: young and old, wealthy and poor united in their adoration. At the far side of this murmuring sea, he saw the frontage of many buildings, all with their strange pyramidal roofs. And then his eyes were drawn upwards. There, above dark trails of city smoke, he saw the tower.

It was colossal, spanning the width of four or five buildings, and when he looked up his eyes followed the perfectly smooth, tapering sides until his neck craned and his back arched. It seemed to reach almost to the clouds, looming over the city.

Simia's whisper joined the thousands of others: "The Temple of Isia!"

He had seen the temple before, but only from a distance. The effect up close was breathtaking. The only breaks in the slick white surface were a series of ribs that ran vertically along its full length until, at the very top, they broadened like the branches of a gigantic tree and sprouted outwards to form great stone supports. These bore a gigantic circular platform, into which was carved a disorderly collection of human figures in poses he could not quite make out, gathered around a tangled mass of symbols and shapes. Even at this distance, he could see that there was something strange and disturbing about the figures — something that was at first difficult to see but which slowly became clear. None of them had faces. In every other way they were lifelike recreations of the human form, but where their faces should have been there was only featureless stone.

Some distance above the first massive stone terrace was another, even larger platform that loomed over the one below, as if to shelter it from the elements. It too was carved with entwined, faceless human figures. It was only here in the shaded edifice between these two platforms that he could see any openings: wide arches showing a core of impenetrable blackness.

He felt a thrill of excitement. Just beyond those arches might be the answers he had been searching for.

"So we just walk up and knock?" said Simia.

Sylas blew out his cheeks. "Well, you heard what Paiscion said when we were in Merimaat's retreat. He said she would know we were coming. That all we should need to do is ask for her."

"Yes, I remember," she said, doubtfully.

"'The Priestesses will know what to do' — that's exactly what he said."

Simia gazed across the square and shook her head. "Seems a little... easy, doesn't it?"

Sylas bit his lip, then he stepped out from the porch. "Come on, we won't know until we try."

They started out into the throng of people and walked around the crowd of worshippers, the whispers becoming louder and louder as they drew close. Soon all they could hear was the hiss of hushed voices, the words merging to form an impenetrable wall of sound, a great gale of words. They made no sense to Sylas but the sound was exciting and magical — an intoxicating murmur of hopes and dreams. But he forced himself to keep his eyes ahead and walk on, making his way as calmly as he could through the praying figures.

Suddenly Simia faltered. She took another couple of steps and then glanced at Sylas.

He followed her eyes towards the base of the great tower and all the air left his lungs.

He could not see the tower because it was surrounded by a wall of scales and gristle and muscle. Scores of gargantuan beasts stood shoulder to shoulder, showing barely a chink of whatever lay beyond. They had all the order and discipline of soldiers, but their appearance was anything but human. Their pale yellow complexion was not skin at all but scales like those of the Slithen, shimmering in the white light of the square. But if they were cousins of the Slithen, their scales were the only sign of it. These were beasts of the land not the waves. They had massive thighs, thick and taut; gigantic, broad shoulders rippling with muscle; and feet and hands that were wide and clawed, tipped with dreadful talons. Their giant heads hung low between their shoulders with a thick-set skull, flaring nostrils and, most striking of all, mighty horns that swept back and then curled down so that the cruel points jutted forward, in line with their dripping snouts.

There was something unnerving about their half-bull, half-reptilian eyes. Like those of the Ghor, they were sharp and intelligent: alert to all the comings and goings of the square.

Sylas drew close to Simia. "They weren't supposed to be there."

She was still staring in disbelief. "They're not supposed to exist at all."

"What *are* they?"

"I've... I've only read about them — in stories about the ancient wars. They were known as Ra'ptahs in the old language, but people had another name for them." She turned to him. "They called them *Ragers*."

"OK..." he said, shifting uncomfortably. "Why's that?"

Simia blinked coolly. "Why do you *think*? They say Thoth made them that way: cunning, strong and full to the horn-tips with—"

"Rage," said Sylas, running his hand through his hair, looking at the mass of terrifying beasts. "OK, so that's good."

36

Ragers

"Ragers are surely fed by hell's own fire. To see their fury is to look into the blazing eyes of Lucifer himself."

SYLAS SQUINTED ACROSS THE square, trying to see a way past. It was hopeless. The cordon of Ragers was so tight that there was no sign of the doorway Paiscion had described, nor the initiate priestesses that he had said would be seated around its entrance. He searched his memory for anything else the Magruman had told him — some hint of another way in, something about the building, Isia, *anything*, but Paiscion had not foreseen this. They had only one plan and this had been it.

"Thoth must have thought we'd try to come," said Simia. "But the *Ragers*... where did *they* come from? And why now?"

"You know why, Simsi. Remember what Triste saw. Thoth isn't just getting ready for us. We're part of it, yes, but he's thinking bigger... much bigger."

"It's real, isn't it?," said Simia, gazing at the creatures. "Everything Triste saw is really happening."

Suddenly there was a commotion across the plaza. One of the traders selling the strange strings of beads had been sidling past the assembled Ragers in an attempt to reach some worshippers, when one of the beasts, irritated by his boldness, growled ominously. Instantly the trader backed away, dropping his stock. Now he was reaching down, frantically gathering up the beads, holding some of them up towards the Rager as an offering – or perhaps he was just trying to put something between him and it. Who could blame him – the beast panted and snorted with inexplicable fury, seeming to swell in size, its chest expanding, its huge shoulders drawing back, and all the while its scaly form changing colour from yellow to pink to a bright, livid red. And suddenly there it was, true to its name: a Rager. There was a movement behind it and something lashed the air – something long and muscular. The tail flew so quickly that it was almost a blur, leaving only the briefest impression of two rows of barbs along its length and a pointed tip.

The Rager stormed forward now, blasting forth a vicious animal snarl, snorting two clouds of vapour from its nostrils as its forked tongue slapped against its wide jaws. It grasped the poor hawker around the neck, hoisting him high into the air for all to see.

The whispers of worship suddenly lulled. Thousands of heads lifted from the stone, but no one did anything: they just looked on as though it were a familiar scene. And then, with a sharp crack of that massive tail, the poor trader was sent spinning across the polished stone, cast aside like so much litter. The beast turned its bulky form and rejoined its ranks, welcomed by a chorus of grunts and the slap of tails against stone. When the hawker came to rest, his body was motionless.

Sylas drew his eyes back to Simia. He saw his own horror written on her face. And there was something else – something he had not seen in Simia before. She looked small. She looked broken. She was no longer holding herself as she always had — shoulders back, head up, taking more space than was possible for such a small person. Her shoulders were slumped and already she was taking small backward steps.

"We'll have to go back," she said. "Find another way in." Her features were clouded and confused.

Without thinking, Sylas took hold of her sleeve. "Come on," he said, pulling her forward.

Simia pulled away. "What are you doing? Let go!"

"We can't just give up now!"

"This isn't giving up, it's staying alive!" hissed Simia. "Nothing's gone to plan! The river, the Kraven, Triste — he's still out there on the Barrens, you know!" Her eyes began to well with tears. "Then there were the Tythish, the sewers, the Slithen and the Black! And now this!"

"But we got through all those."

"You haven't seen the state of your neck! And look at those things, Sylas." She nodded past him to the Ragers. "How are we going to get past *them*? And before you even think of Essenfayle, it's no use. Not with all these people around — and anyway, there isn't anything natural in this hellhole!"

Sylas filled his lungs and put his hands on his hips. He looked from Simia to the cordon of Ragers to the Temple rising above.

"All I know is we haven't come all this way for nothing," he said, grasping her hand. "People are depending on us. There has to be a way through and we just have to find it."

He turned directly towards the line of Ragers and pulled Simia behind him. She struggled at first, cursing. And then, after a few steps, she stopped resisting, as though she did not even have the strength to fight.

They skirted the last of the worshippers and set out over the open plaza, cast adrift in the great sea of white. They were alone now — there for all to see.

The Ragers spied them instantly. They tensed, drawing close, their giant heads following the motion of the pair as they approached. Their forked tongues sniffed the air, their tails squirmed on the flagstones.

Sylas's mind raced. What was he going to do? Fight them? What was he thinking?

But whatever he did he couldn't hesitate. Not now.

Suddenly there was an ear-splitting sound — something between a squeal and a roar. The largest of all the Ragers stomped forward, lowering its horns to reveal a distinctive red crest on the back of its neck, made of sword-like scales. It pounded the stone, its nostrils blasting clouds of vapour, its giant body a seething red.

Simia pulled against Sylas but he kept going.

"Don't show it you're afraid," he said, acting on instinct. "Keep walking. Look it in the eye!"

Simia snatched her arm away. "You're an expert now, are you?"

"No," said Sylas. "But I know this. I don't know why, but this is right! Trust me!"

She shook her head, bewildered and frightened. She gazed at him quizzically for a moment, then wiped her tears on her sleeve. Suddenly she was at his shoulder. He saw her head lift.

"You'd better be right," she muttered.

Now two more Ragers had lunged forward, their gigantic feet pummelling the stone, making it tremble. Their claws scoured the surface as they threatened to charge.

"Keep walking!" said Sylas, his heart hammering. He was surprised by the calm in his voice — the sureness of his step.

They were looking directly into the Ragers' eyes now, past the bloodshot fringes and into the deep, furious blackness.

291

And then they came. The crested leader squealed and snorted then all three of the massive beasts hurled themselves forward into a charge. The stone shuddered and across the square the crowd fell quiet, watching a new drama unfold.

For a moment, everything was noise and fury and motion. The leader was almost upon them.

"Now!" cried Sylas, pulling on Simia's sleeve. "Kneel!"

He dragged her down on to the stone. They hunched forward like the thousands of worshippers behind them, their heads and palms resting on the flagstones, their eyes pressed shut. They could hear the cry of the Ragers, feel the tremor of their charge, but they stayed down, motionless.

Sylas stopped breathing. His mind went blank.

And then something strange happened. Everything around him disappeared. There were no Ragers and there was no stone, there was no noise, there was no fear. His thoughts fell away too, and in their place his mind was filled with darkness. From that darkness he heard a hum and rumble. And then there were distant voices, cloudy and indistinct, with a tide of darkness that ebbed and flowed, as if his mind was on the edge of sleep. He felt warm. He felt safe.

His lips parted. "Believe," he said.

Naeo stirred again. The pain had eased, giving her some moments of reprieve, a space in which to sleep. And in that new and deeper sleep the darkness of her nightmare had long since been replaced by a dreary grey, which had then bloomed into a stark white light. A white that made her wince and set her nerves on edge.

Still she slept, resting her mind against the clean light.

And then something jarred, pounding the edges of her sleep — a thundering whiteness, a whiteness that charged towards her, that consumed her. And then, from the calamitous white, came angry, flaring nostrils and blackened eyes. And somewhere at the fringes of her mind she felt the piercing tips of curling horns and the pounding beat of giant limbs.

And she knew these things.

She knew the bullish huff and squeal that sounded in a far-flung thought. She knew the cool, hard scales that brushed up against her mind.

She knew them from the dark days.

From the Dirgheon.

Ragers.

She knew them, and she knew what must be done. Suddenly she was pushing against the white, throwing back the clouds of her dreams and searching deep for the voice she knew was there.

She opened her mouth and her lungs and let out a silent yell.

Mr Zhi watched her sleeping face twitch and wince. "Even in peace there is peril," he said sadly.

Then her lips moved.

"Believe," she mumbled.

37

The Temple of Isia

*"If there is any hope in these four lands, it rests
with* The Temple of Isia *and the precious
personage closeted within their walls."*

SYLAS COULD HEAR THE pounding beat of giant limbs, the squeal and snort of nostrils, the clatter of claws on stone. Still he shrouded himself in the warmth, in the dullness that ebbed and flowed, lapping against his mind like a dream.

Then he felt a hot blast of breath on the back of his neck.

"Believe," he whispered, lifting his head.

He looked straight into the face of rage.

The Rager was even more horrifying up close: each limb larger than a full-grown man, rippling with muscle; the armoured scales burning with a living flame, which radiated a searing heat. But it was the eyes that halted the heart: rims as red and raw as fresh meat, glassy globes as empty and black as despair itself. In that moment it looked to Sylas like one of hell's own horde — a demon loosed from its halls of fire.

But he looked into those pits of despair and did not flinch. The Rager sent a blast of fiery breath into his face, spraying him with scalding mucous. Sylas wiped it away with his sleeve and kept his nerve. Its forked tongue flicked and probed around his face like a charmer's snake, and Sylas did not recoil. It huffed and grunted, then rocked back and slammed its front feet down on the stone, making the rock tremble. Still Sylas did not move.

But then he heard another grunt behind him and suddenly he felt two piercing points in his shoulder blades.

"What is your business here?"

The voice was gravelly and deep. The rapier points were parting the weave of his coat now, pressing into his flesh. He felt a surge of panic and an instinct to turn and run.

"We're here to worship," he said through his teeth.

There was an angry huff, but the pressure of the horns eased a little.

After a moment the Rager pressed again, harder this time, tearing Sylas's coat and pushing him forward on his hands.

"So why do you not pray with the others?"

Sylas grunted, his face twisting with pain. He felt cool air through the torn coat and a trickle of blood run down his back. He wanted to pull away, but instinctively he knew he mustn't show weakness. Instead he set his teeth and pushed against the horns, forcing himself upright.

The Rager seemed to retreat a little.

"Because..." he gasped. "Because we want... to show our devotion."

The Rager snorted. "Your devotion?" The horns retreated still further.

"To Isia," said Sylas, growing in confidence. "We've travelled a great distance. We want to pay homage. We want to offer ourselves to the temple."

He was aware of Simia rising from her crouch, casting her eyes up at the temple in rather overdone devotion.

The Ragers snuffled and grunted then conferred with one another in a language of hacking stops and snorts. Finally one of them spoke.

"*Where* have you come from?"

Sylas stiffened with panic. To him, this world was the valley, the Barrens and the city of Gheroth. He didn't know anywhere else.

"Llhay," said Simia. "We came from Llhay."

It had only been a moment's hesitation, but it had been enough. Sylas again felt the horns pushing into his shoulders, the full weight of that gigantic head throwing him on to his hands, pressing him into the stone, forcing the air from his lungs. He let out a cry of pain.

"What's happening there?"

It was a soft, feminine voice.

Immediately Sylas felt the horns slip away from his back. There was a shuffling of feet and a turning of bodies.

He pushed himself up and was surprised to see the Ragers bow down, lowering their horns to the stone.

A lone female figure approached them from the direction of the temple, her flowing white robes billowing in the wind. She measured out her step with a golden staff topped by two small circular plates, one above the other in the style of the platforms of the temple. Her appearance was at once beautiful and peculiar. She had pale, delicate features, emphasised by stark decorations: bold make-up around the eyes trailing to points at the sides of her face; heavy jewellery in blue, black and gold; and jet-black hair that had been plaited into braids and drawn forward over her shoulders. In her free hand she held a metallic loop. At first Sylas thought it was a set of keys, but then he saw that it was solid, and that below her hand the loop became three bars of a simple golden cross.

"I believe your instructions were *clear*," she said, her voice gentle but firm. "Worshippers are to be left alone."

"But, my lady, they were approaching the temple! In defiance of Thoth's decree!" growled the Rager behind Sylas, bowing down so that its proud red crest opened like a fan of blades next to Sylas's face.

The woman drew near and cast her pretty green eyes over the two children.

"Have they said *why* they were approaching the temple?"

The Rager huffed and snorted. "They claim they wish to offer themselves, but—"

"That is all you should need to hear," said the woman, growing in stature.

"But, my lady, there's something—"

The woman tapped her staff on the stone so that it chimed out a single, clear note, echoing from the walls of the surrounding buildings. A new hush fell over the worshippers. The Ragers fell prostrate on the floor, tails writhing, as though in agony.

"Do you wish to discuss this with Isia?" she asked sharply. "Or perhaps with the Dirgh?"

The Rager snuffled, then slid its head from side to side so that its crest rattled. "No, that won't be necessary," it grunted.

"Good," said the woman, with an innocent smile. She turned to Sylas and Simia and ran her eyes over their clothes. "Well, you two, if you wish to enter the temple you will first need to change." She sniffed. "And wash. Please come with me."

With that she tapped her staff on the stone so that the chime finally stopped, then turned and walked away, leaving everyone gazing after her.

§

Scarpia's limbs unfolded from the shadows, darting quickly and silently from the darkness of the lane and out on to the pavement.

The fur rose on the back of her neck as she hissed into the empty windows of The Shop of Things. The hiss became a growl as her mongrel eyes lifted to the blank nameplate lit by electric light, and then up to the crooked frontage of Gabblety Row. In an instant she had taken in the labyrinth of beams and drainpipes, cracks and protrusions. Already, she had plotted her course.

She leapt into the air, sinking her claws into the nearest beam while swiping another across the nameplate of the shop, leaving it scarred with three deep gashes. In moments she was up at the first-floor window, and there she lingered, clinging to the windowsill and peering into the darkness with her feline eye. She saw the circle of chairs, the hastily abandoned meal, the many shelves of books. And then she spotted one volume laid on a black oblong. On the cover was an intricate circular symbol depicted in sweeping arcs of black and white. She hissed and spat at the glass.

She continued her climb, slinking sideways as well as up, following the irregular criss-cross of beams down the full length of the terrace. She stopped only once, pressing herself against the jumbled brickwork as the whine and thrum of a helicopter passed over the town, but she was quickly on her way again. She rounded the corner opposite the Church of the Holy Trinity and arrived at the garret room at the very top. She purred quietly to herself, then curled her limbs around the struts that supported the overhanging window. Slowly, she raised her head and peered inside. Her cat's eye quickly spied the mattress on the floor, the old dresser in the corner, the kites on the walls.

In one motion she pulled herself up, threw open the window and slid inside.

Her eyes traced the walls hung with Sylas's squadron of kites, taking in the astonishing array of colours, the symbols, the runes he had crafted without knowing. She regarded them with loathing and flicked at them with her tail, smashing three of them into pieces with a single swipe.

Her eyes travelled on, moving over the neatly made mattress on the floor, the science book on the crooked shelf, the old dresser with a recently repaired fourth leg. And then she saw a photo, suspended above the trapdoor in the corner.

She took a step towards it.

"Sylas?" came a sharp, masculine voice through the trapdoor. "Sylas, is that you?"

Scarpia stopped and cocked her head to one side.

"It's your uncle, Sylas!" There was a brief silence, then the voice came again, louder, harsher: "Let me in! I've... I've been worried about you!"

Scarpia reached down and threw open the trapdoor. In the dark opening below she saw an extraordinarily narrow and gaunt face, the only substantial features of which were the rich plumes of eyebrows, which burst forth like explosions of hair.

Before Tobias Tate could react, she had reached down and grasped his sinewy neck in her claws. With superhuman strength she heaved him up out of the dark staircase, kicking the trapdoor shut after him.

He coughed and spluttered, flailing about with his gangly limbs and reaching for her wrist to try to pull it away. As his hands fell on the soft fur of her forearm, his face filled with new terror. His spectacled eyes widened behind the thick lenses as they passed over her half-human face. He kicked out at her, trying to get away, but in an instant she stepped nimbly to the side and slammed him into the wall, dislodging the picture of Sylas's mother. She caught it before it fell down the stairs.

"My dear Mr Tate, settle down," she purred. "I can see that

you are not a... *resilient* man. Tell me what I need to know and this will go better for you."

Tobias Tate ceased his struggle. This sounded like a deal and deals he could do.

Scarpia gave a fanged smile. "Where is Sylas's mother?" She held up the photo and raised her human eyebrow.

Tate frowned. He glanced around the room, seeing the forced window, the kites broken in the corner, then the picture of Sylas's mother clutched in this creature's claws. His accountant's mind whirred and tallied. It was a blunt tool for such a task, but even Tobias Tate knew that this was all very wrong. Very wrong indeed.

He adjusted his neck to speak. "What do you want with her?"

Scarpia blinked, considering her answer. "She has something I need," she said. "If she gives it to me, no harm will come to her."

Tate scrutinised her face, though with his spectacles halfway up his forehead that was not an easy task. His binary brain began to chunter. This was a problem. Not the kind that he liked – debits and credits, checks and balances. No, this was an altogether more *human* affair. The kind that he detested. How was he to decide anything with no ledger, no account, no tally of pros and cons?

And yet one word played through his accountant's mind again and again:

Risk.

Unacceptable *risk*.

And then something remarkable happened. He had a human thought.

What had all this to do with Sylas? Was *he* at risk? And was that risk something that he, his guardian, should foresee? And perhaps *avoid*?

These were the same questions that had plagued him in the

300

days after the regrettable incident with the letters from Winterfern Hospital — the letters that should never have been seen. He felt the now familiar complaint of something in the pit of his stomach — a pang that he suspected was something like guilt, though having had very little to do with emotions he could not be sure. Whatever it was, that same sensation had brought him up to Sylas's room more than once, and it had made him do such irrational things as look through Sylas's belongings with the care normally reserved for his own files and dockets. It had also made him tidy them carefully away — including the letters, which he had stacked carefully on Sylas's shelf. On the last visit, it had even made him fix the leg on the old dresser. He had mumbled and complained, though there was no one to hear, but at the end of it he had felt unexpectedly better.

Suddenly his calculation was complete. It was not one he would want audited, but he was certain it was correct.

"Why are you in Sylas's room?" he asked, swallowing hard so that his Adam's apple leapt over her claw. He fixed her with a pinprick stare. "Is he all right?"

Scarpia tightened her grip a little. "Now come, Mr Tate, we were getting on so well. Please don't ruin it with tiresome questions!"

Even while being strangled, Tobias Tate did not appreciate being told to shut up.

"I need to know that he is all right," he croaked. "Tell me first…"

Scarpia's grip tightened still further. His eyes bulged and, for once, his gaunt features flushed red. He held out for only a few seconds before he flapped his hands in the air in surrender.

She eased her grip a little to allow him to speak.

Tate gasped and panted but he looked her in the eye. Despite his giddiness, he was resolute. He drew from a deep reserve of spite — a reserve he had cultivated over many years — and turned it to one final heroic purpose.

"Go to hell, you mongrel minx!" He thrust his face into hers. "That boy and his mother are FAMILY, which I don't expect a mangy stray like you to understand! Why don't you get back to the cattery where you belong!"

Scarpia's eyes flared wide and her ears fell against her head. She snarled, revealing her long white fangs and tightened her grip again, relentlessly this time, crushing Tate's neck. For a moment he stared at her, almost seeming to enjoy her reaction, but slowly, inevitably, he started to lose consciousness.

As his mind fogged his guard fell away. His eyes drifted to one side, towards the shelf. Scarpia followed his glance to a stack of papers. To the letter on the top, the letter headed 'Clinical Report'. The letter marked with an address.

Suddenly, as though realising his mistake, Tobias Tate pressed his eyelids shut.

He did not fight in those final moments. He did not give her the satisfaction. When his body slumped lifelessly to the floor, there was a tranquil look on his face, like he had balanced the most difficult of accounts.

38
The Climb

"Our climb into the light will be slow and arduous.
Many will be broken along the way."

As the cordon of Ragers closed behind them, Sylas saw the base of the temple for the first time. It was as smooth and featureless as the rest of the structure, except for a wide stone staircase that led up to a small but ornate arch, also made of white stone. But even at the centre of the arch, there seemed to be nothing but more blank stone: no door, no keyhole, nothing.

"Who do you think she is?" he whispered, nodding to the woman in white robes as she led them up the steps.

"A priestess, I reckon," said Simia. She leaned into his ear. "How did you know what to do? In the square?"

Sylas shrugged. "I *didn't*," he murmured. "There just didn't seem to be anything else for it."

"Well, there was *run away*."

He thought for a moment. "I just knew we could do it. And that we mustn't look scared."

Simia shook her head. "Well just so you know, I think that Black's gone to your brain."

When they neared the top of the steps, the priestess was waiting for them. She raised the metal cross, touched it against the stone and instantly the centre of the arch sank back into the wall, making the grating, ringing sound of stone moving against stone. When it halted it left a deep depression. But still there was no opening.

The priestess turned and smiled.

"Welcome."

And with that she extended the golden staff and tapped the stone with the broad plate at its top. It rang a different note from the one they had heard in the square — a lower and deeper pitch. The depression sank back still further and then swung open like a door. It moved as though it were as light as a feather, revealing a shady interior.

They followed the priestess eagerly across the threshold, noticing how thick the walls were — thicker than Sylas was tall.

As they stepped inside, they slowed to a stop and gasped.

They were standing in a gigantic hollow structure — a massive cylinder of stone rising up and up until it disappeared entirely out of sight. The void was filled with the sun's rays, not travelling between mirrors as in the Meander Mill, but spiralling down from the far roof of the temple, descending in playful turns and swirls, forming a delightful weave.

The beams of sunlight revealed a kaleidoscope of marvels. From a point just above their heads, every part of the tower was alive with colour and form, seething with finely painted images of thousands of people in every attitude of life. There were farmers and hunters, paupers and princes, priests and warriors. There were scenes at sea and on misty mountaintops. There were battles and sieges, pageants and feasts, weddings and funerals. The shimmering light danced over it all, breathing life into face and feature, muscle and sinew. In these magical sunbeams, waves heaved, sails swelled, lovers wept and the vanquished breathed their final breath.

Sylas and Simia gaped in wonder, trying to take in its scale and majesty. Their senses overwhelmed, they turned their eyes to the void – following the path of the light as it cascaded past all the colour and drama of the paintings. It came to rest on the most unexpected of things: a gigantic, ancient tree, growing straight out of the white stone floor.

At first sight the tree was not unlike the one in the Garden of Havens: grand and aged, at once wizened and exquisitely formed. But this tree was taller, reaching high into the chasm above as though trying to touch the faces on the walls. And it bore fruit – thousands of apple-sized spheres in myriad colours and shades: reds and oranges, yellows and pinks, purples and greens. Some were plump with lustrous skins, some younger, smaller and yet to ripen. Then with a chill Sylas noticed something it shared with the one in the Garden of Havens: the thick black veins that marbled its bark, creeping upwards through every bough, branch and twig.

"It is a terrible sickness, this sickness of the Black. And yet still the tree bears fruit," said the priestess, turning her eyes to Sylas, and then down to his neck. "It may even be able to help you."

Sylas raised his hand self-consciously and instantly the pain returned, bubbling beneath the skin. When he touched it, he thought he felt it move.

The woman smiled. "Come, Sylas, Simia, you are expected."

Sylas exchanged a glance with Simia.

"You were expecting us?" he said.

She laughed lightly, her voice ascending the tower. "Isia sees much of most of us but she sees all of some of us." She reached down and placed a soft hand on his cheek, looking at him with interest. "Particularly where you are concerned."

She turned away and walked on under the boughs of the tree.

"This way, please," she said. "We have a long way to climb!"

Sylas and Simia followed in a daze as the priestess stepped on to a staircase protruding from the outer wall. It was made of the same white stone so it had blended with the rest of the structure, but now Sylas could see that it followed the arc of the wall, rising high into the collage of paintings. There, too had been painted with detailed lines and pigments, so that it became part of the great design. It climbed in a perfect spiral, circling the tree until it disappeared far above.

Already the priestess was among the paintings, Sylas and Simia following close behind her. The first of the pictures was a scene of open desert with pyramids rising in the far distance. In the foreground was a stone circle, its high, square-cut stones casting long shadows. At its centre, a circle of robed figures surrounded a small, solitary child.

The hairs rose on Sylas's neck. He had seen this picture before. It was one of the murals in the Apex Chamber — in the Dirgheon.

"What's *that* doing here?" asked Simia, peering over his shoulder.

Sylas shook his head. "I have no idea..."

The images that followed were similar: people worshipping in temples, trading in sandy city squares, building with blocks of stone, sailing ships down a verdant river. Now Sylas was up close, he could see that all the people had a similar look — head to one side, shoulders square, heavy black make-up around the eyes making them stark and piercing. They were, he thought, glancing up at their guide... just like the priestess.

They climbed higher and higher until soon they reached the topmost branches of the tree. Some of the fruits hung tantalisingly close, so bright and colourful that they almost seemed to glow. Just as Sylas began to wonder if he might be able to pick one, Simia slowed, glanced warily at the back of the priestess, then reached out to the nearest branch.

"NO!" commanded a voice that boomed around the vast chamber.

The priestess turned and glared at Simia.

She snatched her hand away, throwing it behind her back as though to hide the evidence.

"We never pick fruit from the tree!" said the priestess. "It must fall in its own time."

"Oh, sorry," said Simia, swinging her shoulders. "Just hungry, that's all."

The priestess's face softened. "Of course, and you'll be eating with Isia very soon."

She continued up the spiralling staircase and they resumed their climb, soon passing the last of the branches and leaving the tree below. As they did so the images around them began to change, becoming more and more sophisticated, showing more detail of the human form. The scenes changed too, becoming warlike, depicting skirmishes in the desert, great battles on a river, the siege of a mighty city and then its defeat: the capture of lords and princes, the burning of temples and palaces, the banishment of its people.

Sylas's eyes followed the long lines of displaced people out on to a desert, the vast painting sweeping around the inside of the tower until suddenly he blinked and frowned. There, protruding from the far wall was another staircase, rising in the opposite direction. He peered over the edge of his own step, down past the branches of the tree far below. There were *two* staircases. Just as theirs had started on one side of the hall, another had begun on the other, spiralling up the length of the chamber just as theirs, but always on the opposite side. The effect was that this second staircase plotted an entirely different path through the collage of images, drawing alongside a string of scenes that were too far away to be seen from where they were standing.

He glanced up and saw the double spiral ascending to the glowing roof of the temple, forming something he remembered from the book of science his mother had given him. The significance of it escaped him, but he remembered the shape very well – delicate and elegant and beautiful. He even remembered its name.

"The double helix," he murmured.

"Two paths to tell two stories," said the priestess a little above them.

He turned to her. "Which stories?"

"The most important of all!" exclaimed the priestess, seeming surprised at the question. "The tales of two worlds!"

She extended her staff and instantly the weave of light above them began to unravel, two of the beams darting out in opposite directions, travelling along the path of the two staircases, climbing the twin spirals. As the light passed over the pictures, faces seemed to shift, muscles twitched, limbs moved, bringing scene after scene to life, tracing a magical path through two human histories.

"Wow!" breathed Sylas. He grinned at Simia and, for the first time in a while, she smiled back.

"Come on now," said the priestess, "we mustn't keep Isia waiting."

She climbed ever more swiftly, so that they had to take the steps in twos to keep up, but still his eyes were drawn to the images. Increasingly they told a single story: a story of empire.

Of one, supreme army and the vanquishing of many. And always the flag of victory was the same: a red background with an emblem at the centre in the shape of a shield, half white, half black.

"Look!" whispered Simia suddenly, pointing excitedly into the chasm of light. "A way across!"

Sylas turned and saw a beam of light reflecting off a long, straight surface. It was a gangway made entirely of glass, leading from the staircase out across the void to the staircase on the opposite wall. Simia pointed upwards towards the glowing roof. There were scores of these floating bridges connecting the two staircases, forming an immense swirl across the space. The rays of light shimmered between them bringing the giant structure to life and making it glisten like a snowflake in the winter sun.

"I really MUST hurry you now!"

The priestess's voice echoed around the tower, but she was nowhere to be seen. She had already looped back above them. They set out at a run, heaving themselves up as fast as they could. Sylas hardly dared look at more paintings for fear of missing his step, but when he did he saw the mark of the Suhl — the white feather on a purple background — and long processions of women, children, the old and the weak, traipsing over mountain passes and windswept plains.

"The Undoing," panted Simia. "The beginning of it, at least."

As they clattered on, the quality of the light began to change: brighter here and cleaner, suggesting an opening just a short way above. They passed many pictures of what looked like Suhl ceremonies around stone circles and beneath each one a glass bridge struck out across the tower, leading to another image of a stone circle on the opposite wall. It was as though the bridges marked moments of connection, moments when the stone circles had brought the worlds together.

As Sylas and Simia rounded the final twists of the staircase, the paintings suddenly came to an abrupt end, leaving only blank white stone, as though waiting for stories yet to be told. Simia stopped, catching her breath, her hands on her hips. Her eyes were fixed in wonder on the wall, on the very last of the paintings.

At her shoulder, depicted in the most vivid of colours, were two silhouetted figures beneath a dramatic sky. Above them, and tracing a dramatic arc across the heavens, was a giant golden bell. It was the shape of a teardrop, and it was suspended from nothing but air.

Sylas felt cold fingers trailing up his spine. One of the figures wore an oversized coat. The other looked just like him.

"Welcome home, my children."

It was not the voice of the priestess. It came from behind and above, but they did not turn. They did not speak. They did not even breathe.

Simia sank to her knees and Sylas's heart raged in his chest.

Each had heard a familiar voice: one they had thought they would never hear again.

To Simia, it was her father.

To Sylas, his mother.

39

Discovered

"The Other is an engine of fables. Like any great truth waiting to be discovered, myth and superstition has taken its place."

THE TATTOOED EYES STARED unblinking into the darkness. All about them blood and sweat glistened in the dying flame: the only trace of life in this place of despair. The rest was stillness and silence.

And then there was a sound.

Shuffle, slide, scrape, gasp.

The silence returned, thick and heavy, but the disturbance had been enough to make the eyes stir. They rolled to one side and a face appeared. The features were drawn and bruised; the lips thick and blubbery; the eyes slits beneath swollen lids. But they lifted and turned.

There was the sound again, louder now:

Shuffle, slide, scrape, gasp.

Shuffle, slide, scrape, gasp.

Then silence. A frown appeared across the battered face. Now came another sound:

Tick... tick... tick... tick...

It was the wooden frame around the giant metal door.

Then there was a creak. A snap. A groan.

Bowe lifted his head, watching the door. All of a sudden he heaved himself on to his elbows, moaning from the shock of pain. In a feat of exertion, he scrambled to the opposite side of the cell.

In that instant the doorframe sent a sharp splinter across the room like a crossbow bolt. The timbers bowed outwards, straining under a devastating force. Cracks appeared, then gaping gashes.

Bowe curled into a ball.

The door screeched, the doorframe groaned and the timber exploded like a gunshot. The bolt snapped with a metallic bang.

The door tipped forward, teetered, then fell, clanging loudly against the flagstones.

It took a moment for the dust to settle and for the lamp to recover its flame, but soon it revealed a lone figure slumped against the opposite wall of the corridor, gazing into the cell. It was a man in wretched, tattered robes, with dark skin and thick-cropped hair. His features were hard to make out in the murk, but Bowe could see the whites of his eyes, the square cut of his jaw, the deep wound across his face.

The two men regarded each other across the threshold, pushing themselves a little more upright.

"Bowe?" murmured the man in the corridor.

There was a pause, then Bowe spoke in a weak, dry voice: "*Espasian?*"

The newcomer managed a dry laugh. "I don't quite cut that figure any more," he said. He started to shuffle into the cell, pulling himself forward with his arm and elbow. Finally he propped himself against the wall. "Call me Espen. I'm happier with Espen these days."

He held out a hand and Bowe grasped it as tightly as he could. They grinned at one another, their eyes taking in the wounds and bruises, scars and stains of blood. They winced on one another's behalf and looked away, turning their eyes to the mouldy walls.

"He got the better of us, didn't he?" said Espen.

Bowe tried to reply, but instead coughed and wheezed. He managed a smile. That had been answer enough.

"He tortured you?"

Bowe nodded.

"What did he want to know?"

"About the valley, Naeo, Sylas," said Bowe hoarsely. Then he frowned. "And Naeo's mother. He wanted to be sure that she was... that she was..."

"That Naeo is the last," said Espen, saving his friend from saying it: that his wife was dead.

Bowe pressed his eyes shut. "I thought if I could hold out... make him think that she was still alive, or perhaps that Naeo was not the only one... that we might have other children, then maybe he would go easier on her." He shook his head. "Desperate really. I could barely think. He used the Black." His face creased and tears welled in his eyes. "Not just on me. He used it on her... on my little girl."

Espen looked down. "You gave her the time she needed; time for Sylas to come," he said firmly. Then he added with a laugh: "And amazingly you're still here, you old boot."

Bowe smiled. "But more to the point, Sylas and Naeo aren't. They're out there somewhere."

Espen grinned. "They are."

They fell quiet. For the thousandth time, Bowe thought back to the giant birds circling the pinnacle of the Dirgheon, carrying that most precious of cargoes. And for the thousandth time, he

313

felt a pang in his gut. Naeo had been just there, so near, her face looking down at him. Oh, Isia, the pain in that face! When she had seen him, when he had wished her away. His Nay-no, alone in this cruel world.

He felt his eyes burning and he bit his inflamed lip. "So what about you?" he asked, wanting the distraction. "What happened?"

Espen smiled. "That story is way too long for me or for you, old friend. But I'm here because I brought Sylas, and then, when they made their escape, I had to stay. There was still fighting to be done."

Bowe's eyes met his. "So… it was you. You saved Naeo."

"In the end, she and Sylas saved themselves."

Bowe smiled knowingly. "With your help," he said. He placed his hand on his heart in thanks. "And you? How did you escape?"

Espen guffawed. "I'm not sure I did!" The smile faded from his face. "They came in such numbers, there was only one place to hide." He set his jaw. "The pool."

"The pool?" cried Bowe, horrified. "The pool of Black? In the Apex Chamber?"

He nodded.

"For Isia's sake! How long?"

"Just until they'd cleared the Chamber. Minutes maybe."

Bowe was aghast. He looked at his old friend more closely, seeing past the scar and the bruises, and for the first time noticing the dark veins in his neck and in his temples. "You shouldn't even be here! How did you—"

"I *am* a Magruman, you know," said Espen. He smiled and slapped Bowe's knee. "I'm OK! And I'll be even better as soon as I'm out of this place."

"But it'll only get—"

"There's no use worrying about it now!" snapped Espen. "We just need to get out of this hellhole!"

Bowe saw his friend's frustration flickering in the dark, his flame-red anger licking up the walls. He knew then that Espen was well aware of how sick he was. He chose not to speak any more of it and they both fell silent, gazing at the damp flagstones.

It was Espen who spoke first. "It's worse than I thought, Bowe. Worse than any of us thought. The birthing chambers are full, the legions are marching, the whole Dirgheon is on a war footing." He pressed his head back against the stone. "I've never seen anything like it."

The Scryer forced himself to sit up. "Worse... than the *Reckoning*?"

"Much worse."

Bowe felt a new chill in his bones. "What do you think he's up to?"

"What he loves," said the Magruman. "War. The real question is, *with whom*? He already has the Four Lands — there's nothing left to fight. Not in this world."

Bowe gaped at him. "In *this* world.... what are you saying?"

"That Thoth is about to start the war to end all wars," said Espen, sinking back against the wall. "And we're stuck here waiting for it to happen."

§

The Rager paced the dark corridor, flicking its tail impatiently from side to side. Everything was wrong. Not just what had happened at the temple, but here as well. Where were Thoth's imperial guards? Why had the oil lamps not been lit? Why was the Dirgheon so quiet? It felt like they all knew something it didn't, and that made it flicker with fire. In a beat of its giant heart, it felt impatience flare into frustration, frustration into anger, anger into rage. It puffed out a blast of air and lashed the wall with its tail, cracking a block of stone. For a moment it gave in to its nature, allowing the wrathful fire to burn, its scales turning from yellow to pink to red, its muscles rippling. But even as the rage began, it heaved a deep breath and worked to settle its nerves, to quench the fire.

Here, its temper could be dangerous. Here, its temper could get it killed.

Suddenly the grand doors opened at the end of the corridor and the silhouette of a Ghor guard appeared.

"He'll see you now," it growled, before disappearing back into the chamber.

The Rager drew in several more draughts of cool air until it was sure that it had tamed its temper, then it stomped up to the ornamental doors. Just before it went in, it reached up and preened the red crest on the back of its neck, making the scales clatter against each other.

As it stepped into the Devotion Chamber, it squinted into the light, quickly surveying the scene. Directly ahead was the Devotion Wall: a vast expanse of dark stone into which had been carved Thoth's three symbols, each twice the height of a man – the hunched bird with its long, cruel beak; two circles, one within the other; and the scroll. Below these symbols was the text of the devotion itself, picked out in red and gold paint:

"Our Dream, Our Fullest Joy, Our Second Soul."

Below this was a vast black table covered with books and papers, strewn haphazardly over the surface. A lone figure stood with his back to the door sorting through these papers, his head bowed, his hands busy. His long white robes were not what the Rager was expecting. And there was something about the figure… It was taller and fuller than that of the great Lord, and one shoulder seemed to be slumped, giving an odd, lopsided appearance.

"Thoth is not here," came a soft, effeminate voice.

Instinctively the Rager flicked out its forked tongue, smelling the air as it calculated and adjusted.

The figure lifted its head and turned.

The chubby face would have been pasty and white had it not been terribly burned down one side, leaving the skin pink and pinched. The same fire had left one eye closed and the thinning albino-white hair entirely missing from that side of the head. One hand bore the same livid burns, the fingers slightly twisted.

The Rager let out a low, uneasy rasp in its throat. It was Thoth's Magruman, Laythlick, scarred and diminished.

"So what is it, Rager?" snapped the Magruman. "Aren't you supposed to be guarding the temple?"

The Rager bowed its head to the floor in full ceremony, allowing its horns to strike the flagstones. "Yes, my Lord," it murmured in its wheezing, gravelly voice, "but I thought I should inform you of something that happened on our watch."

"Well? What is it?"

The Rager drew in a cooling breath. "Some worshippers came to pay tribute to Isia and asked to pass. I would have kept them for questioning, but the priestess—"

"We can't prevent worshippers approaching the temple!" interjected Laythlick, beginning to lose interest and turn away. "Much as we may want to."

"I know, my Lord, but this was strange. These were *children*."

Laythlick drew himself up. "Children?"

"Yes, my Lord. A boy and a girl."

The Magruman turned, his face flushing. "I hope for your sake you didn't let them *leave*?"

"No, my Lord. They're still there."

Laythlick clicked his fingers at the two Ghor guards. "Muster the city guard!"

"But, sir," said one of them with a fearful bow, "most of the guard is gone. The Dirgh has sent them—"

"Then make up the numbers! I want newborn and servant, soldier and jailor! You hear? Every snivelling soul still left in the Dirgheon!" He watched the two guards rush from the room. "And send word to the Dirgh!" he called after them. "Tell him that this time, I will leave nothing to chance."

As the doors swung closed, he turned to the Rager. "You did well to bring me your suspicions," he said with a nod of appreciation.

The Rager puffed out its massive chest and bowed.

"Now," said the Magruman coolly, "start praying that you are right."

40

On the Threshold

"And there, on the threshold *of Setgur,*
he saw his chance for empire:
an empire that one day would span the four lands."

SYLAS AND SIMIA WERE shoulder to shoulder as they climbed the final steps. They paused and looked at one another.

"Go on," murmured Simia, "you should go first."

Sylas took a moment to settle his nerves, then hoisted the rucksack on his shoulder and clambered up into the light.

He found himself standing in a vast circular hall, which rose high above his head and spanned the full breadth of the tower. It was wonderfully bright, lit by a circuit of huge archways that cast a mosaic of light on the white marble floor. The faint rays met at the centre of the chamber, weaving together before diving downwards into the great chasm of the tower, beginning their journey through the history of humankind.

Sylas saw the priestess disappearing through a side door, then he glanced about for the owner of the voice. He looked in one direction, then another, then another.

There was not one face, but thousands.

He saw faces painted on the walls and on the ceiling, gathered between the archways and covering the open spaces. He saw statues, carved from the white stone of the temple, to show all shades of emotion — joy or fear, anguish or tenderness. There were men, women, the young and the old — each depicted in some moment of drama or poignancy. It was a vast collection of the human image, showing every state of mind, every attitude, every thought and emotion.

All of these thousands of eyes seemed now to rest on Sylas.

Any yet he was strangely calm. He knew he was safe. He remembered the voice that had greeted them.

"*Welcome home,*" it had said.

Suddenly the room resonated with that same voice: "I must begin with a warning."

It knocked the air from his lungs. That tone, that trace of an accent... the way it made him feel lost and safe at the same time. It was her, his mother! He was sure of it.

And yet, when he turned to Simia, he saw his own feelings reflected in her face. She too looked bewildered, like the child she really was, young and vulnerable.

"It's him, Sylas," she breathed. "It's my father!"

They stared at one another and then looked all about them, searching again for the owner of the voice, daring to believe.

"In the beginning, you will find me unsettling," said the voice.

Sylas saw a movement in the corner of his eye, among some of the statues. He drew closer to Simia. She stepped into his shoulder.

A figure was walking towards them. They strained their eyes to see, but the bright arches behind made it hard to make out any features.

"My voice is not my own but the voice you most wish to hear," said the figure drawing ever closer. "I am sorry, this will disappoint you. I am Isia and this is the way."

Sylas felt a piercing pang of loss. The hope had been half formed, but for a moment it had been real: his mother, almost within his reach. But then he heard Simia catch her breath and saw her reaching instinctively for the lapels of her missing coat, her lips quivering. And he knew it was so much worse for her. She had heard a voice from beyond the grave.

He reached out and took her hand.

The voice came again: "You will also find my appearance... disquieting."

The figure suddenly emerged into a beam of light and she could be seen. She was young and astonishingly beautiful, with long flowing jet-black hair and eyes so dark that they too looked almost black. Her long doe-like face was fine and delicate, but her features were strong, with high cheekbones and a full mouth. Unlike the priestesses, her fine bronze skin was unpainted, with no heavy make-up around the eyes, no pigment on the lips. Her robes, too, were made of simple white muslin without any elaborate trim, and she wore no jewellery, no headdress, not even shoes. Her manner was bold and commanding, and yet so gentle and graceful that, even across the cavernous room, they felt drawn to her.

But as she had warned — there was something wrong. It was in the way she moved, the way the light caught her form.

Simia shuddered. "Look at her arms!"

Sylas looked and blinked and looked again. There was a blur, a confusion behind the sharp lines of her fingers. Then he saw that it was less a blur than a second image. A repeat. A double. As her hand swung forward, another hand trailed behind. As it paused to swing back, its double caught up and the two became one.

He looked at her other hand, then at her flowing gown and hair. All of them were a blur, all were chased by a second form.

"Do I alarm you, Sylas?"

He started and looked up. "No — no, of course not..." he said, trying not to stare at the way her lips blurred as she spoke.

Isia gave a slight smile. "I would have thought that if anyone might know what it is to have a second self, it would be you."

Sylas was thrown. "Sorry... I—"

She flashed a stunning, unguarded smile. "This is no place for apologies, Sylas! We are alike, you and I. You might even say we are family. You have a unique connection with your Glimmer and the same is true of me, and mine. But in me, there is almost no separation at all. In me, the two are almost one."

She stepped up to them in a blur of motion and caught up their hands in her soft, warm fingers.

"It is wonderful to meet you, Sylas! And you, Simia!"

They suddenly realised they had no idea how they were supposed to address her, and so they bowed awkwardly, muttering a confused medley of thanks and greetings.

Isia laughed a girlish laugh that echoed from the walls and ceiling.

"The pleasure is all mine," she said. She looked at them for a moment, taking in their dishevelled clothes, dirty faces and tired eyes. "Come, you are tired and hungry. We must give you something to restore your spirits."

Naeo woke confused and disoriented. The pain was unbearable at first, scouring her back, across her shoulders and up into her neck. She pushed away from the seat with her elbows and arched her back. That helped a little. She opened her eyes, seeking something to take her mind away from the pain, and found herself staring out of the car window. She saw a pink blanket of light, fringed in amber and yellow. She saw a blur of trees whisking past at impossible speeds. She saw a broad valley, streaked with shadows. And these things helped, because they took her away from the Black. She felt herself falling through the blur of trees, tumbling into the valley of shadows. Slowly, her eyes fell closed. She moaned something, the word barely formed.

"Isia…"

She shifted in her seat, settling into the strange comforts of its springs. Slowly her head dropped to her chest and she slipped off once more into a troubled sleep.

The solitary car wound up the hillside, its twin beams sometimes ranging out into the waking valley, sometimes turning into the dark, forested folds. Above, the pink light of dawn laced the singing treetops, and golden beams rose like a halo across the deep blue sky, crowning this new day as though it were any other.

Tasker held the phone to his ear, steering with a single hand.

"And have we heard from Claude? … There as well?" He glanced across at Mr Zhi, but the old man did not meet his eyes. "And you say you spoke to Jens? … Yes, yes, I understand. We'll find out more when we get to Winterfern. We're just arriving… OK, yes. And you, take care."

He lowered the phone stiffly from his ear. He had barely been off it for two hours. He jabbed at it with a stiff thumb, then dropped it on the dashboard.

"The crisis before the fever breaks," said Mr Zhi quietly.

"And I didn't even know we were sick," muttered Tasker.

"Come now," said Mr Zhi, patting his arm, "we both know that isn't true."

Tasker turned the wheel sharply to the right and the car veered between a pair of high stone pillars, one of which had been engraved in stark lettering:

WINTERFERN HOSPITAL

He peered in the rear-view mirror, watching the high iron gates whirr closed behind them.

"Well, at least we know we're safe here," he said.

Mr Zhi raised an eyebrow. "For now, perhaps."

The tyres crunched and gravel rattled in the wheel arches, waking the sleeping passengers. They blinked blearily as the car trailed down a snaking avenue of trees. Then the driveway wound on through a forest and over the crest of a hill, before finally descending through thinning trees to a clearing. Ash grabbed Naeo's arm and pointed ahead, between the last of the trees.

Something glinted in the rusty light. Rising from a deep bed of ferns they saw a gigantic wall of glistening glass, its wide aspect facing out over the valley. It was a dome many storeys high and twice as wide, but it was not complete: the hillside climbed steeply behind, meeting the steel and glass not far from the apex, giving the appearance that half of the dome was deep in the bosom of the hill.

Mr Zhi turned in his seat. "Welcome to Winterfern," he said, with a growing smile.

Corporal Lucien pushed back on his chair and took a long slurp of coffee from the polystyrene cup. He eyed the doughnut on top of the monitor, the sugar coating winking by the light of the radar screen.

No, one was enough. He drew his eyes away from the doughnut

and back to the monitor. If he wasn't careful, this desk job would make him soft at the edges.

"So do we even know what we're supposed to be looking for?" he asked no one in particular, stifling a belch.

The others gave a general grumble in the negative, none of them lifting their eyes from their screens.

"This is a WS3 nuclear weapons storage facility!" snapped Major Briskett, who had entered without anyone noticing. "All you need to know is that we're on high alert! Now keep those eyes peeled, people, or I'll peel them for you!"

There was a chorus of slightly weary "Yes, sir."

"And Lucien—"

The corporal swivelled in his chair and snapped to attention. "Sir?"

"Remove that doughnut from my bunker, you slovenly excuse for a WASTE—OF—SPACE!"

"Yes, sir!" shouted Lucien, reaching for it and raising it to his mouth.

"Not down your throat, you CRETIN! Throw it away!"

Lucien winced — that was a criminal waste of good doughnut. But he knew better than to argue. It was arguing that had landed him in this pen-pushing detail in the first place. He leaned heavily on his desk to push himself up and glanced briefly at his monitor.

Instantly his eyes drew into sharp focus. He leaned a little closer.

There was nothing there now but he was *sure* he had seen a slight movement at the edge of the screen. He put down the doughnut, wiped his fingers, then swiped them across the image to swivel the camera.

"Lucien! Get your—"

"Two seconds, sir!"

He stared at the screen. The floodlights on the wire perimeter sent great arcs of light out on to the plain, but they showed nothing. Something *had* moved, he knew it — something beyond the light. He shifted to the adjacent screen, tapping it to bring it to life. It glowed with the dull greens and greys of infrared imagery.

"What did you just say, Lucien?" Briskett was at his ear now, standing over him. "Did you just tell me to w—"

"Shut up!" snapped Lucien, bringing everyone in the bunker to a stunned standstill. "Look!"

He drew his fingers across the screen to align the camera, then placed four fingers in the centre and spread them wide.

Briskett brought his shaven head towards the screen. "This better be good, Lucien," he muttered.

The infrared camera zoomed, then focused.

The two men blinked, hardly able to believe their eyes.

41

Salve for the Soul

"What cure is there for a broken spirit?
What salve *for an ailing* soul?*"*

NAEO GAZED UP AT the peculiar structure, wondering at its clinical beauty: its seamless blend of glass and earth. But it was not the imposing building that made her stomach tighten and her mouth run dry: it was the sudden realisation that there, just beyond the wall of glass, was the mother Sylas had thought lost, the mother he had longed for and searched for. The mother she had come to find. And there was something else too, something deep in her still-dreamy thoughts. Now that she was here, could it be that Sylas was in the passages of the Dirgheon, with her father? Could that be why she had felt so suffocated in her sleep? Was that the reason for the darkness of her dreams?

The car drew to a halt by the great dome, gave a throaty growl and fell silent.

Tasker stretched his shoulders and rubbed his neck. "Let's hope everyone else is here."

"Everyone else?" probed Ash.

"The Merisi," said Mr Zhi, opening his door. "This should be quite a meeting."

They all heaved themselves stiffly out of the car, grabbed their bags and made their way along a short gravel pathway that ran alongside the glass wall. Suddenly Naeo felt a knife-edge of pain through her spine. She dropped her bag and arched her back. Ash saw her at once.

"You OK?" he asked, taking her by the shoulders.

As the pain eased, she bent over and rested on her knees, panting. "I think I'm OK," she said.

"You *think*," said Ash. "It's the Black, isn't it?"

"I don't know why but it got much worse in the car, while I was sleeping."

Mr Zhi appeared at her side and bent down to look at her. He brushed the hair away from her face. "The Black, you say?" he murmured, looking concerned. "From the Dirgheon?"

Naeo straightened stiffly, then winced and nodded.

"Indeed," said Mr Zhi, casting a worried glance at Tasker. "We will have to see what we can do about that. Can you walk?"

She picked up her bag. "I'm OK," she said. "I think it's just sitting still for so long."

"Well, either way, you have come to the right place," said the old man. "Come on, let me show you Winterfern."

He took her arm and led her up to the giant glass panes, which reflected the majestic, dawning sky behind them. The interior was masked behind the pink and orange light so Ash walked straight up to the glass and leaned in with cupped hands. Even as his fingers touched the glass there was a loud sigh and a clunk. He jumped back, nearly stumbling over Tasker and treading on his foot in the process.

"Steady!" said Tasker, rubbing his shoe on his trouser leg. "Italian shoes!"

Mr Zhi shot him a sharp look. "Jeremy, really!"

Suddenly there was a whirring sound as the huge glass panel slid slowly to one side. Sounds echoed from beyond the shaded threshold: a deep, ringing roar, like the sound of falling water thundering into a pool; the bright song and chatter of birds; voices, some talking, some laughing and calling out.

"Welcome to our sanctuary," said Mr Zhi with a quick bow.

Ash and Naeo peered past him and were astonished to see a new wilderness beyond the wall, this one enclosed by the vast dome. Ahead was a simple dirt track, winding up a grassy bank to a large pool bordered by bracken, bushes and saplings, mossy rocks and clusters of flowers.

"There's no time for the full tour now," continued Mr Zhi, "but I will show you a little along the way. Only please do remember that this is a hospital." Then he added in a lower voice: "There are patients here who would find the truth about you deeply upsetting. It would be best if you do not speak to them." He paused for a moment, looking with concern at Naeo. "Come," he said, holding out his gloved hand.

Naeo found the gentle squeeze of his fingers strangely reassuring as he led her inside.

"We'll not be seeing Sylas's mother quite yet," said Mr Zhi, seeming to sense her anxiety about the meeting to come. "We'll first go to the Merisi."

Naeo heard him but her eyes were elsewhere.

Everywhere.

Above, fingers of spray curled from a waterfall, which fell the full height of the building in a thin white column of churning foam. Behind it the hillside rose in a steepening bank until it became a cliff, its sheer face climbing all the way to the glassy ceiling. It was at that highest point, just where rock met glass, that the waters cascaded forth, tumbling down in sheets and veils to the plunge pool far below. Perhaps most beautiful of all, the silver falls were girdled by a rainbow, which sent its magical bands of colour far out into the void, almost touching the glass dome.

Around the pool and ranging across the broad sweep of the building, were the most gorgeous gardens. They looked at once wild and carefully tended — great trees laced with vines, verdant undergrowth bordered by splashes of red and white blooms, walkways through rushes and shrubs opening out into lawns of well-trimmed grass.

"There is no balm greater than Nature herself," said Mr Zhi, patting Naeo's hand. "And Winterfern is truly a Salve for the soul."

They heard some voices off to their right and turned to see two women strolling across an open lawn. They were dressed in matching, loose-fitting green clothes.

"Some of our guests," said Mr Zhi. "The gardens are popular at dawn."

The women seemed unaware of the visitors and continued their conversation, disappearing into a copse of trees.

"We have some five hundred guests at present," said Mr Zhi. "Come and see for yourself."

He led them up the winding path towards the plunge pool, and they soon felt the refreshing spray from the waterfall on their faces. Naeo saw more of the hospital's 'guests', some ambling through the gardens, others resting on grassy banks or beds of moss. One man was sitting by the path reading a book. He glanced up and smiled as they approached and they gave a friendly nod in response. Naeo noticed dark rings under his eyes and the sallowness of his skin.

"A new arrival, I suspect," Mr Zhi whispered in her ear.

As they skirted the pool, Ash bent down and scooped up some of the crystal-clear water, examined it, gave it a sniff, then drank it down. He nodded approvingly.

"Spring water from the heart of the hills," said Tasker proudly.

Ash scooped up a little more water and ran it gratefully through his hair, sighing with satisfaction, then shook his shaggy locks, sending out a shower of droplets. Tasker blinked incredulously at his shoes and opened his mouth to complain but seemed to think better of it. Instead he gave Ash a disapproving stare, lingering on his rough boots and ill-kempt clothes. Ash simply grinned, patted Tasker on the shoulder with a dripping-wet hand and walked on.

They made their way around the pool until they could see the full face of the cliff, which swept around behind the waterfall. They saw at once that it was not a rock face at all, or at least, it was a rock face no longer. What had once been a wall of stone was now riddled with openings and galleries, ramps and staircases, all cut into the dark grey surface. It was alive with activity: people walking here and there, leaning over the balconies to watch the dawn, some carrying trays of food, others gathered around in comfortable-looking chairs, deep in conversation. All of them were wearing the same light green clothes that they had seen in the gardens.

Naeo gazed at it in wonder. "And that's the hospital?"

Mr Zhi nodded. "Here, and deeper in the hillside. I do wish I could show you the whole thing but that will have to wait. Nearly there now."

They climbed some turfed steps and entered through a doorway cut into the stone. A twisting stairway carried them up through the cliff face to the light of an open gallery. As they reached the top step, they saw the back of the waterfall off to their side, its spray wafting across their path, casting a pleasant dew. They walked quickly past a number of closed doors to a broad doorway at the end of the gallery. Mr Zhi ignored another staircase and instead followed a passageway that headed directly into the hillside.

Naeo's step slowed when she saw where they were going, but Mr Zhi drew her forward.

"This is no Dirgheon," he whispered.

When she looked down the tunnel, she was surprised to see that it was lighter than the gallery they had just left, lit by broad discs of daylight set into the ceiling. She peered upwards and saw a tiny circle of sky in the far distance, fringed by a silvered shaft.

"Light tunnels," said Tasker. "They take the sunlight straight through the hillside."

"*Through it?*" repeated Ash, squinting to one of them.

Tasker shrugged and walked on. "You have your magic, this is ours."

Ash gazed at the perfectly smooth interior of the shaft, shaking his head in wonderment.

They descended the broad, cool passageway into the hillside, passing many doors and passages leading off to the left and right. They saw more of the guests going about their daily business in their strange garments of green, some accompanied by people wearing a darker green studded with symbols down one arm, which ended seamlessly in a single green glove: a plainer version of the one Mr Zhi was wearing.

"Merisi," murmured Ash to Naeo.

"Not quite," said Mr Zhi, somehow hearing them even though he was some distance ahead. "Though they wish to be. They're what we call Initiates. If they work hard enough and show themselves able, they may join us one day, like Tasker. Until then, their service here is invaluable."

He slowed to a stop at the end of the corridor, beside two large, beautifully carved timber doors. Naeo noticed that one depicted the sun and the other the moon.

Mr Zhi took hold of the two door handles.

"Now," he said, "time to meet the Merisi."

42
The Bond that Binds

*"Isia is the bond that binds all things. Her eyes
are the sun and the moon, her body is the bosom of the earth."*

CORPORAL LUCIEN STARED AT the monitor.

There, just beyond the arcs of the floodlights, were scores of shifting shadows, prowling at the fringes of the security zone. Their shapes were hard to discern, but their eyes were wide and white on the green screen: too large to be human, too purposeful to be animal, too many to be mistaken. They were completely still, as though waiting for something.

Lucien's skin turned to gooseflesh. In one motion, he and Briskett lunged forward and struck the large red button on the back of the desk. Instantly the light in the bunker blinked and dimmed and then a klaxon wail shattered the silence. An automated female voice blasted from speakers in the ceiling:

"ALERT... ALERT..." she declared in a silky monotone. "REPORT TO STATIONS. ALERT... ALERT..."

Lucien and Briskett's eyes were still glued to the screen as the phone on the desk gave a shrill ring. Briskett raised it to his ear.

"Yes, sir, they're all along the Northern boundary... ten, fifteen maybe. I'm just checking the other cameras." He clicked his fingers at his staff. They busied themselves at their screens and then swivelled their monitors in his direction. His eyes moved quickly across them and he paled, shaking his head. "Sir, I'm afraid they seem to be on *all* boundaries. That's right, fifty at least. But they're not doing anyth—" He stopped, swore under his breath, then dropped the phone.

All of the displays were suddenly alive. A surge of dark figures bounded across the open space, illuminated by automatic, high-intensity floodlights. The monitoring station thrummed with the rapid fire of robotic sentinel guns, interspersed with thumps of exploding mortar shells and mines.

"What the hell…" murmured Lucien.

Even under fire, the attackers devoured the open plain, sprinting at inconceivable speeds between the first lines of tracer fire and mortar blasts. Some were thickset and muscular like giant hounds, tearing up the turf with gigantic claws; others were slim and lithe, darting and leaping through the hail of bullets with feline agility. Behind them, still at the fringes of the light, were upright forms, almost human but not quite, with shoulders that were too broad, heads that hung too low. And beyond them were eight or ten slighter, more human forms, their arms held aloft, their hands closed in fists. Suddenly they threw their arms forward and in the same instant something moved in the far darkness, launching up into the air. Whatever it was flew quickly above the range of the camera, so Lucien immediately casting his fingers up the screen to tilt it.

He stumbled backwards into his chair.

There, just passing within range of the floodlights, were dozens of spinning shapes, all of them at least the size of a house. They were colossal clods of earth, torn up from the plain and sent hurtling into the heavens, arcing through the sky.

Lucien glanced at the Major but he was frozen, staring with wide eyes at the screens, still holding the screaming handset.

Lucien turned and screamed at the radio controller at the back of the bunker.

"Send a Mayday! NOW!"

The young private pulled his eyes away from the screens and hunched over his panel.

"Mayday! Mayday!" he bellowed into the microphone as the bunker shook with the first impact. "All stations, this is Weapons Storage Facility Whisky-Sierra-Three-Alpha-Yankee-Oscar requesting immediate assistance. Mayday! Mayday!"

§

Isia led Sylas and Simia across a patchwork of carpets embroidered with yet more images of people, gazing at them with fixed eyes. They headed towards the far side of the chamber, weaving a path through some of the statues. These grand creations of pure white marble were so lifelike that they seemed to look down at them as they passed. Sylas found himself looking into the wizened face of an elderly man with long flowing locks and a thick, tumbling beard. The man's hands were open in front of him, as though making an offering, but his palms were empty. The more Sylas looked, the more he understood that this was a man making a heartfelt, desperate plea.

"Beautiful, isn't he?" said Isia.

Sylas started — he hadn't realised that she was beside him. "Yes. Who is it?"

"I'm not sure it matters!" said Isia. "What I love about these statues, these paintings, is not *who* is in them but *what* is in them. They all capture something very precious."

Sylas looked from one statue to another. "What?"

335

"A moment when someone reaches out and touches us!" said Isia excitedly. "A moment of connection! If you had lived as long as I, you would know that they are the most important moments of all."

"Is that why you have so many paintings?" asked Simia, peering up at the walls.

"They are such a comfort to me," said Isia. "They fill me with hope. After all, if a painter can do this with pigment and canvas, just think what connections we might forge in our own lives. *Real* connections." She looked from one to the other. "But you are students of Essenfayle, I don't need to tell you the importance of connections."

She turned and walked on.

Soon they drew near to a large table covered with silver platters and bowls containing all manner of gastronomic wonders: luscious fruits, steaming breads, fish, meats and cheeses. Sylas and Simia's eyes grew wide — they had almost forgotten how ravenously hungry they were.

"Is this for us?" asked Simia, barely able to contain herself.

"As much as you can eat," said Isia, ushering them with a blur of hands to three places that had been set at the end. Sylas and Simia filled their plates and tucked in ravenously while Isia simply sat quietly, watching, as though enjoying the novelty of sharing her table. The only time her smile faded was when she noticed the black mark on Sylas's neck, now larger than ever, but her composure quickly returned.

It was only after many mouthfuls that the conversation resumed.

"Perhaps we should talk about why you are here," suggested Isia.

Sylas glanced up from a mound of meatballs. "Sorry," he said, wiping his mouth on a napkin. "I haven't had food like this since… well, *ever*, really."

"Then don't let me stop you, Sylas!" she said, laughing and

waving him on. "Just ask your questions as you eat, and I will answer as best I can."

Sylas gratefully took another mouthful and chewed, trying to gather his thoughts. How strange that he hadn't planned what to say — in fact, he realised that he had almost forgotten why he was here. Something about this place — about Isia herself — was so intoxicating, that all his purpose had faded.

He pulled his thoughts into order and said: "We've come here because Paiscion thought you might be able to help me — us, I mean."

"He was right," said Isia.

Sylas gazed at her for a moment, but she just nodded for him to continue.

"Well... Naeo and I found each other," he said, "and we understand that we're supposed to be together, that Merisu was writing about us in his poem when he said '*For then at last we may be one*'. But we just don't understand what our connection *means*. What we're supposed to do with it."

"What they need to know," said Simia, chewing a chicken leg, "is what are they supposed to do next?"

Isia reached across the table for a grape. "Well, I rather think we have been talking about this since you arrived," she said, raising the grape to her mouth in a flurry of hands.

Sylas laid down his fork. "How do you mean?"

"One of the first things I said to you was that I thought you would know what it is to have a second self — do you remember?"

"Yes..."

"And it is the *knowing* that is most important for you now."

Sylas shrugged and shook his head. "But I *do* know Naeo. We rescued her from the Dirgheon, we've travelled together — we were together in the Valley of Outs."

"But do you *really*?" asked Isia, leaning forward. "Do you truly *know* Naeo?"

Sylas looked at her blankly.

"I thought not," said Isia. "The truth is, Sylas, you share so much with Naeo. Her gifts are yours and yours, hers. Can you say that you truly understand that? Can you say you *believe* it?"

Sylas dropped his eyes to his food. He thought about Naeo in the Dirgheon, in the Garden of Havens and when they were leaving the valley. He *had* felt that he knew her. More than that — he had felt part of her. And there had been moments since they had parted when he could feel that connection. But they were just moments. The rest of the time he barely thought of her.

"I suppose not, no," he said.

"Well it is all in the knowing," said Isia in a tone that left the matter beyond doubt. "The two parts of your being should correspond freely, they should connect in you as they do in me. But they are obstructed, frustrated, held apart."

"But isn't that because she's from here and I'm from there?"

Isia shook her head. "No, it's not that simple. You and Naeo have a bond unlike any other. In you, the Glimmer Myth finds its end — it is fulfilled. That is why you are able to meet, to communicate, to act as one. It is no longer the worlds that are holding you apart, it is the knowledge you have lost — the knowledge of each other — of everything you can be."

Sylas leaned on the table and rubbed his temples. "OK," he said, "I think."

Isia seemed to be playing with words, but he knew that she was right, that there was still a barrier between Naeo and himself — a disconnect. His thoughts flew back to his conversation with Triste by the river, when the Scryer had told him he was connected to her in every way, all the time. "*Well if I am, I don't know about it*," had been his reply.

Simia pushed away her plate and looked at Isia. "So if you and *your* Glimmer are one — if you really do know your other self — is that what makes you so..." She fumbled for the words for a moment, and looked increasingly stricken by the course she had taken. "I mean, is that what makes people think you're..."

Isia smiled, reached over and took her hand. "Yes," she said. "My wholeness, such as it is, helps me. It makes me clearer in my mind and stronger in my body."

Simia's eyes sparkled with excitement. "So... is that what makes you *live forever*?"

Isia patted her hand and slid back from the table. "Time for dessert," she said. She leaned over to a large bowl topped with fluffy cream. "You must try our fruit pudding. I have it on the highest authority that it's the finest in this world or that."

She winked at them and spooned out two bowls of opulent pudding that looked like trifle, oozing with cream and custard and packed with diced fruits of all textures and colours. Isia's arms moved swiftly between the bowls so that at times she appeared to have four entirely separate hands and at one point Sylas even thought he might have seen one of the hands reach for something in an adjacent pot, pick it up, and add it to one of the bowls, but it could have been a trick of the eye.

"Eat up," she said, smiling and leaving the table. "We can talk more when you're done."

Then, to their surprise, she left them, walking away through the archway and out into the failing light, trailing an image a little behind. Her shadow was long in the pale dusk and it took a while to disappear, blurring between two forms.

Sylas and Simia looked at each other, a little bemused by her sudden exit.

"You shouldn't have asked her about living forever!" hissed Sylas.

Simia straightened defensively. "Why not? It's true, isn't it?"

They regarded one another for a moment, but their eyes inevitably returned to their dessert. They picked up their spoons and dug in.

Sylas ate greedily. It was, without doubt, the most delicious pudding he had ever tasted. He was soon through the heavenly cream and the velvety custard, then into the sparkling rubies of jelly and the rough sweetness of the sponge. Finally he sank his teeth into the wonderful, sweet, tangy fruit.

The *bitter... burning* fruit.

He hunched forward in his seat and raised his hands to his neck, his eyes staring wildly.

"What's wrong?" cried Simia, standing and pushing her seat over with a clatter. Her face was stricken with panic. "Sylas! What's wrong?"

Sylas could not hear her. His eyes turned to the glowing archway.

He gaped, trying to speak, to cry out, but nothing came.

Then he fell back and exhaled, staring blindly into the dying light.

43
The Merisi

"Here are recorded the chronicles of the Merisi,
begun by our hand in this year of Our Lord
one thousand two hundred and twenty-nine."

MR ZHI PUSHED OPEN the doors emblazoned with the sun and the moon. They swung back with ease, coming to rest with a clunk.

Beyond was a large chamber hewn from the dark stone of the hill, lit by a dim, cool light. At first sight it looked like any conventional room, with square-cut walls, almost-smooth ceiling and polished granite floor, but as Naeo's eyes adjusted to the light, she saw that the walls were alive. They shimmered and glistened beneath endlessly moving sheets of water, which fell from the point where the walls met the ceiling and disappeared somewhere below the floor. The result was that the rock seemed to be in perpetual descent and the cool chamber was filled with the pleasant rush and tinkle of water.

Another sound, the sound of voices, quickly fell silent. At the centre of the chamber a large assembly of thirty or forty robed figures stood around a long table of polished white marble. Each of them wore a single green glove.

When Mr Zhi stepped forward they all bowed.

"Greetings, sisters and brothers. Allow me to introduce some rather special guests," he said, stepping to one side and sweeping his gloved hand towards the threshold. "Ash is a representative of the Suhl…" he paused and gave Ash a kindly smile, then turned to Naeo, "and Naeo, daughter of Bowe, represents herself. Both parts of herself." He turned back to the gathering. "Because, Naeo's Glimmer is none other than Sylas Tate."

The gathering stared at Naeo in astonishment, then glanced at one another. Finally they remembered their manners and bowed.

Naeo nodded awkwardly in response. The pain in her back had started to return and she suddenly felt queasy and faint.

"We are of course hugely honoured by your visit," said a woman with broad, oriental features, who did not seem to notice Naeo's discomfort. "But I am afraid that in the midst of today's crisis it will be impossible to offer you any kind of welcome."

"And yet without the crisis, my dear Kasumi, we would not have the honour of their visit!" retorted Mr Zhi. "Such are the connections of our worlds. Naeo and Ash are well aware of the dangers and difficulties we face — they have already faced many of them alone and without our help."

Kasumi bowed.

He turned his eyes around the gathering. "But is this all? Where are our sisters and brothers?"

"Many have been prevented from answering our call," said Kasumi. "The unrest spread quickly. Borders have been closed, travel restricted — not just here but all across Europe, and now in Asia and the States. Travel is perilous."

Several of the gathering murmured their agreement.

"Then matters are grave indeed," said Mr Zhi, darkly. He cast his eyes over the papers on the table. "You had better brief me in full." He turned to his guests. "I'm sorry, I had hoped that there would be time for some introductions, but it seems not. Ash," he said, gesturing to an empty seat at the table, "if you don't mind I think you should stay and talk with us; you know as much about what we are facing as anyone."

Ash hesitated. "What about Naeo?"

"Naeo's time is better used elsewhere," said Mr Zhi, turning to her. "My child, before anything else, we must have someone look at your wounds, especially if they are infected with the Black." There were whispers of dismay around the room. Mr Zhi silenced them with a dark look. He turned back to Naeo. "You should go directly to see the Seedkeeper."

"The *Seedkeeper*?" she said, dubiously.

Mr Zhi smiled. "Our greatest healer. But perhaps more importantly, she is the person whom you have come to find. The Seedkeeper is our name for Sylas's mother, Amelie." He patted her arm encouragingly. "Jeremy, please show Naeo the way."

Tasker bowed to the room then motioned for Naeo to follow him.

Ash leaned down to Naeo's ear. "Are you all right about this? If you want me to come I—"

She raised her hand dismissively. "I'll be fine," she said, turning stiffly and following Tasker from the room. Ash watched anxiously as she left.

"Your friend is in very good hands," said Mr Zhi, taking his arm and leading him to the table. "There is much more to Amelie Tate than Naeo may realise."

Tasker led Naeo down the passageway as quickly as she was able, passing in and out of the pools of light. Soon they turned into a darker corridor that she had not noticed on her way in. The further she walked — the nearer she came to Sylas's mother — the more her feeling of unease began to eclipse the pain. Why hadn't she thought about this moment? Why hadn't she planned what to do or say?

She became aware of Tasker at her side. "You all right, Princess?" he asked, eyeing her closely.

"I'm OK."

"No, really?"

She shrugged, immediately regretting it as a new pulse of pain shot through her spine.

He leaned forward and caught her eye. "It'll be OK, you know." His tone was caring and tender. "She's a good woman, the Seedkeeper."

"Oh. Yes... thanks," she said, surprised by his attentions. "It's actually more the pain than anything else."

"Well then you're definitely going to see the right person. What the Seedkeeper doesn't know about balms and remedies isn't worth knowing."

"I'm not sure there's a balm for what I have," she mumbled. Then to change the subject she asked: "Why do they call her that?"

"Because she makes these gardens what they are," said Tasker, turning into a sloping passageway. "Everything you saw out there, under the dome — that was all her."

Naeo slowed her step. "She made the gardens?"

"Well, Nature had something to do with it too," said Tasker, laughing. But then his face straightened. "Though if ever I've met someone with the gift to guide Nature's hand, that would be Amelie Tate."

"She sounds... amazing."

He drew a breath. "She is. Come on, nearly there."

They began to descend a staircase, the walls of which were

made entirely of glass. After only three or four steps, Naeo slowed to a stop and stared in wonder. Through the glass she could see a stream tumbling over mossy rocks, flowers drooping beneath a heavy dew, trees and bushes thick with verdant leaves all swaying slightly in an inexplicable breeze. So tall were the shrubs, so lush and richly planted were the banks of flowers, that the rest of the gardens could not be seen at all.

"This is her own part of the gardens," said Tasker, smiling at Naeo's reaction. "She calls it the glen."

Naeo did not notice the wooden door at the bottom of the steps until she was almost upon it.

Naeo stopped and eyed it nervously.

Tasker stepped past her and reached for the knocker. "Let's see if she's in," he said.

It struck a deep, hollow note.

Clunk, clunk, clunk.

He turned and smiled at Naeo. "You're fine, Princess."

She felt far from fine. Her stomach churned and her skin was clammy and hot.

Then there was a voice from the other side of the door: faint but friendly, calling them in.

Tasker turned the handle and pushed at the door. It swung open with a creak.

Naeo stood frozen to the spot, blinking in disbelief.

44
The Glen

"We journeyed through green dale and glen, *each more lush and beautiful than the last. But beyond was an even greater prize: the bright and majestic plains of Salsimaine."*

WHAT LAY BEFORE NAEO was not a corridor, nor a room, but a tiny glen, rising to the left and right from a broad, grassy floor bisected by the stream she had seen from the stairway. The sides were steep but regular, with terraces cut into the soft earth to form wide steps, each thick with riotous life: plants and flowers and herbs of every type imaginable.

Curiously, on the floor of the glen, was a single, brass bed — neatly made with a patchwork eiderdown and plump white pillows — placed right next to the little stream, such that a drowsy sleeper might refresh themselves with its cool waters. Naeo saw other pieces of furniture scattered around: a chest of drawers peeking between two bushes; a wardrobe nestled among a bed of seedling flowers; a dresser half hidden behind a tangle of bushes, the mirror of which seemed to be missing. There was even what looked like an apothecary's cabinet, it's many shelves full to bursting with colourful jars and phials, each marked with a small, handwritten label.

This was not just a glen, or a pleasant retreat from the garden: it was a bedroom, a lounge and a laboratory.

"Sorry, I was planting right at the top," came a cheerful female voice off to their side.

The skin on Naeo's neck pricked and tingled.

She looked around and saw a small, slim woman striding down the terraces, pulling gardening gloves off her hands. She was dressed in the same green overalls as the other guests, but seemed bolder and more vigorous than any Naeo had seen in the rest of the hospital. Her voice was strong and her step was easy and confident. Nevertheless, as she approached, Naeo noticed that her skin was a little pale, her once-beautiful face a little gaunt, her large eyes a little faded and fringed with dark rings.

But then she smiled. Instantly all these marks of fatigue and worry fell away, and she was radiant.

"*Tasker*, isn't it?" she said, cocking her head on one side. "Tasker — from Salisbury? We met the other month."

Tasker beamed, flattered to have been remembered. "Yes," he said, "we didn't talk for long, but you very kindly showed me—"

"I showed you round the gardens," said Amelie Tate, smiling amiably and shaking his hand.

And then her gaze shifted to Naeo.

Her eyes traced the eyes and nose and mouth. Then the neck and shoulders. She gave a slight frown. "And, forgive me," she laughed hesitantly and extended her hand, "who's this? Have... have we *met*?"

Naeo was stricken. The air had left her lungs; her head was swimming. Amelie Tate's face seemed so familiar. Something about her... no, *everything* about her was so... close... so warm.

"I'm Naeo," she managed in a failing, dry voice, offering an unsteady hand.

347

"Naeo?" said Amelie Tate, glancing at Tasker inquisitively. "That's an interesting name. Beautiful, too..."

Tasker shifted. "Amelie, this is Naeo, daughter of Bowe," he said, placing a hand on Naeo's shoulder. He hesitated for a moment then said: "She's from the Other."

Amelie covered her mouth and took two sudden steps back. "Oh God!" she exclaimed, staring at Naeo with wide, frightened eyes. She looked quizzically at Tasker as though asking him why he was subjecting her to this.

He opened his palms and looked apologetically from one to the other. "I think I'd better leave the rest to you," he said, and then turned and left.

Amelie frowned after him for a moment and then tried to gather herself.

"OK..." she said, between her fingers, still gazing after him as if not wanting to look at Naeo. "Sorry, it's just a... a bit of a shock. I haven't had any actual contact with..."

She trailed off. Her gaze turned slowly back to Naeo, tracing her eyes, her forehead, her cheek.

Naeo stared back, limbs trembling. Part of her wanted to run away, but the other wanted to reach out and hold her.

And then Amelie suddenly shook her head. Her lower lip began to quiver. There was fear in her eyes, and pain — so much pain. The pain of a mother who had lost a son; of a woman who had seen too much darkness, too much loss. And there was also something else — a flicker of recognition, the barest glimmer of hope.

Without thinking, Naeo dropped her bag, stepped forward and extended her arms.

Amelie rocked backwards, her mouth open, her arms limp at her sides.

But Naeo took another step.

"I know you," said Naeo. She looked into Amelie's face, her eyes brimming. "You know me."

Amelie looked at her in a bewildered daze, tears rolling down her cheeks. And then, without a word, she raised her arms and gathered Naeo into her chest.

"I do," she said, her voice cracking. "I do."

Simia leaned over Sylas, her eyes wild with panic.

"Sylas!" she cried, holding his face between her hands. She turned and screamed: "SOMEBODY HELP ME!"

A double shadow passed swiftly across the archway, breaking the evening beams. Suddenly Isia was at Simia's shoulder, peering down at Sylas, taking in his taut features, his fixed stare, his empty face.

She did nothing. She just gazed down at him and smiled.

Sylas saw none of this. He saw only colour and form amid a sea of darkness. He saw the world ebb and flow: a great sky of gold, a cavernous pit of fiery red, a dreamy fog of silver.

And then, in this vast nothingness, he saw a face: a face framed in green and burnished with tears. A face that was close and warm, that peered down at him with tender eyes and drew him close. He felt her body and he smelled her skin.

Then he murmured something in a breaking voice.

"I know you," he said.

PART THREE

Knowing

45

The Fruit of the Knowing Tree

"Who would eat the fruit of the Knowing Tree?
Who will savour its sweetness, taste its bitter truth?"

MARTHA DRESCHER ROARED WITH LAUGHTER. "Doctor Helman Schmitz, you can't be serious!" She eyed her colleague, the smile falling from her face. "You... *are* serious."

"Well, I was being a bit serious, yes," said Helman Schmitz, shifting uncomfortably in his seat. He took the glasses off his nose and rubbed them mercilessly with his handkerchief.

Martha pursed her lips in an attempt to lose the smile. "You're really saying, Helman, that we're single because people think we pose a health risk?" She swallowed another giggle.

Helman returned the glasses to his nose. "It's a theory," he said, defensively. "Why? What do you put it down to?"

Martha threw her eyes in the air in feigned thought. "Well, we're hopeless nerds for a start," she said, counting with her fingers. "Second, we haven't exactly been blessed in the looks department. Third, we pretty much live in a laboratory in the backend of Germany. And, I mean, just *look at it*! Is this where *normal* people would choose to spend their time?"

Helman cast his eyes around pathogen lab L65 of the Centre for Infection Research. His gaze fell admiringly on the chalkboards packed with mathematical equations, on the banks of glass instruments lining every bench, on the tubes and condensers, flasks and Petri dishes. Last of all, his eyes came to rest on the state-of-the-art vacuum room, complete with airlocks and a rack of airtight personnel suits. It all looked utterly normal to him: in fact, it looked rather beautiful.

"Plus, there are big locks on the doors," added Martha, "and we wear very weird clothes." She stood up and twirled on the spot, showing off her blue plastic overalls and yellow rubber gloves up to the elbow. "It's not a good look, Helman. And if you can't see that, you've just made my point."

Helman managed a brief, slightly wounded smile. "OK, I see what you're saying," he said. He was quiet for a few moments. "Perhaps I've been going about this all wrong. Perhaps I shouldn't be trying to date *normal* people. Perhaps I should be dating people like me!"

Martha gave him a steady look. "Perhaps," she said.

There was a brief silence.

"Martha?"

"Yes…"

"Do you think you might want—"

"NO, Helman."

"But I thought you said—"

To Martha's intense relief the intercom suddenly buzzed. Then it buzzed again. And again.

"Someone's in a hurry," she said brightly as she walked over

354

to the receiver. "Perhaps it's a secret admirer unable to contain themselves!"

She picked up the handset and the little video screen lit up. She frowned. There was no one in the corridor.

"That's strange," she said, turning around. "Helman, did you—"

When she saw Helman, she froze. He was staring at the laboratory windows, his eyes wide with terror. Martha's skin crawled as she followed his gaze across the workbenches and slowly up to the windows.

She staggered back into the door, trying not to scream.

On each of the windowsills stood a dark cloaked figure, arms braced against the stone uprights, hooded head pressed up against the glass.

She blinked. Impossible. They were four storeys up!

But then, as if to answer her doubts, one of them moved. It lowered one arm and brought it up to the glass. Martha squinted out into the darkness: that was no hand. It was half covered in black fur, and it seemed to have... claws – long, razor-sharp claws – one of which it now extended until it met the security window, then it began to sweep downwards in a wide arc. Behind the claw Martha saw the silver trail of cut glass.

She glanced across and saw the other figures doing the same thing.

"Helman!" she shouted, "the samples! Into the vacuum room! Lock yourself in!"

Helman snapped himself out of his trance. "What about you?"

"Just do it!"

She whirled about and slammed her fist on the red panic button next to the intercom. Instantly the lights dimmed to red and the room was filled with deafening noise. The breach alarm sent out an urgent pulse accompanied by a harsh male voice.

"ACHTUNG – ALERT! ACHTUNG – ALERT!"

Heavy steel shutters began to drop on the cabinets around the room with a series of rattles and bangs.

Martha turned to see Helman fumbling with stacks of vacuum cases.

"Careful!" she shouted over the din. "There are pathogens in those!"

She rushed across to help him and was almost at his side when a new, deafening sound made her stop.

BOOM...

BOOM...

BOOM...

She looked at the windows, but the three figures were still cutting their way through the thick security glass.

Reluctantly, she turned towards the door.

Another BOOM reverberated through the room, making the floor shake.

This time she did scream, but her throat was bone dry and she made no sound. There were four protrusions in the reinforced steel: four impressions of something that had struck with incredible force.

Each was the shape of a head.

A monstrous, canine head.

§

She was not just dreamed, she was there; she was not just seen, she was felt and heard and smelled and known. She was before him and she was everywhere, filling the empty space in his heart, enclosing his world.

She was there. His mother was just *there*.

He reached out with his mind and held her close. He saw her lean forward and he felt her arms about him. He breathed in her presence and drew in her warmth.

356

But there was a rift, a rupture, as though she were seen through a prism. Part of her seemed unreal, unfound. And then, as he looked up, as he drank in the sight of her, he knew that he hadn't moved. That the eyes moving over her face were not his. And although he felt her embrace, he could not raise his arms to return it.

He saw her look down and speak, but he could not hear her words. And then he stepped away from her, even though that was the last thing he wanted to do. He willed himself forward, yearning to return to her, but he was powerless, as though his legs were not his own.

He gasped, feeling the chill of breath in his lungs. Something about that cool evening air made the rupture more real. In the same moment, he felt the tears on his cheeks, the tautness of his muscles, the back of a chair against his shoulders, and he heard a sound: a voice, not his mother's, but Simia's, close at his ear.

"Sylas!" she sobbed. "Sylas, say something!"

His mother faded, drifting into the silver fog. In her place he saw Simia, her eyes bloodshot, her face pale. She was leaning in to him, pleading with him.

"Not you!" she implored. "Please speak to me!"

And in that moment he understood. He knew that he and Naeo were one, that right now he was there with her even as he was here, with Simia. He knew that by some strange twist of Nature, some break in the universe, he was somewhere between the worlds, between himself and his Glimmer.

Then he saw Isia, bold and beautiful, enrobed in a sunset. She gazed at him with ebony eyes and spoke to him with his mother's voice.

"You have eaten the fruit of the Knowing Tree," she said, no longer with the voice of his mother but instead in the tones of a young woman.

He saw Simia turn from him and glare at her. "What have you *done* to him?" she screamed.

"Nothing that will not pass," replied Isia calmly.

Simia hesitated. "What do you mean?"

"I mean it offers a temporary gift. Sylas has been given true knowledge of himself. All of himself. He sees as Naeo sees, feels as she feels."

There was a brief silence.

"I thought you'd poisoned him!" yelled Simia. "Why didn't you warn us?"

"Because the fruit works best with an open mind — a mind free from fear and unencumbered by hope. If I had told you, it might not have worked at all."

Sylas fought a battle with himself, struggling between the image of his mother and Isia's voice. He yearned to return to the warmth, to the certainty of his mother, to her face — that precious face, now marked with care but still beautiful, breathtaking, magical.

But it was distant now, somewhere beyond the silver mist. It was as though Simia and Isia — with their clear, hard words — had sent her back into a dream.

He felt the unwelcome sensation of his own limbs, tense and straining. He felt his stomach tight and bloated — newly filled by the fruit of the Knowing Tree. He felt a trickle of sweat rolling down the back of his neck. He wanted to push these things away, but they became ever more real and his mother was crowded out by these clearer, louder, sharper things.

Suddenly Isia's face was before him, her almond eyes smiling into his, banishing all that was left of his precious dream.

"I must call you back now, Sylas," she said, gently, "back to this world and to this part of yourself." She reached forward and stroked his cheek. "I needed you to see the bond you have with

Naeo with your own eyes — or rather, with *her* eyes. If you are to meet your potential, you must believe your bond, feel it, live it. You must overcome the division of our worlds. Make it irrelevant. Bring it to nothing."

Sylas felt her take hold of his hands and draw him upwards. His legs felt remote and numb, but he found himself rising to his feet. He became aware of a hand around his arm, supporting him, and he heard Simia again.

"Where are you taking him?" she said, full of suspicion.

"He's fine," said Isia, turning her radiance to his companion. "But we must go outside while the effects are still strong."

"Why?"

"Because I have only shown him part of what he needs to see," she said with a serene smile. She turned to Sylas. "Sylas, you have seen how close you are to your Glimmer, even when she is far away. How she is you and you are she, even when you are on two sides of a broken universe. But that is not the whole truth. To understand your gift fully, you must first know a greater truth, the truth of all humankind."

Sylas was still in a shifting, giddy daze. The world was at once dreamy and yet sharp and clear: every sound piercing, every detail precise, every sensation almost unbearably intense. As Isia led him around the table, he saw the dancing light in the crystal, the dusting of yeast on the grapes, the too-bright colours of the cakes. He heard the shuffle of his feet over marble, the halting breath of Simia at his side, the breeze groaning slightly as it passed through the arch.

And then he took an involuntary gasp as a shock of cold wind blew through his hair, fingering his face and buffeting his clothes. Suddenly his vision was clear and he saw Isia to one side and Simia to the other. The wide arc of the circular terrace stretched out ahead — one of the giant platforms that he had seen from the ground. The other loomed above.

Between them, and laid out as far as the eye could see, was the great city of Gheroth. It huddled in the evening light, glowering at the dark horizon, rumbling with activity, churning out countless trails of smoke. Sylas's piercing sight picked out crooked buildings in chaotic streets; tiny figures moving through a busy throng; traders peddling their wares; women hanging washing from their windowsills; children playing in a distant square. He saw all this in a heartbeat, his gaze encompassing all things as though they were near at hand, as though he were walking in the lanes, standing at the windows, playing in the squares.

Isia led him towards the precipice at the edge of the platform. He felt an urge to resist, to keep back from the brink, but his limbs carried him forward until the wind whipped at his body. Soon all that lay between him and oblivion was a narrow ledge of stone.

One final step.

Suddenly Isia let go of his arm. He tottered, trying to find his balance.

When he lifted his eyes, he saw Isia on the very brink, pointing down with a blurred, outstretched finger.

"Behold the plight of humankind," she said, her robes whipping around her in the mounting winds.

Sylas looked down to the plaza, to the expanse of white stone, to the ring of Ragers and the thousands of huddled worshippers arranged around the great tower. He saw with penetrating clarity, looking past and through things, into and between things so that nothing in the world was closed to him.

And then he saw something astounding.

Rising from among the gathered bodies of the worshippers,

there were countless silvery trails, climbing like gossamer strings up and up above the surrounding buildings, above the smoke and bustle of the city, up the flanks of the great Temple of Isia. It was a flux of living lines — one beginning with each person huddled below — reaching up into the void as though seeking something out. They were graceful, ethereal and exquisitely beautiful. Yet something about them made him inexplicably sad.

"The fibres of the human soul," said Isia, "stretched thin between the worlds, searching for what has been lost."

Sylas was transported, his heart aching, his eyes still fixed on the silvery tendrils, tracing their dancing, twisting, turning paths. They climbed ever higher into the sky, curling around one another in a graceful dance, drawing ever closer until just below the platform they formed a shimmering, mystical twine.

"This is my veil of greatness," said Isia, her voice piercingly clear. "They believe I answer their prayers, but in truth the whispers they hear are not mine. And the comfort is not mine to give. They comfort themselves. Their words are their own, spoken unknowingly in another world by another self, resounding across the rift. When they whisper, they speak only to themselves. When they find courage, it is their own. When they discover hope or love, forgiveness or compassion, it is theirs to give. All they seek is in the lost part of their own soul. In their Glimmer."

Sylas turned to Isia. His lips parted to say something, but when he saw her his eyes widened and he staggered backwards.

"Sylas!" screamed Simia, grabbing him around the shoulders and pulling him back from the edge.

He rocked forward, but his eyes never left Isia. To him, in that moment, she was as radiant as the sun, her beauty dimming the rest of the world so that only she mattered. It was not just her shining skin, or her eyes of sparkling black. It was the wide arc of radiance that lay all about her: a seething mass of silvery trails that curled up from the edge of the platform and fell upon her from above, engulfing her in a heavenly light. They were the ghostly threads that he had seen rising from the worshippers far below, but now they were almost one, surging into her as though they had finally found their home.

"It is not me. I am nothing but a gateway, a pathway for lost souls," said Isia, as though correcting his thoughts. "Through me, the two halves may touch. For a fleeting moment, questions are answered, doubts are overcome, dreams are fulfilled."

Simia gazed about her, wide-eyed, looking for these wondrous things, searching for her own thread. "Can I see?" she asked, her voice suddenly full of yearning. "I want to see mine!"

Sylas glanced up and caught a glimpse of a silver trail curling up above her, tracing an arc before darting towards Isia. And then he looked away. For some reason he felt that he had seen something he should not.

Simia hesitated. "Do I even have one?"

Isia moved, making the many radiating trails flex and turn, flashing with a new brightness. "Of course you do, Simia. We all have a Glimmer."

Simia looked at her with wide eyes, struggling to comprehend. "But can I *see*?" she asked again. "I think if I could just see, I might—"

"No," said Isia, firmly. "The fruit of the Knowing Tree would drive most people to madness — there is such a thing as too much knowledge."

The excitement drained from her face. "But Sylas..." she said, turning to him. "*He* can see!"

"He sees because it is his calling. Do not envy him that burden. He and Naeo must heal the division of our souls, or they must try. They may eat from the tree because to find our cure, they must first know our ills."

As Simia gazed at Isia she seemed to grow smaller, the hope fading from her eyes. She began to look as weary as she had before they had arrived at the temple.

"Don't be sad, Simia. You have a Glimmer, somewhere out there, in the Other. Think of that. Your path has been hard, but there is hope and there is comfort. Your Glimmer is proof of that. Your Glimmer is the joy to your despair, the Salve to your pain, the answer to your loss."

Simia gazed into Isia's face.

"Has... has it always been there?" she asked.

Isia knelt before her, drawing her close. "Always. Your Glimmer was there when you were born and when you were a child on the plains of Salsimaine. Your Glimmer was there when the darkness came — there at the Reckoning — there when you were left alone."

Simia's eyes searched her face, as though looking for a lie. "All the time? All that time I was out on the Barrens?"

Isia drew her fingertips across her face, sweeping away tears. "Yes, Simsi. You were never alone."

Simia gulped down a sob. She shook her head, still struggling to comprehend.

"There's something else," continued Isia. "And you must remember this. There is a chance — a distant, half-dreamed chance — that soon Sylas and Naeo may fulfil the Glimmer Myth. And if they do, no one will need the Knowing Tree. No one. Not you, not the worshippers down there, not even Sylas. If that happens, it will be in large part because of you."

Simia lifted her eyes.

"You have already helped Sylas more than anyone could have imagined, and your work is far from done. So do not doubt yourself.

You are caught up in the greatest adventure of a lifetime — of any of our lifetimes — and Sylas needs you." She rose to her feet and smiled down at her. "We all need you."

Something about the strange potion in his blood made Sylas hear this exchange with unbearable clarity, as though it was echoing in the confines of his skull. But now he began to push back, trying to discover his own thoughts — thoughts that he knew were near and important. There was a question — one that he had to ask before the moment passed. He searched for elusive words: words he must form with a tongue that seemed far away.

"Why me?" he said hoarsely. "If you… if you can see all this… if you know… why not *you*?"

Isia turned to face him. "Because I am part of the problem," she said. "Because I helped to make it happen."

The words hammered into Sylas's mind. "What do you mean?"

The last trace of a smile fell from Isia's face.

"I broke the world in two."

46

Trapped

"Now is the time to leave Suhlmeer, and Lhayamtor,
and Babelset — leave for the fringes of the empire, now,
before the entire nation is trapped *and destroyed."*

THE WIND WHISTLED OVER the high terraces of the Dirgheon,
clawing at the stone as it had for centuries. The open flank of
the fortress bore a scar of deep black soot left by furnace-hot
fire, the fire of cascading oil. Otherwise it was featureless, cold
and still, offering its silent defiance to the elements. It loomed
over the busy huddle of the city, mighty and imperious,
dwarfing the puny pillar of the Temple of Isia, mocking the
trifling lives of those who hurried and chattered and bartered
beneath.

And then, something moved.

A faint sound caressed the deserted steps, resonated in the deep
dark stone.

A rustle. A flap.

A screech.

It was distant but unmistakable, and it was coming from a
small opening in the colossal slope of stone. A place where one of

the huge blocks seemed to be missing — at the very centre of that side of the pyramid.

Then it came again, louder. This time more of a flurry, like the frenzied beating of wings somewhere deep in the bowels, where it was forever dark and dank: where the birthing chambers were. Suddenly the black tunnel issued forth a blast of squeals and screeches, a chorus of unworldly, animal wails. And then there was a wind, a gentle but filthy breeze that poured out of the opening. It quickly picked up pace, becoming an ever-stronger gale, blasting forth from the Dirgheon, carrying on its foul currents a hail of flaps and screams and heaving pants. These sounds became a rumble and the rumble became thunder, bellowing at the darkening sky.

A shape erupted from the tunnel, hurling itself far out into the void, rolling and tumbling in a fluttering cloak of blackness. Even as it began to fall, another came, and another, and another. They threw themselves from the side of the Dirgheon, rolling through the air, plummeting towards the city below. And then, just as the first of them looked as though it would be dashed against the terraced steps, it changed shape. Two vast, angular wings unfurled from the flurry and in that instant the creature ceased its descent, catching the wind in its leathery folds and soaring up, over the streets, into the great swirls and thermals of wind above. It flexed the jagged planes of its wings, turning them lightly, gracefully until they caught an upward draught. As it gained height it turned its sharp, pale face to its brethren, watching with bloodshot eyes as they too threw out their wings and caught the air, turning in an arc to follow.

Soon they were a constant stream of black bodies, spiralling up and up towards the heavy clouds, until they passed the pinnacle of the Dirgheon. There, they lifted their heads to the heavens and mounted a triumphal cry, a chorus of squeals that shocked the clouds and chilled the dying rays of the sun.

The bat-like swarm circled around a cloud and sailed out from the city towards the rising moon. They looked down upon the twinkling lamplights of the streets below and the thin silver ribbon of the river winding out towards the distant estuary. They flew on, stretching their newborn wings, delighting in the mounting winds of a storm. A vast dark front loomed over them from the east, and as it flashed and flickered it silhouetted their devilish forms.

They twisted and spiralled upon the fingers of the storm, hungrily upon the dark, rolling lands below, eyeing the vast expanses of the Barrens, and at its fringes the towns and villages, the farms and homesteads. Between the faint lights of distant towns were three columns of blackness, snaking across the countryside, two headed for the silver lines of the coast and one out on to the Barrens. With their bat-like ears the creatures heard the curl and snap of scores of flags, the heave and push of giant bodies, the measured march of troops.

The sight warmed their chilly blood. They were born for war and they would not wait for long.

As the first finger of lightning escaped the towering clouds, the creatures turned a loop in front of the moon and swarmed back towards the Dirgheon, screaming their homage to Thoth.

S

Ash rocked back on his chair, tapping his fingers on the marble table. For some time he had been quietly engrossed in the grand meeting of the Merisi. He had wondered at the careful, decisive exchanges — so much more orderly than the Say-Sos of the Suhl. He had been impressed by the quiet, unassuming command of

Mr Zhi, drawing out just enough information to take decisions. He had been fascinated by the occasional display of a map, or a chart, or a fantastically realistic picture on a piece of glossy paper, normally of a Ghorhund or another of Thoth's creatures. But as the talk turned to the many sightings and incursions and abductions, his face darkened. For a while he continued to listen, but finally he had to speak up.

He rose to his feet. "This sounds like the Reckoning," he said.

The gathering turned to him enquiringly.

"This is how it all started," explained Ash. "Loads of — what did you call them — excursions?"

Mr Zhi smiled and nodded. "Incursions, excursions — all the same. Go on."

"Well, yes, those — we called them raids. Never very big — just a unit of Ghor or Ghorhund. But targeted, and all at once. They knew exactly what they were looking for: food stores, armouries, command posts. And they usually took something back with them — charts, maps, people..."

"People?" probed Kasumi.

"Adepts and Scryers mostly. Spoorrunners and Leaflikes too." His brow furrowed as he remembered. "Quite a few of each, I think."

"What for?"

He shrugged. "To use against us," he said. "When the real war began."

There was a murmur of concern around the chamber. "The real war," somebody said. "You see? It hasn't even started yet!"

Suddenly several conversations began at once. For some moments Ash listened to the mounting alarm, but there was something else he needed to say, something that had been on his mind since their drive to Winterfern.

"But there's another thing," said Ash. The room soon fell silent. "You say that they're coming through all of the stone circles? And some other, new places too — these places where the Ray Reapers have been seen?"

"It seems so," said Mr Zhi.

"Well, in the Reckoning they did the same. Thoth positioned his forces all around the plains of Salsimaine and, before we knew it, they controlled every way in and out. By the time the war began, everyone was trapped; we didn't stand a chance."

"Well, we don't need to worry too much about that," said Kasumi. "He can't exactly trap us in our own world."

Everyone mumbled their agreement. And then, slowly, they seemed to understand. All eyes turned to Ash.

"He can't trap you," he said, "but he can trap Naeo."

Kasumi frowned. "You're saying that Thoth *knew* Naeo would come? That he's trying to keep her here?"

"I don't know if he knew she'd come, but he definitely knows she came. Scarpia knows, which means he knows."

Mr Zhi sank back in his chair. "You're right, Ash," he said, stroking his beard nervously. "Now that Thoth has seen what Sylas and Naeo are capable of, he will do all he can to keep them apart. Whether he intended it or not, this attack is also the perfect defence." He cast his eyes around the room. "And we must decide what to do about it."

47

The Girl

"...a girl, a young, pure girl — a girl in whose veins
ran the blood of all of its nations."

"YOU?" SAID SIMIA, MORTIFIED. "You broke the world in two? *Why?*"

"Because I had no choice."

Simia shook her head. "Why not?"

Isia walked forward and caught up her hand. "To understand you need to reach back into our history," she said, turning and reaching out to Sylas too. "Come, I'll show you."

She led them back towards the arch, away from the windy ledge, from the darkening skies and the mesh of silvery trails. Even as they approached the archway, Sylas noticed that the few tendrils still clear to him were fading, as though they had only been sustained by the full evening light. The day was fading rapidly now, driven away by a vast storm cloud that spanned the sky: a gash of blackness, flickering with distant lightning. The great pyramid of the Dirgheon seemed to draw in the darkness, swelling in the shadow of the storm. Perhaps that was why they did not see a sudden movement on one of its sides: a thin line of black forms trailing from one of the high terraces, spiralling up towards the clouds and then looping around the rising moon.

Isia led them around the great banquet table and guided them back to their seats. The further he walked from the ledge, the more Sylas felt he was coming to his senses. The colours were not so stark, the sounds not so jarring. He was grateful, but he also felt a pang of loss.

Isia reached down beside the table and held up Sylas's bag.

"Would I be right in thinking that the Samarok is in here?"

"Yes," he said.

"Let's take a look," she said, passing the bag to him.

Sylas took the bag and began untying the drawstring, pulling out the ancient volume and laying it carefully on the table.

"Have you read anything of the first part of the book? The passages known as *The Histories*?"

Sylas shook his head. "No, I've read the poem, but…" He hesitated and frowned. "Hold on, yes, I have. When we were on the Barrens — when we camped at the Circle of Salsimaine."

"Which part — the beginning?"

"Yes, just a few paragraphs. They didn't mean much to me."

"About the Priests of Souls?"

"Yes, yes, that's right," said Sylas, rubbing his eyes and then lifting the cover. He turned to the opening page and ran his eyes over the first few lines. Instantly the handwritten scrawl shifted and changed until all he saw was the familiar shape of the Ravel Runes. He recognised the passage at once. "Here, right at the beginning — it talks about the priests and some kind of king…" He hesitated as he waited for the runes to open themselves to him.

"Read it," said Isia. "Just the first page or two."

Sylas glanced up at Simia, who was at his shoulder poring over the page herself, as though the runes meant something to her.

He settled himself, cleared his throat and began to read:

371

"Here are recorded the chronicles of the Merisi, begun by our hand in this year of Our Lord one thousand two hundred and twenty-nine. Know that we, followers of Merisu, Master of the Sacred Arts, do set down this History willingly, in good faith and without evil disposition. In His name, we hereby give witness of the nature of these two worlds, of the history of our peoples, and our account of the evil and cruel infamy of the Priests of Souls, who have brought suffering and misery to the people of all the world such that they are, forever more, the enemy of Mankind.

They came from the cool of the sand-scented temples: from the long dark of the coiling passages and the oily flicker of many-columned halls. They rose as leaders of men in that ancient land, men of words and vision whose mystery brought hope to the squalor-born. But while the people lifted their eyes upon the gentle countenance of these blessed men, they saw not the cool and dark of their hearts, nor the oily flicker behind their eyes.

In the beginning there were twelve: one from each of the great Kemetian temples, devout priests, worthy priests, each and all. So they were until one day summoned by their king to a valley between the cataracts, to a secret place, not known to common men but hidden deep within the rock. There they bound their minds and souls to a great task: to forge a magic true and absolute – a magic of such power that the emperor king would forever reign supreme.

They laboured for one score years and ten, until each grew old and frail and the world had all but forgotten their academy in the hot rocks of the desert. And then, one day, the greatest of all the priests, the priest of Thoth, sent forth a messenger to the mighty king Ramesses, who was yet upon the throne..."

Sylas paused and frowned. He knew that name, *Ramesses*. He was sure he had heard it in history lessons at school. Yes, Ramesses, the Pharaoh of ancient Egypt.

Ancient Egypt.

Suddenly his mind was a whirl of connections: Egypt... the pyramids... the Dirgheon... Isia's priestesses... the Egyptian-looking paintings in the tower. Suddenly all these things seemed far from a coincidence.

"You are beginning to see, Sylas," said Isia, smiling. "But go on, there is more."

He leaned over the Samarok and continued.

"It was a message that told of the impossible, a proclamation that shattered the known and the knowable.

The magic had been found

Only two things would be needed to forge this magic to end all wars, this so-called Ramesses Shield: first, a circle made entirely of stone – stone taken from the four corners of the empire; and second, a girl, a young pure girl – a girl in whose veins ran the blood of all of its nations. So proclaimed the priest of Thoth, scribe to the Academy of Souls.

And so commanded Ramesses the Great.

As work began on the stone circle, thousands of clerks and servants and priests began the search for the child – the girl in whose very being was the perfect union of the empire. This proved the greater task. Long after the stone circle was built and six years after Ramesses' command, a young peasant girl was found. A girl..."

Sylas retraced the line. He glanced up at Isia then spoke the words quietly, breathlessly: *"...a girl called Isia."*

He stopped reading and looked up at her.

"And so you see I am no more a god than you or Simia," said Isia.

Simia stared at her. "You... you were that girl?"

"A normal girl born to peasant parents," said Isia, breaking into a radiant smile. "Just like you."

§

While they had been deciding what to do about Naeo, Ash had been at the centre of the meeting. He had quietly enjoyed being consulted on strategies and tactics, on Thoth and the Suhl, and Sylas and Naeo. But now that the decision had been taken, the meeting droned on about things of which he knew little and his attention started to wander, his mind soon turning to the strange gift Mr Zhi had given him: the golden egg.

"*A Thing for a master of magic; someone like yourself,*" the old man had said. "*Someone for whom Essenfayle is simply not enough.*"

Ash glanced about him and then rummaged in his bag. He felt the cool weight of the egg in his hand and pulled it out. He turned it over, marvelling at the beauty of it, the craftsmanship of its making. It was seamless and untainted, shined to a high polish, seeming brighter than the great discs of light that lit the room. He turned it over in his fingers, the golden light playing over his youthful face.

What's inside? he wondered.

"*That is where the true gold lies,*" Mr Zhi had said.

He laid it on the table and stared at it. Druindil might work. He had done it before — a challenge in the Mutable Inn. He had amazed the Muddlemorphs with his astonishing ability to see through a thick container of stone.

But that would be too easy.

He drummed the table with his fingertips. This was perplexing.

Urgolvane. *That* would do the trick. A little egg would be no match for the way of force, no matter what it was made of.

He placed a hand on either side of the egg, closed his eyes and settled his breathing. He felt the weight of his body in his chair and the great mass of the marble table beneath his fingers. He took all this and he began to press it between the confines of his mind, turning it in upon itself, rolling it up into a smaller and smaller centre of mass — a dense, dark force that shuddered under its own weight.

All this he placed upon the little golden egg.

He opened one eye. Then two.

The egg was trembling a little on the table but its smooth golden surface was still perfectly intact, sending back a laughable reflection of his face.

He snapped his eyes shut.

His mind reached out to the vast granite slabs of the walls, gathering up the might of their ancient rock, folding it in with the forces he had already assembled, pressing it into that tiny space, just above the little golden egg.

He opened his eyes.

It was vibrating now, turning slowly on the spot so that the reflection of his face quivered and warped.

He bit his lip and wiped a trickle of sweat from his brow.

Once again he closed his eyes. He sent his mind still further, beyond what he could see. He reached up, through the great stone ceiling, up into the awesome heft of the hill, into the tons of earth and mud, rock and shingle. His mind spanned so wide that it ached, drawing in soil and clay and sand and stone, binding them up in his thoughts, wrapping them into an ever smaller space: a colossal focal point of force. All this he brought down through the body of the hill, through the ceiling of granite and into the still spaces of that room. Then he lowered it on to the egg.

He opened his eyes.

The egg was spinning, faster and faster, reflecting flashes of golden light around the room. It hummed on the table, growing in volume.

The Merisi's conversation stuttered and fell silent. Ash was dimly aware that they had stopped but he was committed now — he had to see this through.

The egg whirred on the tabletop, making it tremble. Faster and faster it spun, until it was a golden blur, sending out a fizz of air.

Suddenly there was a bang and it was gone. It shot across the room and hit the far wall with a crack, sending out a shower of granite. To his horror, it then darted back, hitting the table and shooting up to the ceiling. There it bounced again and shot down on to the tabletop, before leaping back up to the ceiling. Soon it was bouncing up and down, zigzagging between the table and the ceiling, sending up a flurry of papers and charts.

The Merisi watched this with curious calm, then rather wearily, they lowered themselves beneath the table, apparently taking cover. All except Mr Zhi, who remained seated. He simply placed his palms on the tabletop, and watched.

Suddenly the egg caught an edge and shot across the room, then bounced back and forth across the chamber, then along its length, then between the floor and ceiling until it finally worked its way back to the table.

Ash winced. He was about to lower himself beneath the table in shame when Mr Zhi suddenly leapt into the air, vaulting with unexpected athleticism on to the tabletop and reaching above his head. The egg bounced once on the floor, once on the ceiling, and then shot neatly into the palm of his glove.

He adjusted his hat, and held out the egg.

"I think you had better try again," he said. "*Outside*, if you please."

48

The Beginning
and the End

"Mine was the beginning *and yours must be the* end.*"*

SIMIA PULLED HER CHAIR closer to Isia. "So the Priests of Souls used you in their magic?"

"Yes," said Isia. "I was meant to represent the people of the empire — the people they wanted to keep safe."

"So they were *trying* to make two worlds?" asked Sylas. "One for the people of the empire and one for everyone else?"

"That was the theory, yes. They thought that I would make the right division, because all the blood of the empire runs in my veins. Of course, that's not the way it worked. Instead the magic divided me, and in dividing me, they divided all of humankind."

Simia was fascinated. "So what did they *do* to you?"

Isia opened her mouth to answer, but then seemed to reconsider. She reached over to the Samarok, pulled it towards her and turned the page. She perused it for a moment, then returned it to Sylas, her blurred finger pointing to an indented passage. "Merisu describes it better than I ever could — here, this is his account, as he himself saw it."

Sylas was astonished. "*Merisu... he was *there*?*"

"Of course," said Isia. "He was one of the Priests of Souls."

Sylas blew out his cheeks: this was getting stranger and stranger. "How could he be a *Priest of Souls*?" he said. "The Merisi aren't even *from* this world."

"But Merisu was," said Isia. She tapped the page. "Read from here."

Sylas collected his thoughts then bowed his head. He allowed the runes to reveal themselves.

The heavens boomed with full-throated thunder, making the ground shake. All seemed to morph and shift, a thick yellow vapour rising from the sands, rocks blistering and bubbling, clouds boiling in a blood-red sky.

This we saw as we gathered in our shameful circle of magic, as we played with power beyond our imagining. And yet on we chanted, our voices filled with fear: on and on, lost in the devilry of the Ramesses Shield.

When the thunder echoed into silence, we heard — Isia's cries, her warnings, her desperate pleas. We saw the child's white-robed figure kneeling at the centre of the circle, imploring each of us in turn to stop, stop before it was too late.

And yet on and on we chanted. On and on.

But then Merimis, the Priest of Maat, let go of my hand. She broke the circle and raised her arm, trying to halt what we had begun. I turned and saw her mouth wide, screaming at us to stop. I fought back the trance and I too raised my arm, looking to my fellow priests. But they were lost in the magic. In that moment I was struck by a searing pain. It entered through our outstretched hands and threw us to our knees. I looked up to see a white light, a bolt of fire forking from the sky, scything into Merimis and myself. Our hands burned, and we staggered to one side, crying out in pain. To our shame, we sought to end the pain. We came together, clasping our hands once more.

We resumed our trance-like chant, drifting gratefully back into our unknowing state.

And so we raised a magic beyond our dreams. On we chanted, on and on.

And then we stopped. Our words caught in our throats. Our hands fell to our sides. Our eyes were fixed on the centre of the circle, on the girl, Isia.

For a moment, for the briefest moment, she was not one, but two.

Only then did we cry out in horror. Only then."

Sylas trailed off. For some moments he stared at the page and then he raised his eyes to Isia.

"You were the first," he said, quietly.

Isia nodded.

"And it was all some kind of mistake?" said Simia.

"A terrible, calamitous mistake. The Ramesses Shield did not create a division between the empire and its enemies, it divided *everything*, and worst of all — *us*. Each and every one of us lost part of ourselves into the new, second half of the world — Sylas's half of the world — the place we now know as the Other. Only those who forged the Shield, the Priests of Souls themselves, were spared that fate. They lived on here, more powerful than ever, whole in a world of halves."

For some moments Sylas and Simia were dumbstruck, but finally Simia asked: "And Merisu was part of it?"

"Merisu and Merimaat... each played their part."

"*Merimaat?*" exclaimed Simia incredulously. "Merimaat was there?"

Isia opened her arms. "Of course! 'Merimis, Priest of Maat'. She only became known as Merimaat many years later, when all this was a distant memory."

Simia turned to the open archway, gazing out at the dark skies. "Merimis... Maat..." she murmured. She shook her head. "That doesn't seem right. Merimaat was so... good."

"Who says she wasn't good?" said Isia, surprised. "Remember she did her best to break the circle when she saw what was happening. And the Priests of Souls were not all bad, not then. It was Thoth — the *Priest* of Thoth as he was then — who led the rest astray."

Sylas was still running his eyes over the passage, trying to take it in. "Everyone but the Priests of Souls..." he said, rubbing his temples. "So you were the first to be broken in two. That must mean that your Glimmer was in my world? In the Other?"

"In the beginning, yes. One part of me remained here and the other was lost to the Other. I lived in both worlds, grew up in both worlds."

"But you're together now, aren't you? I mean, your Glimmer came back?"

"Yes, but by then many years had passed. I was a grown woman. I had learned to be apart, lived a full life as two separate people. I even had children, one in each world: my son in the Other, my daughter here."

Simia frowned and screwed up her nose. "That's pretty weird, isn't it? I mean, what would they be? Sister and brother? Cousins?"

Isia smiled. "I liked to think of them as sister and brother. But I think you are missing the point, Simia. In having two children, my single bloodline became two, one on each side of the divide."

Sylas had the growing sense that all this was for his benefit; that Isia was telling him something. And then, slowly, he started to understand. He found his hands clenched, his body tense.

He looked up at her. "A boy and a girl, you say? One in each world?"

Isia sat down and put her hand on his arm. "Yes, Sylas."

His eyes searched her face. "And I suppose... they had children?"

"Yes."

"And their children had children?"

She nodded.

Simia shook her head and threw out her hands. "So?"

Isia answered, but her eyes never left Sylas. "What if my two bloodlines are destined one day to become one? What if that division of blood might be undone, and with it, the division of worlds? The division of souls?"

"But... how?" asked Simia, confused.

Isia turned to her. "Because two of my descendants are not separate at all, but one. They are each other's Glimmer."

Simia's hands fell slowly to her side. "Your... descendants?"

"My children's children, over hundreds, thousands of years."

Sylas lowered his head and stared at the table turning the Merisi Band between his fingers. "You're talking about me," he said quietly. "You're talking about me and Naeo."

She reached over and folded her hands around his. "I am," she said.

And in that moment, as she squeezed his hands between hers — gentle and soft, like his mother's — the confusion began to lift. He looked at her with wide, disbelieving eyes.

"You are my family, as was your mother before you, and hers before her," said Isia. "My blood runs in your veins."

Sylas was stunned, bewildered, but he knew it was true.

She raised a hand to his cheek. "My brave, brave child," she murmured. "We share a destiny, you and I. Mine was the beginning and yours must be the end."

49

Laythlick

"Laythlick is an evil paradox:
his flesh as pale as frost, his heart dark as the Black."

THE STREETS OF GHEROTH were deserted now. Word had passed quickly between hawkers and innkeepers, townsfolk and slumdwellers.

Laythlick is on the hunt.

The city had been sent into feverish panic, people rushing here and there, storekeepers bundling their goods into carts, worshippers leaving their prayers half prayed. In no time at all, lanes and alleys, squares and thoroughfares were cleared. Only the foolish and the weak were left behind.

Laythlick is on the hunt.

Doors had been slammed, windows latched, shutters bolted. Children were pushed into backrooms, livestock crammed into shelters, valuables locked in drawers and hidden under floorboards.

Laythlick is on the hunt.

Occasionally the storm rumbled somewhere over the Barrens or the wind whistled eerily down empty lanes, but otherwise the city was silent. Expectant.

When at last they came, they moved like shadows, creeping along walls, darting between doorways, sloping across open spaces. There were too many to count, but they made no sound. They spilled from the Dirgheon and poured through the alleys like some deathly flood. And yet they moved with purpose, all together, all converging on a single spot.

There they found their master, alone in the Place of Tongues, his robes billowing in the winds.

And his albino eyes, fixed on the Temple of Isia.

§

They had been sitting there for a while now in silence, on the bed next to the stream. After those first, halting attempts at conversation they had given up, but even now, Amelie's gaze barely left Naeo. It was as though if she looked away, this miracle — this impossible, precious piece of Sylas — might disappear. And although Naeo was aware of her staring, although it was uncomfortable, she didn't mind. She understood. More than that — in a strange kind of way, she liked it. It felt as though her own father's eyes were resting on her. As though she was home.

"Such a brave, brave child," said Sylas's mother, breaking the silence. "You came all this way to see Mr Zhi? To find me?"

Naeo shrugged. "I had to do it," she said. "Sylas is doing the same thing: trying to find answers; trying to find my dad."

Amelie looked at her quizzically, still struggling to believe what she was hearing. She looked down at the stream, and when she looked up her eyes were full of tears. "You're both having to be so brave. Brave for us all."

Naeo smiled self-consciously. "Not really," she said, kicking a pebble into the stream.

Amelie's brow furrowed and her fingers fidgeted as though she was fighting an internal battle. Finally it seemed too much. "Is he all right?" she blurted. "Please, just tell me that he's all right."

Naeo saw how desperately she needed to know, the agony in her eyes.

"He's fine," she said, with rather more assurance than she felt.

Amelie put her hand to her mouth and stifled a sob. More tears rolled down her cheeks. She pulled a handkerchief from her overalls and wiped her face. "I can't tell you what it means to me. To know that he's all right. To know for sure." She lowered the handkerchief and stared at it. "You must think I'm a terrible mother."

Naeo stared at her. "No... no, I really—"

"Well I am," said Amelie, meeting her eyes. Her face was full of self-reproach. "If I hadn't let the voice get the better of me, if I hadn't let it take over, they would have let us stay together."

Naeo had no idea what to say.

"But you have to understand," implored Amelie, "once the voice got that bad, I had no choice: I had to go along with it. They said that my —" she winced, as though the word was sharp and painful on her tongue — "my... *episodes* might draw attention. That they might put Sylas at risk. They said the best thing I could do was let his uncle Tobias have him. Then they would be able to watch over him. Keep him safe."

When she finished she wrung her hands and gazed at Naeo.

And then Naeo understood. She was saying sorry. She could not apologise to Sylas, but she could do this. She looked agonised, desperate, and all Naeo wanted to do was to take the pain away. She took Amelie's hand. "He doesn't blame you."

For a moment Amelie looked stunned, as though she had heard something too wondrous and magical to be believed. "Do you *know* that?"

Naeo nodded emphatically. "I do."

And to her surprise, she did know. She knew because she knew Sylas. She knew because, even in another world, in that moment he felt near. He was there to be known.

Amelie brimmed with tears and a big, open, beautiful smile spread across her face. She leaned over and threw her arms around Naeo, pulling her close.

"Thank you!"

Naeo was about to return the hug when Amelie squeezed.

And then everything fell apart.

The pain that she had almost forgotten came roaring and screaming up her spine and raged into her skull, it pulled at her insides and punched the air from her lungs. Her limbs burned and shook, but somehow she heaved her arms before her and pushed.

She felt Amelie release her and then she started to fall.

The last thing she saw was a mother's face filled with horror and the world turning black.

50
Good Medicine

"The Suhl's Salve is a beguiling wonder, but why
is it that I yearn for the good medicine of home?"

WHEN NAEO WOKE SHE was face-down on a soft bed with the pleasant tinkle of running water in her ears. The pain was still there, but as long as she stayed very, very still, it was bearable. Even then the fogginess remained — the numb, confused empty-mindedness that the Black always brought — but she was used to that. She just lay there, listened to the calming stream and thanked her lucky stars that she was still alive.

It was not long before she heard Amelie returning.

"I can't believe you didn't tell me!" she said, still some distance away.

"I thought you had enough on your plate just getting to know each other!" It was Tasker's voice. "Anyway, I thought Naeo would've told you herself!"

"Well, that's the point — she *did* have enough on her plate!" snapped Amelie. "You should've told me everything before I met her!"

There was a silence. Naeo could hear them striding across the grass. She was suddenly aware of the cool air playing over her back and realised that her top was missing. She thought to try to cover herself, but when she remembered the pain, she decided not even to try.

"So you say it's the Black?" said Amelie, just paces away now.

"Yes, that's what she said."

Amelie lowered her voice. "I've never seen anything like it," she murmured. "It's awful!"

They walked up in silence and put some things down on the grass at Naeo's side. There was a white box with a red cross on its lid, and another wooden box containing some of the glass phials and bottles from the apothecary's cabinet – the one Naeo had noticed at the entrance to the glen. Finally, Amelie laid down a large pestle and mortar, checked that she had everything and then looked up at Naeo.

"You're awake!" she said, breaking into a smile. She reached up and drew Naeo's hair away from her face. "You gave me quite a scare!"

Naeo tried to speak, but nothing came.

"Shush, you lie quietly now," said Amelie in a soothing voice. "I'm going to give you something for the pain and then we'll see what we can do about these wounds of yours."

Naeo managed to shake her head a little. "Nothing..." she croaked, "...works."

Amelie frowned. "Well we'll see about that." She turned to the glass bottles and started checking the handwritten labels. "Jeremy, could you get the morphine from the first-aid box? And a syringe?"

Silence.

"Jeremy! Stop staring and do as I ask!" she barked.

Tasker darted forward and bent over the first-aid box. He

flipped the lid off and began riffling frantically through the contents, turning out bandages and packets and bottles. He had almost emptied the box before he found what he was looking for: a tiny bottle and what looked to Naeo like a thin glass tube. It was only then that he looked up.

There were tears in his eyes.

For a moment their gaze met and he smiled tenderly, sadly, but he quickly looked away and busied himself with the syringe and bottle.

Amelie was working at the pestle and mortar now, grinding a mixture of colourful ingredients. She paused, selected another bottle, and added a sprinkling of the grey contents. "I'm making up what we call a *poultice*," she said, apparently to them both. "A mixture of black walnut, lavender and some other good ingredients that we use as an application for wounds, infections, that kind of thing. It's *astringent*, which means that it might help to draw out the Black." She looked up and gave Naeo a wide, reassuring smile. "It'll hopefully give you a bit of relief, if nothing else."

She added another two powders and ground away at them with practised skill. Finally she picked up a bottle of clear fluid and poured it over the mixture, giving it one last stir.

"There," she said. "Now, where's that morphine?" She took the syringe from Tasker, stood up and leaned over Naeo. "OK, there'll be a quick sting but then you should feel much better."

And that was exactly what happened. Naeo felt the sharp prick of a needle and then, almost immediately, a wave of warm, wonderful relief spreading through her back. It was miraculous, as though some magical elixir was washing beneath her skin, cleaning her of the Black.

"Better?" asked Amelie, lowering her face.

"Much!" murmured Naeo.

Amelie grinned. "The wonders of poppy flowers," she said, "with some good chemistry thrown in. And speaking of good medicine, let's try that poultice."

§

Cones of blue-white light carved through the night sky, sweeping the tops of skyscrapers, blazing down wide avenues and dark alleys. The chatter and whine of helicopters was everywhere, competing with the wail of sirens. They were busy and tireless, hornet-like, criss-crossing the vast grid of city blocks, diving into parks, harrying the long lines of traffic. Pilots peered with infrared eyes as their sensors relayed a blur of data; distances were computed, odds were calculated, targets acquired and rejected. A net had fallen over New York City: a net of night vision, rotor blades and chain guns.

And yet in one dark alley in Upper Manhattan, the shadows were moving. They slid between dumpsters, leapt across fire escapes, scuttled along walls. They ran in complete silence and with absolute precision, never breaking their tight formation. Some were larger, bounding on all fours down the floor of the lane, some swung between drainpipes and leapt between sills. Others followed behind, running upright, their large heads thrust forward, giant limbs pounding the tarmac in unison. Some of these carried metal cases, others hastily packed briefcases, while the largest ones had something draped over their shoulders: limp, ungainly forms which were nevertheless carried with ease.

When the figures crossed to the next alley, they briefly passed under amber streetlights. For a moment the burdens were illuminated to reveal arms and legs, hands tied behind backs, some struggling, others still.

On they ran, gliding along the dark veins of Manhattan as though they belonged. They passed in a shadowy blur and a hiss of heaving lungs, leaving as they had arrived: stealthily and quietly, like ghosts. Sometimes they would be seen as they darted across streets or leapt between buildings, but it was a fleeting glimpse — a streak of black, a question rather than a certainty.

And then Central Park opened up before them, the wooded fringes welcoming them into the darkness. It was a sanctuary of deserted dells, lakes and hills. Still they searched the skies for the buzzing beasts that might stray too close, that might spit that metal fire and bring them to a sudden end, like the others. But here they were useless. The park was immense and riddled with places to hide: dense woods and bridges, thick undergrowth and half-lit tunnels.

They were free now, free and in their element, leaping from rock to rock, branch to branch, tearing up turf in a sprint. They were near. They could smell it.

They swarmed through clearings and trees until they reached a place where the ancient rocks of Manhattan erupted from the turf, climbing up towards the sky. There they halted, prowling and panting, breathing deep gasps of the acrid city air.

Only one of their number made the climb — a giant Ghor commander with massive shoulders and a pronounced wolfish mane that rose in black tufts around its ears. Around its neck was a collar of red and gold and beneath one brawny arm it carried a metal case. The steel surface was embossed with the yellow triangle of a warning. Inside the triangle was a black mark surrounded by three black segments.

The mark of a nuclear hazard.

The Ghor commander gave a triumphant huff as it reached the top of the rocky hill and surveyed the scene. All around was the sprawling wilderness of Central Park and along its fringes the giant towers of the city rose like black totems — monuments to mankind's power. The commander's eyes traced the glittering lights of these black slabs of stone and a disdainful laugh gurgled in its throat.

"They built the greatest stone circle of them all," it growled, its mongrel eyes following the ring of skyscrapers, "and they don't even know it."

With that it held the metal case aloft, raised its head to the heavens and howled at the swollen moon.

51
The Motherland

*"No matter how great the empire, no matter how many
lands it consumes, Kemetis remains at its heart.
It is* the Motherland*."*

SYLAS GAZED OUT OF the archway at the criss-cross of lightning,
sharp and bright against the black, billowing clouds.

A storm was coming.

It was gigantic, filling the heavens with a distant rumble, its
heavy brow stretching as far as the eye could see. And yet to
Sylas, it seemed nothing — incidental — a daub across a painted
sky. For him, the turmoil was inside.

He knew it all to be true. He *knew* it. And that was the most
terrifying thing of all.

He was Isia's blood; and she was his.

It was the family that he so yearned for that made this his
destiny. And now he felt sure that this same destiny would break
his family apart. How would he ever be able to be with his mother?
Why couldn't he just have a *normal* life?

He pushed the Samarok away. "But if all this is true, what
should I *do*?"

Isia took his hand. "I know how overwhelming this must be, Sylas, how frustrating, how frightening. I wish I could take the burden away. But I cannot. It was yours to carry before you were even born. You and Naeo must heal the rift between our worlds and, in doing so, end the emptiness in our souls — the doubt that makes us question ourselves and reach for answers in fables and superstitions. You must undo what I have done."

Sylas felt a great swell of desperation. "But *how?*" he pleaded. "I think I know *what* I'm supposed to do, but I still don't know *how*!"

Isia smiled in a way that made Sylas feel that she had seen his thoughts before they had entered his mind. "It will not be easy. It is not simply a matter of combining two halves of a whole. You and Naeo must use what you know of each other and of the worlds to forge a new and greater union."

"But how?" implored Sylas. "HOW?"

"Go to the beginnings of it all," said Isia calmly. "As all things in Nature, the rift has its roots, and it is in those tender roots that the cleft between our worlds found life. That is where you will find its truth. Go to —" she paused and turned in her seat to look out at the storm howling around the terrace — "to the place between the cataracts, to the halls of the Academy of Souls. There you will find the truths that go before me, before Merimaat and the Merisi." She turned back to the archway distractedly then pulled her blurred eyes back to Sylas. "Go there, and take the Samarok. Learn from it what you can of Merisu and of Merimaat. She came to know more of these truths than any other."

"I have to actually *go* to this place?" asked Sylas.

Isia nodded. "It is the motherland, the centre of the Empire. That was where it began, and that is where it must end."

"The Motherland?" cried Simia. "*Kemetis?*"

"Yes."

Simia threw her hands in the air. "That could take weeks — months!"

"Perhaps, though I doubt you have that much time."

Sylas looked from one to the other. "So where is it, exactly?"

"I think you know the answer to that, Sylas," said Isia. "In your world it has a different name."

Sylas sank slowly back in his chair. He hardly had to think about it. Everything led him to the answer; it always had, even before he had read of Ramesses in the Samarok. It was in the shape of the buildings, the clothes of the people, the scripts, the symbols, the paintings, the statues. The truth was in the stark, foreboding shadow of the Dirgheon and now — now that he thought to look — it was in the face of Isia: the tone of her skin, the shape of her features.

"Egypt," he said.

Isia smiled. "Yes. In your world, Kemetis became Egypt, but while the great Egyptian Empire has long since failed, that of Kemetis reigns on and sprawls to the limits of our world. Kemetis is the root of Thoth's empire and the heart of this tragedy. There you will find the final truths you need to..."

She trailed off and turned towards the archway, a flicker of concern passing over her face. She rose from the table. "Wait here," she said.

She walked purposefully through the opening and out on to the broad stone platform. The gale caught her gown and her hair rose in wild, dancing trails.

Sylas and Simia looked at one another.

"What's she doing now?" whispered Simia.

Sylas shrugged. "I have no idea," he said, watching Isia walking out across the terrace. He looked back at Simia. "How are we supposed to get to Kemetis in time? The song said we only have days, not weeks!"

Simia sighed. "I don't know."

For a moment Sylas fingered the Merisi Band, and then he said: "Were you thinking what I was thinking? When she said that stuff about bloodlines and the beginning and the end?"

Simia raised her eyebrows. "Sylas, I *never* know what you're thinking."

"I'm serious, Simsi! Don't you remember the message?" He lifted the bracelet and tapped it. "The one engraved on this? The one from *The Song of Isia*?"

She thought for a moment and then her mouth fell open. "'In blood it began... in blood it must end!'"

Sylas nodded. "It wasn't a warning, it was about the bloodline," he said. "The one that starts with Isia—"

"—and ends with you!" said Simia excitedly. "Of course!"

Sylas turned to the Samarok. "The truth was in here all along." He picked it up and stared at it for a moment, then started stuffing it into his bag. "Come on, we should go and see what's going on."

"Sylas..." said Simia, staring at him.

"What?" He turned and saw that she was staring at his neck. He touched it gingerly with his fingertips. "Is it worse?"

Simia broke into a smile. "No, it's better!"

"*Better?*"

"Completely and utterly better!"

Sylas pressed at his neck. There was no pain, no raised skin, no nauseating slide of Black beneath the surface. It was as though it had never been there.

Simia leaned in. "When did *that* happen?"

He tried to think back. He had felt it when they had been climbing the tower and when they had talked to Isia, and he remembered the dull ache when they had sat down at the table, when they had started to eat...

"The fruit!" he exclaimed. "The fruit of the Knowing Tree!"

"How do you know?"

"Because of how it made me feel — I'm sure of it! The Black made my head all cloudy and confused, but the fruit... I felt free, like I could see everything! It was the opposite! The antidote!"

"The anti-what?"

"The antidote — the cure! It must have—"

He was silenced by a sudden pulse of lightning and a deafening clap of thunder. Their eyes snapped to the archway and they saw Isia, far out on the very brink of the terrace. She was at the mercy of the storm, her body buffeted by the gale, her hair flying wildly like dark flames.

And then she turned to them.

Gone was her softness and serenity.

Her face was as pale and hard as stone.

52
The Silent Surge

"Behind and between these quiet years there is a silent surge, *a gathering storm that will one day engulf our worlds…"*

AMELIE SLID THE FINAL safety pin into the bandage. "There, how does that feel?"

"Much, much better," said Naeo, sitting up on the edge of the bed and flexing her shoulders.

"That's mostly the morphine. Let's hope the poultice gets to work before it wears off, but you'll probably need another dose."

"OK. Thanks for all this," replied Naeo.

Amelie sat down next to her on the bed. "Don't thank me — I feel rather responsible. You'd be all right if I hadn't squeezed you so hard!"

Naeo smiled. "Don't worry, it was pretty bad before the hug."

They both laughed.

Amelie's eyes played over her face. She seemed captivated. "You know, you have his laugh."

"Really?"

"Just the same," she said. For a moment she stared, but then she seemed to realise what she was doing and drew her eyes away.

"A nice thought, isn't it? That we might share our laugh with our Glimmer?"

"I suppose," said Naeo.

Amelie hesitated, and then asked, "Do you share a lot with Sylas? I mean, do you feel connected?"

Naeo looked away and shrugged. "Sometimes. Usually when I'm asleep, in my dreams."

"*Really?*" asked Amelie, leaning forward. "That was how it was for me. The voice I heard — it was always in my sleep." She paused, hoping that Naeo would say more.

But Naeo was quiet. It felt so strange to be talking about Sylas. She hated talking about these things anyway, but this was Sylas's *mother*, desperate to know about her son. How was Naeo supposed to explain this stuff without saying the wrong thing? Without somehow getting in the way? She just wanted to change the subject. She thought for a moment, then pointed to the first-aid box and glass bottles. "So... are you a doctor?"

"Yes... yes, I am," said Amelie, taking a moment to collect her thoughts, "but not the kind you're thinking of. I'm a botanist."

"What's that?"

"It's a kind of doctor of plants and flowers."

Naeo was astonished. "You treat... flowers?"

Amelie gave a hoot of laughter. "Not exactly! I study them."

"Why?"

"Because that's what science is all about: we look for the truth of things."

"Oh," said Naeo dubiously. "Why? What use is that?"

Amelie's jaw fell open. "What *use*? How do you think we know how to make morphine out of poppies? Or that poultice on your back? How do you think I grew the plants in the first place?"

Naeo straightened. "I didn't mean that science isn't useful, I just don't get how *studying things* is useful."

"But science and study are one and the same thing!" protested Amelie. "The word science *means* knowledge. We are only able to do all these wonderful things with medicines and machines and technology by studying how things are made, and what makes them the way they are, and how they are connected to other things."

Naeo frowned as she thought about this. "I guess. It's just that we're so different," she explained. "With Essenfayle we *feel* natural things — the connections between them. We don't have to study them."

"And that's why you don't understand them."

Naeo bristled. "But we do understand them. That's how we communicate. We don't ask Nature to do what it couldn't do itself. We understand it."

"If you say so," said Amelie, curtly. "And yet I'm told that it was magic that shattered our worlds in the first place."

Their eyes met and for a moment both seemed ready for an argument. But then Amelie broke into a smile, her face beautiful once again.

"Sorry," she said, raising her hand to her mouth. "It's just that you look like him when you're angry."

Naeo pursed her lips, still irritated. "I do?"

Amelie nodded. "That thing you do with your eyebrows," she said, spellbound. "And your eyes..."

"You're not going to hug me again, are you?"

They both laughed.

Amelie reached out and took Naeo's hand. "Sorry, I don't want to argue."

"Me neither," said Naeo. They sat quietly for some moments, listening to the sound of the stream.

Suddenly a loud fizz and whistle made them both look up. To their astonishment, something small and golden shot in a high arc

400

over the bushes and saplings, leaving behind a trail of blue smoke. There was a loud tinkle as it struck the dome, leaving a small, irregular hole in the glass.

They looked at one another.

"What was that?" asked Naeo.

Amelie frowned. "I have no—"

And then a tall, athletic figure burst from a clump of bushes on the ridge, running in the direction of the object. Just as he began to descend, he caught a foot on a root, pitched forward and tumbled over and over down the bank in a jumble of blonde hair and flailing limbs.

Naeo cleared her throat. "That's Ash," she said. "I'm afraid he's with me."

§

The winds howled across the Barrens and sang through the stones of Salsimaine, buffeting the rises and screaming through the ditches. When they came to the fire pit, they hit the earthen ring and spiralled up into the dark skies. The flames leapt and danced, but Simia's pit was just deep enough — the walls just high enough — and the fire was not snuffed out.

Not yet.

Triste stirred a little in the failing light, groaning as he turned towards the bundles of wood. He pushed aside the teacup Sylas had left him and slipped down the bank until he was splayed by the fire. He fumbled with some pieces of wood, pushing them towards the embers, but his strength soon failed him. He pressed his eyes shut and then opened them wide, trying to recover his senses, but it was no use: he needed to sleep, just a little.

He stopped fighting and allowed his eyes to close. The sound of the gale became dark waves against an unknown shore, lulling him off to sleep. And for a while, he was at peace.

401

But suddenly the dark sea reared up, filling his mind until it was everything, drowning his thoughts, pressing against the edges of his dreams. He grimaced, thrashing his head from side to side, trying to escape, to shake himself awake. But it was hopeless. Like before, he was lost in a nightmare of shifting darkness: black upon black. Before him, a gruesome black figure rose from the pitch dark, parting its black lips, baring its black tusks. It opened its mighty jaws and spoke with a dripping black tongue.

"Second Hamajaks return to Taganaster!" it growled. "We have the prize, my Lord!"

The creature bowed and fell away, back into the sea of black. Instantly another, canine figure unfolded from the ooze. It parted its oily lips and spoke with a throaty bark.

"First Legionnaires return to Fazgaw! We have what you seek, great Dirgh!"

Again the creature bowed and was lost to the blackness. A moment passed and then another creature took its place: large and broad with a huge, canine snout.

"Fifth Imperial Legion has reached the Westercleft Hills, my Lord!" it snarled.

Triste struggled to think in the fog of blackness. There was something familiar about that place — the Westercleft Hills — but try as he might he could make no sense of his tangled thoughts. He reached through the darkness, searching for his memories, but before they came to him the blackness about him rippled and shifted. The Ghor commander had gone and in its place a new black figure pressed forward: small and lithe, with high, feline ears and an almost-human face. When it gave its report it spoke with a smooth and lilting voice.

"Great Lord, we approach Winterfern! The mother and child will soon be ours!"

For a moment Triste's mind was frozen, weighing the meaning of these words. And then, through the fog, he understood.

He rolled back through the void, straining for his consciousness, reaching for the world beyond his dreams. He surged up, layer by layer, yearning for his living self.

And then he was there, bursting through the surface of the deathly sea, heaving cold, painful air into his lungs. He was struck at once by howling winds and shattering pain, which threw off all that remained of his sleep.

He was shivering in the throat of a storm. But it was the truth of his dream that chilled him to the bone.

Everything was about to come to nothing. Somehow Scarpia was alive and Naeo was within her grasp.

And perhaps even worse, the Fifth Imperial Legion was in the Westercleft Hills — just a day's march from the Valley of Outs! And in the *west* — the elders would never expect an attack from the west. They must have sailed the Narrow Sea.

He had to warn them.

He started rolling his shoulders up the bank, pushing against his heels. He had to get warm and eat something; find his strength. His chest heaved, his burns screamed, but he kept pushing until he was sitting, facing the fire.

There was no fire.

The last embers glowed a deep red beneath a thick carpet of ash.

"Stupid!" he cursed, throwing himself forward, feeling for a bundle of wood. "STUPID!"

He scrabbled in the howling dark before he found what he needed and began sorting frantically through the wood for the smallest, driest pieces.

And then he heard a loud whisper through the storm.

"*S-s-stupid…*" it hissed.

53

The Darkling Horde

"And what would that mean, if one day this darkling horde *broke the great divide and came among us?"*

SOMETHING WAS WRONG — very wrong. Sylas glanced at Simia and saw the same fear in her eyes. They walked mechanically towards the platform edge, knowing that each step took them closer to some new darkness.

The stone rumbled beneath their feet, thrumming with the bellowing voice of thunder, the wind whistling around the tower. Suddenly a flash of lightning lit up the human figures carved into the underside of the platform above, lifelike and detailed in all of their writhing form — all but their faces, which were nothing but blank stone, gaping and ominous.

Sylas and Simia were just behind Isia now.

Another step and they were at her side.

One more and they were peering over the edge into the chasm below.

The square was white and wide and empty. The worshippers were gone.

For a moment Sylas thought that perhaps they had gone to

seek shelter from the storm. But then he saw a movement at the edge of the square. A black shape moving in black shadow. And then he saw another, and another, and another.

Scores of them. Hundreds of them.

The Ghor lined the fringes of the square in neat rows, two or three deep, huddling in the dying light, keeping furtively to the dimmest fringes of the plaza where they might not be seen. They had drawn dark cloaks around their forms, allowing them to fold into the deepening shadows.

With growing panic, Sylas cast his eyes around the square, seeing quickly that the Ghor were prowling on every side, in every corner. And then his eyes were drawn to the surrounding streets, where he saw more dark shapes flitting between the shadows.

Ghorhund. More than he could count.

And between them he saw other stooped and mighty figures: Ragers, their giant, bullish heads glowing red and rocking from side to side in growing excitement. And, more terrifying still — the huge, hunched forms of the Tythish, their prying faces turned upwards towards the Temple of Isia, vast moonlike eyes fixed like telescopes on Sylas as he gazed back at them in horror.

And then he felt Simia's clammy, cold hand around his wrist. She was pointing, not down into the square but to the surrounding buildings.

The houses and shops were alive with a flurry of forms that moved with a loose, loping gait, across rooftops and along ledges, clambering between windows and up drainpipes. They scaled walls and swung between promontories, sprinting with equal ease up the verticals as they did over the flats, devouring the buildings in a swarm of half-human shapes. Then suddenly they all became still, gathering as one into row and rank. Only then did he see their true bearing and form, resting on all fours — their torsos supported by long, powerful arms and hands gathered into fists. This was something new: some new horror from the birthing chambers.

"Hamajaks!" said Simia in a faltering voice.

Then he saw what had drawn them to attention. A lone figure was walking out into the plaza. It was a man dressed in long white robes that whipped around him like pale flames. Sylas squinted, trying to make him out, but all he could see was the glow of his pallid skin in the darkness.

The figure stopped, and slowly, it raised its bloodless face up to the Temple's tower, then further up, to the watching three on the platform.

Spying his quarry, he turned and faced the massed ranks of creatures and with a flourish, raised both hands in the air.

Suddenly the howls of the wind and the thunder of the skies seemed to find their answer. It was a new, more menacing sound: a building, baying call formed of howls and screams and snorts. It rattled the windows, boomed from the walls and echoed in the streets until it shook the foundations of the temple. It jostled the leaves of the Knowing Tree, blared up and up through the painted tower and wailed into the vast edifice of Isia's hall. Finally it screamed out from the archways, meeting itself in the night sky, finding new voice and volume as it echoed in their ears.

It was as though hell itself had opened its jaws and declared their doom.

They watched as Ash emerged from the undergrowth, shaking his shaggy locks so that a shower of leaves fell about him. He was nursing the golden object in his hands.

Naeo glanced at Ash, then back at Amelie. "We haven't known each other for very long," she said, apologetically.

"He's still learning, I see," said a voice beside them.

They both jumped and swung about.

"Mr Zhi!" gasped Amelie. "You mustn't sneak up like that!"

"Was I sneaking?" said Mr Zhi, seeming amused. "I had no idea!"

"Well, perhaps not," laughed Amelie. "But honestly, couldn't you just tread a *little* less lightly?"

"Ah well, my wheels keep to old ruts, my dear!" he pronounced, as though this explained everything. He looked at them both. "Jeremy tells me that you have been getting acquainted, and that Amelie has given you something to make you a little better, Naeo?"

Naeo nodded and smiled. "So much better."

Just then Ash strolled up, still poring over the golden egg. He muttered some greetings and briefly shook Amelie's hand, but then returned his attention to the strange object.

"So you're certain?" he said to Mr Zhi. "It *is* possible to get inside?"

"Of course I'm certain," said the old man. "That is where the true gold lies."

"But if Druindil doesn't work," reasoned Ash, holding the egg up between finger and thumb, "nor Urgolvane, nor Kimiyya, surely that only leaves your science."

Mr Zhi frowned. "Why do you say that?"

"Because you said that Essenfayle wouldn't be enough."

"I said no such thing!"

"Yes, you did," said Ash. He looked appealingly to Naeo, but when she offered no support he wavered. "Didn't you?"

"No, though that may have been what you *wanted* to hear. What I said was that Essenfayle was not enough for *you*."

"That's right," said Naeo. She was rather enjoying this

407

exchange. "'Someone for whom Essenfayle is simply not enough.' That's what he said."

Ash narrowed his eyes.

"I must admit to be having a bit of fun with you," said Mr Zhi, smiling and stroking his beard to a point. "This little egg is really no more than a reminder."

"A *reminder*? Of what?"

"Of the basic things, the natural things, the things you already know to be true."

"And what do I already know?" asked Ash, frustrated.

Mr Zhi turned to Amelie and raised his eyebrows. "What do you think, Amelie?"

She shrugged. "I don't know what all this is about," she said. "But I do know that Nature is more powerful than any of this magic, or than anything we scientists do, for that matter. No matter what we tell ourselves."

"*Precisely*," said Mr Zhi. 'Nature is the root of all power' — that's the very basis of Essenfayle, is it not, Ash?"

Ash had the look of someone being tricked. "Yes..." he said, tentatively.

"So, do the natural thing. Crack the egg."

He frowned. "But that's exactly what I've been..."

"No. Crack the egg as you would any other. Crack it on a rock, say."

Ash's mouth fell open. "It's that simple?"

Mr Zhi grinned and adjusted his hat. "It's a rather special egg, so you may need a touch of Essenfayle, but not too much."

Ash glanced around the gathering and then walked over to the nearest rock. He held the egg between his finger and thumb and tapped it on the hard surface.

With a metallic clink the egg fell neatly into two parts.

For a moment he just stared at them, but then he picked one up. Inside was a perfectly natural, perfectly golden egg yolk.

"'*The true gold…*'" he murmured. A smile spread across his face and he looked up at Mr Zhi. "I get it," he said.

"I hope so, Ash, because you are a gifted young man. Be content with what you know. Essenfayle in your hands is far more powerful than you can imagine. It is the way to heal this world."

The younger man's smile fell from his face. "I understand," he said with sincerity. "I do."

"Good, because now I am afraid we must speak of darker matters. Let's walk and talk." Mr Zhi ushered them towards the side of the glen and a narrow pathway that snaked up between the terraces. As they began to climb, he glanced back. "I have just come from the meeting of the Merisi and I'm afraid that the situation is far more serious than I had thought. You might even say that the worst has come to pass."

His companions exchanged an anxious glance.

"The… *worst?*" said Amelie.

Mr Zhi stopped and turned. "War," he said, grimly. "War that is already spilling between the worlds."

54

Of Glove and
the Hand

"She sings of the lines
Of glove and the hand,
She tells of a time
For one final stand."

AMELIE RAISED HER HAND to her mouth. "War?"

Mr Zhi nodded gravely, continuing his climb. "It seems that, for now, Thoth is merely preparing, gaining his strength, gathering what he needs from each of the two worlds. He has planned this for longer than we know, and his many years have taught him cunning and care. But all-out war will surely follow."

Amelie looked at each of her companions. "But... what's all this about?"

"I have spoken to you about Thoth, have I not?" asked Mr Zhi.

She nodded.

"Then you will know that he is cause enough. He too wants

410

a union of our worlds, but his would be quite different from the one we desire: his would be one of master and dominion, of one world's power over the other." He paused and turned. "This will be a war of devastating consequence; of broken worlds and separated souls; of science and magic; of all the wonders of light and the horrors of the dark."

"Well, I'm ready!" called Ash from behind. "I've always been ready!"

Mr Zhi turned and smiled, though his eyes did not. "And I daresay you will be important to this fight, Ash. But it is not magic or science that will dictate the outcome, nor even the massed armies, though those things will play a part." His eyes shifted to Naeo, who was walking at his side. "No, in the end, the outcome rests on two people. Or to be precise, one."

Naeo slowed. "Me and Sylas?"

"Of course," said Mr Zhi. "If you are able to bring us into union then Thoth no longer has a war to fight. His campaign will fall into its own darkness." He paused to climb up between two deep red Acer trees, then turned and held out his hand to help the others. "So, we must gather our forces, we must prepare to defend ourselves, but more than anything, we must ready our only hope of victory."

"I agree, Mr Zhi," said Amelie as she climbed up behind. "We have to keep Sylas and Naeo safe."

"I'm afraid that isn't entirely what I meant," said the old man. "Certainly we must protect them as best we can, but we must also allow them to. And that means that we cannot keep them safe."

Amelie looked appalled. "Why? What do they have to do?"

"Well, first of all, Naeo must return to Sylas."

"But she's only just arrived!"

"And I would be the first to suggest that she stays a while, that she learns all she can from us before she leaves. But the war changes all that. We cannot run the risk of Naeo becoming trapped here, unable to return to Sylas. We have to believe that they are stronger together."

Naeo listened to this with fighting emotion. From the moment she had met Amelie she had found herself wondering if, at the very same time, Sylas was with her father; if even now her father was making his escape, beginning his journey to the Valley of Outs. And those thoughts drew her back to her own world, to the promise of finding him there, waiting for her. But each time she had remembered that she was here for a reason — and that reason could hardly be more important. She was here to find Sylas's mum, and to learn from Mr Zhi.

"Surely we can stay a day or two?" she suggested. "We're here to find out what Sylas and I have to do — we can't just head back now."

Mr Zhi shook his head. "You must go," he said, resolutely. "Thoth knows you are here and he will act quickly, if not to find you here then to prevent your return."

Naeo thought for a moment. It was so strange to talk of getting back to Sylas when all she had wanted to do when she was with him was get away. And then she remembered something.

"What about this Thing you gave me — the Glimmertrome?" she asked. "I thought that was meant to help us to be together even when we are apart?"

"And so it will. The Glimmertrome may be very important on the quest to come, but don't forget, when you use it you will see as Sylas but not as yourself. It weakens even as it as strengthens."

"So why give it to me at all?"

"Because it will allow you to learn about one another, to *know* one another, and it is only by knowing each other that you can truly work together, act together, be together. You cannot do it all in dreams as you do now. There will soon be no time for dreaming."

Naeo was still confused. "So you think that, in the end, Sylas and I need to be in the same place?"

Mr Zhi paused with his hands on his hips and took some deep breaths. "I think that when all is said and done, *together* must mean exactly that."

§

Their motion was tireless, relentless, unyielding. They devoured the hillside in long, reaching strides and giant bounds, darting through gorse and thicket, copse and hedge. More than once they crossed the winding road, but if anyone had been there to see them, all they would have witnessed was a flicker of shadow, a trick of the eye, a brief chill, best forgotten.

Suddenly they erupted from the undergrowth into the full light of morning, sprinting across the bald hilltop towards the road's end and two high stone gateposts, spanned by an imposing wrought-iron gate. Still they did not pause for breath, one scaling the ornate ironwork, the other turning sharply and leaping into the air, bounding the full height of the gatepost to land neatly on its top. Before it dropped down on the other side, it reached back and swiped at the stonework, leaving three long gashes across the nameplate of the Winterfern Hospital.

§

"So let me get this straight," said Naeo, pushing away a veil of leaves, "the Merisi have been taking care of Sylas—"

"And every one of his ancestors," said Mr Zhi, turning to smile at Amelie. He extended a hand to help her up a rocky step.

413

"And you say Merimaat has been... she's been *taking care* of me?" asked Naeo, struggling to believe what she was hearing.

"From a distance, yes," said Mr Zhi, continuing his climb towards the waterfall. "We could not reveal what we were doing for fear of altering your destiny, or worse, frightening you away from it altogether. In a world where the truth may be too much to bear, we have become accustomed to working quietly, in the shadows. Merimaat kept this a secret from all but Espasian. She had a special fondness for Espasian."

Ash braced himself between two trunks. "Hold up!" he said, looking round at Naeo. "This is like that line from *The Song of Isia*! The one Sylas read in the Samarok! How did it go? '*She sings... of the lines... of glove and the hand...*' You see?"

Naeo pondered for a moment. "Nope."

"The line of the glove — the glove of the Merisi! It's talking about Sylas's bloodline, protected by the Merisi!"

Naeo's eyes widened. "Of course!" She glanced at Mr Zhi. "And the line of... the *hand*! Merimaat's withered hand! Is that what it means?"

He nodded. "You and Sylas have cracked the Samarok, I see!" he exclaimed, grinning. "Excellent. I suspect you will have much need of it yet!"

Ash pulled himself between the two trees. "So if the Merisi and Merimaat had been protecting them all this time without saying anything, how come you told Sylas in the end? I mean, if you were so worried about upsetting things?"

"I'm afraid Thoth rather forced our hand," said Mr Zhi. "We learned from Espasian that Merimaat had been killed and that Naeo had been seized and imprisoned, so we resolved to bring Sylas and Naeo together. We had to take a gamble that they were the children foretold in *The Song of Isia* — that they were *meant* to come together. And, after I met Sylas, I had little doubt that we were right." The old man turned and began walking down a winding path, which led through a grove of trees. The others had to trot to keep up. "But even then, we had to be careful not to say too much," he called over his shoulder. "The truth is difficult to accept — dangerously so."

"Dangerous enough to fill Winterfern Hospital," muttered Amelie. "And plenty more like it."

"Quite, my dear. No, Sylas's journey had to be his own — he had to discover his path for himself — as you, Naeo, must discover yours. Espasian taught you to summon the Passing Bell and then, at the right time, I gave Sylas the Samarok and the key to unlock its meaning. We gave you the beginning, but the end is your own."

"And so... that's all you can do?" asked Naeo.

Mr Zhi turned. "Don't underestimate the importance of that beginning, Naeo. The journey of a thousand miles begins with a single step. But no, that is not all we can do. I have given you the Glimmertrome and we will of course offer whatever protection we can without interfering with your journey. Tasker is already arranging to take you back to Stonehenge. But there is one more thing I can help you with. Step this way, please."

He walked up to a clump of ferns and pushed into them until he had entirely disappeared, then his hand emerged and beckoned to them to follow. They each plunged into the veil of foliage, relying on their hands to guide them.

When Naeo finally stepped out, she found Mr Zhi standing in the centre of a glade waiting for them, his hands clasped behind his back. The gardens were laid out before him, with the waterfall directly ahead, encircled by the colourful bands of the rainbow.

The grove of trees lay off to one side and in the distance she could see the top of Amelie's glen.

"This is what I wanted to show you," said Mr Zhi, reaching back to take her hand.

Naeo looked at him in surprise. "The gardens?"

"Yes," said Mr Zhi, waving for Ash and Amelie to join them, "but you need to look with new eyes. I don't want you to see the gardens. I want you to see how they are made. I want you to see the fabric of the world."

"I don't understand," said Naeo.

"I want you to see like a healer of worlds," he said. "A healer of the body knows how it is made; all of its parts — the flesh and the blood, the skin and the bone. And so I need you to see how the world is made, because it is only then that you will be able to find its ills."

Naeo stared at the plants and the trees, the flowers and the waterfall, but they looked just the same as they ever had. "I really don't know what you mean," she said, growing more and more frustrated.

"It may be more familiar than you think," said Mr Zhi, drawing her forward. "Merisu and the ancients told us that there are four parts to the world, four key elements, just like the flesh and the blood, the skin and the bone."

Naeo's eyes widened. "You mean earth... and air? Fire and water?"

Mr Zhi beamed. "That's *exactly* what I mean," he said, turning out to the gardens. "Everything you see draws from each of those elements, from the fiery sun that warms us and lights our way, to the earth that feeds and sustains us —" he pointed to the thundering waterfall — "from the water that cools and refreshes, to the air that we breathe. These four things are the makings of the world. If you and Sylas are to find its cure, you must master these elements."

Naeo shook her head. "I thought it was enough that Sylas and I... that we're *meant* to do these things."

"To a point, it is," said Mr Zhi, squeezing her hand. "This mastery is yours. You were born with it. But true mastery is in the *knowing*. You must each prove to yourselves that you are able to control the earth, the air, the fire and the water. Only then will you be ready to heal the worlds."

There was a moment's silence. Naeo felt lost. The end of the journey that she had hoped was drawing nearer now seemed to be drifting further and further away.

"Wait a minute!" exclaimed Ash. "Naeo, Mr Zhi's right! You *can* do this. I've seen it myself! Remember at the Reckoning, when you turned the seas? What's that if it isn't mastering the waters? And fire — you used fire to save us all in—"

"...in the Dirgheon," murmured Naeo. She turned to him, her spirits lifting. "That's right, we did!"

Mr Zhi opened his hands. "So you already have two — fire and water. Only the earth and the air remain," he said, gesturing first to the ground and then up to the glass dome squinting into the sunlight.

A frown appeared on his face and he lifted his hand to shield his eyes. Suddenly he retreated towards Naeo, pushing her behind him. "Back!" he cried. "Back! Now!"

She stumbled over her heels, peering over his shoulder at the dome.

There, high on the sparkling surface, was a shape — black and lithe and slick — neither human nor animal. It was a shape Naeo had seen before, in the half-light of the moon.

"Scarpia..." she whispered.

And then she noticed the waterfall.

Something was happening. Something impossible.

The rainbow had begun to warp and twist into a new, writhing shape: no longer an arc, but a curling, twisting spiral of colour, unfurling like a bullwhip of fire.

55

Isia's Song

"Isia's song is not her own; it is billions of straining souls reaching out for something lost."

THE STAIRCASE PASSED IN a whirling rainbow of colour and image, twisting ever downwards into the bowels of the temple. Sylas had given up watching his footing and instead he lifted his eyes and ran by instinct, hopping two or three steps in a single bound, tearing after Isia as she descended with astonishing grace, seeming to float down on a cushion of wind. He could hear Simia behind him, her feet stuttering down the steps, her panting echoing across the chasm.

Down and down they ran, thundering towards the square below.

Sylas barely had a moment to think, to ask himself what they would do when they got there. "It's the only way!" Isia had cried as they left the stone terrace. "We must find a way through!"

The gale outside suddenly blew the door open far below – or perhaps it had been forced – they could not tell. A great wind howled through the opening, buffeting the ancient branches of the Knowing Tree, surging up the tower until it whipped around them and made the walls moan. Still they ran, their eyes fixed ahead, focused on the sweep of the staircase, the nearness of the chasm.

Only when they drew level with the topmost branches of the tree did Isia motion for them to stop. She craned her neck and peered below, then continued alone.

Sylas and Simia fell back against the wall, chests heaving, watching Isia as she stepped cautiously down the final reaches of the staircase. They heard a sound above – a shuffle and a whisper – and they glanced up to see scores of priestesses streaming down both staircases. The women stopped and hushed one another, then gazed down at Sylas and Simia with pale, anxious faces. They looked as frightened as Sylas felt.

"This is it, isn't it?" said Simia, quietly.

She stared at him with wide, terrified eyes, as though it was already over.

He shook his head. "We'll be fine, Simsi," he said, as strongly as he could. "They have to get past Isia first."

They watched Isia walk slowly towards the large oak door, which was banging against the stonework. She moved as surely as ever, without fear. As she reached the threshold she paused, then walked outside. Instantly there was a deafening, frenzied howl from the assembly of creatures.

"Sylas?" said Simia, without looking at him.

"Yes?"

"*Did* I have one of those trails? Those silvery trails?" She turned to him. "Did I?"

"Yes, you did," he said, taking her hand.

She welled with tears and a sob escaped her lips. "Good," she said. "That helps."

"Why?"

"Because part of me isn't here."

The bloodthirsty wail outside had reached a crescendo, echoing through the temple until it was a deafening thunder. Then they felt the stone of the tower resonate to the stomping of thousands of feet: *Boom, boom, boom.*

The horrifying rhythm gained pace, building and building to a gut-wrenching roar.

And then something in Sylas broke. The tension, the exhaustion, the confusion of the past days welled into anger. Perhaps it was Simia looking so frightened, or the thought of Isia out there on her own before Thoth's horde, or perhaps he had just reached the end of his tether. Whatever it was, it burned within him like a kindling fire.

"Come on!" he said to Simia, setting off down the stairs, taking them in twos.

"What are you doing?"

Sylas turned. "We either wait for them to come for us, or we go to them," he yelled. "And we have to help Isia!"

A trace of Simia's spirited smile flickered across her face. "OK then," she shouted.

The two of them ran down through the swirl of wind, their eyes never leaving the dark doorway. They ran without thinking, without measuring the danger. They ran because there was nothing else to be done.

Sylas led the way up to the opening and then out, into the wild black gale. Instantly they were shoved to one side by a vicious crosswind, which almost tore Sylas's bag from his shoulder.

He saw Isia first, standing a little way ahead, out on the open plaza. Her plain white robes were flying about her, furling and snapping in the wind, making her seem larger than she really was. She was framed by a titanic scene: by a black jumble of buildings, towering on all sides; by the immense spectre of the Dirgheon looming in the near distance; by the colossal dark clouds and great streaks of lightning that sliced across the sky.

Then, in a flash of fire, Sylas saw the full force of Thoth's mongrel army. Legions of Ghor and Ghorhund advanced in formation on all sides, heads raised in a triumphal cry. Above them, hanging from the walls of the buildings and screaming deliriously like baboons in an urban jungle, were the giant, apish forms of the Hamajaks. And pressed in among the Ghor were the Ragers and the Tythish, snorting and stomping angrily as they jostled for position behind Thoth's Magruman.

Sylas felt a terror squeezing the air from his lungs and closing around his throat. He stood transfixed as all this thundered and seethed around Isia, vying to defy her greatness, to make her small and frail. But she did not cower nor flinch — she stood tall, facing the Magruman and his army across the open square. Sylas recognised the albino at once from their fight in the Dirgheon, from the deluge of fire. He saw the pinched skin, the scarred features, the missing hair, the gaze of icy eyes.

Thoth's Magruman stared at Isia, taking her measure, considering his next move. And then he raised his arms. Suddenly, the baying, screaming and stamping ceased. All that remained was the whistle and howl of the wind and the deep rumble of thunder.

The Magruman and Isia eyed one another in silence, each seeming to wait for the other to speak.

Finally Laythlick pointed to Sylas and Simia. "Let us have the children, Isia!" he shouted in dry, high-pitched notes. "Our quarrel is not with you!"

Isia tilted her beautiful head to one side. "But, Laythlick, it is."

She did not seem to have raised her voice but nevertheless it sounded across the square, echoed among the rooftops.

Laythlick squared his stance. "Come now, Isia, they may be your guests but—"

"They are more than that."

Laythlick shifted again. "How so?"

Her eyes sought Sylas and Simia and then she smiled and beckoned to them. As they started to walk over she turned back to Laythlick.

"Simia is my friend," she said with icy calm. "Sylas is my blood."

The Magruman was visibly startled. "But he's from…" His wet eyes darted to the boy, then he took an unconscious step back.

Isia ignored him, smiling as Sylas and Simia drew close. "So brave, my young Sylas," she said. "And you, dear Simia."

Laythlick seemed to regain his composure. "Isia!" he cried. "You must obey the will of Thoth! You *must* give them to us!"

Isia paid him no attention. "Remember what you have learned, Simia," she smiled. "Do what I cannot. Take care of my Sylas."

"ISIA!" cried Laythlick. "This is your last warning!"

And then Isia reached for Sylas's hand. "This is your time, my child," she declared. "Remember all that you have learned about me, about us, about yourself. And this, remember this: you have mastered the earth, and the fire and the water. Now, master the air."

Suddenly there was a deafening rumble from behind her. At first Sylas thought it was another roll of thunder, but then his eyes widened.

There, rising high into the air beyond Isia, was a gigantic mass of rubble and flagstones, some broken or shattered, some still whole. Many hung ominously still, others spun and twisted, propelled by the terrible force that had ripped them from their footings. There were hundreds, perhaps thousands of them,

423

shifting in the gusts of wind as one ominous whole. The Magruman bent this perilous mass to his will, his eyes flaring wide, his face set with rage. He stood on the very edge of a vast pit where the plaza had been, his pale skin now a deathly white, his body quivering with the effort.

"GIVE THEM TO ME!" he screamed.

Sylas stared in horror and had to fight the urge to back away. He snatched a glance at Simia and saw his own fear mirrored in her face, but when he turned to Isia, she was smiling. It was a sad but generous smile — one that, in that moment, seemed utterly out of place.

Then she turned to face the Magruman. "No, Laythlick," she said, walking towards him with slow, assured steps, "I will not."

Laythlick's eyelids flickered in surprise. "Then you leave me no choice!" He heaved his hands back and prepared to hurl the swirling mountain of stone. He staggered with the strain of it, sweat pouring down his face, his body trembling.

Isia's step did not falter. "It is time for you to hear what I hear. Hear your crime, Laythlick, Magruman of Thoth, the Slayer of Souls. Then let judgement fall where it may."

She made a gesture as though offering him something, extending her open palms. In that moment everything fell still: the winds died, the thunder echoed into silence, the storm receded. Nothing remained but Isia, and the Magruman, and the hanging mass of rock.

As she reached the edge of the pit, there was a distant sound, like a sigh, or perhaps a whisper. It seemed to come from nowhere and everywhere: from the pit at her feet and the storm clouds above, from the windows of the buildings and the brooding darkness of the Dirgheon.

Words, half formed and indistinct. They drifted from the darkness, an ocean of them, borne up by a thousand whispering breaths. Quick and urgent, pained and yearning; words of love and grief, of joy and despair. They came in a new storm — a storm of feeling issuing from an unknown place, spoken in a million unknowable voices.

Sylas looked at Simia but she was gazing into the skies, into the great darkness around them, and there were tears in her eyes.

"I can hear them!" she said.

In that moment the whispers grew into a murmur, and the murmur grew into a voice, and the voice into a clamorous cry. It shook the buildings and churned the clouds, it rumbled beneath the city and echoed in the heavens. Myriad voices searching for something lost, seeking the answer to a riddle they barely knew was there. These countless voices gathered into a single, human sound — a sound that spoke to the heart and soul of everyone who heard it.

"Do you hear what you have done?" cried Isia over the tumult, her voice thick with rage. "Do you HEAR?"

The Magruman shook under the immense burden above his head, or perhaps it was what he was hearing that had sapped his spirit, because Sylas thought he saw his features crumple a little — and then a tear roll down his albino cheek.

But Laythlick's face hardened. He set his jaw and bowed, as though preparing for a final push. When he rose again, his face was streaming with sweat and tears, but it was resolute. He pulled his arms over his head and in the same instant, the colossal mass of stone shifted.

Just then, the great chorus of voices reached a deafening pitch, hailing down upon the Magruman. He looked stricken, as though the voices had pierced his skull, as though he no longer knew what he was doing or why he was doing it.

He hesitated and looked about him, bewildered. There was a

brief moment of panic written across his haggard face, and then his elbows buckled.

The downpour of rock came in an instant, enveloping him in rubble. The chunks of stone splayed outwards and dust rose in curling plumes, rock crashed into rock, shattering into twisted piles. Soon all that was left where the Magruman had stood was a heap of white debris.

The voices began to fade and as they did so, Sylas felt the first winds returning to the square. Then, as the noise died altogether, Isia took two steps backwards.

For a moment she swayed as though carried on the breeze.

Then she fell.

56

A Proposition

"To one such as Ramesses, this was a proposition *far
too enticing to be resisted, no matter the risks,
no matter the consequences."*

ASH SAW IT EVEN before it entered the dome: a blur, a trick of the
light. He saw the formless thing press itself up against the glass,
and then through it, as though it was not there. He saw the jumble
of light adjust and cohere, gathering itself on the other side of the
glass, shimmering and flaring until it was the shape and size of a
man. And then, as he pointed towards it, as he went to cry out,
he saw it raise two foggy trails that looked like arms towards the
rainbow.

"Over there!" Ash shouted.

As the others turned to see, the rainbow responded, the twisting,
lashing motion of the light beams whipping ever faster through
the air. At the same time the sun's rays were warping and turning,
gathering to feed it, to give it new colour, new intensity, new life.

"A Ray Reaper!" cried Mr Zhi.

Suddenly there was a sound of shattering glass. They all looked
up to see Scarpia's black, panther-like form twisting between the

razor edges of a broken pane. She hung from the framework of the dome, eyeing her prize.

The old man turned and took Naeo by the shoulders.

"Naeo, they're here for you!" he exclaimed, softly but urgently. "I'll defend you as I can, but a Magruman and a Ray Reaper are far too power—"

He was silenced by a sudden flash and hiss. The coloured tail of the rainbow whipped past his ear and struck one of the trees, which exploded into coloured flames and sent up a plume of smoke. It rose first as a misty blend of colours, then a dark grey mushroom cloud, rolling up towards the glass ceiling. Instantly a chorus of terrified screams filled the dome and Naeo saw the guests running across the grass towards the cliff face.

Mr Zhi reached into a pocket and began pulling the green glove over his hand.

Just then there was a loud thump of feet against the turf, and Tasker ran up, his eyes darting around the gathering. "What can I do?"

"Take Amelie," said Mr Zhi.

Amelie raised her hands. "No! I'm staying with Naeo!"

Mr Zhi shook his head. "No. Take her inside, now!" he instructed Tasker. "And get *everyone*! We'll need everyone!"

As he spoke the bullwhip of fire slammed into the ground next to him, sending up a shower of burning grass and scalding earth. He leapt sideways, hurling his body high into the air and flipping about with apparent ease, landing to face the others. Cinders smouldered in his rumpled suit.

"Naeo! Ash! I'm going to have to leave the Ray Reaper to you. I'll try to—"

Suddenly there was a loud crash above their heads. Naeo looked up to see Scarpia hanging from the framework of the dome with one clawed hand outstretched. The surrounding panes of glass had shattered and as they watched a thousand shards fell towards them, not in a straight line but drawing together as they went, forming a dense dagger-point of spinning splinters.

Then a number of things happened at once.

Tasker leapt forward, grabbing Amelie by the waist and dragging her away.

Ash shoved Naeo in the side, pushing her so hard that she stumbled and fell.

And Mr Zhi vaulted, throwing himself in a high arc over the chaotic scene, arching backwards so that his body lay directly in the path of the falling glass. He extended his gloved hand and closed his eyes.

The priestesses came from nowhere, sprinting across the windswept square. They came before Sylas and Simia had time to react, gathering quickly around Isia's slumped figure, some forming a protecting ring, others tending to her. He could see her protesting weakly, but she was soon taken up on a forest of arms. The group started back, their faces strained, some of them weeping as they hurried towards the temple. Isia looked shockingly listless, her arms dangling at her sides, her long locks draped over her features.

Sylas had to know that she was all right. "Wait!" he cried.

The group came to a halt and moved apart. Isia slowly turned her head, leaving the faint image of her Glimmer behind.

Her face was a bluish white. Her cheeks were sunken. A trail of blood flowed from her nose.

"Now you see that mine is a borrowed greatness," she murmured. "I am nothing without the voice and spirit of others."

She smiled, her eyes travelling over his face. "You are truly the best of me, Sylas."

Her eyes rolled and her head slumped until her face was once again shrouded by hair. The priestesses hurried her away.

"Isia!" cried Sylas, stepping out to follow her.

Simia grabbed his arm and drew him back. "This isn't over, Sylas! You have to let her go!"

He pulled away. "I can't just—"

But then there was a new swell of noise: a triumphant howl from Ghor and Hamajak, Tythish and Rager.

"Look!" hissed Simia, tugging again at his arm. He turned to find her pointing up into the stormy skies.

There, framed by the angular lines of the Dirgheon, was a scene from hell itself: a seething mass of giant, bat-like creatures turning in an endless spiral, looping and twisting one around the other until they blotted out all else. Amid this churn of black Sylas could see flecks of white: the pale faces of some hideous new creature, some ghoulish mongrel of man and beast. The swarm sailed from the dark terraces of the pyramid, over the deserted streets and shuttered buildings of the city and came to hover over the square. There Sylas saw the beasts in all their chilling splendour: long, black limbs; vast leathery wings; faces as lifeless as death itself. And he knew then that he had seen them before, in books and in nightmares. They had all the ghastly features of myth and legend, of those that rule the darkness.

He could hardly believe he was thinking it.

Simia raised her hands to her mouth. "Vyrkans," she breathed through trembling fingers.

Sylas glanced at her. "We... we call them *vampires*."

The swarm was descending now, fluttering down to land upon

430

the highest rooftop, breaking apart as it neared the surface, each creature finding its own sill or gable to cling to.

And then, as the last of them landed, the curtain of wings parted. They revealed a lone figure, stooped and frail but dressed in the finest scarlet robes. At first the face could not be seen, shrouded as it was beneath a silken hood, but then two skeletal hands rose and pulled the folds of fabric away.

There was no face at all. There was only an endlessly shifting shape: a brew of pale features that formed two sunken eyes and a black, gaping mouth.

There was a sudden rumble from all corners of the square as Thoth's army bowed to its master: Ragers, Ghor, Ghorhund, Tythish, Hamajaks, Vyrkans, all stooped low in deference to the great Dirgh.

§

"*You forget yourself!*" said the voice, thick and silken.

The oily blackness of Espen's dream rolled back, receding to the fringes of his mind. He felt the advance of the cold, hard world: the chill in his bones; the pain in his hip, and arm, and shoulder; the despair. The voice faded and he waited expectantly, yearning for the blackness, for the return of his sleep, for oblivion. And then it came, slowly at first, through a memory of sounds: *draw, push, slide, scrape.*

Draw, push, slide, scrape.

It was a comforting, reassuring rhythm, and the sounds brought with them a wonderful blackness; the blackness of forgetting, of empty dreams, of nothingness.

But then the voice came again.

"*You forget yourself!*"

It was a smooth, gentle, female voice; one that drew seemed

431

to offer warmth and comfort. But in truth all that happened was that the sleep rolled away once again and the pain came flooding back — the pain, the cold and, this time, a distant awareness of the stench of the cell and the *drip, drip, drip* of some foul slime from the ceiling.

He dispelled the voice and tried to claw his way back to sleep. He filled his mind with the sounds that had first taken him there. The consoling, rhythmic sounds that he now knew so well.

Draw, push, slide, scrape.

Draw, push, slide, scrape.

He was rewarded with darkness: thick, soft, dreamless darkness.

"*Wake!*" came the voice, bolder and louder than ever. "*You forget yourself!*"

Away it went again, retreating like a fleeting tide, leaving him on the cold shores of reality, cold and weak.

"I know myself," he murmured in a half sleep, his lips barely moving.

He stirred, and felt a searing pain slice through his hip. He winced and kicked out angrily.

"I am Espen!" he muttered bitterly, now in the full horror of wakefulness.

He blinked out at the dark cell, at the damp walls, at the broken door by his feet. Then he started. Bowe's face was right next to him, his broken features gathered in concern.

"Are you all right?" asked the Scryer. "You were talking in your sleep."

Espen fell back against the wall and a thin smile creased his lips. "I'm fine," he grunted. "Just losing my mind."

He drew in a long draught of cold damp air, coughed and turned his eyes sombrely around the cell, then out into the corridor. He heard a roll of thunder somewhere in the distance, carried on an echo. Otherwise the Dirgheon seemed oddly still, quiet, expectant.

Then everything faded as though behind a veil. His mind fogged and his thoughts left him. The empty space filled not with blackness but with light: light framing a beautiful face. A woman's face.

Isia's face.

Then came the voice again, her voice, urgent and insistent.

"*You forget yourself, Espasian! Now you must remember!*"

§

Sylas felt his heart begin to fail. He felt Simia's cold, shivering hand slide into his.

Thoth took a step towards the edge of the rooftop. "You should bow to your betters!" he boomed, in the voice of a thousand captive souls.

The words were a shockwave thrumming around the square, humming in Sylas's chest: an agony of shouts and whispers, murmurs and yells. He was terrified, but he did not bow. He would not bow. When he saw Thoth he could only think of the last time he had seen those scarlet robes, that bony, bent figure: high on the Dirgheon, feet planted either side of Bowe's bloodied body, showing him no regard, no mercy.

So instead, Sylas straightened his back and met the Dirgh's gaze.

Thoth cackled, seeming to find this amusing. "I had hoped we might work together, you and I. I had hoped that you might have an eye for greatness; that you might see what your Glimmer could not." He paused, but when there was no response he continued walking slowly to the edge of the roof. "We want the same thing, you and I. We want a union of worlds — no more division, no more doubt — a single dominion ruled by a single power. *Our* power, Sylas — yours and mine!"

The thought filled Sylas with revulsion. "No! That's not what I want!" he shouted, surprised by the strength of his own voice.

Thoth's mouth twisted in a sneer. "Why, how selfish of you!" he bellowed goadingly. "It was always about *power*, Sylas, don't you see that? My power, your power. It is power that decides the reality of our worlds!"

"But I—"

"It is my power, for instance," continued Thoth, "that is even now taking all that is best from your world, preparing it for union — or for oblivion, if it comes to that. I am rather good at oblivion, as your friends will tell you. But then, I am a master of the Three Ways and that is *my* kind of power. It would be quite different for you..." he trailed off, leaving the square to the sounds of the storm.

Sylas sensed that he was being baited. "What do you mean, 'different for me'?"

Thoth opened his palms. "You are a master of the *Fourth* Way, are you not? The way of 'Nature' and 'peace' and 'harmony'." He spat out these words with obvious distaste. "You are the one foretold by the Glimmer Myth, the one who might unify the worlds without war or bloodshed. In this universe of two sides, you are one and I am the other. You are the light and I am the dark."

"You're right," shouted Sylas, "I'm nothing like you!"

"But what if we were to work *together*?" said the Dirgh, solicitously. "Think of it, the might of my empire with the majesty of your greater world! I could show you how to rule! We could share the Sekhemti — the crown of two kingdoms. All without wars or invasions — no darkness, none of the pain of the Undoing, no more mothers separated from their sons!"

434

"Don't listen to him, Sylas!" hissed Simia.

Sylas stepped forward. "It's not me who doesn't see, it's you!" he yelled. "We can't share these worlds because they're not ours to share!" There was a rumble of disquiet from Thoth's army. "You want one world so that you can rule over it. We want one world so that it's not broken any more!"

Simia yanked his arm. "That's enough, Sylas!"

"You are as blind and insolent as your Glimmer!" growled Thoth.

Sylas felt a fire flicker in his chest. "That's right, we're just the same!" he shouted. "I am Naeo and Naeo is me. And we both know what you've done!"

Suddenly Thoth seemed to swell beneath his robes, growing to an imposing height. The hollows of his eyes deepened and his mouth widened into a broad slash. "Your world will weep for your foolishness!" he roared with such power and volume that his words passed in a visible wave through the assembled ranks. "It is a mercy that you will not live to see it!"

With that he held his thin grey hand aloft and closed it in a fist. Instantly the square was filled with a new and delirious battle cry. And as this great onslaught of sound gathered volume, the Hamajaks clambered ape-like down from the rooftops, swinging nimbly from cornices and windowsills, ledges and gargoyles. The Vyrkans threw out their wings and took to the air, circling above the square, while beneath them, the Ghorhund prowled forward, low on their haunches, preparing to lead the charge.

Simia turned slowly to Sylas.

"This is it, Sylas," she said. "This *has* to be your time!"

57
Surge

"If they come, they will not creep but surge. *While we fret about the peace of nations, they will bring a war of worlds."*

SYLAS HAD NEVER FELT so alone. Not since the day his mother had been taken away. And then, the world had only seemed to be falling in. Now, the skies were a boiling black, the ground was shuddering beneath his feet, demons were roaring in his ears. All around him eyes flared, claws lashed, bodies strained. The army of creatures was making its charge, thirsty for the taste of blood: a thousand hungry mouths and just two children to feed them.

And yet the horror was the same as that day, with his mother. It was the same sense that everything was coming to an end and that somehow it was all about him. That everything rested on him.

He mouthed Simia's words under his breath.

"This has to be your time."

He turned to her and saw her wide, staring eyes, her tiny figure, her face filled with fear but also something else — something in the way she held his gaze — steady and still.

Trust. It was trust.

Trust despite the world raining down, and the monsters tearing and tumbling towards them, and the heavens churning with fire and vampire wings. Trust that he would know what to do.

He looked out at the sea of claws and teeth and saw more beasts pouring from buildings and flooding from side streets to join the endless charge. He saw it all as if in slow motion.

Simia was wrong to trust him. He had no idea what to do. He felt only gut-wrenching fear, saw only fury and death.

And perhaps because it was the only escape from the horror, he looked up at the sky; at that vast, murky overhang, shot through with veins of lightning, like a cauldron of fire and air.

"Fire and air," he murmured. "Air and fire."

He blinked at the churning clouds and remembered Isia's words.

"*Now you must master the air.*"

He tightened his grip on Simia's hand.

"Don't let go!" he shouted over the thunder and roar.

She nodded and clamped her hand around his.

And then Sylas turned inwards. He closed his eyes and retreated to the place he had gone on the river with the fleeing Suhl, on the Barrens with the attacking Ghor, on the *Windrush* with Paiscion. He let the snarls and the wild winds recede, and he went to the centre of himself – to the place he and Naeo had found in the Dirgheon, facing Scarpia and the Magrumen. He went to that place and then he reached out with his mind, up, into the skies. He reached into Nature's own fury. It was a discord he knew all too well. The confusion was his, the anger was his. The storm was everything he had felt these past days. It was the storm of his life being turned inside out, of everything he knew about

437

his mother being warped and twisted and turned into something else.

He knew this storm.

He felt the thunder in the pit of his stomach, the lightning in his veins, the rain pricking like sweat. But most of all, he felt its winds. He breathed them into his lungs until they buffeted his ribcage, until they became his breath, until they were his and he was theirs.

And then something slammed into his side, knocking those winds from his lungs. He felt his bones twist, his muscles strain to snapping point. As his back arched painfully towards the sky, he looked down and saw a fiery crest and two gigantic horns slide beneath his arms. The Rager gave a triumphant snort and then, with a flick of its mighty neck it launched him somersaulting into the night. The force almost ripped Sylas's head from his shoulders, his limbs flailing as though he were a rag doll. In the passing blur he saw Simia sliding face-down over the flagstones, the hellish army closing in on her.

And then the ground came rushing up. He threw out an arm to protect himself, but too late: the white stone crashed into his shoulder as he fell heavily on to his back. Pain exploded through him, making him cry out.

He could hear the charge of the Rager, the roar of the army, the thunder of foot and claw.

No time for pain. No time to think.

He was vaguely aware of Simia somewhere near, but he didn't look at her. No time even for her. His eyes were ahead, gazing up at the night sky. Into the storm.

He forced everything from his mind. Everything but the storm.

And when there was only the storm, he found it waiting for him.

He closed his eyes and imagined himself above the clouds, where the storm was the strongest, where the winds reigned supreme. Then he breathed them in, spinning countless gusts and gales into a whirling vortex of apocalyptic power.

And then he exhaled.

The winds came with a full-throated yowl. They crashed down from above, slamming into the ground and wrapping Sylas and Simia in a wailing, raging calamity. It tore their clothes and whipped at their hair. And then gently lifted them on to their feet.

Its fury, it saved for Thoth's army.

When Sylas looked about, he saw writhing streaks of shape and light: a dizzying torrent of motion. It was everything he had imagined: a vast whirlwind, fierce and wild, and he and Simia were at its heart.

He saw the Ghorhund sucked into the tornado of dust and cloud and for an instant they were suspended, claws outstretched, fangs bared. But then they were hurled to the side, whipped around in a vicious spiral. They sailed up, circling and screaming as they were swallowed by the storm.

Sylas was thrilled and horrified as the charging army of Hamajaks, Ghor, Ragers and Tythish ran headlong into the winds. When they struck the whirlwind, it warped and stuttered but raged on, consuming them, throwing them up in the endless churn. Tusk-like teeth punched through, forcing Simia to duck and shove Sylas out of the way, but even as they both staggered back, the Hamajak issued a terrified scream. In a blink it was gone, whipped up in the broth of limbs.

As more and more beasts threw themselves at the winds, Sylas felt his own breath pummelled from his lungs. The tunnel of wind slewed and lurched like a wild spinning top and where it bent and bulged a forest of limbs broke through.

"Down!" he cried, pulling Simia to her knees as the claws swiped overhead. She squealed as a Rager burst into the eye of the storm, its horns flailing just inches above them. They both fell on their backs, staring wide-eyed into the throat of the winds, watching as the Rager spiralled slowly into the skies. Sylas closed his eyes, desperately trying to gather his thoughts, to return to the winds. For a moment all he could think of was the stone rumbling beneath him, the beasts closing around him.

"You're losing it, Sylas!" screamed Simia at his ear.

He blocked out the squeals and huffs and screams. He forgot the pounding of his heart. He thought only of the winds, of their hunger and might, of their endless, irresistible motion. Only when he truly felt them, only when he had pulled them near and made them his again, did he dare to open his eyes. He looked up into the silvery tunnel and saw them begin to respond, shaping themselves between his outstretched hands like clay on a potter's wheel. Soon the protruding claws and limbs were flailing once again, whipping around and around, spiralling up into the night.

"That's it!" cried Simia, pushing herself up on her elbows.

Together they watched the whirlwind gather pace and strength, and as it did so its shape became clean and true: a snaking tunnel, rising high into the jostling clouds and beyond, to the wide-open sky. Finally, in the far distance, it opened to the tranquil moon, which shone down, lacing the tunnel with silver. It was like an eye peering down through the tempest, watching over them.

The sight gave Sylas new hope. He pushed himself up and pulled Simia to her feet. Together, they looked through the walls of wind and into the square.

They could see none of the white stone of the plaza now, nor the buildings, only a rippling sea of bodies surging towards them, pulled ever inwards by the whirlwind. None of the creatures now stood a chance, none came close to breaching the walls. Instead they were ripped up into the air, drawn up and up, high over the city until their screams were lost in the clouds.

Simia turned and looked at Sylas with new wonder. She watched as he moulded the storm, shifting his hands to keep the vortex straight and true. He was aware of her gaze, but he did not dare return it; his thoughts were still in the body of the storm. If he could just hold himself together, it was his to command.

"Follow me!" he yelled at Simia over the wail of the winds.

He stepped out towards the livid wall but did not flinch, because he knew it was with him. As they walked the winds moved with them — surging forward into the sea of bodies, driving a path through arms and legs, tails and teeth. The great whirlwind caught them up, inhaling them into its mighty lungs as Sylas and Simia edged forward, drawing nearer and nearer to the shadow of the buildings on the other side. And all the while, they saw the bodies of the Ghor picked up and hurled skywards, they saw the burly forms of the Hamajaks flicked up into the air like so much litter, they saw the last Tythish and Rager sent sprawling in a tangle of limbs, only to be dropped somewhere far away, somewhere among the skeletons of the Barrens. And for a moment, it seemed it was over.

But then came the voices of many, bellowing through the storm, echoing across the Place of Tongues.

"Vyrkans, rise!" commanded Thoth. "Rise with the winds!"

Sylas felt a sudden chill. And then Simia shrieked, pointing up through the tornado. Sylas followed her terrified gaze just in time to see a stream of distant bodies pass in front of the moon... then turn sharply downwards.

The Vyrkans plummeted into the open mouth of the whirlwind. Once inside, they folded their wings and fell like arrowheads, cutting through the air, keeping clear of the walls. They grew larger and larger, until Sylas thought he could make out white faces in the blackness.

"Sylas, *do* something!" screamed Simia, raising her hands to her face.

Sylas turned his eyes around the vortex. And then he realised: it was easy for them, too easy — all the Vyrkans had to do was fall.

He threw his hand out in front of him, forcing the whirlwind to bulge away, and then he turned on his heel, hand still outstretched, making the winds bow outwards as he went. The bulge circled before him, and as he turned ever faster the whirlwind began to warp, winding into a corkscrew. When he looked up he could no longer see the moon nor the Vyrkans, only a twisting helter-skelter of winds. The tunnel to the skies was no longer straight but a writhing snake, turning ever tighter.

His eyes searched, looking for any sign of the Vyrkans. He expected them to erupt from the darkness any second, stealthy and fast. But then there was a movement high above, in the loops of the whirlwind. He saw black shapes careering across the sky, flung free by the tightening twists.

It was the Vyrkans, their wings flapping uselessly as they were hurled wide of the vortex, their momentum throwing them down into the square so that their black bodies broke on the stone, shattering the slabs.

Still Sylas turned and turned, twisting the corkscrew, feeding the winds. He turned until the rain of Vyrkans ceased, and still he turned, afraid of opening the way to the skies. It was only when he felt Simia's hand pulling at his arm that he slowed.

"OK, Sylas!" she shouted over the gale. "It's OK!"

He drew to a halt, gasping for air, staggering with dizziness. Above him the whirlwind gradually unfurled, stretching itself straight until it once again revealed the moon, glowing serenely in an ocean of stars.

There were no Vyrkans to be seen — only the winds and the skies.

They both looked about them, expecting to see more of Thoth's creatures, but all they saw was stone and brick and shattered windows.

His arms still aloft, Sylas turned slowly and peered through the winds, across the square, to the rooftop. The great Dirgh was standing at the very edge, his hollow eyes fixed on Sylas, his robes flying about him like crimson fire. For some moments he glared in silence, and then he took another step forward until he seemed about to fall.

He tilted his head a little to one side, as though considering an impossible riddle.

"So you wish to live to see the end of things?" he boomed in countless hateful voices. "Then so be it! But know this: before it is done, you will see not one Undoing but five, each measured in agony and loss, each the cost of your defiance! This will be your legacy, Sylas Tate; this, your union of worlds!"

With that he raised his arms so that his robes became a wall of silk, shrouding him from view. And he fell.

For an impossible, thrilling moment Sylas watched Thoth, Lord of the Priests of Souls, falling to his certain death.

But suddenly the robes were no more. Instead, he was shrouded in black: the black of leathery wings and supple limbs, of a dozen Vyrkans swarming like a plague of moths, bearing him up into the night. They swooped from all sides, from their many perches around the square, and now they were one, their wings beating to a common rhythm so that they looked part of the same colossal beast, holding its creator in careful claws. Up and up they flew, circling briefly around the Temple of Isia before disappearing into the clouds.

For some moments Sylas stared in silence, the chill of Thoth's presence still heavy upon him, the horrifying words still echoing in his mind. He was so consumed that he almost lowered his arms, almost let the winds falter.

Simia stepped in front of him. She looked pale and drawn, but then he saw the trace of her fearless smile.

"You did it!" she said. She hesitated then took a step forward. She put her arms around him, burying her face in his shoulder. "You really did it, Sylas!"

He could feel her body still trembling, and then he realised that she was sobbing, openly and freely: sobs of horror and relief.

Only then did he lower his arms from the winds and wrap them around her. "*We* did it, Simsi," he said.

Without its master, the great vortex slowed around them, becoming looser, larger, stretching out before them. The howl began to fade.

And then, somewhere beyond, there was a snort, the thump of giant claws striking stone, the blast of nostrils.

It came so quickly they had no time to react. The Rager erupted from the blur of winds, its scaly face raging red, its horns lowered in a thunderous charge. The remains of the winds caught it in the side, sweeping its legs from beneath it, snapping its gigantic body around and heaving it up into the air.

Just for an instant its horns travelled on into the calm; on, towards Simia.

Sylas pulled her away, but too late. A horn caught her shoulder, slicing through her tunic, hooking her up.

There was a gasp. A shriek.

And then she was gone.

58

Sacrifice

"The truth must come before all else: this is the way of the Merisi. But this kind of truth does not come without cost; these pages are written in loss and bound by sacrifice.*"*

THE GLASS WAS SO CLOSE — so fast and so close.

It glittered as it scythed through the air, heading straight for the outstretched form of Mr Zhi.

But then, to her astonishment, Naeo saw the downpour of glass change its path, parting above Mr Zhi's green glove to fall either side of him. And as the deadly hail fell to the ground so did he, tumbling on to the soft turf below.

She heaved herself up, grimacing from twinges of pain in her back, and turned to look for Mr Zhi.

He lay splayed where he had fallen, and to her horror she saw blood soaking through his jacket. She ran over to him, her heart failing with every step.

She reached him at the same time as Ash and they both crouched next to him. "Mr Zhi!" she panted. "Are you all right?"

He turned away from them, seeming to pull something out from his shoulder and cast it aside, then he looked up, his old wrinkled

446

face wet with sweat. "I'm fine. Just taken a little —" he winced and returned his hand to his shoulder — "a little by surprise."

He pushed himself up on to an elbow. "We seem to be out of time," he said in an urgent voice. He looked at Naeo. "We must work together, you and I."

Instinctively Naeo looked desperately at the shattered dome, the burning tree, the debris all about them.

"Trust yourself," said Mr Zhi, touching her face. "This is your time, my child. Remember all you've learned, all you've done. That's all any of us can ask," he said, looking past her. "Now, I must leave you to deal with the Ray Reaper, while I face an old adversary of mine..."

Naeo turned to follow his gaze.

Scarpia was high in the branches of a nearby tree, prowling along a narrow branch, claws scouring the bark. Her quick, feline eyes shifted between Naeo and Mr Zhi. Her lips parted and her narrow pink tongue slid across her razor-point teeth.

Mr Zhi held his shoulder, swung into a sitting position and then, without pausing, rocked forward and rose to his feet. As he walked off towards Scarpia, he turned and said: "All that comes is meant to be. Now is a time of sacrifice."

Before Naeo had a chance to wonder at the meaning of the words, she heard Ash screaming, "Naeo! Behind you!"

She snapped her head towards the centre of the dome. She saw the rainbow of fire gathered in a tight coil, writhing high above the gardens, curling like the backstroke of a whip. Even as she watched, it darted towards her, unfurling, trailing a fiery tip that fizzed and spat. Tendrils of colour became a horrifying onslaught of flame, stretching out towards her in a single blazing sinew.

The Ray Reaper.

"MOVE!" screamed Ash, pushing himself upright.

But she did nothing. She was frozen to the spot. She watched the approaching fire and she hesitated. If she had any instinct to react, any gift, any calling, it had left her.

Or perhaps it had never been there at all.

She watched in horror as the fire came on, until she felt its blaze on her face, needling her skin, searing her eyes.

And then she remembered.

She remembered this heat.

She saw the lattice of fire in the Dirgheon, twisting and turning above her head. She saw Sylas standing next to her, with her, his strength becoming hers, hers becoming his. And suddenly she remembered how that felt: that quiet, knowing certainty. That absence of doubt. That power.

And that was when she lifted her hand, as though to protect her face from the blinding heat.

The band of coloured flames reached out, seeming certain to find its mark. But then it halted. It hung in the air before Naeo's hand so that it made her open palm smart. But she was not frightened. She knew this fire. It was the fire of the sun, the natural sun, of the painted colours of the rainbow. She knew it, and it was part of her.

She turned her hand and the weave of colours twisted before her. She raised her hand, and the trail of fire rose with it. She gathered her strength and then swept her arm down, starting a ripple in the length of light: a ripple that became a wave, surging back along its length up into the great space beneath the dome and then down towards its end. There, the barely visible Ray Reaper watched with surprise as the curl of beams hurtled back towards it. Moments later the end of the glowing twine bucked, leaping high into the air and snapping back on itself with a deafening electric crack. As a blaze of coloured fire erupted from the rainbow, the Ray Reaper fell backwards through the glass, suddenly engulfed in flame. Naeo heard the creature screech and wail as it disappeared from sight.

And then, wrenched free of the Ray Reaper's grip, the writhing twine began to float upwards, paling as it went, its colours losing their garish glow. Naeo let it drift from her fingertips, allowing the weave of light to rise into the void: to once again become an arc, and then a rainbow.

"How... how did you do that?" It was Ash, standing unsteadily at her side, his clothes still smoking and his cheek and neck a livid pink.

"Essenfayle, of course," said Naeo, with a brief smile.

But there was no time to celebrate, as suddenly they heard a loud sound behind them: a screech and a bang. They turned to see Mr Zhi still walking towards Scarpia, his gloved hand held high. And then they saw why.

The metalwork of the broken dome was buckling and, one by one, the struts were snapping loose, turning in the air and then plummeting to the ground. Scarpia was in the tree, shifting from branch to branch, using one clawed hand and her long, snaking tail to direct her assault. By some feat of Urgolvane, as her tail flicked, the steel of the dome squealed and broke, sending down length after length of steel scything down like spears, their twisted tips cleaving the air, heading straight for Mr Zhi.

But Mr Zhi did not slow his steady march towards the trees. His gloved hand darted about his head, its movements smooth and fluid — like in a dance or martial art — and his fingers opened and closed: grasping and releasing, grasping and releasing. Something about the glove seemed to unpick Scarpia's sorcery, because in response the steel spears checked in the air before they even reached him, changing direction and sinking harmlessly into the turf at his sides.

Scarpia was undeterred, throwing down more and more steel as she edged down the tree branch by branch, until finally she reached the trunk. She leapt lightly on to all fours, crouching down in the grass. Her snarl reverberated through the gardens and she rocked back on to her rear legs and stood up like a woman, a rapacious grin spreading across her face.

"Zhi!" she scoffed in her smooth, velvety purr. "How old you look! How tired and weak!"

Mr Zhi did not slow. "Time touches us all, Scarpia," he said, quietly. "I can't help noticing that it has touched you in... *novel* ways."

Scarpia bared her teeth. "Marked by battle but stronger than ever!" she growled. "You Merisi are such fools! Your love of peace and balance only weakens you. It is *war* that makes us stronger. It is war that will bring balance to these worlds."

"Says one at war with herself!" said Mr Zhi, lunging to avoid another spike. "How could Thoth do this to you?"

Scarpia snarled and reached out to her side. A boulder lying nearby suddenly tore itself out of the turf and hung in the air. "*This* is my war!" she cried, throwing her claw forward and sending the rock hurtling towards Mr Zhi.

He flipped and rolled to avoid it, landing painfully on his shoulder, then staggered to his feet. "Oh, Scarpia, can't you see?" he panted. "You will only reap what you sow!"

Naeo glanced at Ash. "When's he going to *do* something?"

"What *can* he do?" said Ash. "The Merisi won't use the Three Ways — they can only defend themselves. That's the way the glove works."

Naeo shook her head. "Well he's going to get himself killed! We have to help him!" she said, striding out.

"Naeo, no!" shouted Ash.

"Come on!" snapped Naeo, turning back.

"No, Naeo, LOOK!"

Ash was pointing in the opposite direction, back towards the rainbow.

Back to the Ray Reaper.

59

The Elements

"Earth and air, fire and water:
these elements are the pillars of all creation."

NAEO'S EYES TRAVELLED TO the figure of the Ray Reaper. She could just about make out an upstanding form, limbs outstretched as though to catch hold of the leaping ribbons. She thought she heard a laugh – a laugh like the crackle of fire. And then the laugh became a hissing voice, whispering across the gardens:

> *"How feeble the fight, how pointless the ire,*
> *For mine is the light and mine is the FIRE!"*

Naeo and Ash watched in horror as something extraordinary began to happen. The rainbow's bands of colour were drifting, splitting, peeling away from one another to form separate ribbons of light. The unravelling happened quickly, travelling the full length of the rainbow until moments later the ribbons were set loose, each taking its own path, rippling and snapping with a life of its own. The many beams flooding into the dome bent and warped, winding themselves into the laces of coloured fire.

They no longer glowed but blazed, they no longer sizzled but roared.

And then Naeo saw the distant blur of the Ray Reaper lowering its arms.

The sinews of the rainbow bucked, beginning a wave that travelled along their length, each colour splitting off to become its own flailing, hissing whip.

She braced for the onslaught of fire, wincing already from the scorching heat.

The first ribbon of blue fire slapped down into the earth in front of them, sending up an explosion of fizzing earth and burning grass. Then another of yellow surged at them through the cloud of debris. Naeo held out her hand to stop it like before, but this time the flames surged on, fed by a greater fire. Pain raged through her hand and her face felt as though it would melt. A new terror consumed her.

She was powerless to stop it.

She pressed her eyes closed and waited for the inevitable. But nothing happened. She opened one eye and saw it hovering, just inches from her hand, the tip out blazing sparks that landed with a *phut, phut, phut.*

The yellow fire began to fade but there was no time to recover because another ribbon darted through the falling debris — a red fire this time — heading for her chest. Ash threw himself in front of it, holding up first one hand and then two, struggling to repel its flames. They drew closer and closer to him until he was silhouetted in ruby fire, his whole body shaking from the effort.

And then a snake of green flailed down from above, slapping into Naeo's back, throwing her to her knees. The unseen lash sliced across her shoulders, set her tunic aflame and seared the muslin of her bandages. She felt the poultice begin to bubble.

Her mind went white. She was aware that she was screaming, but she heard nothing, as though the fire had burned even that.

She fell at Ash's side and saw that he too was burning. There was a slash of red flame across his chest. And his scream she did hear. It filled her with a new kind of dread, the dread of seeing his end too: knowing that he was there for her, lying with her in the grass, dying with her.

She set her teeth and flipped over, pressing her shoulders into the turf until she heard them hiss. Another orange tendril whisked past her face, scorching her cheek but missing her by a hair's breadth. The green lash reared behind it, preparing to fall like a scorpion's sting.

It was hopeless. There were so many. So fast. So powerful.

There was nothing else to be done. She *had* to believe: believe in herself, in everything Mr Zhi had told her, in everything she was supposed to be. She looked up at the whips of fire cutting across the cascading waterfall.

Fire and water.

Water and fire.

That was when she closed her eyes.

In that moment, she changed. She became something else. She left the one and became the other.

She smothered the fire in her veins, quenched the flames in her chest.

In an instant, her fire became water.

It flushed through her limbs, deluged her thoughts, rushed to her fingertips. She no longer saw the squirming sinews of fire, but instead, the flurry of water from a spring, the babble of a brook, the torrent of a stream and then an abyss: a great cascade... the thunder of a waterfall.

She opened her eyes and saw the green tongue of fire surging towards her, she saw Ash writhing on the ground, she heard the fizz of rainbow lashes closing in. But her thoughts and her body were elsewhere.

They were in the waterfall.

It flowed through her, thundering through her bones, pouring down her spine, cascading over the scars of black.

She sat up and looked towards it, lowering her head. Suddenly the torrent moved as though caught by a great wind, shifting back towards the cliff face until it drenched the galleries of the hospital, thundered down the staircases, washed down the passageways. And then she lifted her chin. Instantly the waterfall surged out and up, leaving the cliff face and heading out into open space, curling skywards like the flick of a colossal silver tail. And even as the ribbon of green fire seared her cheek, making her cry out in pain, the trail of water crossed the flux of flames.

There was an explosion of sparks and steam and a huge cloud rose from its midst, filling the dome with billowing white. The green ribbon died before Naeo's eyes, becoming no more than a ghostly trail, drifting back into the watery cloud. The others followed it — the orange, the yellow, the red — all of them sliding away, and as they did so they gathered together, healing themselves, finding their natural place in the rainbow.

Then came a bushfire howl — a wail of dismay and rage. The Ray Reaper was engulfed by the cloud of steam, the droplets of water clinging to its hunched frame, picking it out in traces of grey and silver. It was a figure of unfathomable age, its wasted limbs bound and wrapped in trailing, rotten rags like a corpse resurrected from a millennium long past. Where its skin showed, it was dry and shrivelled, stretched tightly over crooked bones, and what features of its face could be seen were hollow and empty, little more than shadow, as though they had ceased to be. The putrid lengths of cloth seemed to be all that held it together.

It raised its hands in the steam, searching for its fire amid the thick, cloying damp. But when it curled its rotting fingers, the ribbons did not respond. Instead they continued to settle back into the arc of the rainbow. The Ray Reaper spat and shifted its stance, widening its arms and lifting its mummified head. The entire dome began to dim as all the beams of light swung about, sweeping towards a single point. As more and more beams joined together they became a cone of intense brightness, as though the dome were a magnifying glass, concentrating the sun's rays. Where they touched the ground, the turf began to smoke, and soon the very earth burst into flame, sending up a shower of stones and burning vegetation. Then, as the Ray Reaper moved its arms, the inferno began to advance towards Naeo, grass, bushes and trees exploding in its wake, creating a blazing streak across the gardens.

Naeo watched all this with mounting horror, and as the fire drew close and she could feel its heat, she instinctively drew back her hand, taking with it the waterfall, twisting the silver tail in the air, sending the tumbling waters crashing down upon lawns, boulders and trees, snuffing the fire as it went. Soon she was extinguishing the flames as quickly as the Ray Reaper could make them, crushing the fire under tons of mountain water. And yet still the fire came on, drawing nearer and nearer.

"Naeo, finish this!" yelled Ash, throwing his smoking coat aside and staggering to his feet. "You can do it!"

Naeo became calm. She pulled her smarting hand all the way back to her shoulder, until the waterfall thundered so near to them that they were drenched and cooled by its spray. Then her face hardened and she pushed her hand forward, letting out a defiant shriek.

The centre of the waterfall bowed towards the Ray Reaper, reaching out across the gardens, stretching and warping as it went.

Only when it drew close, only when the Reaper ceased its incantations and turned towards the torrent, did the full length of the waterfall follow, unfurling as it went. And then came the twisting tail, pummelling the trees, snapping them like twigs.

The Ray Reaper staggered backwards into the fog. And then, too late, it threw up its hands to shield itself.

The raging tip of the waterfall struck with crushing force, propelling everything in its path out towards the glass walls and then, amid a crash of breaking glass, on to the open hillside. For some moments the Ray Reaper held its ground, its shape clearly visible now amid the great rush of froth and foam. It leaned into the devastating current, its mouth wide in a defiant scream, its rags tearing away from its body as though it was being eaten alive. In seconds all that remained was a teetering skeleton, and then suddenly it let out a squeal like steel twisting in white-hot fire and disappeared into the maelstrom, carried away through the broken dome.

Naeo stared after it, her chest heaving, her eyes wide and staring. She sank to her knees.

And then she felt hands on her shoulders.

"It's done, Naeo," said Ash, softly. "It's done."

60
Storm

"Still the Suhl marched on, through gale and storm*,
desert and mountain range, bound for the
promised comforts of Salsimaine."*

"WHAT DO YOU THINK she meant?" asked Bowe, wincing as he heaved himself up against the cell wall.

Espen shrugged. "I'm damned if I know."

"But you do think it was Isia?"

"I *know* it was Isia."

Bowe eyed him closely, noting how he had pushed himself up straight, how his head had lifted, how his eyes had suddenly found focus. And his Scryer's gaze saw what lay beneath. He saw the violet stab of pain and the thick, oily greens of doubt. He saw grey clouds of despair clinging like a morning mist. But barely seen, there was also something else: a warm yellow glow of belief — faint but distinct — fringed with the piercing blues of hope.

Suddenly Espen stiffened. "Do you hear that?"

Bowe drew himself back to the physical world and listened. Sure enough there was a low rumble — not the rumble of thunder that they had been hearing for some time, but something new. Something that was now building, growing in volume and force.

"What do you think it is?" asked Bowe.

"I'm not sure," said Espen, biting his lip. He glanced over. "But have you noticed? The guards — they aren't patrolling."

Bowe frowned. He was right. It was hours since he had heard the clawed steps of a Ghor guard patrolling the passageways — even longer since he had been brought food or water. And now he thought about it, why hadn't they come to check the cell when Espen had arrived? He had hardly been quiet about it.

"Wait," he said, "I'll try to see."

He raised his hands to his face in concentration and reached out into the Dirgheon, sending his Scrying mind through its long corridors, its filthy halls, its tunnels and stairwells.

Nothing. Just blackness.

"They've *gone*!" he exclaimed, hardly believing his own words.

They turned and met each other's eyes.

Suddenly Espen reached behind him and, with the heels of his hands, pushed himself up the wall. He slumped more than once, but something kept him going: a new, steely resolve. When he reached his full height he paused, head swimming. He took a moment to steady himself, then extended a hand to Bowe.

"Can you walk?" he asked.

Bowe took the hand and grinned. "I'll carry you if it gets me out of this place!"

It took him several attempts to get to his feet, but eventually the two found themselves standing in the doorway, an arm over each other's shoulder, swaying from side to side. It was sheer will that kept them on their feet.

"Ready?" whispered the Magruman.

Bowe nodded.

They staggered out into the passageway and squinted into the dim torchlight. All they could see was the procession of cell doors. The rumble was louder out here and they could feel a gentle breeze on their skin.

"Sounds like a storm of some kind," muttered Bowe, coughing from the effort.

Espen shook his head. "Not like any I've heard before."

They set off along the corridor, panting as they staggered and lurched, sometimes barely staying on their feet. But soon they developed a rhythm, each helping the other by standing firm while the other moved, or drawing the other along when they lost momentum. They passed door after door, occasionally hearing quiet murmurings from the cells beyond. More than once they thought they heard a quiet call for help, and more than once they glanced at one another and drew up, but always they continued, knowing it would be folly to try anything but escape.

All the while the breeze was becoming stronger, carrying upon it the stench of thousands and thousands of cells deep in the bowels of the Dirgheon. Soon the breeze was a wind, making the torches flicker and spit, whistling across the doorways to the cells.

And then, suddenly, Espen drew them to a halt.

Bowe looked at him, panting.

"You OK?"

"I was here before," said Espen, his eyes fixed ahead as he remembered. "With Sylas. This is the way I brought him in, when he came for Naeo."

Bowe looked back down the passageway, taking in the hundreds of doors, the flickering torches, the lines disappearing into nothingness in the distance.

"Sylas stopped here," recalled Espen, turning to the Scryer.

"He wanted to know about the cells. He wanted to know why we weren't setting everyone free."

"And what did you say?"

"That it wasn't the right time," muttered Espen, almost to himself. "That it all depended on him. And Naeo."

Suddenly he turned and looked Bowe in the eye. "I was wrong."

To Bowe he seemed fuller and broader; even his drooping shoulder seemed to lift, becoming squarer, almost as though he were well.

"'*You forget yourself...*'" murmured Espen.

He helped Bowe to the wall and left him leaning against it, then turned back down the passageway, taking a broad, open stance. The wind whipped at his shoulders and tore at his clothes, but he stood firm. He closed his eyes and filled his lungs, spreading his arms wide. One hand closed into a fist. For a moment he was silent and still, seeming to lose himself in his thoughts. Then his eyes snapped open.

He swung both arms forward, smashing the fist into his open palm.

In that very moment the winds were stunned, hanging in the open spaces, leaving the Dirgheon in absolute silence. Bowe gazed at him in awe and quickly braced himself against the wall.

The Magruman raised his head.

"I AM ESPASIAN!" he bellowed.

And he opened his fist.

Instantly the winds returned, howling down the passageway, buffeting the doorways. They caught up his voice, bearing it off through the Dirgheon, as it went it seemed to grow, until it shook the stones in the walls, until the doors rattled and groaned, until the floor and ceiling thundered his name. And, as his voice grew so did the wind, demanding more space than it had, pressing outwards on the structure that dared to contain it. In an instant, the wind became a wild, unbridled force, charging through the open spaces of the Dirgheon, through corridors and chambers, stairways and halls. And all the while it carried a voice on its back, a bellowing, warlike cry:

"I AM ESPASIAN!"

Suddenly bolts snapped, hinges broke, doors flew open. The sound of shattering metal echoed like gunfire down the passageway. Bowe threw his hands over his ears, but Espasian did not flinch. He stood firm as exploding metal ricocheted down the corridor, sending out a shower of sparks so that for once that deathly place glowed like day. Soon the Dirgheon was filled with a rat-a-tat roar of sound as the same happened in the next passage and the next, on the floor above and the one below.

And then, as quickly as they had come, the winds began to subside, dropping to a gentle breeze. The Magruman's voice too trailed off and began to fade, though it could still be heard echoing through the furthest corners of the Dirgheon.

Espasian staggered against the slimy wall of the passage, then slowly slumped back down on to the floor.

He looked at Bowe, a smile forming on his lips. Bowe grinned back.

Just then there was a movement further down the corridor.

A pale hand appeared around one of the doorways, followed by a gaunt, white face. It was a woman, her dark hair falling in greasy knots around her shoulders, her pale eyes blinking into the corridor. Then another face appeared further down: a child this time. Then another in the far distance. Slowly the passageway filled with more and more forlorn figures, their eyes wide and disbelieving, their movements furtive and frightened. And as they came, something else emerged from the cells.

Whispers. Whispers of thousands of weak voices, like dry leaves on the wind. At first they were just a rush of sound, but slowly they became one voice.

And it spoke one word.

"ESPASIAN!"

§

It would not leave her. It washed through her thoughts and gushed down her spine. The Ray Reaper was gone, but the deluge thundered on, racing through her limbs, stirring the pain in her back. Ash's words were warped and watery, his face bleary and distant.

"It's done, Naeo," he gurgled. "Are you all right?"

But she was fathoms deep, held in the great cascade. She saw him kneel down next to her.

"Let it go, Naeo," he said, cupping her cheek. "You've done enough!"

Perhaps it was that touch, or his words, but suddenly Naeo felt something beyond the cool, airless veil, something vital and human to cling to. And in that moment the waters began to leave her, ebbing from her mind and draining from her chest, taking with them the creeping chill.

She met Ash's eyes for the first time.

"That's it," he said, smiling. "Come back."

His voice sounded clear and crisp, and it came with other sounds: the roar and splash of the waterfall, the tumbling of water over rocks.

And screams. And shouts. And a deafening, crashing sound, like the sky was falling in.

She saw Ash look over his shoulder, and then she watched him stand.

Reluctantly, she turned her eyes.

She saw fifteen, perhaps twenty Merisi emerging from the trees, Tasker at their lead, breaking into a run. She could see the whites of his eyes, his features slack with horror.

And then she saw Mr Zhi, bloodied and bruised, fighting on many fronts. The ground buckled beneath his feet, great clods of earth flew at him from each side, an entire tree flipped towards him, careering over the hilltop.

There before him was Scarpia, directing her devastating power with graceful sweeps of claws and tail, her sleek flanks writhing in an elaborate dance. Mr Zhi performed a dance of his own, extending his gloved hand to each threat, halting it in its tracks, casting it aside.

But he was losing the fight.

Suddenly he was battered by a blizzard of rocks and earth, sent sprawling by the tree trunk, whipped by plants and branches. And then Scarpia threw back her head and let out an animal snarl. There was a metallic screech and a crash of breaking glass. A vast section of the glass dome scythed down, collecting into another lethal column of razor shards.

In an instant Mr Zhi had fallen on his back and raised his hand. In a trice the glass column began to divide, falling either side of him in a flurry of slicing splinters.

For a moment, it looked like he had done enough.

But one piece of glass fell straight.

One piece of glass fell true.

The final flurries of winds would not leave Sylas. They whipped at the corners of his mind and squalled in his chest. He tried to set them loose, free them back to the storm, but for some reason they held on, as though reluctant to let him go. Still they whipped about him, turning in a vortex of dust and debris, keeping him from seeing where Simia had gone.

In the end, it was not he but Simia who quelled the winds. When he thought of her face, of her scream, he felt something beyond the winds, something close and real. It was a feeling that all was undone. It was despair.

The winds slowed and for the first time he thought to breathe out, to relax his shoulders. They did not go quickly, but slowly, inevitably, they lost their force. The detritus of the city fluttered down through the air: papers and peelings, the awnings of stalls, garments from clotheslines, rags from the nearby slums. He peered through them, turning on the spot, waiting for the first attack, readying himself to run, to fight. He peered between the falling trash, into doorways, among the rooftops.

There was nothing.

No sign of the Ghor, nor the Hamajaks, nor the Ragers.

Nor Simia.

He looked up and saw the whirlwind retreat into the clouds, gathering into the rumbling dark. Lightning streaked across the sky as if sewing it back together.

He was alone. Horribly alone.

61
Shattered

*"Oh what it would be to wake now —
wake from these* shattered *dreams!"*

SYLAS LOOKED AROUND IN growing desperation.

There was nothing in the Place of Tongues, nor in the nearby lane, except for a few scattered, limp bodies, lying lifelessly on the white flagstones. The rest of the creatures seemed to have disappeared, ripped up by the devastating winds, hurled skywards only to be lost in the heart of the storm. Was it really possible? All those creatures — the whole seething mass of them, carried off by winds alone? *His* winds?

And then he had a chilling thought: had the winds taken Simia too? His eyes were drawn up to the clouds, boiling and bubbling like a devil's brew. It was too horrifying to contemplate.

He skirted the buildings and entered the lane, legs quivering beneath him, a knot in his throat. He looked quickly over piles of rubbish, through broken windows, past doors that flapped and banged in the storm's winds. Still nothing.

He remembered Simia's face as Thoth's creatures had charged: that expression of absolute trust. It made him feel sick. How could he have lost his concentration? Why hadn't he stayed with the winds?

He felt panic pressing on his chest and he became ever more frantic, peering into corner and crevice.

And then he froze.

There was something next to a shattered stall. Something large and living.

Its flank heaved with slow, laboured breaths. It was slumped against a wall, its scaly flesh glowing pink between pieces of wood and scraps of awning. And he could hear it now, over the whistling wind: a strained whine as it breathed in, a spluttering huff as it exhaled.

A Rager.

Cautiously, he walked towards it, noticing that the breaths were coming ever more slowly and its exposed flank was fading from pink to grey. He saw the tail quivering against the wall; the huge, armoured head twisted at an odd angle; its massive, demonic features staring blankly. The colour drained from its brow and cheeks and as it did so, the beast let out a last, violent huff. Suddenly it too was still and silent.

Sylas leaned forward. Could this have been the one? The one that took Simia? He shuddered at its flesh glistening with a final sweat. It was dead because of him, because of what he had done. He was aware of a distant notion that he should be horrified, but that was not how he felt. He felt glad.

Then something caught his eye.

There was a patch of red on the creature's neck.

Vivid, burning red.

He steeled himself, expecting the Rager's eyes to blink, its chest to heave, its mighty tail to lash out with a deadly blow. But it was still and lifeless.

His eyes moved back to the patch of red, and in the same instant he realised what it was.

Not scaly skin, but something lying across it. A splash of red hair, trailing over the creature's neck and into the shadows beyond.

Breathlessly he clawed at the debris of the mangled stall, throwing aside planks of wood, lengths of fabric, broken pottery.

At last he could see her face — motionless and deathly white. But he could not free her. She was trapped, her arm twisted between the wall and the Rager's tail.

Tears welled in his eyes. "No, Simsi!" he cried, hurling more wood over his shoulder. "No! No! No!"

He pushed at the beast with abandon, his words echoing down the lane.

And then his words seemed to come back, loose and unformed, grunted rather than spoken.

"Uh! Uh! Uh!"

And then again, louder this time: "UH! UH! UH!"

He did not hear them at first. He heard only his heavy pulse, his panted breaths. He clambered on to the beast's flank and then behind, pushing himself into the small, dark crevice, kicking out at the tail, desperate to free her.

"UH-UH-UH!" came the voices, too loud now to be denied. "UH-UH-EEEH-EEEH-EEEH!"

The shrieks finally drew his eyes away from Simia's twisted form, up to the surrounding buildings. There he saw eight, perhaps ten Hamajaks clambering down from the rooftops, swinging between windowsills and ledges, some climbing with their hands, others, bloodied and injured, hanging upside down by their feet or tails. Their gums were pulled back, their yellow teeth bared and drooling. For the first time, Sylas saw that their features were

468

almost human, their eyes focused and bright. But everything else about them was animal, hungry and cold.

He turned away, looking back to Simia's tiny form, broken and still.

He hardly cared what happened now.

He crouched down to be near to her. And he waited.

"No... No... No..." she murmured.

For some moments Naeo just stared at Mr Zhi's form, enshrined in a circle of broken glass. It was a strange, almost beautiful scene: the old man, quiet and serene, encircled by shards that showed fragments of his small, resting form — a little of him but not too much, as though he were already a memory.

But one detail betrayed the jarring, horrifying truth. One single shard, long and thin, rising like a dagger from the centre of the circle.

The flood had left her now but her limbs were heavier than ever, her heart as dark and cold as the deep. Tears welled in her eyes as she remembered his last words to her:

"*Now is a time for sacrifice.*"

And then she thought she saw a movement. A flicker in the glass. Something shimmering from one sliver to another: a moving shape, a dancing flash of colour. Her heart leapt.

But then she saw another and another: reflections, flitting between the polished planes — not Mr Zhi at all, but something happening beyond, at the edge of the glade.

Her eyes lifted to the tree line, to the dark figure of Scarpia crouching and leaping, twisting and turning, casting a hail of magic.

And before her, the Merisi.

All of them were there, arranged in a wide ring of dancing bodies and fluttering robes, shifting with every missile thrown, rippling as they jumped and crouched with gloved hands outstretched.

They leapt over spinning boulders and crouched beneath twisted beams, parrying swarms of pebbles that shrilled through the air like bullets. Sometimes the ring of Merisi broke, parting for a cartwheeling tree or a rift in the earth, but always it closed again, drawing tight, moving ever inwards, step by hard-fought step.

And at their centre Scarpia raged and snarled, throwing up a cloud of dust as she dispensed her magic, calling upon all the power of Urgolvane to lift what may not be lifted, throw what may not be thrown. She tore at the earth and ripped at the trees, gathering them up in her wild pirouette to hurl them outwards, sending them clattering into the unwavering line of Merisi gloves, only to see them thrown aside or halted in their tracks. She split the earth, pummelling it until it became a pool of mud, only to see it settle beneath a Merisi palm. She threw down glass and metal from the roof, only to find her deadly hail turning in the air and spearing the ground around her, forming a mesh of razor edges.

And then Naeo realised what was happening. The Merisi were turning Scarpia's magic against her: letting her hem herself in, defeat *herself*. They closed in steadily, mercilessly, like a noose about a neck, and soon they were so close that Scarpia's missiles were halted before they took flight, falling almost at her feet. She let out a wailing, furious shriek, wheeling about and kicking at the mounting pile of debris about her. Then she squealed and raised a claw to her face, a bleeding claw, caught on one of her own shards of glass.

"'You will reap what you sow'," murmured Naeo under her breath.

She tried to climb to her feet, to join the fight, but she found herself falling back down, her limbs still stiff and heavy.

"Stay here," said Ash at her shoulder. "I've got this."

He strode out ahead of her, straight towards Scarpia — straight into the fight.

The Merisi were shoulder to shoulder now, their ring a solid wall. Scarpia's ears were back and she snapped and lashed. But she could not reach them: she was surrounded by a jagged enclosure of steel and glass, rocks and branches. More than once she flailed into it, catching her arm, leg or tail. She tried to jump clear of it, but landed squealing on a criss-cross of metal, sliding back into her self-made stockade.

But then there was a strange pause. The Merisi hesitated, seeming unsure of their next move and Scarpia used that moment of indecision to hit out at her bonds. She changed her tactics, using her strength alone to dislodge the debris. She braced her back and pushed out with her legs, sending a slew of rocks and glass and metal outwards into the approaching Merisi.

A triumphant grin over her face.

"You cannot hold me!" she shrieked. "I am a Magruman of Thoth! My power is older than rocks and rivers, older than petty clans and pretty tricks!"

She sent a boulder rolling between the Merisi, a branch scudding across the glade, a shower of earth into the face of one nearby. The Merisi line began to falter and suddenly the side of the stockade broke open, leaving the way clear.

Then Ash stepped into the breach. He lifted his head and raised his arms, his stance wide and assured, his features set and determined.

Naeo's breath caught. He looked like a Magruman.

There was a rumble in the earth — deep in its bowels, far below the gardens. The trees that were still standing began to shake, shedding leaves and twigs. For a moment, Scarpia ceased her scrapping and fell silent, looking about her like a cornered animal.

Then the rumble became a roar: the roar of grinding rocks and fissures snapping shut, of half-fallen trees heaving themselves upright and roots slithering back to their rightful place. It was the sound of Nature healing herself.

The tangle of weeds and branches around Scarpia suddenly came to life, twisting and writhing around her like a nest of snakes. Grass wormed and wriggled, stems reared into the air, branches clawed.

"That's it, Ash!" murmured Naeo, a smile curling her lips.

Scarpia froze, ears up teeth bared.

The gardens roused themselves, seeking revenge for the hurt and harm. Roots and stems and leaves crawled like a net across her chest. Twigs became her bonds, branches her shackles. She lashed out at them with tooth and claw, struggling to hold them back, but their power was too great. She sank down amid the writhing pile, into the things she had so abused.

Ash looked on, his shoulders heaving, his eyes wide and shot with red.

"Reap what you sow, Scarpia!" he cried. "Reap what you sow!"

§

Now he knew the touch of death.

He had seen it, of course he had. Everyone had seen more than their fill of death at the Reckoning, and the Scryers more than most. He had seen fields of death, rivers of death, days and nights of death. And his Scrying eyes had seen all that came with it: the anguish, the confusion, the hate, the loss, the love never expressed, the words never spoken.

He had seen death and his young heart had broken more times than he could remember.

But this… this was what it *felt* like.

Empty. Cold. Numb. Blank. Black.

Black.

But it was not complete. Not yet.

Somewhere there was a radiance. A hint of warmth. A glow. And Triste curled towards it, drinking it in.

He rolled into the ash of the campfire and pressed himself against the warm stones, clinging to life.

He could not be sure when the Kraven had left him. The attack had been endless, and the darkness since, endless too. It was one infinity.

But he knew why they had left him.

They left because of the one who had spoken. The one who had touched Sylas hours before. The one who knew Sylas's promise. Sylas's greatness.

It had been a woman's voice; dry and hollow, but feminine. First she had spoken to the others, telling them to release the Scryer, to leave him be, and thankfully — miraculously — they had done as she commanded, rising through his chest and shoulders, tugging at his insides, reluctant to let go. Some had lingered a little too long and the voice had come again, sharper and harder, and he had felt the remaining Kraven shiver and start, spiralling up into the night.

Only when they had gone had he felt her near, cold and lifeless. She trailed against his leg, brushed up his side, nestled into his shoulder. He felt her dead lips at his ear, heard her breath, like air escaping a tomb.

"*As you are life, we are death*," she had whispered.

And then there were icy fingers against his cheek.

"*Tell the boy to let us die!*"

62

The Source

"Even the mighty Nile, that fount of life and spine of the empire, has a source *that somewhere trickles meekly from the earth."*

SYLAS RESTED BACK AGAINST the corpse of the Rager, its scales pressing between his shoulder blades. He heard the Hamajaks draw ever closer. He heard the scrape of their claws against stone; the shuffle of their giant bodies as they swung towards him; their shrieking cries.

But he did nothing.

Instead his gaze was fixed on Simia's ashen face.

She looked so calm, so peaceful now. None of the fight. None of the fire. Now, at the end, she looked like the young girl she really was: quiet and frail.

He felt as crushed and broken.

"Please don't leave me, Simsi," he said, reaching out to draw the red curls from her face.

"I can't. There's a Rager on my arm."

He threw himself back, slamming against the flank of the Rager. Simia's eyes blinked open and focused on him.

Sylas struggled to find his voice. "I thought you were..."

"So it seems," said Simia, with the trace of a smile.

"Are you… OK?"

She blinked. "Well I can't feel my leg and I'm under a Rager, but otherwise I'm fine."

"Well you definitely *sound* yourself," he said, laughing in relief.

She grunted, wriggling her shoulders and trying to move. "Are you just going to talk or are you—"

Suddenly she looked up above his head, her eyes widening.

Sylas turned, the smile falling from his face.

He looked straight into the face of a human ape, looming over the back of the Rager, its great silver mane flared, its yellowing incisors dripping drool. Its eyes flicked between him and Simia, then it reared back on its hind legs and thrashed its chest with its fists, letting out a mighty, triumphal scream.

Instantly two, three, then four more appeared at its sides, silhouetted against a maze of lightning. All of them thumped their chests and screamed their victory.

In those precious moments with Simsi he had forgotten all about the Hamajaks. He shifted towards Simia, putting his body between her and the beasts, raising his hands. But he knew it was too late.

The leader surged forward, its fists crashing down on the Rager, breaking bones where they fell. Sylas could reach out and touch it now. He could smell its breath: the stench of festering gums and the rotting flesh of its last meal.

And then it hesitated.

Its giant arms fell to its sides, its screams fading to a panting huff.

The others too had frozen, looking up the lane. There was something almost human in their expressions, something that betrayed their surprise, their fear. And then they each began to shuffle anxiously, drawing closer, into a pack.

The leader chattered in a half-animal, half-human voice. It thumped its chest as though to rally its troop, but the rest did nothing. Their eyes shifted to their companions and then back up the lane.

"What's going on?" murmured Simia from behind Sylas.

He started to push himself up. "I don't know," he whispered. "They've seen something — up the lane."

He edged ever upwards, over the round ribcage of the Rager, until his eyes peeked over the top.

He blinked in disbelief.

Ghosts.

Hundreds, perhaps thousands of silent ghosts.

They were walking shoulder to shoulder down the middle of the lane, their pale faces looming out of the dark, their unblinking eyes seeming to stare straight through the creatures. Their bodies, such as they were, were wasted and thin, shrouded in filthy rags, their skin sallow and grubby, their hair long and matted. All this gave them the appearance of wraiths, of a deathly host emerging from hell itself. But as they approached a row of flaming torches, light glistened on clammy brows and sparkled in staring eyes. It played across forms that were solid and real, across muscle and bone. There were men and women, the young and the old, those who limped and stumbled.

And as they came, Sylas realised that they were not silent at all. They brought with them the sound of hushed words and the patter of countless feet against rock.

These were not ghosts.

This was an exodus. And it was coming from the Dirgheon.

The Hamajaks began chattering loudly among themselves, their great manes on end, their eyes furtive and frightened. Then one of them bolted up the street, back in the direction of the square. The rest hesitated, looking from one to the other, and then they too turned, bounding away as fast as their feet and fists could carry them. The leader paused a little longer, its eyes shifting between the advancing army of spectres and Sylas, as though weighing what to do next. And then, with an almighty shriek, it flung itself about, tearing off along the lane.

Simia hit Sylas's leg. "What's *happening*?"

He looked down and shook his head.

"You won't believe it," he said.

"Try me!"

"It's them, Simsi. It's the Suhl."

She blinked up at him. "What do you mean? *Which* Suhl?"

"All of them!"

They passed in a fog of whispers — the whispers of those who had not raised their voice for years, who had almost forgotten how to speak. Some glanced at Sylas, some even nodded and smiled, but none of them stopped — they all moved on, intent on leaving the Dirgheon far behind. Many held hands or linked arms, comforting one another as they headed out into the unknown. Grown men threw arms around shoulders, supporting each other as they took their first steps in years.

"Help me up!" demanded Simia. "I want to see!"

Several of the passing prisoners stopped and turned. They frowned and looked over inquisitively towards where Simia lay.

"I mean it, Sylas, get down here, right now!"

Sylas watched nervously as the closest among the passing crowd stepped forward and clambered up on to the Rager, peering into the crevice behind.

Seeing the ghostly face, Simia shrank back, pressing herself into the shadows.

The man raised his hands and retreated a little. "It's OK," he said, in Simia's, rich, rolling accent. He knelt down. "I heard you — you're Suhl, aren't you?"

She gazed at him, her face filling with emotion. "Yes, I am."

"Are you all right?"

"No, I'm not," she said. "Not at all, really."

"You'll be OK, little one," he said. There was something in that husky voice that was to be believed — to be trusted.

"She's trapped," said Sylas. "Can you help me move this thing?"

The man nodded. "We *all* can."

He looked back into the lane and gestured to his companions. After a brief exchange they arranged themselves around the Rager, and in spite of shaky limbs and wasted muscles, they began heaving with all their might. Sylas leaned his back on the beast and planted his feet against the wall, pushing with the rest of them. Slowly but surely, the gigantic corpse began to roll away.

Simia grimaced as the weight shifted off her arm and her cheeks drained of their little remaining colour, but she did not cry out. She would not show her pain, not in front of these people — these people who had suffered so much.

And then with a final twist of the body and a slap of the tail, the Rager fell away. Simia huddled over her arm, cursing under her breath. Her wrist was blue and purple and there was a deep gash near her elbow.

Sylas took her round the shoulders. "Come on, Simsi."

With his help she was soon pushing herself up, flinching as she put her weight on the twisted knee.

But when she finally looked up she forgot her pain. She gaped at the endless procession of whispering figures, at the stiff bodies wrapped in rags and the drawn, tired faces showing their first flicker of hope. For a moment she just watched, soaking in the sight of them. Then her eyes filled with tears.

"Did *you* do this?" she asked, quietly.

"I don't *think* so," said Sylas.

An old woman was hobbling by, using a broken plank as a crutch. She slowed and turned to them. "It was him!" she whispered. "Espasian! Espasian has come!"

The Merisi stood around the circle of glass, their eyes fixed on its centre, their faces sombre and drawn. For some time, none of them moved. Finally it was Franz Veeglum who stepped into the circle and knelt, folding his long thin form to sit cross-legged at Mr Zhi's side. He attended to the old man as best he could, pulling out and casting aside the shard of glass, cleaning his face with water collected at the waterfall and covering the wound with white muslin cloths. They were not bandages — it was too late for bandages.

Only when these things had been done to his satisfaction did the undertaker bow his head to his leader and friend.

Naeo felt tears rolling down her cheeks. She hardly knew Mr Zhi, but in their few hours together he had made her feel safe; she hadn't felt that way for a very, very long time. But it was more than that. She knew he had done this for her. He had walked into Scarpia's hellfire knowing that she was more powerful than he; that he did not stand a chance.

Again his parting words played through her mind: "*A time of sacrifice*," he had said.

And then, suddenly, Mr Zhi's hand quivered and grasped Veeglum's arm.

There was an excited murmur among the Merisi and many stepped forward to try to see his face. Veeglum seized his hand, leaning closer.

Words seemed to be exchanged — slow, halting words, spoken so quietly that all that could be heard was a murmur. Veeglum nodded his head and removed his jacket, rolled it up and then eased Mr Zhi up a little to use it as a pillow.

Everyone saw his face then, and any hope fell away. His skin was white — not pale, but marble white — and the many folds and lines that told of a long and important life seemed deeper and darker, as though they had been etched into his face. If there was one hint of the Mr Zhi that everyone knew, it was in his eyes. They at least were still quick and bright. And they turned towards Naeo.

"Mr Zhi vishes to speak vith you," said Veeglum, beckoning with long fingers.

Breathlessly, Naeo stepped into the circle of glass, hearing it crunch and tinkle beneath her feet. She flinched — it seemed too loud, too hard. She walked to Mr Zhi and knelt next to him. His kindly old face broke into a smile.

"I'm so sorry!" she blurted. "I... I just couldn't..."

Mr Zhi's hand slid across and fumbled into hers. It was frighteningly cold and clammy.

"No, NO!" he whispered, faintly.

"But they came to find *me*! If I hadn't—"

"They came to wage war," whispered Mr Zhi. He looked at her keenly, as though willing her to understand. "A war on us all. On our future. On all we might be."

She met his eyes, but then looked down. "I'm just so sorry..." she said, sobbing.

He clasped her hand tightly and lifted his head. "No, my child. All is as it should be. This is your journey now; I am at the end of mine." He winced, closing his eyes and taking shallow breaths. He lifted a finger and pointed out at the gardens. "That must be my way now."

Naeo followed his gaze as it moved from the grasses by his feet, to the long fronds of flowers on the hillside, to the pool at the base of the waterfall.

"I don't understand!" she said. "*Where?*"

"The source of things," he said, with a faint smile, his eyes dancing with the ripples, shifting in the dappled light. Then he looked up the great column of water, up and up that dazzling spire of foam until finally he gazed at the endless bubbling torrent high above, leaping and sparkling between rocks and moss and grass.

"There!" he murmured.

And then his eyes faded and closed.

63

Burdens to Bear

"And so it must fall to these, the Bringers. They bear the burden of a truth we are not ready to believe."

THE CROWDS PARTED BEFORE them like two great rivers, flowing with a shuffle and a whisper. Some stopped to watch their passing, looking curiously at the two children who fought against the tide. Some seemed concerned, eyeing Simia's cuts and bruises, her injured arm and leg, and Sylas, bearing her weight across his shoulders. One tall, thin man approached to see if he could help, but when Sylas insisted on continuing towards the Dirgheon, the stranger gazed at him in bewilderment and carried on alone.

And then, finally, they rounded a corner and saw the Dirgheon towering above them, black and menacing.

"There!" exclaimed Simia. "There it is!"

It was strange to look at that evil place with anything other than dread and even stranger to feel a flood of relief, but that was what they felt. They saw its massive ebony sides rising above them, its highest reaches wearing the storm clouds like a crooked crown. They saw the vast red banner hanging down the nearest of the terraced sides, and at its centre the immense and empty face of Thoth glowering down upon them. They saw all this and they were glad, because they knew that the worst was behind them and that the end was near.

They stumbled on up the lane, heading for a broad space at the foot of the Dirgheon, which flickered with firelight. They could hardly believe that they were so close.

"Simsi?" he said.

Simia glanced up at him.

"I'm just thinking, what if Bowe's not there?"

She blinked at him irritably. "Why wouldn't he be?"

"What if we passed him along the way? What if he's in one of the other lanes?"

Simia thought for a moment. "Well, he's a *Scryer*," she said with a shrug. "He'd probably have seen us even if we didn't see him."

"Really? With all these people around?" said Sylas dubiously. "Remember in the Meander Mill, at the Say-So? I asked you why he was hiding up in the gallery and you told me he couldn't—"

"...he couldn't bear to be too close," said Simia, nodding slowly. "Because it was all such a muddle. You might be right."

Sylas gnawed his lip nervously. "Well, I suppose if he got out, that's a good thing, whichever way you look at it."

"I suppose."

"Come on, we've got to try," said Sylas, starting out again.

But after a few paces Simia said: "If Triste was here, he'd be able to find him."

"You think?"

"One Scryer looking for another — how could they miss each other?"

Sylas grunted. "See what you mean."

Simia slowed a little. "Do you think he's all right?"

"Who, Triste?"

She nodded.

Sylas looked away, feeling a pang of guilt. He had to admit he had barely thought of Triste since they arrived in Gheroth. "I'm sure he is," he said, vaguely.

She shook her head. "Out there on the Barrens, on his own, with the Kraven. And those burns!"

Sylas stopped and met her eyes. "Simsi, I think if anyone can look after themselves out there as well as you, it's Triste."

She looked at him doubtfully and he saw the anguish in her eyes.

"Seriously," he insisted, "I bet he's already on his way back to the valley!"

She gave a heavy sigh. "If he isn't, I'm not sure I'll ever forgive myself."

She let him lead her on and together they staggered up the final stretch of the lane. As they went they did their best to keep their eyes up, to scour the faces of the stragglers as they traipsed away from the Dirgheon. So intent were they on the faces that the end of the lane came upon them suddenly, leaving them blinking into bright torchlight.

Before them was a small plaza lit by burning urns dotted about its perimeter. At its centre, wide steps rose to the Dirgheon's entrance, which towered darkly above them, its gigantic doors thrown back. A few weak, limping figures were still emerging from the black interior, but they seemed to be the very last: an old man, leaning heavily on a stick; a terribly thin woman looking lost and dazed; a man crawling on all fours, a smile spreading across his face as he saw the light.

Below them, the steps were teeming. These were the old and the weak, the injured and the diseased: the last few for whom the prospect of escape was simply too much. The promise of fresh air and an open sky had brought them this far, but now they just gathered in small groups, staring gratefully at the world that had become a distant dream, taking deep breaths of air that they had almost forgotten. Their expressions betrayed their thoughts: however this might end, it was worth it for this moment.

Some of their younger, stronger companions moved among them, talking to them, reassuring them, trying to persuade some to make the journey onwards. But it was futile: there were hundreds and they were not for moving.

Sylas and Simia began limping towards the nearest of the groups, searching through the many faces, hoping against hope that Bowe might be among them. A host of hungry eyes blinked up at them as they approached but then paid them little more attention, assuming them to be more recruits to their hapless band.

Sylas was about to speak to some of them when there was a commotion at the top of the steps. At first all he could see was an excited crowd jostling near the entrance, but then some stepped to the side, as though making room on the steps to allow something or somebody to pass. A whisper went up among them, a whisper that quickly became excited chatter.

And then the crowd parted.

Two large figures staggered forward, each the other's support, arms across one another's shoulders. Both dragged limbs and had a sickly complexion, but that was where the similarity ended. One had a long pallid face and doleful eyes; the other a powerful build and glistening mahogany skin. One had the tattoos of a Scryer around his head, the other a diagonal scar across his face.

Simia squeezed Sylas's arm excitedly.

The chatter swelled into a chant.

"Espasian! Espasian! Espasian!"

The two men eased one another down the steps, turning to nod at those who bowed as they passed. Still the chant grew in volume, filling the square, singing between the buildings.

"ESPASIAN! ESPASIAN! ESPASIAN!"

And then the Scryer stopped, dragging his companion back. Espasian looked at him in bewilderment and then glanced around the square.

The chant faltered and then stopped. Everyone was watching the Scryer.

Bowe's deep green eyes were fixed on two children at the bottom of the steps, two children holding each other across the shoulders just like them.

Espasian looked down at them. For a moment he blinked, seeming barely able to believe his eyes. And then his scarred face crumpled into a grin.

"Sylas!" he bellowed, his voice dry but full, echoing around the square. He turned his eyes to Simia and his grin broadened. "And young Simia, of course!"

"Espen!" cried Sylas, helping Simia up the steps. "Bowe! You're alive!"

The two men staggered down to meet them and when he was close enough, the Magruman reached out and gripped Sylas by the shoulder.

"Call me Espasian! Today I feel more worthy of that name." He looked at them both. "So you came to set us free!"

Sylas grinned. "Well, you beat us to it!"

"I wouldn't say that," said Bowe, his features alive with a new excitement. "Did you draw Thoth's guards out of the Dirgheon?"

"And did you call these winds?" asked Espasian.

486

"He did!" said Simia, proudly.

Sylas glanced at her and grinned. "Well, I couldn't have done it without Simsi."

"Then you have done more for us than you know," said Espasian. "Both of you."

Sylas felt a flush of pride, but he tried not to show it.

Bowe was exploring Sylas's face. "Do you know how Naeo is?" He looked across the square. "Is she... with you?"

Sylas shook his head. "No, she's gone to try to find Mr Zhi. We're trying to find out—"

Espasian raised his hand. "Not here, Sylas," he said, glancing at the many faces gathered around them. "Leave the rest until we're alone."

Bowe leaned forward. "But she's *all right*, Sylas?"

"Yes," he said. He was sure of it. "She's OK."

Espasian was looking around, his face darkening as he weighed the task ahead. "We need to get out of here," he said quietly. "And we have to help the people who can't help themselves."

Sylas and Simia looked at each other and smiled.

"We can help with that," said Simia.

Espasian raised an eyebrow. "Everyone?"

"Yes, I think so," said Simia, looking at the crowd.

"Does this have anything to do with canvas birds?" asked Bowe nervously.

Sylas laughed. "Not quite."

"Well, if you really can help them," said Espasian, "I'll attend to the rest."

The smiles faded from everyone's faces.

"What do you mean?" asked Bowe incredulously. "You can't be thinking of crossing the Barrens with the others?"

"That's exactly what I'm thinking," said Espasian firmly. "Can you imagine what would happen if Thoth caught up with them? Out there on the wastes? They'd be defenceless."

"But you're in no fit state!" exclaimed Bowe.

"I'll be all right."

"Espasian, you can barely walk!"

"And yet look what he did," came a deep voice from behind. Everyone turned.

A giant figure mounted the steps towards them. He had bushy brown hair, a great mane of a beard and a bear-like build made all the more imposing by thick leather armour on his shoulders, chest and flanks. It was the armour of a Spoorrunner.

His face was set and stern, but as he reached them it broke into a guarded smile.

"I will walk with you, Espasian," said Bayleon, extending a hand.

§

The General hunched over the feasting table, tapping a claw impatiently on the wooden surface. He had no appetite. How could he eat at a time like this?

He threw himself back in his chair and raised his massive arms behind his head. His canine eyes travelled around the field tent: over the banquet of meats, the empty seats around the table, the entrance flapping in the wind and then out on to the hillside.

Where the hell were they?

He heaved himself to his feet, ornate armour clattering as he rose. He threw his clawed fists behind his back and paced up and down the tent, his wolfish muzzle hanging low and trailing drool. It was not the feast that made him salivate: it was the promise of battle. He could smell it now. War was so close he could almost taste the blood.

Then one of the sentries ducked inside the tent.

"Sir, they're here," it growled in the language of the Ghor. "Lord Grak is outside."

"What took him so long?" snapped the General.

"They had casualties, sir."

The General grunted his disapproval. "Show him in."

The sentry took its leave and moments later a giant figure stepped inside. It bowed deeply, revealing a high, crested mane.

"Great Lord," it said.

The General waved impatiently. "Were you successful?"

Lord Grak stood to his full, intimidating height, showing his muscular chest, broad shoulders and scarred face: half man, half hound.

"Yes, sir. We have the weapon." He lifted the steel case at his side, turning it to reveal the yellow and black symbol on its side: three black segments radiating from a single point.

The General eyed the case. "You're sure? It seems... small."

"The rest will be built," said Lord Grak. He prodded the case with a claw. "But this is where the power lies."

The General growled, the fur rising on his mane.

"Good," he snarled. "And the scientists?"

"All as the Dirgh commanded. They are in the stockade. We'll soften them up and then get them to work."

The General strode forward then, snatching up a half-plucked chicken from the table and ripping it in two.

"You have done well, Grak," he said, chewing and walking towards the entrance. "Come, address the troops with me." He tossed half the chicken to Lord Grak.

Grak caught the half-carcass in his jaws and devoured it with a snap, then licked his lips. He snatched up a skinned rabbit and followed the General.

"I lost forty in New York," he said at his commander's shoulder. "Good fighters, all of them."

"Only forty?" scoffed the General, drawing back the flaps of the tent.

They strode out into the wind and made their way between rows of saluting officers until the hillside opened before them. The ground fell away to a vast, open landscape, spanning in all directions. Before them, at the bottom of the hill, was something extraordinary.

It was a gigantic oblong enclosure, bordered on all four sides by colossal uprights of stone. It was so immense that a haze almost obscured its furthest reaches, but its sides were as straight and true as the New York blocks on which they were modelled. Between the mighty stones was a shifting sea, not liquid but rippling nevertheless with muscle and sinew and steel.

"Forty is a drop in the ocean," said General Hakka, First Lord of Horugur.

With that he lifted Grak's arm in the air and with it, the steel case.

Instantly there was a roar from the assembled thousands, and the sea became a tempest of raised fists and swords and spears, of gnashing teeth and flailing tails. Myriad flags were lofted in the air, bearing the emblems of countless regiments of all of Thoth's creations: the Ghor, the Hamajaks, the Ragers, the Vyrkans, the Slithen and many others besides. And between each of these flags were standards in red, bearing a simple image: the empty face of Thoth, with hollow eyes and mouth.

Grak grinned with jagged teeth. "When do we go?"

"Tonight," said the General.

They exchanged a smile and then both arched their backs and lent their howls to the cries of war.

64
Gather the Suhl

"Gather the lost and gather the damned,
Gather the Suhl, *for here we will stand."*

"COME ON," SAID ASH, taking Naeo gently by the elbow. "Let's walk — they want us outside."

Naeo was relieved that he was there to tell her what to do next. She stirred for the first time since Mr Zhi had spoken his last words, pushed herself up on to her feet and then, without thinking about it, she gave a slight bow. It was what the Merisi had done and it seemed right.

As they walked away they passed the tangle of roots, earth and metal that now cocooned Scarpia. Somewhere deep in its centre they heard muffled snarls and the impact of her thrashing limbs. Naeo was glad to see a small group of Merisi standing guard, wearing their gloves in readiness.

Just then another of the Merisi approached from the direction of the waterfall. Ash recognised her as the oriental woman from the meeting, the one called Kasumi. She was carrying what looked to be a fine circular necklace made of a metal that glowed in the sunlight. She nodded politely as she passed and continued purposefully towards Scarpia.

Ash and Naeo exchanged an intrigued glance and they watched to see what would happen next. When Kasumi reached the guards she handed one of them the necklace, pulled on her green glove and then, with great care, started to climb the mound. When she was near its top, she turned back and took the necklace. Then she looked at each of her colleagues in turn.

"Ready?" she asked in a hushed voice.

They all nodded.

She transferred the necklace to her gloved hand and drew a deep breath.

"Now!" she cried.

Seeming to sense danger, Scarpia suddenly struck out at her bonds, making the mound shudder and shake, but the Merisi had already stepped in closer, their heads bowed in concentration, gloved hands extended. At the same moment, Kasumi thrust the necklace down into the heap. She was wrenched forward so that her upper body disappeared entirely and, for a moment, it looked as though she might be dragged in. There were snarls and shouts from within and leaves and branches flew up in the air. Then Kasumi cried out and everything fell still.

Scarpia's growls and screams died away and all that could be heard was a complaint in feminine tones. The mound ceased its quivering and then something strange and magical began to happen: the roots and branches began to peel away, reeling back from the tangle. Kasumi raised her head, revealing three deep scratches across her cheek. But she did not pause to nurse them — instead she quickly clambered down off the shifting pile.

She shot a triumphant glance at her fellow Merisi. "Let's see how the cat likes its collar," she said.

As stems and leaves retreated, a figure began to appear, a figure with jet-black hair that crept down over a fine-featured face, with tapering eyes, one of which looked less than human. But even as they watched, the fur seemed to recede a little across the face, revealing dry and pinched skin, scarred by terrible burns. The cat's eye slowly closed, the eyelid wrinkled and scarred. Scarpia cried out in anguish, not a bestial snarl but rather her own voice, the voice Nature had given her.

"You have nothing to fear!" shouted Kasumi over the shrieks. "You are wearing a band of quintessence. It will do no more than return you to yourself!"

And then, as the final twisted branch released her, Scarpia raised her scarred hands — claws no longer. She pulled at the necklace, which had drawn tight about her neck like a choker. But the more she pulled, the more it seemed to tighten, stifling her cry, and she quickly gave up her struggle.

She lowered her head until she regained her breath and then looked up. Her disfigured face turned about, looking hatefully at her captors. And then she looked beyond, across the glade, at Naeo. She tilted her head a little to one side, her good eye travelling, taking in every feature. When finally she spoke, it was with her old voice — not a feline purr, but a purr nevertheless.

"A saviour of worlds?" she sneered. "You can't even save an old man!"

Ash linked arms with Naeo. "Come on," he said, drawing her away. "Let's go outside."

Naeo held Scarpia's glare for a moment, but then allowed Ash to lead her down the slope.

Scarpia heaved at her restraints. "This world is already lost!" she cried. "You'll see! Soon Thoth will reveal his great design! Then you will bow! Then you will weep!"

Ash squeezed Naeo's arm. "Keep walking."

"You won't even make it back to Salsimaine!" Scarpia called after her. "You're no match for the Priest of all our Souls!"

Naeo slowed her step. Ash tried to keep her moving, but she freed her arm and whirled about.

Scarpia gave a maniacal laugh. "You do, don't you? You actually think you stand a chance!"

Afterwards, Naeo was unsure why she had said it. It was a feeling rather than a thought.

It was an absolute absence of doubt. A quiet certainty so clear and true that it might shake the foundations of the world.

"I know I do," she said.

The grin fell slowly from Scarpia's face. Her good eye narrowed. "What makes you so sure?"

"Because of Sylas," said Naeo. "Because I'm not alone."

"I can't," said Sylas. "I'd like to come, but I can't."

"Why not?" asked Bayleon, frowning. "We could use you out on the Barrens."

"Because of Naeo," said Sylas. "We said we'd meet back at the valley as soon as we could and decide what to do next."

Espasian bowed his head. "You're right, Sylas, you must continue your journey — we'll only slow you down." He tensed a little and glanced at Bayleon. "Much as I hate to disagree with my friend the Spoorrunner."

"It's never stopped you before," grunted Bayleon, and then his expression softened. "But yes, I'm sure we'll fare well enough without you, Sylas. After all, we have a worthy Magruman to keep us safe."

Espasian gave a playful bow. "And an esteemed Spoorrunner to show us the way."

"Well you will have to make do without a Scryer," said Bowe. "I don't think I have the strength to walk the Barrens."

Espasian smiled and nodded. With that all of the companions reluctantly bid each other farewell, hardly believing that they must part after such a brief reunion. Espasian grasped Sylas by the shoulders and to the boy's surprise, drew him close.

"You've already done more than any of us could have asked, Sylas," he murmured. "See you at the valley. Then you can tell me about Isia. I'm very, very intrigued."

He smiled, turning to shake Bowe's hand.

Simia meanwhile had thrown her good arm around Bayleon and buried her face in his chest.

"You have nothing to be sorry for, child," said Bayleon, placing a large hand on top of her head. "They'd have caught me anyway and you got Sylas to safety, which is what matters. And look what you've done since. It's a miracle!"

She looked up at him and when she saw earnestness, she smiled. "We haven't done too badly, have we?"

"Not badly at all." He ruffled her hair. "Now just get on and finish the job!"

And so all too soon, Sylas and Simia said goodbye and began making their way slowly and unsteadily back down the steps. The crowds parted before them, whispering about the two children who seemed so friendly with the Magruman, staring with interest at the boy he had embraced.

As they reached the bottom of the steps, Espasian's voice boomed, echoing loudly around the square.

"Listen well, my friends!" he bellowed. "It fills me with great joy to see you here, beneath the sky, free at last. But we must not linger. It is not safe. Those of you who are well enough to walk a distance must come with me. We will stop for Salve and refreshment in the slums, and then we will walk on, to the Valley of Outs!"

There was a rumble of excitement around the square.

"Those of you who cannot travel so far must take a different path," he continued. "You must follow young Sylas and Simia here." He pointed in their direction and all in the square turned to look. "They will take you to safety. There will be a short walk, so those who are able must help those who are not."

He paused as the air was filled with murmurings and the sound of people hauling themselves to their feet or helping others to do the same.

"Best of luck, my friends!" he shouted over the hubbub. "We will meet again in the valley!"

This time there was a chorus of hopeful and excited cries, of "Good lucks" and "Farewells", of "Isia watch over you!" and "Long live Espasian!"

Then a single voice rose up — louder and more resonant than all the others. It was a deep baritone singing a slow, haunting melody:

> "*In far lands of dark and high lands and low,*
> *I hear songs of a place where none ever go…*"

Sylas looked about for the owner of the voice and saw Bayleon leading Espasian down the steps, his burly shoulders carrying the Magruman's weight with ease. His head was high and his mouth wide.

> "*…Locked in the hills, 'midst green velvet folds,*
> *A treasure more precious than gem-furnished gold…*"

Even before he and Espasian reached the bottom step, the

assembly had taken up the song, their dry, unpractised voices managing little more than husky whispers, but together, they made a rousing, unearthly sound. Bowe too had found his voice, and as he and his helpers joined Sylas and Simia, he led his fellow Suhl in song:

> "...For there dwell the Suhl, the last broken band,
> There dwell the lost and there dwell the damned.
> Tis their fortress, their temple, their garden of grace,
> Their last earthly haven, their glorious place."

So it was that Bayleon and Espasian made their way from the square towards the slums, and Sylas and Simia and Bowe led their following in the opposite direction, carried forward on the strains of an ancient song. Despite its sadness, it seemed to give the Suhl new life and hope, to lift their tired and ailing limbs for one last effort. The song rose among the sounds of the storm, filling the streets and passageways, halls and bedchambers, waking any citizen of Gheroth who still slumbered. It swept through the grand entrance of the Dirgheon and crept along deserted corridors, up dank stairwells, into empty cells and silent galleries. It whispered into Thoth's library and murmured in the Apex Chamber, caressing the pool of Black until it stirred and bubbled.

> "In far lands of dark and high lands and low,
> I hear songs of a place where none ever go;
> Twixt Nature's fair arms and held to Her breast,
> 'Neath the smiling moon and the sun's warming crest:
> A valley of comfort, of gifts full and fair,
> Born of the earth and the rains and the air.

And here rest the Suhl, the lost and the damned,
Here is their haven, their one promised land."

As Sylas walked along the canal towards Ending's Gate, he found himself sharing a grin with Simia. He turned briefly to see the long line of struggling, limping, lurching figures making their way along the towpath, their faces bright and animated, singing as they came. They sang as though the song were their anthem, as though they finally had a home to go to. Nearest of them all was Bowe, his great bulk supported by two older men but his face joyful, tears in his eyes.

Leading Naeo's father to freedom, leading the Suhl to new hope, Sylas felt full and free. The song swelled around him and, for that moment at least, he allowed himself to believe that all was well.

"In far lands of dark and high lands and low,
I hear songs of a place where none ever go;
A place with no walls and no roof but the sky,
Where goodness may linger and evil must die.
Here is our essence, our home and our all,
Here hope fills the breast with a full-throated call:
Gather the lost and gather the damned,
Gather the Suhl, for here we will stand."

65
Journey's End

"And thus at this, our journey's end,
is another just beginning."

IT WAS EVACUATION ON a massive scale. Two lines of vehicles had been brought to the front of the hospital, one consisting only of cars and the other of larger vehicles with long, high roofs and closely packed seating. Between the convoys, people in dark green overalls busied themselves with bundles and bags, hoisting them into compartments then packing them down to make room for others. All this was done quickly and quietly, with only the occasional instruction or correction from one of the supervising Merisi. The faces of the workers were grim and pale, but they carried on without a fuss. This escape had been drilled many, many times.

Naeo and Ash stood with Tasker, watching as the first of the guests were brought out and taken to the large vehicles. Their expressions were anxious, their movements furtive and frightened.

"You did well in there," said Tasker, rocking on his heels. He adjusted his tinted glasses, which hid his eyes. "Both of you."

"I'm just sorry that we brought all this with us," said Naeo.

Tasker gave a mirthless laugh. "'*A crisis before the fever breaks…*'" he mumbled.

"Sorry?" said Naeo.

He glanced at her. "Just something Mr Zhi said on the way here, Princess. His way of saying that this had to happen for things to get better." He turned his eyes up to the broken dome, still belching smoke and steam. "Still, I wonder if he knew it would come to this."

Just then there was a flurry of activity by the entrance to the hospital and they turned to see a group of Merisi forming two orderly lines either side of the doorway. Shortly afterwards the gaunt figure of Franz Jacob Veeglum emerged from the doorway. To Naeo's surprise, both lines bowed to him as he passed and he began making his way along them, shaking each gloved hand in turn, murmuring in each ear.

Ash raised an eyebrow and turned to Tasker. "Your new leader?"

"It seems so…" he said. "Mr Zhi always said that Herr Veeglum would be good at a time like this."

"Good in a crisis?"

"Good in a war."

Herr Veeglum reached the end of the line and for the first time they saw a coffin behind him, carried by four of the Merisi. It was draped with a green cloth, which was embroidered in black and white.

Veeglum saw Naeo, Ash and Tasker and made his way past the waiting convoy, walking up to them with long, confident strides.

Tasker straightened his back and as they met he gave a bow, which Herr Veeglum acknowledged with a quick nod. The new leader turned to Ash and Naeo, his expression amiable but cool.

"So, zis must be farevell," he said firmly. "Tasker and as many others as I can spare vill come vith you to ze stone circle. Zey vill do zer best to ensure your safe passage back to ze Other."

He glanced at Tasker, who nodded solemnly.

"Any questions?" asked Veeglum.

"What are *you* going to do?" asked Ash.

"Ve vill prepare as best ve can for vot is coming," said Veeglum matter-of-factly, "and ve vill fight." He blinked at them both, his green eyes showing no emotion at all. He looked at Naeo. "Anysing else?"

Naeo's mind went blank. She glanced at Ash but he shook his head.

"Good zen," said Herr Veeglum, bowing his head. "I vish you all ze luck in ze vorld." For the first time he smiled. "In *both* ze vorlds."

With that he turned on his heel and walked away, joined quickly by an escort of Merisi.

Ash raised his eyebrows. "Zat vas a bit brief!"

"*That* was Franz Jacob Veeglum," said Tasker, with an admiring smile.

Suddenly Naeo took two steps forward. "Herr Veeglum!"

He stopped and turned.

"Can you stop him?" asked Naeo. "Thoth — can you stop him?"

"No," he said. "Zat is for you to do."

Naeo's heart fell.

Then Veeglum added: "But ve vill give you and Sylas ze time you need." He paused. "And now ve have another Magruman to help."

Naeo frowned. He was looking past her, at Ash.

Ash blinked and jabbed his chest with his thumb. "*Me?*" he

cried. He laughed hesitantly. "You can't mean *me*! I'm more Muddlemorph than Magruman!"

Herr Veeglum shrugged his shoulders. "As you vish, but Scarpia vud disagree. As did Mr Zhi."

Ash's mouth fell open. "*Mr Zhi?*"

"He said you are a Magruman, if you choose to be one," said Veeglum. "And for vot it's vurth, I agree."

Ash was dumbstruck. He turned and stared at Naeo and found her smiling: not a mocking smile, but a genuine one.

"See what you can do when you stop peddling the Three Ways?"

He narrowed his eyes.

They all watched as Herr Veeglum and his escort reached the waiting coffin and the bearers fell in behind, forming a grand procession.

And then Ash blurted out one more question: "Where are you taking him?" he called. "Where are you taking Mr Zhi?"

"To ze East," called Veeglum. "To ze place he most loved to be."

And with that he turned away and led the procession around the broken frontage of the hospital, people bowing respectfully as they went.

The moment they disappeared, Tasker clapped his hands.

"Right then! We need to make tracks!" He strode over to the nearest of the cars — a long, black one with tinted windows — and pulled the rear door open. "Your carriage, Princess." He doffed an imaginary cap, but his tone was friendly.

"No," said Naeo, flatly.

Tasker turned to her slowly. "And you ask why I call you Princess?"

"I'm not going without Amelie," said Naeo. "Sylas and I had

a pact. We agreed that I would find his mum and he would find my dad and I'm not leaving here—"

Suddenly a face appeared in the doorway of the car.

"Did you really think I was going to let you go without me?" said Amelie, arching her eyebrows. She extended her hand. "Come on — it took a little female persuasion, but they've put us in the same car."

Naeo looked at Tasker, who grinned. She cleared her throat and took Amelie's hand.

They took their places on shiny leather seats: broad and luxuriant like sofas. There was a little table and what looked like a drinks cabinet, and up ahead, next to the driver, there was even one of those large oblong *televisions* that they had seen in the shop window. The driver sat quietly in the front seat, but he did not turn: he gripped the steering wheel with leather-clad hands, and waited.

Naeo leaned towards Amelie. "I thought I was going to have to persuade you. I thought the Other was the last place you'd want to go!"

"It's the last place I want to go and it's the only place I want to go. It's where Sylas is." She smiled. "Just keep away from me with all that magic. Both of you."

"If you think we're bad," Ash murmured, playing with his armrest, "you should see your son!"

Tasker walked round to the front of the car and fixed something to one corner — a green flag, drooped so that its design could not be seen. Once it was in place, he turned and spoke to a group of Merisi, who quickly dispersed to the other cars in front and behind, and began fixing more flags to each of them. The design was still hidden in the limp folds of fabric, but they could see glimpses of black and white embroidery on a green background, like the drape over Mr Zhi's coffin. Once all were in place, the Merisi pulled on their gloves and climbed into the vehicles.

Tasker jumped in beside them and slammed the door.

"Right, seatbelts on!" he instructed. "This is going to be quite a ride!"

The car suddenly growled into life, its voice deep and powerful. There was a roar from the rest of the convoy and then Naeo felt herself thrown into the back of her seat as they surged forward on juddering tyres and a cloud of dust. She felt the familiar pain slice through her back, though thankfully the morphine or the poultice seemed to be taking the edge off it. She gripped the armrest and wrestled with the clasp of her seatbelt until, with relief, she heard it click into place. Three or four cars squirming up the track ahead, setting a terrifying pace, so that their own driver struggled to stay behind them. When she looked through the rear window, she saw two more cars skidding at every turn and Winterfern disappearing out of sight.

The cars bucked and veered as they tore into the tree-lined driveway, the convoy writhing along its length like a snake of steel, rasping and snarling as it went.

Ash nodded out to one of the following cars. "Isn't that the Yin thing Mr Zhi showed you?"

Naeo turned and saw two flags fluttering and snapping from the roof. There, at the centre of an expanse of green, was the black and white disc that Mr Zhi had pointed to on the book cover.

"The Yin Yang symbol," said Tasker.

"What's it for?" asked Naeo.

"It's the mark of the Merisi."

Naeo turned back to watch the convoy. Then she asked: "But why do you need all the flags?"

"They may just save our lives," he said.

Just then a new sound pierced the rumble of the car – a howl from above. Everyone pressed their faces against the windows and saw a strange shape streak across the sky. Naeo squinted at the pointed nose; the flat, outstretched arms, two larger and two smaller; the dark circles along its flank that looked like portholes; and at the rear, its flat, upright tail, marked with a symbol: a disc, half black and half white, on a background of green.

Tasker appeared at her side and they both watched it disappear into the distance. As it was swallowed into sunlight Tasker bowed his head.

"Goodbye, Mr Zhi," he said. "Fly home."

Sylas could still hear the last strains of the song as he stepped on to the quayside and looked into a wall of blackness. He could smell the stench of the river and ahead there was the glint and swirl of an inky surface.

"What do you reckon?" said Simia quietly, between clenched teeth.

Sylas swallowed. "I reckon we'd better start hoping."

They fell silent and waited. In the distance they could hear the many thousands of Suhl beginning a new song: a lighter, more rhythmical melody that sounded more like a march – a chorus to bear them on, through the slums and out on to the Barrens.

But the weak and sick did not take it up. They shuffled to a halt behind their young guides and peered ahead into the blackness. Silence poured back into the narrow canal.

And then there was a noise in their midst – a commotion that travelled up the ranks towards Sylas and Simia. They turned and looked back along the line and saw someone in the thick of the crowd pushing their way through, muttering and chattering.

It was an old man with long flowing locks, walking with a slight stoop and a perpetual frown, as though pondering an impossible riddle. He murmured a jumble of words to people as he passed: long, fussy words like "salutations!" and "humble apologies!" and "extenuating circumstances!" And as he lifted his wrinkled old face towards Sylas and Simia, the locks fell away to reveal a large nose and little wire-rimmed spectacles.

"Fathray!" they cried in unison.

The old man beamed. "Any use for an old Scribe?" He opened his arms, taking them in a rather unsteady embrace. "To corrupt an old saying from myth and legend," he chuckled, "'so, at last, we are one!'"

Sylas laughed. "Good to see you, Fathray! We were so worried about you at the Mill."

"No need to worry about an old octogenarian like me! We're infuriatingly hard to get rid of!" He hooted into his moustache. "Now, let's look at you! What a splendiferous sight for sore old eyes!" He frowned at Simia's injuries. "Sorely ruffled, young Simia?"

"Sore for sure," grinned Simia, "but you should see the Rager!"

"That's the spirit, little one!" laughed Fathray. He patted her arm, his eyes travelling to her companion. "And so here you are, Sylas, the boy extraordinary!"

Sylas smiled. "I'm not sure about that."

"But look what wonders you have done!" said Fathray, gesturing to the long line of freed prisoners. "And the rumour is that you have seen Isia herself!"

Sylas nodded, feeling rather proud. "We've just come from the temple."

"What auspicious times!" cried the old scribe, clapping his hands in delight. Still beaming, he turned to look out into the black expanse, the smile fading a little. "So... what is your *plan*?"

Sylas exchanged an embarrassed look with Simia.

Suddenly there was a noise somewhere out in the blackness. It was faint but definite, and everyone on the quayside turned and gazed out into the night, searching for its source. It was more harmonious than the noise of the storm, more measured than the sounds of the river. It sounded like the high strains of violins, ebbing and flowing as though drifting upon the waves. And then Sylas thought he heard the rise and fall of cellos, then horns — lots and lots of horns.

They all looked at one another, wondering if it was imagined, but then, in an instant, any doubt fell away. The sharp report of a horn, or something sharper — a cornet — pierced the night: six rapid notes, cutting through the whirl and flurry of the winds.

Then again. And again.

Responding to the cornet, the violins and cellos and horns surged, their voice singing through the blanket of darkness, their pitch soaring, rising and falling, then building, up and up and up until they were joined by oboes, clarinets, and finally, as they climbed to a deafening crescendo, the magical metallic swell of the cymbals.

Sylas turned to Simia, his eyes bright and expectant, and he found her grinning back at him.

"A symphony!" she whispered, looking out into the blackness.

As the instruments tumbled over one another towards their zenith, as giant drums rolled like thunder and the strings reached new heights of a final, soul-shattering note, something moved in the night.

It was a ship of astonishing beauty, with elegant lines and intricate carvings, glorious paintwork and gilded designs. And of all these designs, none were more exquisite than the bold and looping nameplate, its letters picked out in pigments of green, purple, silver and gold:

The *Windrush.*

Standing high on the prow next to the gleaming horn of a gramophone was a lone figure, one foot up on the railing. He wore long, black flowing robes, which billowed in the breeze, but it was his dark hair and round spectacles that drew a murmur from the gathered Suhl.

"Paiscion!" they whispered. "It's Paiscion!"

The Magruman smiled a fatherly smile and raised a single hand in greeting.

Sylas waved excitedly, his eyes drifting upwards to the rigging and sails, along the great girth of the mast as it tapered into the gloom high above. At the fringes of the lamplight, he could see the brassy gleam of the crow's nest and above, fluttering and furling in the wind, a gigantic flag.

There, in an expanse of green and picked out in purple braid, was the bright white feather of the Suhl.

66
The Perilous Path

"But is this not a perilous path*? What will come
when these two parts meet? These parts that stand
entire in separate worlds?"*

THE MERISI FLAGS SNAPPED and cracked as the convoy sped along
the open road, passing the last of the hills. Ahead, the open plains
were broad and bright and the sky was cloudless but for an ugly
smudge of black smoke on the horizon. It was a tranquil lowland
scene of open countryside and empty rural roads with not a soul
to be seen.

Naeo gazed into the blur of hedgerows, playing idly with the
old bootlace from her pocket, weaving it into an ever more complex
design.

"It's so quiet," she said.

"*Too* quiet," said Tasker, gnawing his lip.

He turned to rummage in a compartment at his side and
produced a black oblong, which he pointed at the *television*
mounted behind the driver. The black screen beeped and sprang
into life, revealing the head and shoulders of a woman who

appeared to be speaking directly to the occupants of the car, her voice charged and urgent.

"—*reports from as far afield as Germany, the United States and Russia. All speak of some kind of attack, always brief, always very targeted. In most cases the phenomenon seems to be linked to stone circles, but in others, most notably New York City*—"

Tasker pressed a button and the image changed. This time a man was talking to them, against the backdrop of a glass and steel building.

"—*broke into the Berlin-based facility late last night and caused massive destruction, killing several security guards and stealing objects described as 'of tactical military value'. A spokesman for the*—"

Tasker shook his head and jabbed at the oblong. The screen flickered and changed again, this time to a man standing at a podium in front of a shiny black door bearing a stark white '10'.

"—*above all, I urge you to stay in your homes. Lock your doors. Do not venture out unless you are told to evacuate by a member of the security forces. We are working with the United Nations, allied governments and other friendly forces to*—"

Tasker ran his fingers through his hair and pressed more buttons, changing the image several times.

"What was that?" said Amelie, suddenly leaning forward and waving at the screen. "Go back!"

Tasker pressed another button and suddenly they saw an image taken from the air, drifting high above open green plains as though looking down from the clouds. Naeo stopped breathing. There, surrounded by what looked like hundreds of uniformed figures and a ring of blockish dark green vehicles, was Stonehenge. And at the centre of the circle of stone were more figures: large and black, their bodies stooped and muscular, defending the central space. There were scores of them.

Amelie was the first to speak. "Isn't… isn't that where we're going?"

The others nodded without taking their eyes from the screen.

"So how are we—"

"I have no idea…" murmured Tasker.

Suddenly the screen went off and there was a click and whirr from the direction of the cab. The glass partition slid down.

"You need to see this, Tasker!" shouted the driver, pointing ahead.

Everyone peered past him. The road in front curved off to the right, and just after the bend they could see scores of the uniformed figures arranged in military order across the road. They were gathered around gigantic, camouflaged vehicles, which formed a formidable barricade of steel. Each of the figures was carrying a black, stick-like weapon, which they held to their shoulders. They seemed to be pointing in the direction of the convoy. Above the roar and rumble of the cars they could hear a solitary voice, sharp and metallic, as though spoken by a machine:

"STOP!" came the command, the voice steely and calm. "STOP YOUR VEHICLES! WE ARE AUTHORISED TO USE DEADLY FORCE!"

All eyes turned to Tasker.

"Keep going!" he shouted at the driver. "Radio the others! No one is to stop!"

Amelie was horrified. "Jeremy, you can't be serious! They've got TANKS! We don't stand a chance!"

"It's *Tasker*, and I'm deadly serious!" he snapped. He looked back to the driver. "I said, tell the others!"

The driver turned in his seat, his face ashen. "But, Boss—"

"They'll make way!" he shouted. "TELL THE OTHERS!"

The driver raised a black oblong to his mouth. "We're to keep going! He says they'll make way!"

They were drawing close now, the tyres screeching as they rounded the bend. They could see the soldiers' helmets, the whites of their eyes, their glances and shifts as they realised that the convoy was not going to stop. The turrets on top of two of the giant vehicles started to swivel, pointing their long barrels at the lead cars.

Ash turned on Tasker. "What are you *doing*?!" he cried. "You're going to get us all killed!"

Tasker held up his hand. "The flags!" he shouted. "Just wait!"

Naeo looked from Ash to Tasker and, almost without thinking, she pushed the bootlace into her pocket and began to raise her hands. She looked out into the countryside, seeing trees and bushes, turf and hills. Essenfayle should walk, but surely there was no time.

"STOP!" The metallic voice was no longer calm. "HALT OR WE SH—"

There was a sudden hesitation.

The convoy thundered on, careering towards the wall of steel.

And then one of the military vehicles shifted, lurching on its tracks, rolling out into a field. Then the other did the same, growling off in the opposite direction. Suddenly the soldiers lowered their weapons, rose to their full height and in good order, jogged at double time to the roadside, lining up in formation. They were not running but withdrawing, responding to some unheard command.

Naeo lowered her hands.

Only one man remained, tall and stiff-backed in the centre of the road. As the convoy swept between the assembly of soldiers, he shouted something to his men and instantly heels were clicked and hands snapped up in salute, then he too quickly stepped to the roadside. At the instant they swept past, he stood perfectly to attention, lifted his chin and gave an unflinching salute.

"Godspeed!" they heard him cry.

And then they were gone, tearing out on to the open road.

Ash peered out of the rear window then turned to look at Tasker. The two regarded each other for a moment and smiled.

"I'm sorry," said Ash. "I should've had more faith."

Tasker shrugged. "Ah well, trust is earned," he said, then added: "I just hope this does it."

Ash laughed. "So... 'Other friendly forces'... that guy on the television — was he talking about the Merisi?"

Tasker nodded. "We're known to most governments," he said, matter-of-factly.

Ash settled back, but Amelie looked unconvinced. "But I still don't understand what we're going to do when we get to the circle," she said anxiously. "You saw the pictures — they make that roadblock look like child's play! All those soldiers and tanks and guns! And even if we make it past *them,* there are those things in the middle of the circle..."

"I know," said Tasker, pushing himself back into his seat. "The truth is, I'm not sure what we'll do."

For a long time there was silence. And then suddenly Naeo sat bolt upright.

"I have an idea!" she cried.

Paiscion, Sylas and Simia leaned over the railing, watching the last of the Suhl helped aboard by the crew of the *Windrush*. At the very back, waiting for everyone else, was Bowe, murmuring words of encouragement to the old and feeble.

"I hope you liked the music — I chose it for the occasion," said Paiscion, as the final strains faded and died.

"What was it?" asked Sylas.

The Magruman smiled. "It's a ballet called *Spartacus* — do you know the name?"

They both shook their heads.

Paiscion filled his lungs with the damp air. "An ancient Roman warrior, who freed his people from slavery." He turned and winked. "So, not unlike yourselves."

"I don't know about that," laughed Sylas. "It was Espasian who got everyone out."

"Well I'm sure he had more than a little help," replied Paiscion. "I've never seen anything like that storm! We hoped that you might be able to free Bowe and a few others but *this* —" he swept his hand out over the *Windrush* — "this is beyond our wildest dreams!"

The ship bustled with activity. The crew were leading the weakest to the many berths below and laying out mats and cushions for those strong enough to stay on deck. But what made the scene truly remarkable were the expressions on people's faces. Eyes sparkled, heads lifted and once-weary faces shone with hope. Even here, in the heart of Gheroth, beneath the shadow of the Dirgheon, there was a sense that anything was possible.

"Things are changing, everyone can feel it!" exclaimed Paiscion. "We could never have dreamed of this a few weeks ago — never!"

Sylas smiled at Simia and she grinned back. She was the old Simsi again, bold and fearless, her face open and her head high. He felt a great flush of affection for her then, his companion through each of these incredible, bewildering, horrifying days, and he thought he could see the same warmth in her.

514

"But still there is much to be done and more we cannot see," said Paiscion. He patted the handrail of the *Windrush*. "Before we came here, we prepared this old girl for a fight — we worked day and night to get her shipshape. But the river was open all the way here. Even as we passed through the Barrens we saw nothing: no Slithen, no Ghor patrols, nothing. Something is afoot — something with its beginning and end in Thoth's own darkness."

Sylas's smile faded. "I think we know what it is," he said.

He told the Magruman about Triste's conviction that Thoth was about to wage war between the worlds. And then Simia told him of their encounter with the Dirgh in the Place of Tongues, and about the warning Thoth had given as he had been borne away: "*not one Undoing but five, each measured in agony and loss.*"

The more he heard, the darker and more brooding Paiscion became, and when Simia recounted these final words, he leaned heavily on the handrail and bowed his head. "So much hate," he murmured into the darkness. "So much pain. Why can he not let us be as we are meant to be?" He lifted his head and turned back to them. "Well, if all this is true," he said, a little wearily, "the dangers are far greater and the time even shorter than we thought. We need to set sail without delay."

He led them back to the quarterdeck, issuing instructions to his crew as he went: "Raise the gangway" and "Cast off the ropes" and "Ready the passengers". But as they reached the wheel, a cry went up from the bird's nest high above. They looked up and saw a sailor pointing out across the city.

Sylas's skin prickled and turned slowly, preparing himself for the worst.

But what he saw was quite wonderful. There was a blaze of light high above Gheroth: a ring of exquisite archways floating over the city, flooding the rain-filled skies with a hopeful light.

They sent out long beams above the highest rooftops, across the teeming streets and on to the dark flanks of the Dirgheon.

It was the Temple of Isia, shining like a beacon above a soulless city. Silhouetted against the bright archways, they could see scores of priestesses, standing shoulder to shoulder on the great stone terrace, like sentinels. They watched over the streets full of freed prisoners, singing as they walked; over the Suhl of the slums, joining the mighty throng; over a ship setting sail under the forgotten standard of the Suhl.

A cheer rose from the front of the ship, sweeping like a wave along its length.

The light sparkled in Paiscion's eyes. "In the darkness, there is the light!" he said, smiling at his companions.

Then he turned to the crowds gathered on the decks. "Friends, prepare to set sail!" he cried. "The valley awaits!"

67

The Glimmertrome

"...and so this marvel, this Glimmertrome,
is at once here with this and there with that. In its to and fro,
it holds the Yin and the Yang, the me and the you."

AS THE CAR PRESSED on towards the stones, Naeo curled on her luxurious bed of leather and dreamed. She dreamed of Mr Zhi, somewhere high and free, looking down upon the distant shores of the East. She dreamed of the countryside, passing in a blur of fields and hedgerows, streams and open plains. But most of all, she dreamed of a watery darkness; of sails filled with buffeting winds; of faces, white and wasted, peering out towards an unknown shore. And beneath her she felt the heave and yaw of a ship, bearing them onwards to sanctuary.

It was the pain that pierced her sleep, creeping up from the small of her back in needling fingers, reaching up her spine and out to her shoulder blades. It had found her again, and this time it gripped like an icy claw, making her wake with a gasp.

She saw her singed bandages on the floor by her side, no longer white but stained with black. So much black. Her stomach turned as she realised that it had come from her, drawn from her own foul wounds. She had told herself that they were superficial — just scars — but this was an infection. The Black was consuming her.

"Relax, try not to tense. I'm going to give you some more morphine." It was Amelie, her voice close and soothing. Naeo tried to slacken her muscles, settling back on to the car seat. She found it damp with her own sweat.

"You cried out in your sleep," continued Amelie. "I had to change your dressing. Don't worry, I sent the boys away."

Naeo looked ahead and saw Ash and Tasker crammed into the front with the driver. They looked so uncomfortable that she smiled in spite of the pain.

"Did it work?" she asked. "That police thing?"

"The poultice? A little. It certainly drew out some of the Black, but there's more. I wish we could get you to hospital." She paused. "Do you even *have* hospitals in the Other?"

The Other. In her pain Naeo had almost forgotten where they were heading. "Are we there?" she asked, pushing herself up. "At the stones?"

"Yes, but hold on, I haven't given you the morphine yet!"

"I don't want it," said Naeo. "I can't, I need to focus."

Amelie took her arm. "But, Naeo, you're in no state to—"

"I'm fine with clean bandages," she insisted, leaning over to the window to peer out. "That's more than I've ever had before."

The convoy was parked on a grass verge at the side of the road. Ahead, across some fields, was Stonehenge, its majestic stones jutting like ghostly totems. But they were not alone. All around and forming a neater, sharper circle, was a cordon of steel. It was made of vehicles of all kinds, bulging with all kinds of strange, angry-looking objects, most of them pointing into the middle of the stone circle. Between them, figures marched and scurried, bearing with them more hard-looking things: things on their shoulders and things under their arms — things of weaponry and war. And above, buzzing and thrumming in the midday skies, was a great swarm of machines, turning about like hornets over a nest.

All this angriness was not directed at the stones themselves, but at what lay within. The Ghor paced the fringes of the circle, marking their territory, snapping and lunging at anything that drew too near. Other, cat-like creatures had climbed the stones and arched their backs, clawing and hissing at the buzzing hornets above, sometimes leaping the height of a house to ward off those that swooped too low.

And at the centre of all this, in the very heart of the stones, was a gigantic pile of bounty — a haul of shiny steel cases and large wooden crates, of vessels and flasks, weapons and instruments. Between them, bound and gagged, cowering in small groups of two or three, were people. Hostages. Hunted and seized by Thoth's creatures, snatched away against their will, now waiting; waiting for who knew what.

It was a horrifying scene — a scene of two worlds in a mortal lock, fingering the trigger of war.

Naeo felt gentle, soft fingers take her hand. She looked across to see Amelie's troubled face close to her own.

"You don't have to do this, Naeo," she said with a worried smile. "We can wait — wait until they've fought it out. Until you're better."

Naeo shook her head. "I have to go," she said.

"No, you don't. We can—"

"I do," said Naeo, looking out at the stone circle. She squeezed Amelie's hand. "We both do. Sylas is there."

Amelie gazed at her, her eyes glistening. "You really are like him, you know."

Naeo smiled. "I know."

Amelie made her way up the length of the car and knocked

on the partition. Ash and Tasker peered over their shoulders and nodded.

Once everyone was back in their seats, Naeo reached into her bag and pulled out the package Mr Zhi had given her. Her companions watched expectantly. She pulled away the paper and ran her fingers over the face of the Glimmertrome: the two plates, one white and one black, and between them, the beautifully ornate needle, rising in shiny twists and swirls to a tiny clasp, made of the same exquisite metal.

"Do you think it'll work?" asked Ash.

"It's from Mr Zhi," said Tasker, arching an eyebrow. "Of course it'll work."

Ash turned to Naeo. "But are you sure about this?"

Naeo lifted her eyes and smiled. "No. Are you ready?"

"I'm *serious*, Naeo," he insisted. "If you're busy seeing what Sylas is doing, how will you see what's going on here? How will we make the passing?"

"What choice do we have?" said Naeo, exasperated. "If we get as far as the circle, we won't make it through without taking them with us," she nodded towards the Ghor and Ghorhund prowling through Stonehenge. "Look at them all! As soon as we're through, they'll be all over us! They'll slaughter us! I'll need his help on the other side."

"And you really think if we get to Sylas quickly enough, you'll be able to stop them?"

"Who knows?" said Naeo anxiously. "But it's the best hope we have."

Amelie sat forward. "I still don't understand how the Glimmertrome fits into this."

"Because if everything has gone to plan," explained Ash, "then Sylas should be on the *Windrush* by now, on his way back from

Gheroth. And if he is, then the river will bring the *Windrush* near to the stone circle, and if we know exactly *when* it's near, we might be able to get to it — and to Sylas — before those things get to us." He glanced at Naeo. "Is that right?"

"That's the theory."

"That's a lot of 'ifs'," said Amelie.

"Right," grumbled Ash.

Tasker cleared his throat. "Well, I think Naeo's right, this is still the best hope we have. We need to see where Sylas is, then wait and pick our moment. Then it'll be down to Naeo and Sylas to —" he took a long breath and exhaled — "to do whatever they can."

Ash turned back to Naeo. "OK. But be careful with this Glimmertrome thing. I mean, if it doesn't feel *right*, you have to stop, OK?"

Naeo shrugged. "Sure," she said, wondering how any of this was supposed to feel 'right'. She had no idea what the Glimmertrome would do, nor how she was going to get them through Stonehenge, nor what she and Sylas would do if they found one another.

She turned her eyes around her companions. "OK, everyone? Ready?"

Amelie, Tasker and the driver nodded.

"Right then," she said, and she snapped the clasp off the needle of the Glimmertrome.

Sylas rubbed his eyes and laid the quill carefully on the deck. It was hard to concentrate on writing; he was so, so tired. The newly written Ravel Runes writhed and settled before his weary eyes, and then became still.

He set the Samarok to one side and turned around, sliding his legs beneath the railings of the *Windrush*, so that his feet dangled over the dark waters. For a while he sat there in silence, resting against the rails, peering out over the froth and chop of the ship's wake. Both banks of the river bristled with the shacks and stalls of the slums and he enjoyed listening to the sounds of preparation, the bustle of activity, the sense of change in the air. Word had reached the slum-dwellers and they were on the move.

He soon heard some steps behind him. It was Simia, supported by another of the passengers. She thanked her helper and then sat down next to Sylas, handing him a tankard of Plume and a piece of bread.

Sylas smiled his thanks. "Looks like everyone in the slums is getting ready to leave," he said, nodding towards the riverbanks. "You can hear them packing up. They sound pretty excited."

"Good news travels fast with the Suhl," said Simia with a smile. "They've waited long enough. And they know this is it — their chance to get to the valley."

"I hope it goes OK," said Sylas.

They gnawed on their bread and sipped at their Plume, gazing out at the passing hovels, listening to the chatter on the riverbanks.

"Been quite a journey, hasn't it?" said Simia after a while.

Sylas laughed and nodded. "It really has."

"Do you think we got what we needed?" asked Simia. "From Isia, I mean?"

He shrugged. "At least I know why all this is happening now." He thought for a moment. "And I know where we've got to go next — after I meet up with Naeo."

Simia nodded and rested her chin on her arms. "I wonder how she's getting on."

For some moments they both looked out at the dark river, watching the last buildings of the city slide past them.

"It's been quite a journey for you too, Simsi," said Sylas, without looking at her.

She grunted. "Quite a journey..." she murmured, thoughtfully. "Feels worth it though. Not just because of all this —" she glanced back at the teeming decks — "though this is great, obviously. But also because of what we found out."

"About Thoth? This Academy of Souls?"

She shook her head. "What Isia told us about Glimmers — that we're never alone. That I was never alone — even when I was out there, after the Reckoning. That there was part of me that was free from all this." Her eyes remained fixed on the black expanse, seeming to turn the idea over in her mind. "My Glimmer, living my life, but... differently — like you and Naeo."

Sylas nodded slowly. "It's quite a thought, isn't it?"

"It really is," she said, wistfully. "I just wish I'd known it. That in all that darkness, there was part of me in the light. Or... or that when things were really bad, it might have been different for them. It would have been something — really *something* — to know that when I was lost, they were safe... or even that when I... when I couldn't do this or that, perhaps they could." She turned to him. "Know what I mean? I think it would've given me a whole lot more hope."

He met her eyes, thinking of Naeo out there, somewhere in the Other, perhaps with his mother, perhaps with Mr Zhi, perhaps with neither but out there, doing what he could not.

"I know exactly what you mean," he said.

For a while they fell silent again, lost in their own thoughts. Then Simia said: "Do you know what I wish?"

"What?"

"I wish that right now, Triste knew what we know. It isn't right that he's out there on his own." The words caught in her

523

throat, but she swallowed them down. "You know? I just hope he doesn't feel as alone as I did."

"I know, Simsi," said Sylas.

They fell quiet again, watching the Barrens open around them. They ate no more of their bread and drank no more of the Plume. They had no more stomach for it.

After a while they heard the approaching roar of tumbling water, and at the same time the air filled with the familiar gut-wrenching stink of sewage.

"Sewage outlets from the city," said Simia, pinching her nose.

The ship rolled as it passed a thunderous torrent, which crashed down from a gaping back tunnel in the high riverbank. As it met the river it formed swirls of putrefying foam, coating the surface of the river. They drew up their feet and retreated a little from the railings. Sylas found himself willing the *Windrush* to speed up.

Soon enough the horrifying torrents began to retreat into the darkness and the stink began to disperse. He was about to slide his legs back over the side when Simia reached out and grabbed his coat. She leaned forward and peered into the half-dark.

"Look!" she exclaimed, pointing at the churn of filth.

Sylas looked where she was pointing. The lumps and grime on the river's surface were *moving*, drifting as one in the direction of the *Windrush*. Drifting *upstream*.

He staggered to his feet. "Slithen!"

In that moment, as though they had heard his cry, the lumps of detritus reared in the waters, rolling back to reveal their bulging eyes.

For a moment there was a strange, eerie quiet. Simia pulled herself up. Paiscion ran up behind. A hush fell over the *Windrush*.

It was broken by a hissing, whining, gurgling cry: a cry that chilled the bones of the Suhl. And with that, the Slithen came on, thrashing their limbs in the mire as they advanced on the ship. Hundreds of them.

Sylas turned to Simia and opened his mouth to speak.

But nothing came.

His arms dropped to his sides and his eyes fell closed.

Naeo slapped her hand down on the needle.

"They're on the *Windrush*!" she cried, blinking in the bright light of day. "They're already on the Barrens!" She looked at the driver. "Go now! Go! Go!"

The driver nodded and picked up the oblong. "This is it!" he shouted. "Everyone follow me!"

Suddenly the car roared and they were thrown back into their seats as it surged forward, its wheels sending up flurries of mud and stones. They tore out on to the road, quickly picking up speed. The other cars snaked in behind them, their tails swinging wide until they came under control.

"What did you see? Is he OK?" asked Amelie anxiously.

Naeo winced with pain. "He's OK," she blurted. "He's near. We haven't got much time!"

Everyone clung to door handles and armrests as the car veered around a bend in the road. The stone circle was close now and they could see the soldiers in the rearguard turning towards them and then running to their positions.

"Don't stop for anything!" shouted Naeo at the driver. "Whatever happens!"

"But what do we do when we get there?" asked Tasker, eyeing the shadows between the standing stones.

"You're just going to have to trust me."

Tasker regarded her for a moment. "All right, Princess."

68

Our Riven Soul

"What it would be to unite our riven soul *and then, perhaps, to see with truer eyes, feel with a fuller heart!"*

"HOLD ON, EVERYONE!" SHOUTED the driver.

Suddenly the car swung to the right, missing a bend in the road and hurtling into a wooden farm gate. The timbers smashed into pieces, sending shards flying in all directions. The car dropped into the grassy field beyond, digging into the turf before bouncing and swerving. The occupants were hurled from side to side and Amelie yelped as she hit her head against the window. Ash lunged to help her, but she raised her hand.

"I'm fine! I'm OK!" she cried.

They all looked out of the front window towards the military cordon just ahead, across a stretch of open grassland. The soldiers had spread out in a long line and were kneeling with their weapons to their shoulders. Behind them some of the military vehicles were manoeuvring about, their turrets turning to face the approaching convoy. Over the rumble and thunder of the wheels, they heard another metallic voice commanding them to halt.

"Don't stop!" shouted Naeo.

And then there was a loud bang. The front window shattered, leaving a white impression in its middle and cracks emanating in all directions.

Suddenly they heard a deafening clatter on the front of the car and sparks flew up in the air.

"They're firing at us!" screamed Tasker.

"The flag!" shouted the driver, gesticulating frantically towards the front of the car. "It came off when we went through the gate!"

As more volleys hit the car, Tasker scrambled to the little table. He reached beneath and pulled out a piece of paper and a pen then crouched on the floor and began scribbling furiously. After a few moments he looked up towards the driver.

"Open the window!" he shouted.

"But, Boss, it's bullet proof—"

"Open it!"

The window by Tasker started to slide down. He reached for the armrest, took a deep breath, and then threw his arm out of the window.

The paper flapped back in the wind, revealing a hastily drawn symbol in black and white – the Yin Yang symbol.

"Blast!" cried Tasker. "They won't see it like that!" He drew it in, took the paper in both hands, glanced quickly at his companions, then rose to his feet and pushed his arms and upper body out of the window.

The volleys suddenly ceased. Then one more shot rang out.

Tasker paused in the window for a moment longer, before dropping back into his seat. "That should do it," he said.

Everyone looked ahead and saw soldiers running from their positions, vehicles starting up and rolling back, a single figure running forward to wave them on.

"Well done!" shouted Ash, turning to slap Tasker on the shoulder.

But he stopped short.

Tasker's shoulder and chest were covered in blood. Ash lunged forward and began tearing at his shirt.

Tasker was already pale and sweating. "Just a graze!" he said with a smile that looked more like a grimace. He turned to Naeo. "Keep going, Princess, remember? Whatever happens!"

Naeo shook her head. "I know, but—"

"You don't have a choice!"

Naeo looked desperately towards the standing stones. She saw the way clear now, flanked on both sides by green vehicles and soldiers. She saw the circle, huge and imposing, towering above the scrambling convoy, the baying Ghor, the bewildered soldiers.

She released the needle and raised her hands.

She reached out with her mind, beyond the steel shell of the car, ahead of the scrambling, twisting convoy to the cool surface of the stones. To the ancient, chiselled, weather-worn rock; timeless, knowing and magical. And then her thoughts soared, flying up past the screeching cat-like mongrels on the topmost stones, up into the great blue void, up and up into the sunbeams. She reached for the source of that bright clear light, and she found it waiting for her. She found the rays yielding to the touch, willing to be taken. She found them spiralling down now, following her back down to where she had started. Back to the stones.

And then, as she opened her eyes and saw the stone circle shimmering in great pools of golden light, as she saw the archways fill to the brim with its radiance, the needle of the Glimmertrome passed the centre point and everything disappeared.

"Sylas!" she heard in the blackness. "Sylas! What are you doing?"

"What are you doing?" shouted Simia, shaking his shoulders.

Sylas blinked, fighting to find his own thoughts. For a moment he was caught somewhere between light and dark, between warmth and cold. And then his body became his own again and his mind began to clear.

He shook his head. "It was like... like I was with Naeo!" he said. "Like I was in the other world — my world!"

Simia gave him a steady look. "Well, you weren't, you were here! And here is not a good place to lose your senses!" She pointed over the ship's railing. "LOOK!"

He squinted into the blackness, his eyes adjusting to the dark, taking in the Slithen, writhing through the froth and leaping over the waves. The *Windrush* was travelling so much faster now, carving through the river, sending a wash high up the slimy riverbanks, but still the Slithen were gaining, reaching out at the keel of the ship, sliding over one another to be the first to gain hold.

"Paiscion brought the winds to make us faster," shouted Simia over the gale, "but it's still not fast enough!"

Sylas turned and saw the Magruman standing close by, one hand on the wheel of the ship and the other held aloft, summoning the winds, filling the great sails of the *Windrush*.

"Can we go faster?" yelled Sylas.

Paiscion shook his head. "I'm doing my best."

"But if there was more wind?"

The Magruman glanced at him. "If there was more wind, of course! This is the *Windrush*!"

For the second time that night, Sylas raised his hands and closed his eyes, turning his mind into the heart of the storm. He lifted his thoughts into the clouds, gave himself up to the thunder and the lightning, breathed deep of the mighty swirling winds and called them to his aid. He tumbled down with them, gathering them to his flanks as they swept towards the ship, feeling their power in the pit of his stomach, and then he opened his eyes.

He saw the sails lift and leap, the rigging twang tight, the stern of the ship begin to rise. He felt the deck surge beneath his feet, the wind and rain blast at his face.

And then he felt something cold and slimy reach around his neck.

As it squeezed tight, his world was filled with light.

Naeo raised her hands to her neck, but felt nothing there.

She forced herself into the moment, turning her mind away from the ship, from the Slithen, from Sylas.

She squinted ahead, trying to get her bearings, to remember where she was.

The light was like a searing fire, blazing through the shattered window, so bright that the driver had his arm over his eyes. She could just about see the stones amid the dazzle and glare, looming in silhouette, but everything else had disappeared: the wall of steel, the grassland, the Ghor — all had been consumed by a flood of the sun's rays.

"Keep going!" she cried. "Between the stones — there!" She pointed ahead. "There, where there's a gap!"

The driver turned the wheel. "Hold on!" he shouted as the car leapt and lurched.

Everyone braced themselves, squinting ahead into the liquid light, which rippled before them like the surface of a lake. Naeo turned and saw Amelie clinging to the seat, her knuckles white, her body stiff with fear.

Naeo reached out and took her hand. "It's OK," she yelled. "It'll be OK!"

And then, in an instant, everything changed. Light became dark, the rippling surface disappeared, the car no longer lurched ahead but skidded, veering to one side. It plunged into the darkness of another world and suddenly Stonehenge was no more. Instead the steel flanks screeched against the stones of Salsimaine.

"My God!" screamed the driver, pressing himself back in his seat.

Naeo peered past him into the gloom. All around them were shapes that were not stones. They were moving and muscular, loping into a circle around the car.

The Ghor and Ghorhund lowered their canine heads, scuffed the dust of the Barrens, and charged.

69
A Light in the Darkness

"And there beyond the verdant maze was the valley of legend,
glowing green like a light in the darkness."

SYLAS FELT THE COLD grip loosen from his throat, leaving a trail
of slime around his neck. He heard a squeal, a shriek, a thump.
His thoughts were still a jumble of here and there but as he
came to, he saw a figure wrestling with the Slithen, pushing it
over the railing as its limbs scrabbled and its jaws snapped. And
when the Slithen fell away Sylas saw the figure at the railing
lose its balance, its legs giving way until it crumpled down to
the floor. There the man rolled and turned, revealing broad but
crooked shoulders, a tattooed head, a long face grimacing with
pain.

Sylas ran over. "Bowe! Are you all right?"

The Scryer nodded. "Go!" he cried. "Help Paiscion! Go!"

Sylas stood looking about him. The *Windrush* was charging
down the river now, forging a path worthy of its name, carried

onward by the full force of the storm. He saw Paiscion, no longer at the wheel but arms cast to the skies, using all his might to conduct the winds. Beside him Simia clung to the wheel for all she was worth, doing her best to follow the Magruman's commands, her hair wild like red flames. The *Windrush* was at a precarious tilt, thrown forward by the winds but somehow it sailed on, skipping over the black surface as though she had been built for it — crafted to harness the greatest of gales.

But that was all that Sylas could see. He could not see the Circle of Salsimaine, nor Naeo and her companions, even now in the clutches of the Ghor. But he knew they were near, shrouded somewhere behind the high riverbanks and the thick blanket of night. He had to find her, to help her. But how?

Suddenly his eyes flew upwards, up the length of the mighty mast to the glistening brass of the crow's nest, swinging and heaving high above the ship.

He set off at a run down the deck, pushing through the passengers, staggering as the hull lurched and bounced. Then he skidded to a halt, put his foot on the railing and launched into the air.

"Sylas!" shrieked Simia, somewhere behind him, but her voice was snatched away by the winds.

For a moment his hands flailed, clawing at the darkness, but then his fingers closed around a rough hemp rope. He gripped it and swung himself around, bracing against a ladder. He gathered his courage and began clambering up as quickly as he dared, trying to ignore the buffeting winds, the heave of the ship, the horrified shouts of those below.

Three rungs — five — ten. Finally he allowed himself to look down: down to the windswept decks, to the desperate faces, to the inky river far below.

To the door of the car buckling and the window smashing in.

"Sylas!" screamed Naeo desperately.

She looked at the Glimmertrome clutched in her hand, watching the needle swing slowly from the centre point.

For a moment her cry drew confused glances, but there was no time to explain. Claws ripped the car door from its hinges, revealing a tangle of gnashing yellow teeth, bloodshot eyes and snapping muzzles. The car lurched and swung about, veering towards one of the standing stones until it slammed up against it, sending the Ghor tumbling into the darkness.

Tasker groaned, clutching his chest. Amelie unclipped herself and crouched forward, taking off her scarf and pressing it against the wound.

"Everyone still here?" shouted the driver.

"Yes! Go!" yelled Ash, waving a hand in the air. "GO!"

The driver turned on the headlights and slammed his foot down. The engine roared and sent the car weaving between stones and black bodies, swinging in an arc around the inside of the stone circle. Naeo looked back and saw the rest of the convoy twisting and swerving behind them, black bodies tearing at their roofs and trailing behind them.

Suddenly they heard a clatter of claws and teeth hitting the sides of the car and a screech on the roof like nails on a blackboard. A strange, mongrel face appeared upside down where the door had once been, its cat-like eyes scanning the interior of the car.

Ash slammed his hand down on his belt buckle and lunged, kicking out with a single boot. He caught the creature on the furry side of its face, snapping its head around, briefly revealing a human cheek and eye before it flipped off into the dark.

The car hurtled on, bounding out of the stone circle and into the blackness, bouncing and bucking over the broken remains of rocks, the creatures tearing along behind them.

Their headlights reached out into the void, meeting nothing but the night. Soon a crazed mesh of beams of light fell about them as the convoy scrambled behind, careering out across the dark of the Barrens.

The mesh became ropes in Sylas's hands, twisting and bucking in the wind. His arms ached from holding so tightly, his hands burned, chafed by the coarse weave. The pain brought him quickly to himself and he felt his own limbs beneath him, the cold blast of the gale on his face.

He gritted his teeth and clambered on up the ladder. As the *Windrush* lurched on a wave he stumbled, but he did not dare slow down — he had to reach the crow's nest before it happened again. The ship was rocking like a colossal pendulum: he wouldn't be able to hold on for long.

He climbed quickly, hand pumping over fist, rung after rung. As he passed the top of the mainsail, he chanced a look down and saw the deck floating in a sea of blackness, and on that deck a jumble of frozen white faces looking up at him. He could see their horror and confusion. He shut his eyes and sucked in three deep breaths, then pushed on.

Five more steps and he was at the bottom of the crow's nest. He paused, working out how he was going to climb inside, and as he did so he became aware of the sway of the ship — so much worse up here. He waited for it to steady a little, closing his eyes, gathering his strength.

And then he looked up, eyeing the brass rail.

He crouched down and then threw himself upwards.

His palms slapped on to the bar and he curled his fingers.

Then he felt the chill of rain: wet, slippery rain.

One hand slid away, sending his arm swinging into the winds. He tried desperately to hold on, but he felt his shoulder twisting too far, sinews being wrenched, pain shooting up his arm.

As he felt his fingers slipping, everything went quiet and calm.

It was as though the world was waiting. As though it was holding its breath.

Then he heard a snap and a flutter. He felt something trace across his face.

It was fabric, embroidered fabric, soft and smooth. He looked up and saw the Suhl standard, the white feather bright and vivid even in the night. It curled down from the mast above, sending out a tasselled finger as though offering its help.

He snatched at its folds with his free hand just as the winds caught it up. It surged towards the storm clouds and carried him with it, sailing out over the ship, ripping his other hand free of the crow's nest. He glanced about in panic and saw the basket drifting away, leaving him at the mercy of the winds. He looked down to where he was sure he would fall, along the length of the giant mast, past the bulge of the mainsail, through the lattice of rigging. He saw Simia, staring in horror from the wheel; Bowe, slumped in anguish against the railing; Paiscion, conducting the winds.

Paiscion, conducting the winds.

And sure enough at that moment those winds shifted and turned, pulling him back towards the mast. He felt the standard lift as though guided by a gentle hand, carrying him towards the crow's nest. And then, miraculously, he felt the handrail in his palm. With a final effort he swung his legs up and over and let go of the standard, sending it back to the heavens, high and proud.

536

He bowed his head for a moment, gathering himself, fighting through the flood of adrenalin. Finally he stood.

The crow's nest swung wildly but he held on, setting his hands wide on each side. He kept his eyes up, searching the blackness, looking for any sign of Naeo.

And then he saw the headlights, carving through the nothingness like swords of light battling the dark.

"There!" he yelled down to the deck below, pointing frantically. "There!"

Naeo slammed her hand down on the needle.

"There!" she cried, pointing out into the darkness. "They're ahead of us! We have to catch up!"

The car veered over the dry, packed earth, sending up a vast cloud of grey dust as it sped towards the riverbank.

Naeo looked down and fumbled with the Glimmertrome until finally the catch snapped over the tip of the needle, locking it in place. She exhaled a deep sigh of relief, turning now to look with her own eyes, knowing he was close, praying he would find them.

After a moment peering ahead into the darkness she looked around the car. Tasker was limp and unconscious on the far seat and Amelie was busy bandaging his wound; Ash was up ahead, leaning through the partition, talking to the driver and pointing out on to the Barrens. She glanced behind, out of the broken window, looking for the lights of the other cars.

Four beams. Only two cars.

The others were gone, lost somewhere out in the blackness.

"Look! There!" bellowed Ash. "There! Do you see?"

Naeo scrambled to the window, her eyes searching through the shattered glass.

And then she caught her breath. She *did* see.

It was a miracle. A beautiful, wonderful miracle.

High above the Barrens and lit by the leaping beams of light, was a gigantic white feather.

The feather of truth. The feather of the Suhl.

70
At Last

"Reach for the silvered glimmer on the lake,
Turn to the sun-streaked shadow in your wake,
Now, rise: fear not where none have gone,
For then, at last, we may be one."

THE CAR SKIDDED TO a halt on the riverbank, its wheels pushing dust and ash into the waters below. The others tore up behind, slamming on their brakes just in time to avoid plunging into the river. They were hardly cars at all now, but monsters of twisted metal, of gashes and punch-holes and shattered glass. Their bruised and broken engines spewed clouds of blue-black smoke, like flares calling for rescue.

The occupants tumbled out into furious winds, scrambling from the nearest door or window, gathering at the water's edge. Tasker was the last, still unconscious and deathly pale, borne between the shoulders of Ash and Amelie. And there they waited, whipped by the winds, gazing out into the dark. The flag had disappeared, no longer lit by the gathered headlights but out there, somewhere – close but out of sight.

No one could speak. They waited in quiet, collective

yearning, trying not to listen to the howls and the wails out on the plains, or the rumble of claws in the dust, getting closer every second.

And then they saw it, like a spectre through the dark, silent and vast. It rode water and wind as lightly as the feather that fluttered from its masthead. As it turned towards them, passing through the golden beams of the headlights, Naeo felt the pain in her wrist — that familiar ache around the Merisi Band. It seeped into her bones and up her arm, but how welcome it was now.

The winds suddenly seemed to drop and as they did so the keel rocked and veered, turning swiftly to draw up to the bank. The colossal sails sank back, the rigging fell loose, and in moments it was there, striking the earthen bank with a boom. They heard a sharp snap from above — a bolt being drawn. There was a clatter of chains and a gangway fell at their feet, gouging into the dust as the ship came to a stop.

A lone figure stood in the shadowy opening. He had a proud, sallow face and his spectacles caught the light.

"Paiscion!" cried Ash, stepping forward.

The Magruman opened his arms to the gathering. "Come aboard, all of you!" he said, flashing a warm, welcoming smile.

Suddenly the Barrens seemed to let out a moan.

Paiscion squinted past them into the darkness. The moan quickly became a chorus of howls.

"ON BOARD!!" he cried, waving them on. "NOW!"

Naeo could not help herself — she turned and gazed out into the night.

The darkness was no longer still and featureless but a muddle of shadow shifting against shadow, of dark forms bounding on dark earth, black claws tearing at black dust. And in the midst of the frenzy, hundreds of pale eyes, cool and unblinking, bounding towards their prey.

"Naeo!" shouted Paiscion urgently. "Hurrry!"

Naeo whipped about, stumbling on to the gangway just behind her friends as they were hurled into the belly of the ship. Paiscion reached out for her, seizing her hand and yanking her forward so that she almost tripped into the passageway. Even as her feet slapped down on the timbers of the *Windrush*, the chains roared around her and the gangway swung into the air, slamming shut with a deafening bang.

She heard howls and wails outside and then something new: shrieks and cries from above her head, from the passengers of the ship.

"Cast off!" cried Paiscion, scrambling past her then up some narrow steps. "Cast off NOW!"

Sylas heard the terrified cries and looked out from the rope ladder, across the decks, following the gaping faces and frightened eyes. Most were looking out at the Barrens, at the halo of light cast by the headlights. There were too many creatures to count, some running as men, heads up and eyes fixed on the ship; some sprinting on all fours, using their arms to gather speed. There were hundreds of them, and they were gaining fast.

Some of the passengers were staring out at the river, where the Slithen had made up for lost time. They were too close now, their spiny backs forming an endlessly breaking wave. Sensing their victory they gargled their battle cry, their screeches and whines joining howls and wails in a monstrous chorus.

Suddenly Paiscion leapt from the hatchway, raising his arm to direct the winds.

But Sylas was not frightened. He felt calm and strong.

He felt whole.

His gaze turned to the hatchway, to that small patch of darkness in the middle of the deck from which Paiscion had emerged.

He knew that below that deck, through that doorway, they were there; that both of them were there.

He clambered down the ladder, jumping the last few rungs at once and landing on the deck. As he did so, a figure stepped up from the darkness of the hatchway — strode towards him — took his hand, her bright bracelet shimmering like his own.

As one they turned their eyes to the great lungs of the storm.

The Suhl were silent now. No one whimpered, no one cried out. They were watching Sylas and Naeo.

"Ready?" asked Sylas.

"Ready."

The question and the answer came in the same instant, so they could not be told apart.

They closed their hands through the pain of the Merisi Band, and held on.

For each of them it started like before, when they had reached up beyond themselves for the sun's rays or for the ravenous winds. They felt themselves become larger than they were, stretching up into the skies until the skies became them and they the skies. But then it changed. For a moment, up there above the storm clouds, they felt warm and welcome. They felt as though Nature herself was there to meet them.

The Ghor snarled lustily as they leapt from the riverbank, sinking their claws into the smooth timbers of the *Windrush*, tearing at the gangway until it sprang ajar. The Slithen hissed their delight as they spidered up the hull, swarming up the stern, tumbling over each other in their thirst for blood.

But they were not heard.

Nothing was heard but the voice of the heavens, screamed in strains of thunder. It was a yell of fury, the command of Nature herself. She reached down from that highest place with a seething fist of wind, lashing out at the *Windrush* with a blow of awesome, crushing force.

And yet it was as though that charmed old ship was waiting; as though those ancient timbers and well-worn ropes had always known that this would come. Because when the wind struck, the masts did not splinter, the rigging did not snap. Instead the *Windrush* creaked and groaned, gathering the gale in those grand old sails, catching it in rope and canvas and twine. The bow lifted, the wheel turned, and she set sail.

The Ghor and the Slithen cried out in horror as claws were torn free of timbers and slimy palms were wrenched loose from railings. Bodies black and grey were thrown from the ship's sides, sent spinning into the waters below. Some clung on, digging their claws deep into the bucking body of the ship, biting down on the anchor chain, wrapping themselves around the tiller. But soon they felt the winds curl about their limbs, whipping at their flailing flanks, sucking them down. They raged and snarled at an enemy they could not see and, one by one, they lost their battle. With a desperate howl or shriek they spun off into the darkness, twisting in the tumult, tumbling into the waters below.

The *Windrush* sailed on into the night, carrying its precious cargo of the sick and the wounded and the free, of not one Magruman but two, of the Merisi and a mother from another world. Of Naeo and Sylas, standing bold at its helm, their minds lost in the storm.

And as time passed and the ship steadied on its course, as it skipped lightly over the glassy waters, the two children opened their eyes for the first time. They saw the passengers staring at them in wonder, they saw the bow leaping on a cushion of air, they saw the shadows of the passing Barrens. And they saw Paiscion, his face full of emotion, his eyes glistening behind his glasses.

He looked from one to the other. "At last we may be one," he murmured.

They both smiled.

The Magruman looked up at the straining sails. "The *Windrush* hasn't sailed like this since —" he laughed — "in truth, I'm not sure she's *ever* sailed like this!"

But when he looked down, he saw that neither had heard him. Naeo was gazing towards the stern of the ship, to a figure propped against the railing; and Sylas's eyes were on the dark hatchway, peering into the gloom.

Their two hearts pounded in unison, the excitement almost unbearable, but they hesitated.

"Come," said Paiscion. "I should be able to manage the winds for a while."

And then a new voice chirped from the direction of the hatchway.

"I'll help!"

They all turned to see a great crop of blond locks rising into view, dancing in the winds.

Sylas grinned. "Ash!" he cried.

Ash heaved himself out of the hatch and straightened his clothes. "The very same," he said with a grin, walking up and placing a hand on Sylas's shoulder.

Paiscion smiled knowingly. "Made your peace with Essenfayle, have you?"

544

Ash turned to Naeo. "Let's just say I've learned that there are more than Three Ways to skin a cat."

Naeo laughed, and glanced briefly in Sylas's direction. Then they both took a breath and began lowering their arms.

And as they ceased their conjuring, Ash and Paiscion began theirs.

The winds raged on, sweeping down from the heavens and filling the wide span of the sails. For a moment, the gale faltered a little, no longer a mighty surge but a squall, spilling from the sails. Howls became wails; the thunder, a distant rumble. The ship shuddered and veered, dipping for a moment back into the waters so that Simia cried out, wrestling with the wheel. Many of the passengers had to lunge to steady themselves and a shout of fright went up from the decks.

Paiscion and Ash eyed one another, but neither wavered. They lowered their heads, closed their eyes and set their arms wide, reaching into the furthest flurries of the storm. The winds began to come in gusts, making the ship leap and buck, but slowly the gusts became longer, picking up the bow, holding the sails taut. And then the gusts became a sustained wind, steadying the grand old ship, holding it to its course. The *Windrush* gathered pace and forged on, not as swiftly as before but still dancing with the winds, skipping lightly along the river.

The two men exchanged a triumphant smile.

"It seems we have a new Magruman," murmured Paiscion.

Sylas and Naeo had already walked away, Sylas one way and Naeo the other, their eyes fixed on a single spot. The Suhl spoke to them as they passed, whispering their heartfelt thanks, asking them to stop a while, but they did not pause.

Sylas saw a movement in the hatchway and was struck by a

sudden fear, a fear that after all this, after everything that they had been through, she would have changed: that she would be different from those precious, well-worn memories of her.

His step faltered and in the same instant, so did Naeo's.

She could see her father clearly now, bruised and broken, his knees shaking, his face beginning to crumple. And it frightened her. He had always been so strong, so constant and true. And she his Nay-no — his little Nay-no.

What had happened to him?

How could she have left him like this?

But then, in an instant, the doubts and questions disappeared. He started to fall, to slip down from the railing, unable to stand tall for his girl any longer. She rushed forward, darting between the remaining passengers, catching hold of him so that they fell together. They slumped down on the decks and they held on, so tightly that Naeo could barely breathe.

She sobbed into his heaving chest and then looked up into his face.

Into those deep, deep eyes.

It was her eyes that broke Sylas. Her eyes, looking up at him as she climbed on to the deck. They were no different from his memories, no different from the picture above the trapdoor in his room, no different from the last day he saw her — that day in black and white.

Except that *these* eyes, *these* were vivid and bright.

And they were *blue*. How had he forgotten? The blue of a summer sky.

They held him before he felt her embrace. They drew him close and told him he was home.

S

Simia leaned on the wheel and watched, her throat tight, her eyes heavy with tears. They were tears of joy, she told herself. Joy at seeing Sylas so happy. And Bowe with the daughter he had lost. They looked so joyous, how could she not be?

But there was sadness too. She turned her eyes up to the rigging, frowning at a perfectly sound knot as though it needed her immediate attention. She would allow herself a tear or two, but later, not now. Now wasn't the time.

And when she had checked the rigging and examined the sails and tweaked the wheel, she cast her eyes further afield, out on to the Barrens, to see if that might take her away from the sadness. And the happiness.

But she should have known better. As her eyes searched the pitch-black, her heart became leaden and her spirit failed. It was not just the deathly dark, nor the looming presence of the endless plains. It was the thought of the one they had left behind. Of Triste, who might even now be battling for his life against the Kraven, or his burns, or worse.

This time, though, she did not turn away. This unhappiness she had to face, and do it without tears. This unhappiness she had caused.

And so she steered the ship on towards the Valley of Outs, looking between the pale glimmer of the river ahead and the Barrens. She sailed as Sylas and his mother walked the decks, deep in conversation. She sailed as the decks filled with lively chatter, which turned eventually to song: that same sad but hopeful song that they had sung beneath the shadow of the Dirgheon — the song of the Valley of Outs. And slowly she was pulled in by these sounds of life and laughter, drawn back to the decks of the *Windrush*.

Then she saw it. Out there in the blackness, far ahead of the dancing ship. It was barely visible, but it was there.

A flickering glimmer of light. A winking orange flame.

It was moving, winding towards the riverbank.

She heard a voice at her ear. "There's a Scryer out there!" declared Bowe, leaning his weight on the wheel.

And then Simia let herself cry.

She smiled a smile of tears.

"I know," she said. "I know!"

Epilogue

THE CORDON OF SOLDIERS advanced slowly but purposefully, lowered in a crouch, weapons tucked tight into shoulders, safety catches off. This is what they had trained for. It was training that made them move as one, that steadied their hand, that helped them fight the urge to run.

It was training that made them walk towards the impossible.

They peered along the barrel of their guns, surveying the scene, searching for a target. They saw standing stones veiled in a fading light, they saw the tracks of the beasts gouged deep into the plain and the marks of skidding tyres converging on a gap between the stones. They saw where the marks stopped in the exact same spot, as though several vehicles had become one and then disappeared. And now, as the light faded still further, they saw the centre of the circle, churned into a muddy mess by claw and talon, rutted and furrowed by the devil's own spawn.

But that was all. There were no dark, prowling beasts, no huddling prisoners, no crates or cases. There was no mysterious convoy of vehicles shrouded in tinted glass and flying a foreign flag. There was nothing but the standing stones, silent and strong, whispering in the wind.

A radio command crackled in their earpieces and at once their walk became a trot, the cordon closing like a noose around the hanging stones. Barrels swept left and right, readied for the unthinkable, primed for beasts rising from the earth or descending from the heavens. But nothing came. The cordon reached the stones and shouts went up from all directions:

"CLEAR!"

"CLEAR!"

"CLEAR!"

And then, "HOLD! ALL UNITS, HOLD!"

A lone soldier lowered his mouthpiece and stood staring at one of the stones, his eyes trained on the spot where it met the ground.

"What the..." he murmured to himself.

Something was oozing up from the base of the rock, something smooth and slick, like oil. It glooped as he watched, surging as though fed by some underground spring.

And then it pooled outwards, coating the turf in a thick, impenetrable black.

Acknowledgements

Acknowledgements

I USED TO THINK that a book was a solitary effort, but that is very far from the truth. While most of the work is done alone and a writing shed certainly comes in handy, this book has been touched by many people along the way, so I have plenty of thanking to do.

I have to begin with my agent, Ben Illis, who was there at the start and whose inexhaustible energy and enthusiasm has propelled this trilogy onwards from the first draft of the first book. Without him as its champion, there is a good chance that it would never have seen the light of day. I also owe a great debt of gratitude to the publishing team at HarperCollins Children's Books for their patient support, and in particular, to Nick Lake, who first saw the potential of *The Mirror Chronicles* and shared my excitement for all it might become. His expertise and creativity has helped me to bring the story ever more vividly to life and this trilogy would not be what it is without him. Thanks, too, to Lily Morgan, who copy-edited *Circles of Stone* with great sympathy and insight (and prevented it from being even longer!) and to Sam Swinnerton, who brought all the editorial and design efforts together to make the book in your hands. Finally, I am very grateful to Matthew Kelly, for the stunning cover illustration, and to Mary Byrne, Nicola Carthy and Hannah Bourne for all their marketing and publicity skill and pizzazz.

I am hugely indebted to my early readers, who have helped to shape both my ideas and my writing, and have made the whole process a lot less lonely and a lot more fun. Thanks, in particular, to Ben Truesdale, David Williamson, Melinda and Marc Dresser, Chris and Mike Paris-Johnstone, Ed Moran, Adrian and Heather Rosser and my mum, Barbara Johnstone.

A month before the publication of *The Bell Between Worlds*, when I was about halfway through the writing of *Circles of Stone*, my wonderful wife, Emily, suffered a very serious stroke. Her courageous struggle has dominated our lives from that day to this, and neither of us could have kept going without the kindness and support of many around us. So this book owes a great deal to Alyrene, our ever-smiling sister, for being there and putting up with me; to Adrian and Heather, for their tireless support and for sharing this hardest of journeys; to my mum, for Tuesdays, and all the other days; to our little girl Ella, for making each and every moment better; and to all the dear family and friends who have gathered us up and helped us along — I can't name you all but you know who you are. Thank you.

Last but by no means least, I want to thank Emily, who through it all has been the best companion, friend, confidante, critic and editor I could ever hope for, and who thought of others, and me, and this book, even as her world fell in. Thank you for staying with me, Emily, and for making this and everything else, possible.